HOUSE

- A Name Lost in Time -

Cecil P Saunders

KLOPT0N Books

First published in Great Britain in 2021 by
KLOPTON Books, Warwickshire, England
www.Klopton.co.uk

KLOPTON is a Registered Trademark at the IPO under number
UK00003468238

A Cataloguing in Publication data record for this book
is available from the British Library
ISBN 978 1 7399092 0 8

Printed and bound in Great Britain by
KMS Litho Ltd, Station Road, Hook Norton
Oxfordshire OX15 5LS

In loving memory

of

Frances Mavis

20th Century map

of

Stratford-upon-Avon

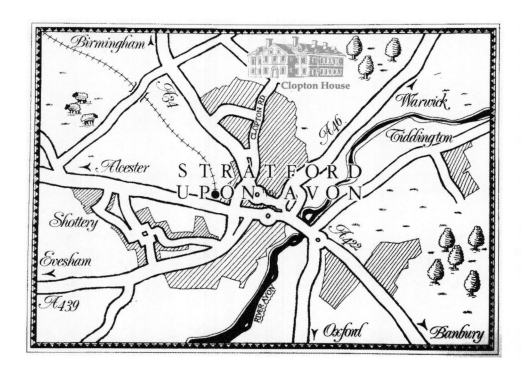

showing the location of

Clopton House & Clopton Park

Prologue

The County of Warwickshire is located in the English Midlands and amongst its many historic places there is none more famous than Stratford-upon-Avon, which in the C12th became a thriving market town after King Richard granted it the right to hold weekly street stalls.

Whilst now known around the World as the C16th birthplace of William Shakespeare, the town also owes much of its historical growth and prosperity to the aristocratic Clopton family, some of whom are buried in the family chapel built alongside the main aisle of the Collegiate Church of the Holy & Undivided Trinity and close to the chancel where the 'Bard of Avon' is also laid to rest.

In the C13th Sir Robert de Clopton was granted a vast country estate on the Northern edge of Stratford-upon-Avon by King John, which grounds comprised hundreds of acres of land and low lying hills centred around an old Manor House and deer park, that became known as Clopton Park.

Over the many centuries that followed, the family's wealth eventually diminished due in part to their decadent lifestyle, until in the C18th Sir John Clopton became the last recorded direct male heir.

After his death, the estate was transferred through successive female descendants to their respective husbands, until by the end of the C19th it was sold off and no longer held in the ownership of any remaining Clopton relative.

When war broke out across the World at the beginning of the C20th, it was time for Katrina and her husband Tarak to travel back to England from Ireland with their teenage twins and stay on the Clopton estate.

Once there, they were to help look after the injured soldiers in the field war hospital being built within the grounds of where Katrina originally lived with her parents, but was now owned by the Reverend Francis Hodgson.

Kane & Kara would both soon be sixteen years old, but they had never been told anything about their true ancestral birthright.

Reluctantly however, Katrina knew the time was coming for her to disclose this and in doing so she would send them on a journey they would have to complete together, if they were to uncover the destiny that fate had set them.

Whilst only known to a few scholars of medieval history when the **HOUSE OF KLOPTON** was re-discovered by Sir Robert, its long forgotten secrets still remain concealed deep within the heart of the Clopton Park estate today, despite the Manor House and its extensive lands having been converted into late C20th residential properties with an adjoining local Nature Reserve.

Book Contents

Full red lunar eclipse over Clopton Park

Part 1

HOUSE OF CLOPTON

- 13th Century -

Chapter 1 : **Passage of Light**

In thirteenth Century Britain, war threatened to break out between the Monarchy and the rebel Barons and although King John of England had the Magna Carta drawn up by the Archbishop of Canterbury to try and appease the rebels, shortly after signing it in 1215 the Barons War still happened.

The following year King John died from a fatal illness he caught whilst leading a campaign with his soldiers against the rebels and his son Henry became King at only nine years of age.

The Magna Carta was amended for King Henry III of the House of Plantagenet in order to satisfy the rebel Barons and after he signed it in 1217, the war soon ended.

Robert had always been one of King John's most bravest knights who served in all of his campaigns against the rebel Barons and was knighted for his loyalty by King John before his death in 1216.

He continued to serve King Henry with equal devotion, but shortly before the war ended he and several other knights were ambushed near Warwick Castle by a large rebel force and after a fierce battle, just seven of them managed to escape along the river bank to the east.

They were all injured during the fight and needed to find somewhere they could shelter before the sunset and also attend to their wounds.

Sir Robert was not born into an aristocratic family unlike most other knights, but his late parents Matthew & Janet Parker were instead farm workers who lived on the Clopton Park estate and lands near Stratford-upon-Avon.

On his mother's death bed however, she told him that Matthew was sadly not his actual father and that she had been assaulted whilst working alone one day in the stables, by a visiting Lord from the local gentry who would not even let her know his name.

This man did however threaten her by saying that if she ever tried to tell anyone they would not believe her, but instead both her and Matthew would be thrown out of their workers' cottage and off the estate.

Matthew therefore never knew what had happened and always believed Robert to be his son.

2

During Robert's youth, after he had helped out with his various daily jobs around the estate, he would often spend time in the nearby Oat Hill woodland covert and also the fresh water stream along its edge.

He therefore knew that this should be an ideal place for him and the other knights to rest overnight without hopefully being disturbed.

The surrounding fields and Stony Hill covert also close by, contained a variety of wildlife plus assortment of berry bushes and edible plants, which together should help provide them with the opportunity to gather some food for eating that evening.

It was late as they approached the Clopton estate and there was a full Moon rising from the east which had already started to turn red in colour as it moved slowly across the early night sky and in doing so began transforming the surrounding fields with its eerie glow.

Sir Robert had seen this red Moon evening phenomenon several times before over the years whilst resting outside during his numerous military campaigns and he knew that the red glow would become much brighter and make them all more visible as its vibrant colour reflected off their shiny metal armour.

Over the brow of the hill they could see the estate Manor House in the distance with smoke coming out of the chimneys and flickering lights in the windows, but Sir Robert did not know if the present occupants were loyal to the King or to the rebel Barons.

Not wishing to take the risk in case they were the enemy however, the knights slowed their horses to a quiet canter and rode further around the outskirts of the estate than original planned to hopefully reach their intended destination without being seen.

Thankfully, it only took a few more minutes for them to arrive in the woodland on the edge of a covert, where they dismounted straight away and tethered the horses amongst the numerous lush trees for cover.

After a quick reconnoitre around their new secluded surroundings, it was agreed that they could not be seen from the Manor House and should therefore be relatively safe for the night, but nevertheless two of them would stay to guard the horses whilst the rest of them looked for a more sheltered spot where they could hopefully get some sleep without being disturbed.

Sir Robert and four of the other knights set off along the edge of the nearby stream until they came to what appeared to be the source of the water as it rippled gently over some rocks, behind which was the grass covered side of the small hill to the west of the woodland clearing protected by thick overgrowth.

This area was still too open for their purpose however and so needing to find somewhere less exposed, they continued to move forward by cutting a small path through the large brambles with their swords and using their armour to protect them as they pushed their way past the long sharp thorns.

Just up ahead they saw an exposed jagged rock face along the hillside behind the brambles that was also partly covered with thick ivy, but after a few more steps they suddenly stopped to crouch down as Sir Robert signalled for them to remain still and be quiet.

He then pointed over towards a strange red glow coming from the inside of a partially hidden tall narrow crevice in the rock face to the front of them and waited patiently to see if there was also anyone else nearby.

They all stayed there for another minute until after seeing no movement nor hearing any other sound, Sir Robert decided they should continue on their way again as he started cutting back more of the overgrown bushes blocking their path.

He then moved cautiously towards the red light, whilst the other knights followed closely behind ready to help protect him should there be any danger up ahead.

The crevice entrance however, was far too narrow for Sir Robert to enter without removing his body armour, so he reluctantly took this off and laid it on the ground, whilst still keeping his chainmail on.

Armed with just a sword in his hand, he then let out a deep breath and slowly pushed his way through the tight opening in the rock, where he found himself in an underground passageway illuminated by veins of glowing red crystals embedded within the rock walls and ceiling.

Upon realising that the red light they had seen outside the crevice entrance was being caused by the glow of these bright red crystals from the Moon and there was probably no-one else around, Sir Robert called back to the other knights to let them know that everything was alright, but to wait there until he had explored a bit further inside.

He then started off again along the small passageway, until it opened up to become much larger and he was able to stand upright, at which point he managed to walk at a quicker pace to where the red light was shining a lot brighter and he could also hear some running water.

Sir Robert soon found up ahead of him a red glowing stream that flowed along the left-hand side of the passageway, which he followed a short distance more until it reached a rock wall and then stopped, with its underground source seeming to have originated from somewhere down beyond this wall in front of him.

Meanwhile, the passageway itself veered off to the right-hand side and into a rock cave, which was only dimly illuminated by a few glowing crystal veins on its walls plus a few beams of red light shining through some small cracks in its ceiling.

As he stood there in this empty void, Sir Robert replaced his sword back into its sheath whilst he collected his thoughts for a few moments and decided that the crystals, beams of light and stream waters must all be glowing red because of the full Moon's bright red colour shining onto the Clopton hills from up above them in the night sky.

There were no visible signs around him of anyone else having been inside this cave and apart from the remains on the floor of some small wildlife creatures which must have wandered in along the passageway sometime in the past, everywhere else appeared to be remarkably clean.

Sir Robert then turned around to go back outside and tell the others what he had found, but as he walked down the passageway towards the entrance he heard Sir Peter shout out his name, having evidently also now made his way through the crevice gap to see if he was alright.

Upon calling for Sir Peter to wait where he was, they soon met up again and after Sir Robert had told him about what he had just seen inside, they both squeezed back through the entrance and once outside made their way over with the other three knights to rejoin the two still waiting in the woodland.

When all seven of them were back together again, it was agreed that Sir Robert and three of the knights would go back inside the passageway to bathe in the red glowing stream waters, whilst Sir Peter would remain outside to guard the crevice entrance and another knight would look after the horses.

Meanwhile, the remaining knight would forage close by for any food he could find for their meal that night after they had all finished bathing and also before they subsequently took it in turns to get some sleep in readiness for their long journey the following morning.

Sir Robert and the other three men soon entered back through the narrow crevice gap without wearing their armour and then slowly walked along the red crystal lined passageway until they reached the rock wall.

At the end, they stopped in-between the red glowing stream and the illuminated rock cave to discuss how old the place probably was and who else may have been there before them.

In the 13th Century, knights were particularly religious men and not only did they fight for their King but also for God, so all four of them then knelt down together with the cross on the handle of their swords facing upwards, before bowing their heads and quietly saying a prayer to their saviour.

They then all walked back over to the stream where its clear water still glowed red, but looked ideal for them to bathe in and also clean their wounds from the blood of their recent battle.

5

Not knowing how deep the stream was or how strong its underwater currents were however, Sir Robert went in first as he was a good swimmer and once he had checked that the waters were indeed safe, the other three knights would then be able to join him.

After removing his chainmail and other garments, Sir Robert carefully climbed down the jagged rocks standing along the edge of the passageway to the stream, from where he then lowered himself into the water until he was submerged up to his neck.

As soon as he began washing off the dirt and dried blood with the red water however, he felt some unusual tingling sensations coming from within the deep open wounds that he had on his body.

A short time later, whilst this unexpected experience continued, the birthmark which he had long forgotten about underneath the upper part of his sword arm, began to swell up and cause him an acute pain, before also spreading from there across to his chest and in doing so made him breath quite erratically.

He immediately tried to call out to the other knights for their help, but he could hardly speak and then as quickly as the pain had begun, it stopped and his breathing returned to normal, to which he uttered a sigh of relief.

Being unsure about what had just occurred however, Sir Robert checked under his arm and saw that his birthmark had changed colour from its original dark brown to a bright red and also its hexagonal shape had become much bolder and clearer.

The three knights standing on the rocks watching over Sir Robert had also noticed his distress, but before they had chance to ask him what had just happened, he felt all the pains from his wounds and battle-weary bones dissipate away and for his whole body to be totally invigorated.

He then looked up at the other knights who were all clearly concerned, but being unsure how best to explain to them what had just happened, he decided instead to tell them to enter the red glowing stream with him and see if they too benefitted from its healing properties.

As they all lowered themselves down the rocks onto the waters edge, Sir Robert watched and waited with trepidation to see how they would feel, especially since he doubted whether any of them also had an hexagonal birthmark similar to his under their arms too.

Within a relatively short time all three knights stated they were feeling more revitalised, although it was not evident to Sir Robert that any of their wounds were healing up as quickly as his did.

Nevertheless, as they continued bathing along the edge of the stream to recuperate for a while longer, they all agreed that the red water must have special healing powers and so began drinking some of it as well.

After a short time, one of the knights decided to go for a swim, but after diving into the stream from the rocks he was resting on, he felt an underwater current start to carry him down with it.

He then became even more concerned as the water dragged him even deeper under the surface and it was now so strong that he could not pull himself back up to the top and thought he was going to drown.

Thankfully, Sir Robert soon realised that his fellow knight had been underwater for too long and deciding that he must be in some sort of trouble, dived into the stream to find him.

It was not until he was much further under the water however, that Sir Robert saw the knight's limp body was being carried along within the strong current.

He immediately swam over to rescue his friend and eventually managed to grab hold of his body tightly, before pulling him up to the surface where the other knights were all waiting to help lift him out of the stream and back onto the rocks.

After a period of frantic resuscitation by each of them in turn, the knight managed to expel the water he had just swallowed and to everyone's relief started breathing normally again.

Without knowing why their fellow knight had almost drowned in the red water when Sir Robert had not been affected, they all nevertheless agreed that none of them would swim in the flowing stream anymore.

Instead, they remained on the rocks by the edge of the red glowing water whilst they continued to rinse their wounds, since this still made them feel quite revitalised.

As soon as they had all finished, it was time for them to get dressed again and return back down the passageway to swap over duties with the other knights who were still keeping guard outside.

Upon meeting up again, Sir Robert explained what had just happened in the strong underwater current, after which the other three knights set off up along the passageway to also bathe themselves in the red glowing stream waters, but only from beside the rocks.

Meanwhile, Sir Robert took up guard duty outside close to the gap in the crevice, whilst the other two went back over to the woodland with the horses to start preparing whatever wildlife, berries, mushrooms and other food could be gathered for their meal.

Sometime later, after the knights had finished bathing, they rejoined Sir Robert at the entrance and then went back over to the woodland clearing where the others had lit a small open fire and were cooking some meat, which included a couple of conies (*rabbits*) and a fox they had managed to trap and kill.

They all sat down together under the glow of the full red Moon and quickly devoured what unfortunately was only a small meal when divided amongst seven hungry men, before then deciding what to do next.

It was agreed that five of them would take some of the burning logs and a few extra branches back to the rock cave at the far end of the passageway to make a fire for extra warmth, whilst the other two knights would alternate outside between watching over the horses and the rock face entrance.

Several hours later, after managing to get some much needed sleep, it was Sir Robert and another knight's turn to keep guard and once they were both through the crevice gap, they put their body armour back on over their chainmail before taking up their respective positions.

A short time afterwards however, as Sir Robert looked up again at what seemed to be a finite number of stars still glistening in the darkening red coloured night sky, he realised that the Moon was no longer directly overhead.

Instead, he saw it had moved across the hills towards the horizon, whilst its previously vibrant glowing red colour was starting to disappear as the Moon slowly began to turn back to its various normal shades of grey.

Sir Robert immediately headed back over to the crevice, where he picked up a large rock and banged it repeatedly against the edge of the entrance in order to wake up all the other knights further inside

After putting the rock back down again, he then shouted out loudly along the passageway for them to come and join him as fast as they could.

Fearing that they had been discovered by the rebel Barons, the knights picked up the remaining armour they had not been sleeping in and after squeezing through the crevice gap, helped each other put it back on over their chainmail as quickly and quietly as they could.

They then took hold of their swords in their hands and upon Sir Peter's command, all charged out together through the overgrowth ready for a fight.

Once in the open however, instead of finding an enemy waiting for them, they saw Sir Robert bending down on one knee by the side of the stream with the point of his sword in the ground, whilst gazing upwards into the sky and saying a prayer.

As all of the other knights looked over in the same direction, they too realised the Moon was descending into the west and no longer glowing such a bright red light as when it shone across the night sky into the passageway that evening.

They immediately knew why Sir Robert was praying and all knelt down beside him to offer their own prayers to God and thank him too for the healing powers of the red glowing water.

Only Sir Robert knew about the unusual birthmark underneath his arm that had changed to a bright red colour that night and he decided not to tell any of the other knights about this, as he believed he had been blessed due to his exceptional valour in battle.

All of the seven knights continued to kneel for a short while longer until they saw that the Moon was no longer glowing red, when they all stood up together.

It was then agreed that they should not stay there much longer, but instead would set off before sunrise in order to avoid becoming more visible in the daylight to any enemy soldiers nearby.

During the short time they still had left however, Sir Robert and Sir Peter decided to go back inside the passageway to check that nothing had been left behind in the cave and also ensure that the entrance to the crevice was well hidden by overgrowth to help it from ever being discovered again.

Once they had both entered through the small gap in the rock face, they saw that it was much darker inside than the night before, with the crystal veins in the walls no longer glowing bright red, but instead they had changed to now become a dull rose pink colour.

As they continued on towards the stream, they found that although its flowing waters remained quite clear, these too was not coloured red anymore and instead this section of passageway and cave were lit by just a few beams of white light reflecting through the ceiling cracks that no longer illuminated the rose pink crystals.

Inside the cave, the crystals were now hardly visible, but there were still a few glowing embers from the fire they had lit during the night and after putting these out, they moved the remains to the rear of the cave amongst the jagged rock walls so they would not be seen.

After one final look around, they both returned back down the passageway and once outside, pushed back the thick brambles and bushes they had moved when they first arrived, before also covering up their foot tracks in the ground to the front of the rock face.

They then made their way over to rejoin the other knights who had been tending to all the horses in readiness for the long journey ahead.

After everyone was ready, they all mounted their horses and set off together over the Clopton hills to rejoin King Henry's loyal Barons and soldiers in Oxfordshire for the next battle.

They had a long and dangerous ride ahead of them.

Chapter 2 : **History in the Making**

In 1217 the Barons War ceased, but a couple of years later when Sir Robert was still only 35 years old, the numerous injuries he had received during battle were taking a heavy toll on his body, to the extent that he could no longer fight effectively, particularly in the heavy knight's armour required and so decided that he had no option but to step down.

King Henry was very disappointed that he had to lose one of his most trusted and bravest knights, but as a reward for his loyal service he granted Robert full ownership of the Clopton Manor and its extensive lands including a large deer herd, together with the title of Sir Robert de Clopton, which estate along with his title would then pass on to his male heirs.

Although Sir Robert was saddened to learn that the previous owner of the Clopton Park estate who he remembered from his youth, had been killed along with his family by the rebels during the Barons War, he was nevertheless greatly honoured by this gracious gift from the King.
In less than a week Sir Robert had sorted out his temporary accommodation and financial affairs in London, whereupon he set off to Stratford-upon-Avon with his wife Lady Marsha and their three children John, Sofia and Kate to take up their new permanent residence in the old timber built Manor House.

Upon their arrival, Sir Robert quickly realised that the whole property had fallen into considerable disrepair during the Barons War, but he soon set about planning the restoration of the main House for his family and also the addition of replacement outbuildings needed for all the various workers required to help look after the Clopton Park estate.
Additionally, replacement fencing was required around the estate's perimeter so cattle and sheep could be bought and graze securely, whilst new stables and pens had to be built for all the livestock and poultry.
The remaining fields on the opposite side of the estate were to be furrowed in readiness for seeding and the growing of all the different crops needed to make the estate self-sustainable as far possible.

Before the workers had the chance to start on all of their jobs around the Clopton Park estate however, Sir Robert took his whole family over with him to where the Oat Hill woodland clearing and nearby stream were located on the North side of the fields.
This was the place where he and the other King's knights had rested overnight in 1217, whilst avoiding the rebel Barons who had been pursuing them after a battle.

He also showed them the thick bramble and other bushes close by, that were covering the outside of a rock face and hidden entrance he had discovered that evening, which overgrowth he replaced the next day before he left in order that the crevice gap would not be discovered again.

Sir Robert then explained to them about both the red glowing stream and illuminated cave at the end of the crystal lined inside passageway, which he and the knights had used that evening before they headed off in the morning to rejoin the Baron wars.

Finally, he told his wife and children to ensure that the rock face crevice was always kept covered over and that the enclosed passageway was never entered into without his specific permission, as it was a very dangerous place where one of his fellow knights nearly died.

As they returned back to the Manor House, Sir Robert also revealed to all of them the bright red hexagonal birthmark he bore underneath his right arm.

Then, one at a time, he rolled up the sleeve covering each of the children's right arms to show them that they too had been blessed with such a birthmark, although theirs were still a deep brown colour like his had originally been.

He further explained that once their hexagons had turned bright red, they would help protect them when the time was right and they had entered into the cave during the time of the red full Moon.

Sadly, Lady Marsha did not have the birthmark, although this was hardly surprising since she was not of the same bloodline as either of Sir Robert's parents, from whom he had inherited his.

Over the next few months the planned restoration work on the estate progressed rapidly and as the weather was getting a lot drier, Sir Robert decided that it was now time for him to enter the main passageway again, but on this occasion he would go on his own so he could try and explore it more thoroughly.

Early one morning of the following week, whilst most of the workers were either looking after the stables or out collecting essential goods from town, Sir Robert checked that no-one else was around and then set off pass the Manor House gardens to the fields beside the stream, until he reached the Oat Hill woodland covert.

Once there and certain that he had not been seen, he collected a few fallen branches so he could make a small fire once he was inside the dimly lit cave section.

He then made his way towards the entrance, where he pushed the overgrowth away just far enough to reveal the hidden crevice set back inside the jagged rock face.

11

Sir Robert then squeezed himself through the small entrance gap and began to make his way slowly along the passageway.

As soon as he was no longer in line with the daylight coming from outside however, it became too dark for him to see anything up ahead and so he stopped to create a small fire using the wood he was carrying.

Once he had managed to get a couple of branches burning and his eyes adjusted to the relative darkness around him, he started to see the rose pink crystal veins in the rock walls glisten slightly and provide some light along the tunnel.

As he then began moving forward again, he soon heard the stream water flowing up ahead of him and knew that he was not too far away from that section of the passageway.

Upon reaching the rock wall at the very end, Sir Robert saw numerous beams of white light coming through the small cracks in the ceiling that reflected onto the surface of the water, although this was nothing like the dramatic sparkling red colours he remembered from his original visit.

To the rear of the small cave he could see a few dark shadows which he had especially come to have a look at and so set about building a larger fire using the remaining wood he had brought with him.

As soon as this was lit and the flames came alive, so did the extra illumination caused by the embedded rose pink crystals reflecting the light around the rest of the walls.

After just standing there for a couple of minutes whilst taking in all of the surroundings, Sir Robert turned his attention to the rock wall leading into the cave, where he could now see a flat silver edged crystal hexagonal device, glistening amongst the jagged rock edges.

This object was no longer hidden by the dark shadows, but partly lit by the flickering flames coming from the fire Sir Robert had built in the cave and intrigued by what it could be, he walked over to have a better look.

As soon as he got close, he discovered that protruding from the centre of this hexagonally shaped device was a smaller but similar designed hexagonal shaped stud, except this one also had a silver letter 'K' embedded on its top within the crystals.

Sir Robert stood there for a few moments fascinated by this and then decided to take hold of the stud to see if he could remove it from the rock face, but no matter how hard he tried it simply would not budge.

Still convinced however, that this stud would come away, Sir Robert tried again, but this time he also turned it in an anti-clockwise direction whilst he pulled.

With utilising both of these movements together, not only did the stud begin to slowly turn, but he also felt his birthmark swell up slightly.

Buoyed by his progress though, he grabbed hold of the stud even tighter and with all his strength repeated these movements again, until gradually he managed to turn it upside down where it came lose, enabling him to remove an elongated hexagonal shaped object from the centre of the device .

As Sir Robert physically held this rather unusual object in his hand, the swelling he had felt on his arm went away as quickly as it came, but with no explanation as to why, he chose to simply ignore this for now and instead continued to examine the object more closely by turning it upside down.

He discovered that the underneath section comprised a group of four intricate silver stems, three of which were about the same length as his thumb, whilst the fourth was slightly longer.

All four stems however, were fixed at different angles to each other and yet when combined together, they created a very unusual key in the same outline as the letter 'K' embedded on top of the stud.

Intrigued by what this key would actually open and why it had been created to such a specific 'K' design, Sir Robert held it back up to the hexagon device on the wall and saw that the hole in the centre which he had removed the stud key from, was upside down compared to its stems.

It was then he decided that not only could the key be turned around even further once replaced back into its hole, but also realised that both the hexagonal shaped stud top and wall device in which it was held were the same shape as the birthmark underneath his arm!

Unable to understand what this all meant and yet just as surreal as his first visit to the passageway the previous year, Sir Robert saw the light from the fire begin to flicker and knew it would soon go out as he had no more wood left with which to keep it burning.

Reluctantly aware that it was therefore now time for him to return back to the Manor House, he picked up the last remaining couple of lit branches in his hand and started to leave the cave, but within a few steps he spotted a second silver edged rose pink hexagon glistening amongst the rock crevices.

Upon getting closer to this, Sir Robert saw that it was an empty 'K' shaped key hole similar to the other one, except this hexagon was located in the middle of a rectangular block of rock surrounded along its edges by a band of silver protruding slightly above the crevice surface.

Sir Robert suspected that this might be a small alcove with something of value inside it, but the rim edge was far too thin for him to grip with his hand and so he tried pushing himself up against the piece of rock instead, but it would not move.

Deciding that he must have to use the 'K' key to open it, Sir Robert placed this up to the hexagon and instantly felt his birthmark swell up again as the key shot into the hole, where he managed to slowly turn it.

On this occasion, he also heard what sounded like a rusty metal wheel slowly turning inside the wall, as he noticed a rectangular piece of rock gradually start to move forward towards him.

This block soon became loose and Sir Robert then managed to pull it out the rest of way with his hands, after which he put it down onto the cave floor so he could examine the large hole now open in front of him.

Unfortunately, it was too dark for Sir Robert to see anything in this alcove, so he felt around its inside walls instead and towards the back, past what he thought must be the wheel mechanism that he had just heard, he came across what felt like a parchment scroll.

After removing this, he saw that it was indeed a very old looking manuscript rolled up tightly and held together by a narrow silver band securely fastened with a silver rimmed buckle, which again was embedded with a letter 'K' amongst a few rose pink crystals.

Hoping that this scroll would contain some answers to the many questions he had been asking himself ever since he first discovered the crystal passageway and cave, Sir Robert decided to take it to the Manor House with him so he could study its contents in the daylight.

Before leaving however, he lifted the block back into its rectangular hole in the wall as far as it would go and then locked it again, after which he removed the 'K' key to also take this with him and keep secure.

After extinguishing the final few embers still lingering inside the cave, Sir Robert made his way down the passageway to the crevice entrance, where he paused to look through the gap and check that no-one else was anywhere nearby.

Seeing that it was all clear, he stepped outside and immediately pulled back the bushes and shrubbery again to ensure the entrance would remain well hidden behind the overgrowth covering the rock face.

He then made his way across the hillside next to the stream and was soon walking into the gardens, where some of the workers were busy going about their daily chores.

Once back inside the Manor House, Sir Robert went straight upstairs to his private chambers, where he put both the key and scroll into a lockable metal chest concealed in a floor space behind a large wooden wardrobe, in order to keep them secure with all his other valuables.

Frustratingly it was not until later that afternoon after completing his checks on the progress of the renovations still being done around the estate, that Sir Robert got the chance to sit outside in the sun on a log close by the lake, where he could be alone to examine both the 'K' key and parchment scroll, without being disturbed.

As he first of all held the key up to the daylight, Sir Robert was captivated by the sheer intricate beauty of the rose pink crystals embedded within the silver rim of this unique design, which he had never seen anything like before.

Whilst studying the key more closely, he then noticed what appeared to be some text engraved along both sides of the longest stem, each of which comprised a series of three words in an unusual font that looked similar to a medieval style he had once come across.
When all these six words were put together, the combined text read

'only the key ... will passage allow'

No matter how much Sir Robert pondered over different ideas in his head, he could not unravel the significance of why these words were being used together in this short cryptic message, unless the 'key' also opened another 'passage' he had not yet found hidden somewhere else inside the passageway.

He did however, whilst examining this longest key stem up closer, also find at its very end a small crescent shaped symbol which again was etched onto both sides.

This object's design reminded him of the Moon when it was only partly lit up in the night sky and although this appeared to have nothing to do with either the key or its cryptic text, Sir Robert thought that it must have something to do with the crescent shape of the partial full red Moon he saw during the cycle of its eclipse.

As he continued to turn the whole key over slowly in case he had missed anything else, Sir Robert suddenly noticed a narrow beam of daylight shine through a small round hole below its top, which ran through the whole width of the main silver stud just beneath the pink crystals.
He instantly realised that this hole would be the perfect place to add the silver chain he had recently bought as a gift to give to Kate on her twelfth birthday and that with the key also displaying the letter 'K', it would make a wonderful pendant for his daughter to wear safely around her neck.

Sir Robert then changed his attention to the old scroll he had also brought back with him from the cave and it quickly became apparent that in order to see what was displayed on this parchment, he would first of all need to open the silver rimmed 'K' buckle that securely fastened the silver strap together.

Unfortunately however, he could neither lift nor undo this buckle, even after putting on his leather gloves for a more secure grip, but then not wishing to break it open he thought it best to release his tight hold, especially as he had another idea to try instead.

He quickly noticed that there was a single slim rectangular shaped hole on one edge of the buckle which looked very similar in size to the end of a silver key stem and as he brought them closer, he saw they were indeed the same width.
Upon pushing them both together, Sir Robert again felt a slight swelling around the birthmark on his arm, as the longest key stem slotted straight into the hole and the buckle immediately flipped open.

After undoing the silver strap, the scroll loosened up sufficiently to reveal two separate sheets of parchment, both of which displayed along their top in a single line, seven different letters all embossed in silver onto the paper.
Each of these silver characters were enclosed in the centre of adjoining rose pink stone layered hexagons, apart from the silver 'K' which lay within ruby red stone fragments instead, but when all put next to each other created the word

Sir Robert assumed this to be an historical spelling variation of the name 'Clopton', but was intrigued as to where this may have originated from.

He remembered back to when he had fought alongside King John during their overseas battles together and how they entered several old French monasteries, where he came across some medieval manuscripts which occasionally had the letter 'C' at the beginning of certain words replaced by the letter 'K'.

The only symbol Sir Robert had encountered however, was the letter 'Phi' from the Greek alphabet on some ancient scrolls and he was very perplexed as to why both of these two letter variations would appear together within the same local name, deep inside a hidden Warwickshire hillside cave.

He then unrolled the parchment sheets fully to read their contents, but was hugely disappointed to see that they appeared to be blank apart from the name and a beautifully embossed black & red coat of arms at the bottom, which resembled in design but not in colour, that of the House of Clopton.

Sir Robert held the sheets up to the light, hoping that he might find a watermark or similar faint text hidden within the body of the paper, but he could find nothing.

Reluctantly, he wound the two parchments back up together tightly using the silver strap and then re-locked its buckle with the 'K' key's long stem, before putting it back inside his jacket.

A few moments later he was disturbed by Lady Marsha, as he was needed in the main courtyard to sort out payment for various livestock that had just been delivered to replenish the stables and pens.

Sir Robert got up and returned to the Manor House where he put both the scroll and 'K' key back away securely in his room, whilst also collecting some coinage in order to attend to the estate matters that had summoned him back.

Later that evening, after the family meal was finished and the children gone to bed, Sir Robert sat down in front of the flickering flames of the dining room log fire and stared at the 'K' key again, whilst his mind thought back to the other six knights who were with him on that night a couple of years earlier, when they first discovered the passageway.

He decided that all of them should have something unique with which to remember each other by, not only because they had fought side-by-side for many years, but also because they were such good friends who had shared the glowing stream waters created by the red full Moon overhead.

As this experience would remain with them for the rest of their lives, Sir Robert wanted something that would last forever too and came up with the idea of having seven identical hexagonal shaped signet rings made from silver and rose pink crystals, to match the design on top of the key stud he had just found.

These would also display the same letter 'K' too, since this would help identify them to be the Knights they all were.

In London there was a silversmith Sir Robert knew, who could make these signet rings for him and as he also had a couple of old silver goblets in his metal chest which he never used anymore, these could be smelted down and used for this purpose.

His next journey to the capital was not for another few days however, so Sir Robert had time to go back inside the passageway beforehand and chisel sufficient rose pink crystals from the rock walls to take with him.

After a restless few weeks later, the silversmith completed all seven signet rings and arranged a horse rider from London to deliver them to Sir Robert personally at the Manor House.

Upon receiving them all, he was so delighted with their design and excellent workmanship, that he immediately put one onto his finger to start wearing straight away.

Next, he got a quill and parchment paper to write letters to each of the other six knights, inviting them all to join him at the Manor House so he could give them their new signet rings personally and also re-visit the crystal passageway together.

Several weeks passed before he received a couple of letters back, one telling him that three of the knights had died sometime ago when fighting for King Henry in France, whilst the second letter informed him that two other knights had also died, but only a month earlier from severe injuries they had sustained just recently.

It took yet another week before a final letter arrived, this one advising that Sir Peter had gone missing during a battle and was presumed dead, although the sender did not know this for certain.

Upon receiving such tragic news about his fellow knights, Sir Robert was distraught and became very depressed, spending a lot of time in the tranquility of the rock cave in prayer for his friends' souls and also that Sir Peter may yet still return one day.

Shortly afterwards, he decided to give his only son John one of the signet rings for him to also wear, whilst he locked the other five away inside the heavy metal chest hidden in his bedroom to keep them safe for use by future knights of KLOPT0N.

Deer herd on Clopton Park estate

18

Chapter 3 : **Inconsolable Despair**

It was mid-afternoon one day in early Autumn that Sir Robert was sitting outside next to the Manor House lake with Lady Marsha and Kate, when he suddenly noticed the rose pink crystals on his silver 'K' signet ring start to glow bright red.

Immediately looking up into the sky, he saw that the Moon was slowly breaking through the thin cloud cover as it rose in the east over the brow of the distant hills and glowed a weak red colour across the early evening sky towards the Sun, which was only just starting to set in the west.

Sir Robert instantly realised what was happening and as his heart started beating faster, he left them both beside the lake as he set off as quick as he could in the direction of the Oat Hill woodland and crevice entrance along the side of the rock face.

Before he got too far though, he thankfully remembered that Kate was wearing the 'K' key around her neck as a pendant and that he would need this once he was inside the cave, so he quickly turned around and went back to retrieve it from her.

When he reached Kate however, she told him that she had lent her pendant to Sofia to wear for the week and instead Kate was wearing Sofia's silver bracelet, with the two sisters apparently often swapping their jewellery.

Sofia had stayed inside her room that afternoon to finish reading a school book she had been given and Sir Robert therefore set off in that direction to find her.

As he approached the Manor House however, he saw that Sofia was actually outside in the courtyard chatting to one of the young farm workers and upon seeing this, Sir Robert quite sternly called out her name and clearly startled her as he had intended.

Sofia stood there quite still as she saw her father coming towards her in a hurry, whilst the boy set off quickly in the opposite direction towards the stables.

Once Sir Robert caught up with Sofia she asked him what was wrong, but before he could question her about the boy she was talking to whilst unsupervised outside at that time of the day, he saw the rose pink crystals on the top of the key pendant around her neck were also glowing red.

He asked her if she had discussed the pendant and crystals with the boy she was with and whilst she said no, Sir Robert was not totally convinced by her answer and decided to take her with him to the cave so he could keep watch over her for the rest of the afternoon.

After following the side of the stream for a while, they soon reached the woodland clearing and continued walking over to where the overgrowth was covering the rock face, but they could now see the red light glowing through the gap in the hidden crevice.

Sofia was full of trepidation as she had not been inside the passageway before, whereupon Sir Robert assured her that she would be perfectly safe since not only would he stay with her, but she also bore the same hexagon birthmark under her arm as his which he had shown her.

He then pulled away some of the bushes covering the entrance before smiling at Sofia reassuringly and taking her by the hand as he led her carefully through the narrow crevice gap and into the passageway.

Once inside, he kept a tight hold of her as they stood there for a while so their eyes could adjust to the dim red light coming from the glowing crystal veins within the rock walls, after which both of them slowly set off on their way again.

Upon reaching the glowing stream waters and beams of light shining through the cracks in the ceiling, where they combined with the glistening crystals and illuminated all of the rock walls around her to a brighter red colour, Sofia became mesmerised by the whole picturesque scene.

After a few moments she bent down on her knees and closed her eyes as she prayed to God for such a wondrous place, whereupon her father knelt down beside her and also said a short prayer.

Sir Robert stood up again first, before lifting his daughter onto her feet to stand beside him and asking her for the silver key pendant she wore around her neck, which Sofia passed to him.

He carefully walked over to where the hexagonal device was located on the rock wall close to the cave and saw that the crystals around the upside-down empty 'K' hole were also glowing bright red.

With the 'K' key now in his hand, Sir Robert placed it up to the hole in the centre of the hexagon, but before he had the chance to align it correctly, he felt the key being pulled away from him as it flew straight into the hole and locked itself the right way up.

After just standing there for a few moments contemplating what had just happened, Sir Robert decided to take another firm grip of the protruding stud and try to unlock it again, since he was convinced that this key would open another passage somewhere in order to fulfil the cryptic text etched onto its longest stem.

As he started to both pull and turn the key stud at the same time, these two movements together again caused the key to slowly move in an anti-clockwise direction, whilst he once more also felt his birthmark swell up slightly.

This time however, once the key would turn no further and Sir Robert had lifted it back out of its hole, a very loud thud suddenly echoed around the whole chamber, which noise was like the passageway rock wall in front of him had just split wide open.

Immediately afterwards, as he listened intensely to various other new sounds, he heard water gushing through an underwater passage somewhere within the rock wall, whilst the stream had also clearly begun to flow a lot faster.

Instantly remembering that he had left Sofia sitting near the edge of the passageway overlooking the red glowing stream below, Sir Robert turned around to make sure that she was alright, but could not see her anywhere in the dim red light.

He frantically began shouting out her name as he quickly made his way over to the stream, but there was no response and she was still nowhere to be seen.

Upon stopping along the very edge of the passageway however, he looked down over the side and with a huge sigh of relief saw Sofia smiling back up at him from the rocks at the water's edge, having obviously climbed down there by herself.

Seeing that the stream water level was rapidly rising however, Sir Robert called for her to stay where she was whilst he came to fetch her, to which Sofia waved at her father and told him she was fine.

Instead of waiting as she had been told however, Sofia decided to take a step back up onto a higher rock to stop her feet getting wet, but with not realising how slippy this now was, she lost her footing and fell into the red glowing water.

Sir Robert heard a loud splash and instinctively looked down to see that his daughter was no longer standing where she should be, upon which he knew she must have fallen into the stream and despite the obvious danger, he immediately dived in off the rocks along the top to rescue her.

Upon entering the water he could not see Sofia in the downstream current, so instead he looked upstream towards the rock wall where there was a very bright red light glowing through a large gap underneath the water.

As he looked on more intensely in that direction, he saw his daughter being carried away towards the red light and after taking another deep breath of air from the surface, he swam off after her as quickly as he could.

The underwater current was flowing quite fast as it swirled around Sir Robert and helped pull him along through the water where he soon caught up with Sofia, but upon grabbing hold of her body he instantly realised that she was no longer breathing.

21

Realising that this current was too strong for him to carry her back up to the passageway in time to save her, he decided instead to continue following it and the bright light through the open rock passage in the wall.

Once on the other side of this wide gap, the underwater current took them both a further short distance, until Sir Robert re-surfaced inside a brightly illuminated magnificent red cavern, which was much larger than the small cave they had just left behind.

The rock walls and ceilings of this cavern were covered with thousands of glistening red crystals, whilst beams of light again shone through cracks overhead and most of its stone floor was nearly knee deep high in glowing bright water.

Towards one edge of the cavern there was also a spectacular rock pool, from which red water sparkled indiscriminately as it came out of the ground.

Sir Robert quickly carried Sofia in his arms over to a dry stone flat area close by this, where he laid her down and immediately started to try and resuscitate her.

It was more than five minutes later that Sir Robert knew he was not going to be able to revive his precious young daughter and as he sat there helpless on the stone floor next to where her delicate body lay motionless, he looked at her beautiful but pale white face and started to shed some tears.

Sir Robert had experienced the death of many close friends during the numerous bloody battles he had fought in, but none had ever been so heartfelt and distressing as loosing his beloved Sofia.

He stood up and started wandering aimlessly around the inside of the cavern for a while, whilst he tried to compose himself before having to set off back to the Manor House and explain how she had died.

As he reached the opposite side, Sir Robert noticed a group of flickering crystals surrounded by bright silver shining from amongst the hidden crevices along one of the rock walls and walked over to have a closer look.

He soon discovered a series of seven hexagonal crystal and silver edged devices all grouped together to form a symmetrical, but jagged circular shape, with a silver letter 'K' at its centre.

The other six hexagons also contained either a single silver letter or symbol, which when read clockwise from the 'K', altogether made the word 'KLOPTON' as it was also spelt on the scroll parchment that Sir Robert had seen previously.

Furthermore, whilst both the 'K' and 'P' hexagons glowed bright red, the other five remained rose pink in colour, yet the 'K' and '0' key holes were the only two not containing a key stud.

Remembering about the text etched onto the 'K' key stem, Sir Robert wondered if removing the 'P' key would open the next passage, but he knew that now was not the right time for him to find out.

Upon walking back over to where Sofia lay, Sir Robert knelt down beside her to say a short prayer, before picking her up in his arms again and making their way back over to where they had entered the cavern.
Holding her body tightly, he re-entered the water and swam off by the side of the current through the underwater passage, until he surfaced again amongst the rocks standing along the edge of the stream.
After climbing back up these onto the passageway, Sir Robert walked over to the nearby cave entrance and locked the hexagonal device on the side wall again with the 'K' key.
He immediately heard another loud thud coming from within the rock wall, which he knew this time was the sound of the underwater gap closing shut.

With Sofia's body in his arms, Sir Robert left the passageway through the crevice opening and once outside, he covered up the rock entrance with various flora again, before setting off slowly down the hillside to the Manor House, where he had the unenviable task of telling his wife and children the tragic news.

All of the family were unconsolable as Sir Robert lay Sofia onto her bed so they could kneel down together beside her body in reflective prayer, but as tears of sadness continued to be shed, this just became far too difficult for everyone to cope with.
Whilst Sir Robert tried to comfort them all, Lady Marsha stood up after less than five minutes and took both John and Kate with her back to one of their bedrooms, where she stayed with them until they eventually managed to fall asleep.
It was still late at night and there was much to do in the morning after sunrise, but for now Lady Marsha needed to wash Sofia's body before changing her into some of her favourite clothes in readiness for the funeral the next day.

Sir Robert also had things to do, but before he left Sofia's room he wanted another look at the hexagonal birthmark under her arm, as he wondered why this had not protected her when she was in the red glowing waters, as it did for him.
He waited for his wife to return with some clean cloths and together they rolled up Sofia's sleeve, where they both saw that her birthmark was still a deep brown shade and not the bright red colour which Sir Robert had under his arm.
Lady Marsha suspected that she might know the reason for this however and slowly started to explain her thoughts to her husband, as they both stood by her bedside overcome with grief.

23

Sofia was still only twelve years old and had not yet reached puberty, but at the age when she would have started bleeding, her birthmark would have also turned bright red upon her entering the glowing waters during the time of the red full Moon.

Sir Robert looked at his wife and became even more forlorn as he realised she must be right.

He totally blamed himself for taking Sofia into the cave with him when she was far too young, since otherwise she would still be alive and have her own future to look forward to.

They then went over to the bedroom where both the children were thankfully still fast asleep and not wishing to wake them up, gently rolled their right sleeves up one at a time.

Kate was older than Sofia, having turned thirteen that year, whilst John was fourteen, but both of their hexagonal birthmarks were still a deep brown colour.

Sir Robert knew however, that it would not be too long before they both reached the age of puberty and could then enter the passageway when the full Moon shone red, so their birthmarks could also change colour and thereafter enable them to swim safely in the stream whenever it too glowed.

It was late the next morning when Lady Marsha and the children awoke, but Sir Robert was used to having much less sleep and as soon as the sun rose, he sent one of his squires off to fetch the priest from the Holy Trinity Church in Stratford to perform the funeral service that afternoon.

They decided to bury Sofia's body on the edge of the Oat Hill woodland clearing near to the old rock face and after the private burial, they would also have Kate re-christened with the extra middle name of Sofia, so that in the future she would always carry this with her in memory of her younger sister.

Sir Robert also hoped that one day in the future, both John and Kate would find their way through the stream's underwater passage into the larger red glowing crystal cavern where Sofia died, and explore all of the wonders this magnificent chamber had to offer.

Over the years that followed, whenever Sir Robert saw the full Moon glow red again overhead, he would take the whole family into the crystal lined passageway and up to the rock wall at the end, where the stream water and cave were also that colour.

Whilst he would never turn the 'K' key in the wall device himself to access the large cavern, they would all instead kneel down for a short period of quiet prayer in remembrance of Sofia, before soon returning back to the Manor House.

Once the children had both gone to bed, Sir Robert & Lady Marsha would then go back outside to sit near the lake and look up at the night sky until the red full Moon had gone again and everything returned to its natural colour.

During such periods of time however, Sir Robert could never find any pattern for when the full Moon and rose pink crystals would both glow bright red together.
He therefore decided to have a wooden clock made that would let him know beforehand when these overlapping events were going to occur and in doing so, hopefully prevent him from not being in Clopton at the correct time to witness them.

Sir Robert's first job was to go back inside the passageway during the day and to chisel off some of the rose pink crystals lining the various rock walls.
Then, whilst on his next trip to London, he took these crystal pieces with him and went to see a craftsman in the art of clock making, who had been recommended by one of his aristocratic friends.

After listening to all of Sir Robert's requirements, the horologist drew up a design for an exquisitely carved wooden clock, on the face of which would be displayed three individual circles.
Each of these would contain one of three separate dials at their centre, all of which inset with some rose pink crystal fragments that would glow bright red in time to announce the period of the next red full Moon:
- a small circle with a silver dial to point to a day of the week.
- a medium sized circle with a silver dial to point to a KLOPTON letter.
- a large circle with a silver dial to point to a date in the month.

To create such a clock, the horologist used the rose pink crystals Sir Robert had collected from the rock passageway and fixed them to all the various specific points around the clock face circles.
Two months later the wooden clock was delivered to Clopton House and Sir Robert was so delighted with this, that he proudly displayed it on top of the fireplace in the main dining room for everyone to see and where it remained from that day.

The following month was Kate's sixteenth birthday and Sir Robert knew that it would be the right time for him to return the 'K' key pendant to her to keep, which he had locked away and never let be used since Sofia's tragic death.
He also decided that whilst opening the metal chest, he would remove the five remaining silver signet rings, plus the 'K' scroll and a bag of silver coins he had been storing inside it.

Instead, Sir Robert would put all of these into the alcove in the rock wall, where they would be locked away in a much safer place and only accessible to a descendant in possession of the 'K' key and KLOPT0N family birthmark under their arm.

That afternoon, he set off over to the rock face crevice and as soon as he had reached the passageway cave wall, he opened the alcove and placed all of the items inside, after which he put the rectangular piece of rock back into the hole and turned the key again to lock it shut.

A few weeks later Kate was sixteen and that evening after the birthday celebrations had finished, Sir Robert & Lady Marsha sat down with her and John to all say a family prayer together for their deeply missed Sofia.
Sir Robert then handed Kate the 'K' pendant and silver chain for her to start wearing again, although initially she was very reluctant about taking them.

Upon seeing the sadness etched across her young face, Lady Marsha explained the full reason why Sofia had died so tragically and told her that by wearing these again, she would be honouring her memory.
After shedding a few tears, Kate took the pendant and chain from her father and clasped them in her hands whilst she said a short prayer for her sister, before placing them both around her neck.

Sir Robert then told her and John about the spelling of the name KLOPT0N he had discovered on the scroll in the alcove and how this 'K' key would also open the hexagonal device nearby, to give them safe access along the stream's current and through the underwater passage in the rock wall.

It was up to each of them if they wished to follow this path during the period of the red full Moon and by doing so, enter the vast illuminated cavern where the long forgotten history of KLOPT0N and its ancestors was there to be discovered.

Sadly, Sir Peter never returned to Stratford and in 1247 Sir Robert died, leaving his son Sir John de Clopton to inherit both the Clopton Park estate and his title.

Sir Robert already had the black & red coat of arms for KLOPT0N copied from the 'K' parchment and painted onto a wooden shield, with instructions that upon his death, this was to be laid over his body together with his House of Clopton shield, as they had both helped protect him during his life.

Lady Marsha also placed by her husband's side his favourite sword and a wooden cross, both of which she had engraved with his name as a loyal Knight of England and the ancestral family Houses.

In addition, the 'K' signet ring was left on Sir Robert's finger, as she knew how proud of this he had been, whilst Sir John would be keeping the identical 'K' ring his father gave him all those years earlier.

Sir Robert's final wish was for him to be buried next to the body of his beloved Sofia on the edge of the Oat Hill woodland clearing, where they would both lay facing towards the rock face and the hidden crevice entrance of the crystal lined passageway.

His wooden coffin was to be covered by a slab of stone to match that on top of his daughter's grave, where they would then both wait for the rest of the family to one day join them and thereafter, all spend the rest of time together watching the Moon whenever it glowed red in the night sky overhead.

20th century Clopton Manor House

Part 2

HOUSE OF CLOPTON
- 20th Century -

Chapter 4 : **Journey Home**

It was a cold New Year's morning on 1st January 1915 as Katrina and her husband Tarak stood together outside their old fisherman's cottage in the small quiet coastal town of Queenstown close to Cork in Ireland, whilst sipping a hot drink as they watched the strong waves from the Irish Sea splash over the narrow beach and against the sea harbour wall to the front of them.

The distant stars and constellations shone brightly up above in the clear night sky, as they watched the full Moon move slowly overhead in alignment with the Earth and the Sun, causing it to glow bright red due to the refraction from the Earth's shadow whilst it remained between it and the Sun.
This full lunar eclipse made the visible night sky appear red too, which colour also reflected down onto the sea as far as they could see up to the horizon.

Katrina knew that this phenomenon would only last for a few hours as she looked down at the silver letter 'K' pendant she wore on a silver chain around her neck and was captivated by its rose pink crystals which had been glowing a bright red colour all that time.
She also reflected on her ancestors family traditions and knew that the time would soon come for her to pass this extraordinary piece of intricate jewellery onto her daughter Kara.

Their friends had now left for the evening after enjoying a rather muted New Year Eve's party buffet with just a few fireworks, whilst their teenage twins Kara & Kane had gone upstairs to one of their bedrooms from where they could still be heard talking to each other.

This picturesque setting could not have been more distant from the bloody War that was now raging in Europe and rapidly spreading across the rest of the World, with troops from all nations of the British Empire providing unwavering support to King George V (House of Windsor) and the Allied Powers, against the might of the German armies and the Central Powers.

Tarak & Katrina looked over at each other and both knew that very soon their lives would never be the same again.

Katrina had been sent off with her maid Laura by her parents in June 1898 whilst she was still sixteen, as she had become pregnant out of wedlock and as such would bring shame on the aristocratic Clopton family name if she remained.
A private room in a Catholic convent in Cork had been arranged for her and once she had settled into her new accommodation, Laura returned back to the family at Clopton House again.

Tarak was born in India in 1877, but left there at the age of fifteen with a group of Jesuit priests on a pilgrimage overland into Europe, before eventually arriving at a Catholic monastery in Cork in 1897.
During his five years of travelling he had worked in many different hospitals and being a very intelligent person, soon became highly skilled, so much so that the Cork hospital were delighted to have someone with his expertise working there.

Katrina & Tarak met each other at the hospital where she had gone for a routine examination that he was to carry out, but which Katrina soon had to admit to him was because of her pregnancy, as it was evident Tarak quickly realised her true condition.
As they talked more however, he quickly became besotted by her and made numerous excuses to check her medical condition again as often as he could over the following weeks.
What he had not realised though, was that she was infatuated with him too and equally delighted to keep returning back to the hospital to see him.

Katrina was a very pretty, well spoken and athletic English girl with beautiful long brown hair and blue eyes, who was especially good at horse riding.
Tarak was a tall handsome Indian man with black hair and brown eyes, who had a muscular physique and also enjoyed sport, particularly fencing.
They were both clearly perfect for each other and soon fell deeply in love, whereupon realising the timescale of her pregnancy and not wishing to let any further shame fall upon her, Tarak asked Katrina to marry him as soon as they could, to which she readily accepted!

A week later, after Tarak had left his Jesuit brothers and Katrina had told her Mother Superior, they were married in the convent chapel.

The convent also agreed to let them stay in a fisherman's cottage they owned in Queenstown and the following year the twins were born to everyone's delight.

Once the children were old enough to go to school, Katrina started working at the hospital with Tarak and soon became a nurse, with which qualifications she was determined to help repay the kindness shown to them all.

It was nearly sixteen years after Katrina's arrival in Cork that it was time for them to leave back to England and safe passage across the Irish Sea from Dublin to Liverpool was arranged for the four of them.
Fortuitously, they had both secured medical positions in the field War Hospital that was soon to be opened in the grounds of the Clopton Manor House for wounded soldiers, through the generosity of the Reverend Francis Hodgson who now owned the whole of the Clopton estate.

Katrina & Tarak returned the Queensferry cottage which had been their home since they got married, to the convent together with virtually all of their possessions, since they would only be able to carry a few small personal items with them on their journey.
The long drive and sea crossing would however provide Katrina with some time to tell the twins more about both Stratford-upon-Avon and Clopton House, so they would have a much better idea of what to expect upon their arrival.

There were however, some ancestral family secrets Katrina & Tarak would not let the twins know about until their sixteenth birthdays had passed, whilst there was also a long forgotten history to Clopton which Kane & Kara would need to discover more about themselves once they were there.

They eventually landed by transport ship in Liverpool military docks on a cold damp early February morning in 1915, where there was a military vehicle waiting for them on the quay side.
After their documents had been checked, they had time for a quick bowl of soup and hot drink with the driver, before being taken off to the site of the field War hospital in Stratford-upon-Avon.

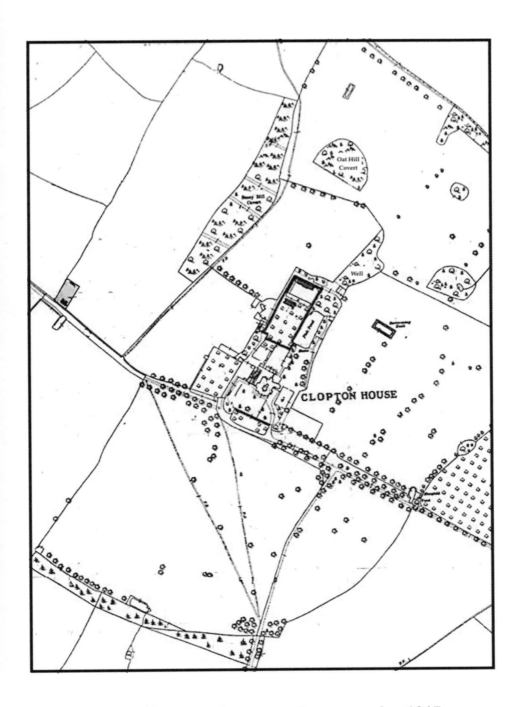

Clopton House and surrounding grounds c1915

Upon their arrival at Clopton House later that evening, they were shown into the field War hospital temporary office where they were greeted by Avis Hodgson, daughter of Reverend Francis & Elizabeth Hodgson.

She was delighted to have two extra trained medical staff available to help look after all the wounded soldiers they were still waiting for, as the field hospital accommodation was not fully built yet, nor had all the necessary medical equipment arrived that needed installing.

After brief introductions, Avis could see that all four of them were very tired and so took them over to the Manor House, where on the first floor they were provided with a large fully furnished family sitting room and two bedrooms, meaning that the twins would have to share with each other as they did in Queenstown.

All three of the rooms had log fires that had already been lit for them, which they were grateful for as the winter climate was very cold, especially at that time at night.

Their cases and other bags had already been delivered to the suite by the driver and so they quickly sorted these all out and then each unpacked their fresh clothes to change into.

Once something had been prepared for them to eat by the kitchen staff, they all went downstairs to the dining room together, where in front of a roaring log fire they were served their hot food and drink.

Avis and another nurse Kathleen Talbot also joined them for the meal and quickly turned the topic around to discussing the family's time in Ireland, which they both found very fascinating.

After they had finished their meal, the four of them expressed their grateful thanks to Avis for the food and then retired to their rooms for some long overdue comfortable sleep, with all of them agreeing that everything else could wait until the following morning.

Upon sunrise the next day, they heard a military bugle being blown outside in the field and as they looked out of their windows, they saw the Union Jack being hoisted up a flag pole in front of the main field War hospital construction.

At the same time, a group of men who were helping to erect the hospital structures, saluted and gave three cheers to King George V.

The morning sky was very clear and as they all left the Manor House to go for a quick walk around the gardens before breakfast, the crisp cold weather hit them and it was not long before they all headed back inside to the kitchen and cooked themselves a hot meal.

They soon ate up all of their food and straight away afterwards Katrina & Tara went off to find Avis again, in order to discuss more about their new roles and also meet some of the other field hospital personnel.

Meanwhile, Kane & Kara put some thicker clothes on and set off outside again to explore the many outbuildings and grounds surrounding their new home.
Fortunately, it was a weekend, so the twins would have a couple of days to also hopefully meet some of the other teenagers living and working on the estate, before they both had to start their new schools on the Monday.

The Manor House comprised a splendid Restoration style three storey white washed brick mansion, which had been rebuilt together with further significant restoration work during both the 16th and 19th centuries.
Most of the rooms overlooked the inner stone courtyard which had a small well at its centre, whilst every room had a view over different aspects of the extensive large gardens, various outbuildings and surrounding countryside.

The main function rooms included the glorious wooden panelled Great Banqueting Hall with window seating in front of several stained glass windows and crystal chandeliers hanging from its ceiling, plus numerous family portraits on its walls.
The polished wooden floor was partly covered with luxurious patterned carpets and had a stone fireplace at one end, with a carved mantelpiece and a splendid old clock, plus various other ornaments spread around the room.

There was also an impressive large dining room and stone fireplace, next to which was a fully functional kitchen with a narrow stone passageway down to the cellar for storing food and wine.
This basement also led to a concealed outside doorway and steps back up to the edge of an ornate walled garden.
Finally, there was a smaller separate sitting room with several book cases containing a well stocked library of intriguing reading books.

The first floor comprised of the main living accommodation and bedrooms, whilst on the east wing of the second floor inside the tall roof space were small rooms for the house servants.

Also on the second floor in the corner of the West wing was a small private Chapel, but this was kept locked by the family for their own personal use.

Outside, there was a variety of well stocked landscaped gardens, including miniature bushes bordering the stone paths and a large selection of fruit trees, whilst to the north east was an ornamental fish lake with a small boat store, surrounded along two sides by stone balustrades, with steps down to the water's edge and overlooked by a series of carved white marble statues.

The small lake and a separate rectangular pond built in the field nearby for bathing, were both fed by a fresh water underground stream, which ran down through the nearby lush hillside fields from somewhere deep inside the overgrown rock face of the south facing Oat Hill woodland covert.

The spring water for the lake however, resurfaced separately via a small brick built arched well, where it crossed over the rear North corner of the lawned gardens and through a couple of small ponds, before flowing into the lake.
Both water sources soon merged again to form a single stream, that ran down across the field on the eastern side of the Manor House, before eventually entering the Bluecap woodland covert and then down the hills on the opposite side.

Along the edge of the trees stood Clopton Tower, which was mainly octagonally shaped and built in stone as a belvedere back in the 1850's due to its prominent location.
This primary single turret structure displayed a British flag from its meagre battlements, whilst also providing excellent views over Stratford-upon-Avon town centre and much of the surrounding countryside.

On the north eastern side of Clopton Tower was the Welcombe Hills estate, which lands bordered Clopton Park and were separated by a thick belt of trees and pathway, which formed a small part of the Monarch's Way trail along which King Charles II escaped in 1651 after the Battle of Worcester.
This large private estate, together with the magnificent Welcombe House built on the lower grounds during the 1860s in a neo-Jacobean style, were owned by Sir George & Lady Caroline Trevelyan.

The main building was rather flamboyantly designed as a 'Calendar' house, comprising 7 entrances, 12 fireplaces, 52 chimneys and 365 windows!

Overlooking the house slightly further north up on the hillside, stood a tall memorial monument built in 1876 by the then owner Robert Philips, which imposing obelisk could also be seen above the trees from Stratford-upon-Avon down below.

Back in the Clopton Park grounds of the Manor House close to the western side of the lake was a walled kitchen garden, together with a large brick outbuilding that had two tall chimneys and furnaces at its centre to provide most of the hot water required by the Manor House via a series of narrow metal underground pipes.

These outbuildings also provided much needed indoor working space and dry storage, plus living accommodation for the estate manager.

The walled gardens were used to grow a large variety of vegetables, with greenhouses built for fruit such as grapes and tomatoes, whilst a chicken coup and pig sty were also well stocked.

There were also two other small outhouses nearer to the Manor House, whilst the main coach house was built close to the main rear entrance and courtyard.

The surrounding fields were mainly fenced in, with cattle on some of the lower fields and sheep on the upper hillside, whilst other parts of the estate lands were used to grow most of the crops needed.

In addition, the main stables, paddocks, farm buildings and other workers cottages were kept just over the brow of the Stony Hill covert to the west in Lower Clopton.

Overall, the estate was reasonably self-sufficient, but as the War got worse a lot of this would be about to change with food and labour shortages causing much more demand.

Reverend Hodgson was often working away in London due to the War, but before he left he organised for all the field hospital structures and tents to be spread around the Clopton grounds close to the front and side of the Manor House, thus enabling direct road access for deliveries and everyone else who was helping with the building work and all the various medical requirements.

He also gave permission for some of the more senior medical staff to live in the Manor House spare rooms, along with his few remaining servants who would also help to maintain the property.

It only took a few days for all the family to settle into their new home and surroundings, whilst Katrina & Tarak got used to their respective job responsibilities and the twins decided on which local schools they wanted to attend.

The following week Kane started at King Edward VI School for Boys in Stratford-upon-Avon where he would continue with his education.
He was used to single sex schooling back in Ireland and as his new school syllabus contained many subjects at which he was proficient, including his favourites Mathematics, English and History, he quickly settled into his new environment.

Kane also spoke very eloquently and although he had a slight Irish accent, his pronunciation was always precise and he soon started making many new friends, particularly in the sports teams as he was a strong all-round athlete and highly skilled in fencing which the school also excelled at.

This boys school dated back to the 13th Century, having been re-founded in the 16th Century by King Edward VI and was where the playwright William Shakespeare was partly educated.
Over the centuries the school had built a variety of extra buildings including a Guildhall, a half-timbered schoolroom, the teachers' offices and also the Old Vicarage where the Headmaster lived.

Next to the school stood the historic Guild Chapel to which Sir Hugh Clopton had been a generous benefactor in the 15th Century and was now also regularly used for school services and prayer.

Kara also started her school that week, but she had to travel over to nearby Warwick instead, where she joined The King's High School for Girls.
Although Kara had many similar traits and skills as her brother, she also loved music like her mother did and over the years had learnt to play several musical instruments.

She equally loved the theatre and was thrilled to have the opportunity to learn more about William Shakespeare than she did in Ireland, whilst she also hoped that one day she would be able to take part in one of his plays which the school performed every year.
In addition, Kara took the opportunity to read as much as she could about the Clopton family and chose this as one of her history topics, whilst most of the other girls mainly studied parts of Warwick history.

Kara also preferred swimming to athletics and had won many tournaments back in Cork, which ability quickly made her a prominent member of the school swimming team.

The girls school was only established in the late 18th Century, having originated when the boys left to form they own separate Warwick school and then by subsequently also combining with the girls and buildings from two neighbouring schools.

Katrina accompanied Kara to Warwick on her first day at school so she could also use the opportunity to go and visit her parents Kathleen & Andrew nearby, who she had rarely seen since she was sixteen when they sent her off to Ireland.

Although they had also exchanged a few letters and black & white photographs, it was always going to be an emotional reunion and one which Katrina decided it would be best that she should do on her own, before her parents met Tarak and the twins for the first time.

After the initial trepidation and tears of joy, the day went very quickly with so much to talk about and Katrina was sad to see how poorly her father had become.

Being a nurse, Katrina promised that she would come back and visit them as often as she could and also see what medicine she could obtain from the field War hospital to help, although she knew this could be difficult due to the general shortage of medical supplies.

It was then time for Katrina to leave as she was meeting Kara after school so they could travel back to Clopton together, but she told them that it was the twins birthdays in a couple of weeks and they were invited to the Manor House, whilst hoping that they would be well enough to make it.

The time passed by quickly and the day of the twins sixteenth birthday was upon them all.

Avis had agreed that they could use the hospital canteen tent for a small party and invite a few friends from their schools plus some other teenagers from around the Clopton estate.

Kane had become best friends with the stable lad Stuart who was of a similar age to him and lived in the farmhouse with his parents.

Stuart had two older brothers Luke and Mark, plus a sister named Helen who was only a year younger than him and she soon became close friends with Kara too.

38

Over on the Lower Clopton farm Stuart also looked after the sheep dog kennels, so Kane & Kara would try and join them whenever the dogs were needed to bring in the sheep, as it was always a great experience.

However, Kara had started getting some feelings for Stuart and was thrilled when she could join up with him and her brother, but she also knew that she would have to keep these thoughts to herself for now as her future was so uncertain.

Katrina's parents Kathleen & Andrew arrived at the Manor House early in the afternoon before the party started so they could spend some more time alone with their daughter, but also meet their grand-children and son-in-law who they had never met before.

It was another emotional meeting, but everyone made a real fuss of them both which really helped lighten the occasion, especially as Kathleen became very anxious every time she mentioned about a dangerous journey the twins would soon be going on and how they must always look after each other.

Kane & Kara had no idea what their grand-mother was talking about and assumed that she must be confused with the journey they had just undertaken back to England across the sea from Ireland.

Andrew and Tarak got on particularly well with each other and spent a lot of time talking about their respective home countries, especially since Andrew had never visited India before and was fascinated to hear some of Tarak's stories from when he was younger.

They were also both interested to learn about each other's present day armies and how Britain and India were fighting together against their common enemies in the Great War.

Unfortunately, with Andrew not being too well he soon became tired and Tarak took him to their bedroom so he could have a rest.

He then went to the hospital to get some medicine he had put to one side after Katrina had previously described her father's symptoms.

Later that afternoon Kane & Kara got ready for their birthday party in some new clothes they had borrowed from the house keepers.

Upon Katrina & Tarak seeing them looking so smart and grown up, they were so proud of them both and finally realised how they were not young children any more.

The twins had been born several hours apart and looked quite identical during the early years of their childhood, but they were no longer that similar with Kara now taking after her mother much more than Kane did.
Although both of them had brown hair and blue eyes, Kara was more petite than Kane, who was tall and muscular with strong facial features.
It was therefore usually considered that Kane took after Tarak in his physique, although not otherwise in appearance, whilst Katrina knew her husband was not the true birth father to either of the twins!

Even so, Katrina believed there was something very special about them both and often wondered if her journey through the red cavern waters on the night of the full lunar eclipse when she was pregnant, had somehow impacted on the twins creation.

. . . .

Despite rationing having been partly introduced due to the war, everybody helped with the party food and the cooks even managed to make a birthday cake for them to share out with as many guests as it would go around.

The medical staff had previously collected several musical instruments and together with a few of the stewards already made their own small band, so those who could dance would also be able to join in the birthday celebrations for at least a couple of hours.

The day was a great success, but unfortunately Kathleen & Andrew had to leave before the early evening weather got too cold and after a few emotional farewells, they were driven home to Warwick in an army vehicle Tarak had organised for them.

Thankfully, the weather continued to stay dry and as soon as it got a bit darker, the birthday party went outside for a short time to watch a few improvised fireworks.
They all then returned back indoors for a couple of last dances, after which everyone left to either return home or go to their rooms.

It had been a wonderful evening, but it was not until they had all gone to bed that the realisation of what Katrina & Tarak had to tell the twins the next day really impacted on them.

They both knew it would be difficult to get much sleep that night.

Chapter 5 : **Clopton Generations**

The following morning soon dawned and after finishing their breakfast in the hospital canteen, everyone returned to the private sitting room in the Manor House so Katrina could tell Kane & Kara about their more recent Clopton family history, which she had not told them before.

Katrina's grandmother Lady Katherine was born in 1838, the daughter of Sir John Clopton who inherited the family estate upon his birth in 1818, but who's father Sir Edward Clopton (birth name Ingham) sold it a few years later to the Meynell family.
The estate was subsequently sold to Fisher Tomes and again five years later to John Lloyd in 1830, who died in 1863 when the estate was inherited by his nephew Charles Warde.

During these years of ownership changes, the main Clopton family continued to live in part of the Manor House buildings and when Katherine was old enough, her mother Lady Karen Clopton would teach her the household responsibilities expected of a lady of the House.
In addition, she also helped her gain a more complete education compared to that she was getting by just attending the local school.
In 1860 Lady Katherine married Sir Thomas and the following year Katrina's mother Kathleen was born.

It was a few years later in 1871 that Sir John's wife Lady Karen was tragically killed in an accident on the estate, when a herd of startled cattle stampeded through the main farmyard and trampled her to death.
He was totally distraught by her agonising death and it took him a long time after the funeral before he felt able to talk freely to his daughter Lady Katherine again about any family matters.

Whilst in one such conversation, Sir John reminded her that the middle name of 'Sofia' which both she and Lady Kathleen were born with, also belonged to Lady Karen whilst she was alive.
Indeed, many female descendants of the original Clopton bloodline would have this extra middle name, since it also helped to identify their true ancestral family birthright.
This tradition continued to remain significant as Sir John had no male heir and also because the Law of England during those times decreed only men could legally own any such assets.

It was Sir John who therefore insisted that Lady Katherine's husband Sir Thomas also change his married surname to Clopton and that all of their future daughters' husbands must do the same, especially if they or their sons were to ever inherit the family House and grounds.

In 1879 Sir John passed away peacefully in his sleep and it was Sir Thomas who therefore acquired all of his financial estate.

The following year Lady Kathleen married Andrew in the small private chapel on the top floor of the Clopton Manor House, after which they also moved into one of the main family accommodation suites on the first floor.

Unable to cope with the Clopton status bestowed upon him however, Sir Thomas had in the meantime already started drinking and gambling excessively, so much so that within only two years he had virtually spent all of the monies he inherited from Lady Katherine's father.

In 1881 the whole of the Clopton estate was sold to Sir Arthur Hodgson who was the High Sheriff of Warwickshire and he initially allowed them all to continue living in part of the Manor House with him, as he was not always there.

Unfortunately however, there was not really enough space for everyone, especially as the family now also included Katrina Clopton who was born to Sir Andrew & Lady Kathleen in August of that year.

It was therefore decided with Sir Arthur Hodgson's agreement, to evict Sir Thomas from the estate in disgrace for losing the family fortune and also because he was not a true descendant of the Clopton family.

Thomas subsequently died nearly three years later in a hostel for the homeless in nearby Warwick town, where he also sadly ended up being unceremoniously buried in a pauper's grave.

In 1889 at the age of fifty-one, Lady Katherine sadly died of pneumonia, although Kathleen believed this was also partly due to her broken heart.

Sir Andrew & Lady Kathleen continued to stay in their accommodation at Clopton House until 1898 after Lady Katrina had left to stay in Ireland and they then moved to Warwick, where they stayed as honoured guests in part of the castle outbuildings for many years.

. . . .

The two children already knew how their parents Tarak & Katrina had met each other in Cork and that they got married soon afterwards, with both of them being born the following year.

However, the very difficult news for Kara & Kane to now learn was the real reason why they got married so quickly, which was that Katrina was already pregnant when they met and Tarak was not their actual true birth father.

Katrina had conceived at the age of sixteen whilst still living in England and upon realising this, her parents sent her off to a convent in Ireland with a trusted maid to support her whilst she had the baby, not knowing that Katrina was actually going to have twins.

Through working closely with Katrina in the hospital, Tarak quickly realised that she was pregnant, but he had fallen in love with her from the moment they first met and wanted to bring up her children as their own.

Tarak, however, was born the first nephew of an Indian Hindu Maharaja and at that time he would be disowned by his family if he married outside of his class, especially to a white Christian girl, even one born into an English aristocratic family.

Whilst Katrina was very unhappy about Tarak's decision to accept such a dishonour when she agreed to his marriage proposal, he was adamant about his feelings for her and she knew that not only was it true love between them, but they were obviously destined to be together.

Kane & Kara looked at each other and then back at Katrina & Tarak, before with tears in their eyes they stood up together and gave each of their parents huge hugs, whilst telling them both how much they loved them.

After what seemed like an eternity, the twins sat back down again and after everyone had composed themselves, Kane spoke first and asked who their birth father was?

Katrina explained that his name was Richard and he lived and worked on a farm just outside Stratford-upon-Avon, although she first met him whilst he was helping to sell produce on a food stall at the town market.

He was just seventeen at the time, but after she was sent off to Ireland, she never heard from him again and also never wrote to tell him about the twins.

This however, was not the whole story, but Katrina & Tarak knew that it was not the right time to tell the twins the rest, especially as although they both knew where Richard probably was, this would be very difficult to explain and they also did not know if he was still alive.

It had been an emotional morning for everyone and as the clock struck twelve noon, they all agreed that it would now be the right time to go outside for a break and have some lunch, after which Katrina had some more Clopton family history she needed to tell them.

As it was quite a mild day with the winter sun breaking through the thin cloud cover, they decided after finishing their meal to sit down outside on one of the benches overlooking the lake to continue their talk, with the twins quite apprehensive about what else their parents still had to tell them.

Katrina began by removing the 'K' silver pendant and chain from off around her neck and upon handing it over to Kara, told her that now she was sixteen years old this belonged to her.

43

Whilst she knew that her mother always wore this, Kara had never been able to hold it up so close before to examine its intricate silver work and see an hexagonal layer of rose pink crystal fragments on its top surrounding an embossed silver letter 'K' shape.

Kara also noticed that the four slim silver stems protruding underneath the pendant were designed in the shape of a 'K' and that in fact the whole of the pendant appeared to be a key.

Before Kara could ask any questions however, Katrina told her to look closely at the two-part inscription engraved in an unusual font on either side of the longest metal stem.

As Kara held the pendant up to the light to see, her mother recited the phrase out loudly so everyone could hear her say:

'only the key ... will passage allow'

Both of the twins looked puzzled as Katrina explained that only during a specific short period of time would they be able to turn the lock which this key opened and only then would they be able to proceed on a journey through a hidden passage to discover their destiny.

Realising that this pendant was a lot more precious than either of them could have ever imagined, Kara & Kane listened intensely as Katrina went on to explain that it had been passed down through the generations to the daughters of the Clopton bloodline only and that she had been given it when she was sixteen by her mother, being the family tradition at that age.

The pendant was also much more than just a piece of jewellery or a key, as the rose pink crystals had special properties which would only reveal themselves when the Moon glowed red overhead in the night sky during a full lunar eclipse.

The twins remembered back to when they were all living in Cork and how their mother would take them outside whenever a red Moon appeared over the horizon, to tell them how the full lunar eclipse changed its colour.

What she had not previously told them however, was that the rose pink crystals embedded in the pendant would also glow red during such an eclipse and that more of these crystals could only be found in one location on the Clopton estate, which secret was only told to true descendants of the ancestral bloodline when they came of age.

Katrina also had something else to reveal about the 'K' key however, as she told Kara to look again at the very end of the longest stem, where she would find a small crescent shape etched onto both sides.

This symbolised the Moon just before its full lunar eclipse and was very relevant to their journey ahead.

44

The weather started to go cooler outside and so Katrina said they should continue with the family history back inside the Manor House, to which they all agreed.

After a quick detour via the kitchen to get themselves some much needed hot drinks and cake, they joined each other again in the dining room.

Once everyone had sat down, Katrina went over to the stone fireplace on top of which stood an antique wooden clock with unusual dials and markings, none of which however, seemed to tell the time.

She began by explaining to both of the twins about the clock and how it worked:

- the small silver dial on the right hand side of this clock face which had just seven points, would only move when it was time to show the day of the upcoming lunar eclipse.

- the large silver dial in the centre would move around the inside of the clock's outer edge and had just 30 points to show the actual date the eclipse would occur, although twentieth century clocks now had up to 31 days in some months.

- the medium sized silver dial on the left hand side of the clock face however, was the most intriguing, as this comprised seven small hexagons linked together in a symmetrical circular type shape, with each one containing a different letter or symbol.

When starting from the letter 'K' in the centre hexagon, they all together spelt the word 'KLOPTON' when read in a clockwise direction.

Almost as if they were one voice, Kara & Kane both asked why Clopton was spelt with a 'K' instead of a 'C' and Katrina explained that this was an historical anomaly, although she knew this was not the only reason, but would not tell them more just now.

Also, the second letter 'O' had a vertical line through its centre and Kara noted that this was of the same design as the letter 'phi' from the Greek alphabet.

Kane, pointed out however, that such a symbol was also referred to as the 'golden number' being an infinite mathematical figure he had once calculated to fifty digits whilst at school.

Katrina smiled at her clever son & daughter and told them that this medium length silver dial arm would also move in the same direction as the six other letters, with each one identifying a different period of time throughout history.

Furthermore, once a full lunar eclipse had begun and the Moon started to glow red, the rose pink crystals in each of the clock face's three dials would also shine bright red.

In fact, the same would happen to all of the other rose pink crystals embedded within a few random objects discretely displayed around the Manor House, which also had the unusual KLOPT0N spelling of the family name carved onto them.

Tarak then produced a signet ring from out of his pocket and gave it to Kane, telling him that this was now rightly his and he should always wear it from then onwards.

The ring was made of silver just like the pendant and also had a letter 'K' embossed on a hexagon shaped top surrounded by the crystals.

Katrina explained that when Sir John Clopton died without a direct male heir, he bequeathed this signet ring to Lady Katherine for her husband Sir Thomas to wear, before it was subsequently passed on to their daughter Lady Kathleen to give to her husband Sir Andrew.

The ring was eventually passed on to Katrina by her parents when she left for Ireland, so she too could let her husband wear it when she got married.

When Kane was born however, he was the first male Clopton heir in many generations and now that he was sixteen, it was time for him to inherit the ring and thereby display his true family lineage.

There was a sudden knock on the door and Avis Hodgson entered the room as she needed to discuss some hospital matters with Tarak & Katrina before dinner, so it was agreed that the four of them would continue with their family discussion after breakfast in the sitting room.

The twins however, stayed up late that night wondering about what else their parents were going to tell them, but were still downstairs first the following morning as they were very keen to find out.

Katrina entered the room shortly after them, but was on her own as Tarak was needed in the main field hospital tent and she surprised them by being dressed in her overcoat and boots.

She told them they were all going for a walk and she would wait for them in the hallway until they had put some more suitable clothing on.

A few minutes later the three of them were outside in the main courtyard, as Katrina explained that it would be a lot easier for her to show them what they needed to know, instead of just discussing it.

They then walked over to the garden area at the back of the lake where water was seen flowing out of a small arched brick well up ahead, close to which stood a glorious red cherry blossom tree that had been planted there in memory of Lady Margaret Clopton who drowned in 1590.

As they stopped for a short while, Katrina pointed up to the Oat Hill woodland covert on the side of the hill where the spring water stream originated from and which was to be their next destination.

Once they all set off again, she continued to tell them how the stream used to flow downhill over the Clopton Park fields, but to prevent any more tragic deaths, Margaret's father Sir William had it diverted to run underneath the surface along the same route instead.

They soon reached the edge of the woodland, where the twins discovered that part of the terrain was quite steep and the ground much more twisted than they had originally thought.

As they walked slowly through the trees and closer to the centre of the covert, Katrina guided them through some of the flourishing shrubs and thick bushes running across the front of the main hillside, where she pointed out the strata of vertical rocks protruding from amongst the thick moss and wild grasses growing over them.

She then instructed Kara & Kane to follow her along this line of rocks a bit further, but in single file, until after several more yards they all came to a halt as Katrina stopped and crouched down in front of a jagged edge crevice, which was hidden by various flora covering the rock face.

Katrina explained that in the dark shadows at the back of this deep crevice was a narrow gap, which provided a small entrance into a rock passageway on the other side.

This was not very well illuminated however and once inside, they should stand still for a short while before walking any further, to let their eyes adjust to their new surroundings and not injure themselves.

After their mother had disappeared through the crevice ahead of them, Kara & Kane quickly followed her through the gap in the rock face, where even despite the lack of light inside, they were both intrigued by where this rose pink crystal lined passageway might lead.

As soon as they could all see a bit better, Katrina led them slowly along to where the stream waters ran down one side of the passageway, whilst a small cave stood on the other, before turning to Kara and asking her for the 'K' pendant she was wearing around her neck.

Katrina then walked over with them to where a single 'K' hexagonal device was embedded on the rock wall and explained how during the full lunar red eclipse, it's key would open an underwater passage inside the red glowing stream, through which they could swim into a much larger cavern.

Once there, they would find a group of seven hexagonal devices in the same circular shape as on the clock face, another one of which would also be glowing bright red and upon removing this second key, a different underwater passage would open to take them on to the next part of their journey.

She continued by saying that they must always remember to close all of the key locks behind them and to ensure that they leave the cavern before the Moon stopped glowing red.

If they failed to do this, they would become trapped inside and probably end up starving to death before the passageway was opened again.

They must also retain the letter key with which had just opened the new passageway, so they could subsequently return to the main cavern during the next lunar eclipse and continue with their journey.

Finally, they should always keep the 'K' key, so every time they returned to the large cavern, the passageway back home to Clopton time could also be re-opened too, if necessary.

Katrina then showed them the wall location for an alcove with another 'K' hexagonal device where a 'K' scroll was stored inside, but she explained that this parchment's text could only be read during the period of the red full Moon and should be locked away before they left.

It was now time for all of them to go and make sure that the crevice entrance was covered over again with bushes after they had left, in order to help prevent it and the passageway from being discovered by anyone else.

They then made their way back down the hill to the Manor House for lunch with Tarak, after which they would help out in the field hospital during the afternoon and then discuss any questions the twins had after dinner together.

The main topic of conversation that evening Kara & Kane wanted to talk about was the destination of their forthcoming journey through the passageway, which Katrina had kept mentioning to them that morning.

Unfortunately however, the answer they got was not what they expected, since neither of their parents truthfully knew where the twins would end up!

Katrina explained that only after the full lunar eclipse began and one of the seven keys glowed red, would that letter point to their next destination, but they did not know where all of the keys pointed to.

When they did arrive at the location however, they must never disclose where they actually came from since to do so would be very difficult and even dangerous for them, although thankfully they should meet up with other family descendants and therefore be looked after during their stay.

When she was young, Katrina travelled through the passageway on her own, but found it very difficult with no one to support her and she returned back home as soon as she could.

48

If however, the twins were to set off together, they would be able to help each other complete the whole journey and in doing so, fulfil the destiny set for only true blood ancestors, although rarely had anyone ever achieved this over countless generations.

Whilst she could tell them more about the lunar eclipse when the full red Moon was actually over Clopton, they had now visited the passageway that morning and everything else would become clearer once they had made their way into the main cavern and begun their journey.

It was getting late as Katrina & Tarak said goodnight.

They had a very busy day ahead of them preparing for more injured soldiers than originally planned for, so they all retired back to their rooms.

Kara & Kane however, stayed up talking for a bit longer, as there were many questions their parents would not answer and those replies they did were often cryptic or incomplete.

They both wondered what else lay ahead of them to discover once the full red lunar eclipse did appear, but decided that with school the next day, they too should now get some sleep.

Meanwhile, the War around the World kept getting bloodier and more desperate, with thousands of troops on both sides continuing to either die or become seriously wounded.

It was going to be a particularly difficult time for everyone and Katrina had a very selfish reason for Kara & Kane starting on their journey through the cavern during the period of the next red full Moon, to a different era in time.

She also knew that upon Kane turning eighteen he would be called up to serve in the Army and had already made it clear he wanted to fight on the front line for his King and Country.

Katrina however, like most mothers, did not want her son to become another young casualty of the deadly battles being fought across Europe and therefore hoped that by the time the twins returned back home, the War would be over.

Shakespeare's house in the 20th Century

Chapter 6 : **Stratford-upon-Avon**

At the weekends, after Kane & Kara had finished their school work and household chores, they would both go around the Clopton estate to help with some of the ongoing preparation work for the launch of the new field hospital.

They also took every opportunity available to learn some basic medical skills from the nurses, so they could assist them once the wounded soldiers started arriving.

In particular, they wanted to help those with badly injured limbs to start exercising again and so quicken up their physical recovery time.

Any other spare time Kane & Kara could find they would use researching the history of both Stratford-upon-Avon and William Shakespeare, especially due to the connections with the Clopton family. Indeed, the small private chapel on the top floor of the Clopton Manor House was the very place where William married Anne Hathaway in 1582, although no specific record of this had ever been found.

The twins also learnt that William Shakespeare had been buried in 1616 inside The Collegiate Church of the Holy and Undivided Trinity, which stood alongside the River Avon close to the town centre.

This was also the same church as where Sir George & Lady Joyce Clopton had been entombed inside the Clopton family chapel in 1635, and where other ancestral tombs also lay reverently on display behind ornate gated railings.

Kane & Kara were equally delighted to be able to visit the Shakespeare Memorial Theatre which had only opened in 1879 and they hoped that one day soon they would be able to see one of his plays being performed by some renown actors on the specially built circular wooden stage.

The rest of Stratford-on-Avon was similar in many ways to other English market towns of that era with an eclectic mix of historic, Elizabethan and modern architecture.

It had originated as a medieval village in the 7th Century, until in 1196 King Richard I granted it a charter to hold an open market every week which changed its status to that of a market town and it prospered with better hotels opening up.

The main bridge across the River Avon for trade was re-built in stone in 1480 by Sir Hugh Clopton, who went on to become the Lord Mayor of London, and the Clopton Bridge as it was renamed, helped the town to flourish even more.

Meanwhile, back at Clopton House, the field hospital had already started taking in a few injured soldiers as the War continued to get much worse and additional tent structures were being erected to cope with the anticipated need for extra beds.

Despite all the sadness that was happening around them, the people of Stratford-upon-Avon were not going to let the War spoil their annual celebration of William Shakespeare's birthday on the 23rd April.
Although it was a much smaller event than usual, once the British flags were being flown along the streets and people arrived to join in the occasion, Kane & Kara with other pupils from both their schools also took the opportunity to visit Shakespeare's birthplace too.

By the end of May as the weather became much warmer, the field hospital was formally opened and an influx of badly wounded soldiers arrived that afternoon, which continued regularly thereafter.
Both Tarak & Katrina worked long hours together with all the other doctors and nurses, whilst after school finished the twins would often sit by the side of the hospital beds of those soldiers who were too poorly to walk and keep them company by just talking or reading books to them.

With summer having now arrived, Kane & Kara were pleased at being able to spend more time outside again, especially as they had made several friends on the Clopton estate and their school sports teams also kept them both very active.

It was one day whilst they were both swimming in the pool near the Manor House however, that Kara first realised the faint coloured hexagonal mark underneath the upper limb of her right arm was now a darker shade of brown and when she told Kane, his too in the same place under his arm had also changed to an identical colour.

That evening, after they had all finished eating, Kane & Kara asked their parents about these brown marks, to which Katrina reminded them that the hexagon shape was an hereditary birthmark for all children born directly from the original bloodline.
Additionally, this mark would change colour as they got older and she then rolled up her sleeve to show them that she too had the same birthmark underneath her upper right arm, but her's was now bright red in colour.

As the months passed by, everyone kept hoping that the War would soon be over and the horrific carnage stop, but sadly the news they kept receiving from everywhere gave no indication that the fighting would finish for at least another year.

Furthermore, whilst there was some good news from the field hospital as many of the wounded soldiers managed to recover from their injuries and were able to be returned back to active duty, distressingly others could not be saved and eventually died.

Every time this happened, a solitary soldier would blow his bugle as the British flag was lowered to half-mast and those available would step outside into the courtyard for two minutes respect, whilst the deceased's body was carried away to the temporary morgue for collection the following day.

As October arrived, it was agreed that despite all of the despondency caused by the war, the annual Mop Fair would still be held in Stratford-upon-Avon town centre the following week and so help give everyone a bit of cheer and light relief from the sad news being received far too frequently.

The event was first granted a Royal Charter by King Edward IV back in 1553 and although it would be smaller than usual this year, the funfair still provided a great deal of joy, especially for all the children who were given a free slice of meat from one of the oxen being roasted in the open streets.

One morning at the end of that month, Kane & Kara went downstairs to the kitchen as usual to get something to eat, with the field hospital canteen staff now being far too busy preparing food for all the nurses and injured soldiers, to help them.

As they crossed over the hallway and into the dining room carrying their food, the twins saw that the middle dial on the wooden clock was glowing red and pointing at the letter 'P'.

They also noticed the other two dials had both moved and were pointing to the day and date, whilst the rose pink crystals in both Kara's 'K' pendant and Kane's signet ring had also started to glow red.

Suddenly, Katrina burst through the door to join them and before they had chance to say anything, she excitedly said "It has begun and we have a lot to do!".

They all realised that the next full lunar eclipse would be starting that afternoon as the Moon moved over Warwickshire, until rising in the sky above Stratford-upon-Avon and directly in line with the Sun on the other side of the Earth.

Katrina had of course already experienced what was going to happen next when she was just a teenager herself, but for the twins and also Tarak who had now just joined them in the dining room, it was much more difficult for them to fully appreciate the magnitude of this ancestral event as it unfurled in front of them.

Whilst they all ate their breakfast together, Katrina reminded them that neither Kara nor Kane would be going to school anymore from that day onwards.

Letters had already been prepared for delivery to both of their head teachers, advising that the twins were having to return back to Ireland for personal family reasons and they might not be back in England again for a long time.
This would also have to be the story told to everyone on the Clopton estate and in the field hospital, even though it was not true, but otherwise it would be near impossible for them to try and explain the real reason for the twins upcoming prolonged absence.

After the finished eating, Kara & Kane went off to say their goodbyes to all of the friends they had made, which was a very uncomfortable, drawn out experience, as they did not want to lie about why they were leaving, but knew they had no other choice.
Kara was especially sad to be be leaving Stuart, as despite her best efforts to remain just good friends, her feelings for him had become much stronger and she knew that he felt the same way towards her.
She was going to miss him the most.

The morning passed by very quickly and it was soon time for lunch as the four of them had their final meal together, after which the twins said farewell to all of the staff and nurses who were in the field hospital canteen with them.

Next, it was back upstairs to their rooms, where the twins got changed into some very old fashioned clothes and walking shoes which Katrina had especially chosen for them both, whilst she explained that they would be going on a long journey and needed much more practical outfits.
After they got dressed, Tarak gave Kane his old pocket knife and an even older compass to take with him, whilst Katrina gave Kara a thick leather belt to wear around her waist, which had a few hidden pouches with some old silver and gold coins inside of a design Kara had never seen before.
The twins looked at each other quite confused and wondering where their extraordinary journey that night would end up taking them.

With winter now only a month away, the afternoon was getting dark much sooner due to the sun setting earlier in the night sky to the west.
As dusk approached however, they could see a faint glow appearing from over the eastern hills in the distance, as the red colour from the edge of the full lunar eclipse reached the early evening sky far off on the horizon.

All four of them agreed that they would need to get to the Oat Hill woodland rock crevice entrance whilst it was still light enough to find it safely, but dark enough for them to hopefully remain unseen crossing the fields by any of the workers still outside on that part of the estate.

Kara & Kane chose to leave the Manor House first via one of the more secluded side doors and hopefully avoid any of the nurses and other staff from seeing them.
They then made their way over quickly past Margaret's Well and up the hillside, where they waited shielded amongst the trees and bushes for Katrina & Tarak to come and join them.

As they both stood there quietly, they looked back towards the lights which had been lit around the Manor House and the field hospital structures, whilst in the distance they could hear the farm dogs on the estate barking loudly, in a way they had never heard them do so before. It was all quite eerie.

About ten minutes later the twins heard someone walking through the woodland overgrowth towards them, but fortunately it was a clear sky that evening and with the benefit of the red glow from the full Moon, they saw that it was their parents who were approaching.
After they had arrived and greeted their children with a quick hug, Katrina said that they would all now be better off inside the passageway, especially as the red glow had started shining from out of the crevice gap and should anyone else walk too close to the rock face, they may see this red light and decide to have a closer look inside.

Tarak had never been through the crevice gap before during the full lunar eclipse and so he let Katrina go in before him, with Kara following next and Kane entering last.
Apart from Katrina, none of them had ever seen the passageway whilst it was coloured bright red by the rock crystals and beams of ceiling light, that they were very surprised to see this and stood there for a short time taking in the scene as their eyes adjusted to the different light.

After a while, Katrina told the twins to follow her up to the end of the passageway, where they saw that both the stream waters and small cave entrance were also glowing bright red.
Whilst Tarak had stayed closer to the crevice gap, Katrina took the twins to the side of the passageway from where the three of them all climbed down the rocks to the waters edge.

Once there, she told Kara & Kane to both roll up their right sleeves and to each place their arm under the red water for a least a couple of minutes, during which time their birthmarks started to swell up and cause them some acute discomfort.

This pain then spread across their chests and made them both breath erratically for a short time until everything returned back to normal apart from their birthmarks, which hexagon shapes were now more defined and also displayed a new bright red colour.

Katrina explained that only the descendants of the true KLOPT0N bloodline were blessed with this gift when they came of age and meant they would forever be safe to enter the red glowing spring water during the full lunar eclipse and also benefit from its many healing properties.
Anyone else who entered the red waters however, would very probably drown and this was why Tarak kept his distance that evening.

The three of them then climbed back up over the rocks and once on the passageway again, Katrina took the twins over to where the two 'K' key devices were that she had shown them during their previous visit, whilst Tarak stood patiently further down the passageway watching them all.

On this occasion however, the crystals around both 'K' key holes glowed bright red and Katrina took the three of them over to the alcove first, where she asked Kara to put her 'K' key into the hole and then pull and turn it at the same time, whereupon she would be able to open the alcove whilst also feeling a slight swelling around her birthmark.
Kara looked slightly puzzled by her mother's instructions, but did as she said and was surprised when the key shot from out of her hand into the hole before she had chance to place it there.

They then heard some sort of mechanical grinding noise coming from inside the alcove as the rectangular piece of stone moved slowly forward on its own, until it stopped at the edge and Kane had to physically lift it out the rest of the way.
From inside the alcove, Katrina took out a few more silver 'K' signet rings identical to the one Kane was wearing and told him that they were there to be used if he ever needed another.

After putting them all back inside the alcove, she then removed a scroll and showed Kara where the small single hole was on its 'K' silver latch for the longest key stem to open it with.
Once the silver strap was loosened, Kara took hold of the two pieces of parchment and as she unrolled them both, they could all see the letters of KLOPT0N embossed across the top inside seven adjoining hexagons, together with the black & red coat of arms.

The rest of the parchment appeared to be blank, but then remembering what her mother had told her previously, Kara held both sheets up into the red glowing light, which revealed some hidden text that had probably been written in a very old medieval script.

Unfortunately however, neither she nor Kane could decipher what this said and were very disappointed, but Katrina told them both not to be too upset and to put the scrolls back into the alcove for another time, when they had found an ancestor who could read them.

Once the alcove was closed shut again, they all walked over to the other hexagonal 'K' device, where Katrina said it was now time for Kara & Kane to undo the main 'K' lock.
In doing so, they would open up a new underwater passage through the red stream into the main cavern, from where they would begin the next part of their journey.

Kara & Kane always knew this moment would come, but the sudden realisation that it was actually going to happen clearly hit them, as they started hugging Katrina and it proved difficult to hold back their tears.
Despite the significant risk, Tarak had also walked along the passageway to join them and say farewell too, but after a couple of minutes Katrina said it was time for him to go as the key lock now had to be opened.
He slowly released the twins and once he had walked far enough away, she told Kane to take hold of the key this time and place it towards the hole, where it shot out of his hand just like it had done for his sister.

With one last nod of agreement between them after which there could be no turning back, Kane pulled and turned the 'K' key to open the lock, whereupon he felt his birthmark swell up like Kara's had when she opened the alcove lock a few minutes earlier.
Kane then took the key which had lifted itself out of the hole and put it back around Kara's neck to take with them, but as he did they all suddenly heard a very loud thud echo around the passageway chamber, which sounded like the rock wall in front of them had split apart.

Katrina told them both to walk back over to the side of the stream again, but this time they would see the red water level rise as it started to flow faster and once it had reached halfway up the rocks, they needed to climb down the edge and swim off with the strong current through the new underwater passage.
They would soon arrive at the large cavern which she had mentioned to them before and once inside, they needed to find the seven hexagon device in the rock wall and remove the red illuminated letter 'P' key indicated on the Manor House clock that morning.

Whilst they then waited for a different underwater passage to open up, they were to use the 'K' key to lock the previous passage shut before swimming off in the new current with both keys, until they resurfaced inside another rock passageway that would lead them outside again.

After one final wave to their parents, the twins climbed down the rocks and dived off into the red glowing stream together, before disappearing under the water and they were gone!

Katrina & Tarak remained by each other's side in the passageway for a couple of minutes, quietly reflecting on whether Kara & Kane would safely complete their ancestral journey and also if they would ever see either of them again.
They then left through the crevice hole at the end of the passageway and after pulling back some shrubs to cover the gap, they slowly walked down the fields to the Manor House, whilst overhead they could still see the full lunar eclipse as the Moon continued to glow bright red.
Upon entering the sitting room, they both sat down with a drink as they watched the old wooden clock dials moving slowly around and both of them knew that their lives would never be quite the same.

Meanwhile, back in the fast flowing red stream, Kara & Kane were both being pulled along quickly by the strong underwater current towards another bright red light, which shone through an open passage in the rock wall up ahead of them.
Once through this gap, the twins continued swimming with the current for a bit longer, until the water level of the stream started to decrease all around them and they re-surfaced inside a red glowing rock cavern.

As they both stood there for a while to take a few deep breaths after their underwater swim, they were captivated by their new surroundings, as thousands of glistening crystals and beams of ceiling light combined with the sparkling spring water, to create a wondrous bright red illuminated spectacle that was truly surreal.

They then walked out of the remaining stream water together and set off around the cavern walls, where they soon found within one of the rock crevices the KLOPT0N seven lettered hexagons, all grouped in a circular configuration to the same design as they saw on the old wooden clock.
As Katrina had just told them, the 'P' letter hexagon contained a silver key stud that was glowing bright red, whilst both the 'K' and '0' hexagons also glowed too, but their key holes were empty.

Kara took the 'K' key from around her neck to place into its hole, but as she got closer this was pulled out of her hand and just shot in by itself, whereupon she took hold of it again and after feeling the usual swelling around her birthmark, turned the key to lock the passage they had just swam through.

She then removed the 'K' key again and they both heard a loud thud come from within the underwater rock wall, whereupon they knew that

58

the gap behind them had now closed shut as the stream entering the cavern floor started flowing off somewhere else.

Whilst the water level continued to go down, they both went over to look at a separate single hexagon device they had seen glistening on another part of the cavern rock walls nearby.
They found this to be the silver hole for an alcove lock displaying the '0' symbol, but as they did not have the key to open this with, they could do nothing and so walked back over to where the main seven hexagon device was instead.

After a few more moments just talking, they both decided with a certain amount of trepidation that they should now continue to the next destination on their journey.
Kara took hold of the 'P' silver stud this time and as she pulled and turned it, she once again felt her birthmark swell up slightly, before the key opened the 'P' lock and lifted itself out of the hole for her to also put on the silver chain around her neck.

Suddenly, they both heard another thud in the rock wall which echoed very loudly and seemed to vibrate around the whole cavern, whereupon they knew the rock wall had just opened up again to create another underwater passage, but from its water flow this was evidently not the same one they had just arrived through.
They watched for a couple of minutes as the water level in the cavern started to rise again and the location of the new current became more apparent, whereupon they both waded through the water across the stone floor to where this was and after a deep breath, dived into the red glowing stream to join it.

This time the strong current took them in the opposite direction along the stream, through the passage in the rock wall and then carried them back up to the surface, where they came out in a red illuminated rock lined passageway that looked very similar to the one they had just left.
However, after climbing up the rocks along its side and over to the red glowing hexagon device on the rock wall near a small cave, they saw that this hole was for the 'P' key and not the 'K' key, clearly meaning they had arrived somewhere else.

Before they could set off to discover where they were however, Kara took the 'P' key off her chain and used it to turn the lock in the hole again, whereafter they heard a loud thud come from within the rock wall and knew that this underwater passage must also now be closed.
Up ahead at the very end of this crystal lined passageway, they could see a bright red light shining from outside and they realised this must be their new destination - wherever that was!

Oat Hill woodland covert on Clopton Park

Part 3

HOUSE OF **PLANTAGENET**
- 14th Century -

Chapter 7 : **Family Uncovered**

Upon walking down the passageway towards the glowing red light, Kara & Kane soon arrived at a narrow gap in the rock wall through which they would be able to climb.

Outside however, they could see that this hole was more overgrown with wild brambles, thistles and tall sharp grasses than the previous entrance they had just left behind.

Kane went ahead first to push his way through this overgrowth as carefully as he could without trampling it down too much, since he knew they would need to put most of the flora back in place once they were out, in order to ensure that the rock face crevice remained hidden.

In the clear night sky up above, the Moon was still glowing red from the lunar eclipse, but a dark crescent shape had started to reappear across its surface as the Earth spun around on its axis and the red colour created by the alignment started to diminish.

The crystals on Kara's two pendants and Kane's signet ring were also starting to slowly lose their red glow and gradually turn back to their original rose pink colour.

It was also at this moment the twins realised that once this eclipse was over, they would probably not be able to leave the place they were in again until the next full red moon appeared, whenever that would be?

In the distance, they could hear what they initially thought were some wild dogs barking, but as the baying became louder they decided the animals sounded more like a pack of hunting hounds.

Closer by, they also heard some running water and after walking a few more steps around the outside edge of the jagged rock face, they discovered a clear water stream flowing briskly from out of the ground and over some large rocks, before running down across the fields in line with some woodland trees along the slope of the hillside.

The twins agreed that this stream was probably from the same underground source as they had just left behind inside the cavern and passageway, although neither of them recognised where they were.

Fortuitously, the early morning weather was quite mild and their wet clothing began to dry as the sunrise in the distance started to light up the morning sky with a glorious assortment of colour.

Kara & Kane had experienced some dramatic sunrises like this back in Ireland, but they were rarely as spectacular and nothing like the mainly overcast ones they had seen so far since their arrival in England.

After taking enough time to enjoy the splendid scenic views, they decided to set off and follow the stream near the cattle grazing in the long lush grass, to see where they ended up.
Before getting too far however, they suddenly heard men's voices shouting loudly as a couple of riders on horses appeared from over a ridge, with several vicious gnarling hounds running in front of them.
They were all chasing a vixen and its two cubs across the meadows, with these dogs presumably being the ones they had just heard before in the distance.

Not wishing to be seen, the twins instinctively crouched down amongst the tall grasses next to the stream edge and could only watch on as the hounds caught up with the cubs and ripped them both to shreds, whilst they sadly yelped their last painful breaths.
The vixen could do nothing to help and kept on running for its life towards the comparative safety of the hillside trees, but the riders and hounds continued their pursuit and followed her into the woods, before all disappearing out of sight.

After waiting to ensure that the horse riders and hounds did not return back their way, the twins stood up again and looked over in the direction of the ridge where the riders had come from to check if there was anyone else about, but thankfully the fields were clear.
In the distance however, they did now notice smoke rising out of some chimneys belonging to a small group of timber built houses and decided that they would head off in their direction.
With a degree of caution after what they had just witnessed, Kara & Kane hoped they would be able to find something to eat and also a place for them to sleep that evening.

As they got closer, they could see that the stream ran through a couple of small ponds before flowing into a large lake surrounded by a small woodland, on the far edge of which stood the largest of several very old styled buildings.
The twins stopped walking and looked at each other quite bewildered, before Kara quietly said "We must be in Clopton!",
to which comment Kane immediately nodded his head in agreement.

What neither of them could understand however, was why the original brick Manor House and other buildings plus the tented field hospital, were no longer there, but in their place were some wooden thatched cottages and one much larger timber framed house with a slate roof.

Additionally, the landscaped grounds and walled kitchen gardens they had left behind only that morning were now mainly grassland surrounded by trees, with various rustic open stables, wooden paddocks for livestock including pigs and some smaller pens for both chickens and a few sheep.

They agreed that this must have been where the horse riders came from, but realising that they had no other obvious choice, they decided to go over to what they assumed must be the main house and see if they could find someone to help them.

As they approached the front entrance they looked up over the top of its large ornate wooden oak door and stood there quite still in disbelief.

Above the front door ahead of them, carved into the outside timber frame of the house, they saw the name of KLOPTON boldly displayed across the centre of a large hexagonal shape.

After a few moments, Kara who was always the more forward of the two siblings, knocked loudly on the door and after a short time they heard someone walking across the stone floor inside towards them.

The front door was opened slowly and they were greeted by a young woman, who from the style of the old fashioned clothes she wore, appeared to be the maid.

She looked straight past Kara and instead turned towards Kane before asking him politely what they wanted, to which he replied that they would like to see the master of the house.

The maid said that her master Sir James Klopton was away on business in London, but that she would fetch his manservant and then went back inside before closing the door again behind her.

The twins looked at each other as Kara repeated out loud in astonishment the name of KLOPTON again, to which Kane nodded his acknowledgement to what they had both just heard.

It was not very long before the front door was opened again and this time a quite smartly dressed middle aged man appeared, who upon seeing the twins, just stood there staring at them both rather quizzically.

After a short while Kane said hello to the man, who upon regaining his composure, responded by welcoming them both to KLOPTON House and then asking how he could help?

With everything that had just happened to them over the past twenty-four hours, neither of the twins had thought what to say to anyone about who they were supposed to be and so they needed to make up a story very quickly if they were to answer the man's rather obvious question!

Kane started off by stating both their first names only and then continued to explain that they were siblings who had travelled from Bath with their parents on their way to York.

Whilst on the road outside Stratford-upon-Avon however, their coach was stopped by some robbers, who mercilessly killed both their parents and took all of their valuables.

Kara then picked up the story and using a very emotional voice, said how their father had confronted the robbers, but they hit him over the head repeatedly and when their mother went to try and stop them, they murdered her too.

Being unarmed and knowing there was nothing they could do, they both ran off across the fields from the opposite side of the coach as quickly as they could and into some nearby woods, fearing for their lives too.

Kane then continued their elaborate story with equal trauma in his voice as he explained how they hid amongst the trees until they saw the robbers ride off with their coach and horses, before they made their way back to where their parents lay lifeless and all covered in blood.

After a short time for grieving, they knew they had to get away from the road and so they picked up their parents bodies and headed off to a small brow at the top of the field.

Once there, they found a hollow amongst a large tree's roots, where they lay the bodies down side by side before covering them with soil and stones, followed by a layer of branches and overgrowth.

They stayed there for several minutes to say prayers for their parents and then headed back down the hillside, not knowing where they were going.

After a couple of hours walking they noticed this small settlement of houses, so they came here in the hope that they might be able to find some accommodation for the night, even in one of the barns or stables if necessary.

They then stopped talking and the man gently smiled at them, which made them both think he did not believe a word they had just said.

Instead of being sent away as they thought he might however, the man asked them politely if they would like to come inside and stay there for the night.

The twins could hardly contain their relief as they instantly said yes and thanked him for his kind hospitality.

The man opened the door wider to let them enter and as they walked in they saw that the house was much larger than they had realised from outside and also lavishly furnished, although very dated in style.

Hanging around the walls they saw several paintings of battle scenes with portraits of knights, plus others of ladies and children who were presumably their families.

The man called the maid over to join them and introduced her as Frances, before telling her to make up the spare rooms for his guests to stay in that night and also to cook extra food, as they would be joining him for dinner later that morning, followed by evening supper too.

He then commented on not only how damp and dirty their clothing looked, but also how unusual their garments were compared to those usually worn by most families of Warwickshire.

Turning back to Frances, he instructed her to get some clean dry clothes from the spare dressing room and to lay them out on the beds in the two rooms for their guests to change into.

He also told her to get another servant to boil enough hot water for two baths and after they had changed, clean their existing clothes for them.

Facing back towards the twins, he then asked if they would like a drink before they bathed as it would be a couple of hours until lunch, to which they both said yes and Frances went straight away to fetch them something from the kitchen.

He then told them that he had some estate duties to finish off before their meal and would therefore rejoin them at noon in the dining room at the end of the main corridor, whereupon he stood up to leave, but just before closing the door he casually introduced himself as Richard Greenway.

Once he had left the room, Kane & Kara looked at each other enquiringly, as they realised they might have an answer to a question both of them had at the back of their minds ever since Richard first opened the front door to the house.

Before they had time to talk to each other about this however, Frances came back into the room with two goblets of fresh water and asked them to follow her upstairs to the landing, where she took them to their respective bedrooms.

Once inside, they both found some fresh clothes laid out on their beds as Richard had instructed, whilst a few pots of hot water were being brought in by another servant to fill their baths in readiness for their much needed soaks.

Whilst they waited for sufficient hot water to be poured, they both sat in Kara's room with their drinks and as soon as they were alone for the first time since they entered the house, Kara spoke very excitedly to ask Kane just one rather cryptic question, "Could it be?".

He knew exactly what it was they needed to talk about, but suggested that they should bathe first, to which Kara readily agreed.

They decided to meet up in Kane's room in an hour's time after they had washed and changed, so they could focus on the enormity of the truth that might be waiting to reveal itself downstairs during their meal.

Unsurprising to Kane, his sister knocked on his door before the time they had agreed, but he let her inside anyway whilst he continued to get dressed, as he knew she would only pester him otherwise.

Kara was wearing a single cream coloured full-length woven dress with a simple embroidery along its hemline and a thin brown leather belt around her waist, which she really liked and strangely reminded her of a similar casual outfit she had sometimes worn back in Ireland when she was younger.
She had also done her hair up and gave Kane a quick twirl, to which he warmly smiled back at her.

Kane meanwhile finished putting on a pair of single pleated brown trousers, together with a loose fitting beige woollen shirt and a dark coloured stylish long jacket, to which Kara nodded her approval whilst also being quite surprised how different her brother looked.

After they then sat down together on the end of the bed, Kara passed to Kane the letter 'P' pendant she had taken from inside the cavern, for him to look at. This was very similar in construction to the 'K' pendant, apart from the silver letter on top and four long key stems underneath which were designed in the shape of a 'P'.

Kane next read out the two-part inscription engraved separately on either side of the longest silver stem, which when put together read:

'only the past ... will death revere'

They both looked at each other and with their usual inquisitive minds, wondered if this phrase might refer to the deaths of their ancestors, since this seemed to be a quite plausible explanation.
Additionally however, the two keys cryptic texts they had now seen could combine with the remaining five keys texts to provide some sort of historical prophecy or hidden message, but if so this would only presumably become apparent once all seven texts had been read.

Kane then held the 'P' key up closer to examine the very end of the longest stem, where the 'K' key displayed a crescent shape.
On the 'P' key however, he saw a different symbol etched on both sides, which basically comprised a circle on top of a small cross.

Whilst he recognised this, Kane could not remember where he had seen it before and turning to Kara, she too did not know what this unusual symbol represented.

Both of them agreed that these conundrums would have to wait for another time however, as there was something much more important to discuss and Kara could not contain herself any longer.

Unfortunately, just as she was about to ask her brother about what they had both sensed that morning upon meeting Richard, there was a knock on the door and Frances had come to take them downstairs.

As they walked into the dining room there was a log fire burning within a stone surround, on top of which stood an antique wooden clock that appeared identical to the one displayed on the Clopton Manor House mantelpiece just the night before.

They were both bewildered by this, but before they got chance to take a closer look at this clock, Richard entered the room and welcomed them, before asking what they wanted to drink with their food.

Neither Kane nor Kara usually drank alcohol and they were both given a cup of thick squashed apple juice instead, whilst Richard was served a tankard of ale.

For their substantial meal they were served roast pork with duck eggs and a selection of fresh vegetables with newly baked bread, followed by a plate of cheese with fruit and berries, which they both quickly ate as they had not eaten anything since they left Clopton.

Once the meal was finished, they both thanked Richard for the excellent food and felt a lot more at ease.

Sensing however, that his guests were anxious to ask him something and also wanting some questions answering himself, Richard prompted the conversation topic by looking over towards Kara and with a smile on his face called her by the name 'Sofia', as he said how wonderful it was to see her.

Kara was totally taken aback by him knowing her middle name and after glancing over to Kane, she could not contain herself any longer as she turned to Richard and asked him if they were related?

He responded by saying that she reminded him of someone he used to know very well and then asked what her mother's name was, to which she replied 'Katrina'.

After sitting there for a moment as tears appeared in his eyes, he asked if Katrina was still alive and well, to which Kara calmly replied yes.

Richard then clearly became even more emotional as he slowly stood up and walked over towards Kara, where he gently took hold of her hands and said to both her & Kane that he believed he was their father.

Kara instinctively knew that he was the Richard who their mother Katrina had told them about and she responded by squeezing his hands too, as she replied that they also believed they were his daughter and son.

Kane stood up and walked over to join the two of them, with the facial likeness between him and Richard being very apparent as they came so close to each other.

After a short while, they all sat down again and Richard asked how old they now were, which initially seemed a strange question for a father to be asking his children.

As soon as Kara had replied that they were both sixteen however, she remembered from their new surroundings that they were clearly no longer in the same period of time as they had been the previous day when they left Clopton.

Kara therefore quickly added that they were both born in 1899 during the reign of Queen Victoria and then asked Richard what date it was now, which previously would have also sounded an unusual question.

He smiled and calmly said it was October and that they were all together there in the year of our Lord 1348, during the reign of King Edward III of the House of Plantagenet.

The twins were astonished by his answer, but immediately realised that this was probably the only logical explanation for what they had experienced that day and equally raised many more questions, not only about KLOPTON but also about their mother.

Anticipating their need for more information and not knowing how much they had already been told, Richard started off by explaining how Katrina had also visited fourteenth century England in 1332 by using one of the KLOPTON keys, when she was still a teenager.

She too had come through the hidden cavern on the hillside before arriving at the Manor House where she was met by Sir James Klopton, who quickly realised who she truly was and invited her in.

There she stayed and was very well looked after, especially by Sir James's wife Lady Susan who delighted in her company and often took Katrina with her on many journeys around Warwickshire.

It was during one of those journeys that Katrina found out that Sir James & Lady Susan had their own daughter Khloe.

Earlier that year just before she turned sixteen however, Sir James sent her off to live with her mother's parents in Oxford, as he did not want her to travel through the crystal cavern and possibly never come back.

The following year Lady Khloe married Frederick and they had two children Kathryn & Ryan, who were now fifteen and thirteen years of age respectively.

Lady Khloe was now thirty-three years old and still lived in Oxford, but she would visit Stratford-upon-Avon with her family every year, although she never met Katrina during her stay as Sir James would not let them return to KLOPTON whilst Katrina was there.

Sir James also had a son Stephen, who became a squire when he was seventeen, then knighted six years later and was now twenty-nine.

At the beginning of 1347 only a few months earlier, Sir Stephen's uncle Sir Thomas de Beauchamp 11th Earl of Warwick was one of only twenty-six Knights Companion to enter the noble fraternity of the Order of the Garter, founded by King Edward III in recognition of their chivalry at the Battle of Crécy in France during 1346.
This extra responsibility to Sir Thomas meant that Sir Stephen had to stay away for longer periods of time in London, but he would still always make time to travel up to KLOPTON to see his parents when he could.

He too had married, but sadly his wife Christine died without bearing him any children and he never re-married, due partly to his duties keeping him very busy, but also because he never got over her death.
Sir Stephen did however manage to meet Katrina during her stay and Richard remembered them often going off horse riding together across the KLOPTON estate hills whilst she was there.

Katrina subsequently met Richard when he worked on the KLOPTON farm, as he would visit the Manor House on most days to take fresh meat and vegetables for the cook to use in Sir James' meals.
They soon became inseparable and spent as much spare time as they could together, when she would tell him all about the KLOPTON history, including the story of how she inherited the birthmark under her arm.

He paused the story for a moment to ask if they too had an hexagonal shaped birthmark, to which they both rolled up their sleeves and showed him their red marks that were identical to the one Richard remembered his Sofia had.
He then continued to explain how Katrina had asked him to call her by her middle family name when they were with other people, in order to help keep their close friendship a secret and hopefully enable them to spend more time together without suspicious eyes watching them.

As the months passed by they fell deeper in love and with the old wooden clock dials still not turning red, Katrina decided she wanted to stay with Richard in KLOPTON forever.
It was another month later however, before she realised that she was pregnant, although she did not tell him immediately.

Later that same week, the dials did then finally turn red and when he saw Katrina outside in the courtyard that morning she was clearly distraught, despite her having been so happy all of the days before.
Richard did not know the reason why and she would not tell him when he asked, but instead she walked off with her thoughts obviously somewhere else.

They did not see each other again for the rest of that morning with Katrina clearly avoiding him, until early in the afternoon she came to find him on the farm and asked that they go for a walk.

Once they were out of sight of the buildings and there was no one else around to see them together, Katrina took hold of Richard's hands as tears started running down her face and she said that she could no longer stay with him in KLOPT0N.

Richard was devastated by what she had just told him and upon seeing the reaction in his face, Katrina took the 'P' pendant key off from around her neck to show him its red glowing crystals.

Then without saying a word, she lifted up her other arm and pointed over to the hills in the distance where the full red lunar eclipse had started to appear overhead in the sky.

Looking up across the fields, Richard's heart sank as he saw the red glowing full Moon and knew why Katrina wanted to go, but he also realised that if she left then he would probably never see her again.

After a few moments, Richard said that they both knew this day would come eventually and asked why she changed her mind so soon after saying she would remain with him forever in KLOPT0N.

Katrina did not answer and instead just kept walking until they reached the hidden crevice in the rock face, where Richard helped her clear away some of the thick overgrowth outside the entrance.

They both went inside along the rock passageway covered with red glowing crystals, until they reached the rock wall and the sparkling red stream running by its side.

Richard had never seen such a mesmerising scene before as Katrina stopped and turned to hold him in her arms, where she said that although she would always love him, it was now time for her to leave KLOPT0N and return home for the good of her family.

Richard was confused by what Katrina had just told him since both of her parents were well when she left them less than a year earlier, but before he could ask her anything else, she pulled him towards her and kissed him passionately.

After what to Richard was far too short a time, Katrina stopped their embrace and moved away from him with a brave smile, as she said that it was now time for her to go.

Katrina then walked over to the rock wall where she showed Richard a single red glowing hexagon with a hole at its centre, into which she placed her 'P' key and unlocked it, before then removing it again and putting it back on the chain around her neck.

A few moments later, they both heard a loud thud as Katrina took Richard over to the edge of the stream, where the red glowing water level had started to rise and flow faster, before explaining to him how she had to dive into the strong current and continue with the stream through the underwater passage.

Once she resurfaced on the other side, Katrina would then lock the passage again and upon Richard hearing a second loud thud, he would know that she had safely reached the next stage of her journey home.
She then told him that he must not try to follow her through the red stream or else he would drown, as only KLOPTON descendants born with the hexagonal birthmark can survive the strong underwater current.

With another difficult smile, Katrina looked into Richard's eyes to tell him she was pregnant with their baby, but promised that she would make sure their child knew all about him when she was old enough.
Richard just stood there for a moment completely overwhelmed by what he had just heard, as Katrina said she loved him again for one final time and then dived off the rocks into the stream, before disappearing with the current under the water.

Despite her specific warning however, Richard dived in straight after her, but as soon as he entered the stream, the current started to wrap itself around him and pull him under the water.
Thankfully, Richard was a very good swimmer and quickly realised how strong the current was before he got dragged down too deep, whereupon he managed to swim back up to the surface and grab hold of the rocks along the edge of the stream.

After he climbed out onto the passageway floor, Richard just sat there for a while praying that Katrina and their unborn baby would make it home, when suddenly he heard the noise of another loud thud in the rock wall and knew they were safely through the underwater passage.

Sadly, as Richard finally realised there was nothing else he could now do apart from hope that one day he would meet them both again, he slowly walked back along the crystal passageway and at the end squeezed himself through the narrow crevice gap.
Once outside, he then covered the rock face entrance with thick overgrowth and various flora as Katrina requested him to do, before she had said her tearful goodbye.

Chapter 8 : **Time and a Word**

Richard set off down the hillside and across the fields to where he lived, but he struggled to get any sleep that evening as he could not stop thinking about Katrina and their unborn child.

The following morning he was up early to continue with his work on the farm, when to his surprise he received a message from Sir James Klopton requesting that he come over to the Manor House.
He headed off straight away and was greeted at the back door by one of the servants, who invited him inside to wait in the sitting room whilst she went to fetch Sir James & Lady Susan.

A couple of minutes later they both entered the room and upon seeing them, Richard became clearly concerned about what it was he had done wrong.
Upon sensing his anxiety, Lady Susan gently asked him to take a seat whilst she instructed the maid to fetch them all a drink and then told him that they had invited there as they wanted to talk to him about Katrina.

They both knew that Katrina & Richard had fallen in love with each other, whilst Lady Susan also suspected that Katrina was pregnant before she returned back to her own time the previous evening during the red lunar eclipse, to be with her parents again.

After they had finished discussing matters, Sir James invited Richard to work in the Manor House instead of the farm house from then on, since that would also give them the opportunity to talk more about Katrina and some of their other KLOPTON ancestors.

. . . .

Having finished talking to Kane & Kara about the time he had spent with Katrina before she returned home sixteen years earlier, Richard now wanted to know all about them and also what had happened to their mother ever since.

The twins took it in turn to tell him all about their lives in Ireland and how their mother had married a Doctor named Tarak, despite him knowing that she was pregnant with them at the time.
Katrina however, never had any more children and she now lived in the Clopton Manor House, where she worked as a nurse in the field War hospital with her husband.

After taking a few moments to compose himself, Richard said that he had all but given up any hope of ever seeing any of them again and to now find out that he had both a teenage son and daughter was truly a wonderful gift, which he will treasure forever.

What made their existence even more precious to him however, was that after Katrina did not come back to KLOPT0N, he too got married a few years later, but tragically both his wife Rosemarie and three year old son Jack died when their cottage caught fire and Richard never remarried.

It was after this terrible accident that Sir James invited him to come and live in the Manor House from then onwards, as his full-time manservant.

There was however, something else Kara & Kane needed to know, which Sir James told Richard after he found out that Katrina had returned home whilst pregnant.

Apparently, it has never been disclosed by any of his ancestors from their knowledge of the family history, that a baby has ever been conceived in one era of KLOPT0N time and then born in another, after having travelled across the void of time during pregnancy.

Sir James has always therefore questioned, what impact such a journey during the full lunar eclipse would have on Katrina's offspring, especially should he or she ever enter through the red water cavern again after reaching the age of sixteen.

Just as significant however, he also wondered that if the child did survive, would he be the one to fulfil the ancestral KLOPT0N prophecy, although no-one knew of course that Katrina was going to have twins!

As both Sir James & Lady Susan were currently staying away in Suffolk, it would probably be a few days before they received Richard's message despatched by horse rider telling them of their arrival, but then maybe a couple of months before they returned home to meet them.

In the meantime, Richard decided it would be prudent to warn Kara & Kane that they should always be cautious during their travels around Stratford-upon-Avon.

Many town's people were very suspicious of strangers and it would be at least another year before the next full red Moon appeared for them to leave again, should they chose to do so of course.

Meanwhile, he would make sure that they both had appropriate clothes to wear, but there was nothing he could do about their unfamiliar Irish accents and they should therefore learn to mimic the way everybody else around them spoke as quickly as possible.

Then turning to Kara with a gentle smile, Richard apologised in advance for what he was about to say, but just like he remembered her mother to be, they were both quite outspoken women.

Unfortunately however, such behaviour was not acceptable to most men of that time and as difficult as it may be, she needed to appear much more submissive in front of people who she did not know and especially the men.

Kara could not hide the wry smile on her face as she acknowledged what Richard was saying and added that she would always try to be on her best behaviour whilst there.

Kane however, was unable to contain himself, as he looked over at Kara and remarked that he might like to live in KLOPT0N more permanently if all the women there could be made to be so obedient, which flippant comment prompted Kara to throw a cushion at him through the air!

For the first time since they had all met, Richard laughed out loud at the light banter between the two siblings, but he then reverted back to a more serious mood as he reminded them that any out of the ordinary behaviour or discussions about what they knew in the future, could easily get them noticed by the wrong people and possibly lead to serious consequences for their wellbeing.

Richard then told Kara that she must always keep the two silver lettered KLOPT0N pendants and chain out of sight around her neck, as there were lots of robbers around town and the twins would not be able to get back home to Clopton without both of them.

In addition, Richard still had Rosemarie's wedding ring, which he now wanted Kara to wear so that when other men saw it they would believe she was married and hopefully stop pestering her, especially as she was an attractive girl of the right age of consent.

Kara reached over to take the gold band from her father and after delicately sliding it onto her third finger, told him how proud she was to wear such a precious possession and that she would ensure it was safely returned to him before they left on the next part of their journey.

Finally, he also told Kara that she should say she was Kane's wife if the need arose, since it was quite common for people to get married at such a young age and this would mean Kara was Kane's property to be left alone by other men.

This further comment brought yet another wry smile to both of the twins faces.

Richard next told Kane to always wear the 'K' signet ring he already had and ideally on his wedding finger too, if it fitted.

74

He must also not be afraid to display it prominently if any problems arose, since its significance was well known around Stratford-upon-Avon and few people would want to cause any trouble with Sir James Klopton in view of his position and connection with the King of England.

The afternoon passed by very quickly and it was then time for their evening meal, which thankfully comprised of a much lighter selection than their dinner feast had earlier when they were really hungry, as the twins were now both quite full.

The conversation became much more about Stratford-upon-Avon as the town had significantly changed since the 20th Century when Kara & Kane had left.
After a couple of hours and nothing much else to discuss that evening, everyone agreed that they were tired, so they all said their goodnights and went upstairs to their respective rooms for a long overdue sleep.

The following morning Kara & Kane were both awakened in turn by Frances who brought them some more casual clothes for them to wear during their stay and after they got dressed in their new 14th Century garments, they went downstairs to join Richard for breakfast and talk about what they should do during their time in KLOPT0N.

As it would be virtually impossible for either of the twins to continue with their education, since whatever they were taught would now be almost 600 years out of date and Richard knew from when he was with their mother, that both Kara & Kane would also be too knowledgeable for any of the available tutors and most scholars of that era.

The one topic they may want the opportunity to study however, was the actual history of that time, with Richard remembering how Katrina found it fascinating for her to be learning whilst actually experiencing aspects of 14th Century Warwickshire first-hand.
They would need to be very careful who they talked to without raising any suspicion however, but when Sir James & Lady Susan got back they would no doubt be delighted to tell them all about Stratford-upon-Avon and other recent historical events.

Richard then remembered how the twins had told him about their upbringing in Ireland and asked them about their education, as although he knew Katrina had been brought up a Christian, he was not sure what impact Tarak's religion may have had on both of them.
Kara answered by saying that they had been taught both Catholicism and Hinduism by their parents whilst growing up and they therefore fully respected both religions, whilst not proactively practising either.

75

Upon hearing their opinions on faith, Richard explained that they must not mention this to anyone else and whilst living in KLOPTON must go with him to the Collegiate Church of the Holy & Undivided Trinity in town every Sunday, where they will have to be seen praying to God and probably on occasion take Holy Communion.

If they were ever seen doing anything else or overheard not reciting the Bible text, they could be considered as heretics and probably sentenced to death.

Richard then left the room and returned shortly afterwards with Sir James' hand written copy of the Bible, which he gave them and pointed out which scriptures to learn first, so they could quote these passages if ever challenged by anyone.

In the meantime, they were welcome to explore the surrounding areas including nearby Warwick and maybe even spend some of the smaller silver coinage which Katrina had given to Kara before they left, but they must always remember not to bring any attention on themselves.

He then asked if they could both ride a horse, which they told him they could and he said that they would all go to the KLOPTON stables later that morning to choose a horse for each of them.

Next he enquired if they both knew how to handle swords, as there were a lot of robbers around and when they were on their own they might need to scare off any potential attackers or even physically defend themselves.

Kane replied that he was part of both his previous schools fencing teams, whilst he also had some sparring sessions with Kara during their spare time back in 20th Century England.

Richard explained that whilst he was pleased Kara could at least look after herself a bit, ladies were not expected to either display or fight with swords in 14th Century public and he would therefore organise a smaller discreet sword for her to conceal under her outer garments.

However, he also wanted her to have some extra practice with her new sword before she left KLOPTON so that she could defend herself if necessary, although she should never go out alone either on foot or by riding, as sadly it was far too dangerous for a young lady to travel anywhere in that century without an escort.

Turning back to Kane, Richard was intrigued to hear about his prowess with a sword and said he would take him to the blacksmith that afternoon to find which sword he preferred, after which he looked forward to them fighting each other so he could see how good his skills really were.

Kane replied that he accepted the challenge and looked forward to their duel, whilst with a grin he also promised to go gentle on his father.

Richard gave him a wry smile back and retorted that after waiting sixteen years to find his son, he would promise not to injure Kane too much during their very first fight!

A couple of hours later they were all at the stables trying out some different horses, with Kara eventually selecting a chestnut mare and Kane choosing a sturdy black steed.

After Richard also got onto his own horse, the three of them rode off together across the fields and over the hills around KLOPTON estate.

On their way back, they rode past the stream and overgrown rock face where the twins had first arrived, after which Kara & Kane both felt a bit saddle weary from their long ride, but really enjoyed it and Richard said he was very pleased how well they had both rode their new horses for the first time.

After a short rest and some food, they all went off to select the swords Richard had discussed with them earlier.

The blacksmith only had a few smaller swords for Kara to try out, which had been made primarily for youngsters to practice with and were not much bigger than long daggers, so whilst Kara soon choose one, she was not that comfortable with it as she was used to larger better balanced modern swords.

Choosing Kane's sword however, was much more difficult, as he was used to a much lighter modern sleek sabre design, rather than the large two-handed heavy long sword frequently used by knights and soldiers in 14th Century combat, especially when they were fighting against heavily armoured opponents with shields.

Richard helped Kane try out a few different sword styles in mock combat scenarios and after a while they both realised that he was better off with a short handled long blade design, similar to the sword he was already used to handling, although much heavier and less balanced.

However, since the sword Kane chose was essentially for self-defence rather than taking part in any full-bloodied battle, it was better for him to have one he could confidently adapt to as quickly as possible.

This choice prompted Richard to grin slightly as he said he would hold off from the sword fight Kane had challenged him to until he had the chance for some much needed practice, to which Kane cheerfully agreed.

Richard quickly followed up his remark in a more serious tone however, as he told the twins that they also needed to learn some of the tactics robbers used, especially when there were no soldiers about and that he would accompany them on their first few visits into town to help them recognised such dangers and keep them safe.

Over the next couple of months Kara & Kane kept themselves busy helping around the estate with many of the daily duties, but they especially enjoyed working with the horses in the stables and going for long rides in the surrounding countryside whenever they got the chance.

In addition, Richard helped them both learn some effective sword fighting skills and although Kane was clearly the stronger swordsman, Kara was much more agile and the duels between the two siblings soon became quite intense with neither wanting to give the other any advantage.

Richard was very impressed how quickly they both improved and it was not long before he realised that they should be able to look after themselves in most hand-to-hand combat situations.
He reminded them however, to continue avoiding any groups of men they did not know and also not to engage in any activity which might attract unwanted attention and potential conflict.

Later that month, during one brisk afternoon a few days before Christmas whilst it was still light, the twins were riding their horses across the estate as usual, when they heard a lot of commotion at the Manor House and turned back around to find out what was going on.
As they got closer, they saw a group of horse soldiers had dismounted in the courtyard and were standing to attention next to a horse driven large ornate coach, which displayed the KLOPTON red & black crest on both its doors.

Kane & Kara rode their horses back to the stables as quickly as they could and then went straight over to the front of the Manor House, where they saw Richard and Frances greeting a very smartly dressed couple as they alighted from the coach.
The rest of the household servants all stood very still as they created a welcoming line up to the front door and Kara & Kane assumed it must be Sir James & Lady Susan Klopton who had arrived back from Suffolk.

Richard nodded towards the twins as they approached and immediately invited them to come over and join everyone.
Before he had the chance to introduce either of them however, Sir James lifted his arms up towards Kara and after taking hold of her with both hands, called her Katrina and said how wonderful it was to see her again.
Kara smiled back at him and replied that he was unfortunately mistaken as she was in fact Katrina's daughter, before she then also introduced Kane as her twin brother.

Sir James instantly apologised for his error, especially since Richard had told him in his letter who they both were, but in that moment of joy he mistook Kara for Katrina and forgot otherwise.

He then shook hands with Kane too, after which he introduced them both to his wife Lady Susan who also greeted them both very warmly.

Richard then interceded to take Sir James & Lady Susan inside as they were tired after their long journey, whilst asking the twins to join them in the dining room a few hours later for an evening meal when they could talk more.

That evening lasted late into the night as they all had so much to talk about, with their hosts both intrigued to hear all about Katrina and the twins personal stories, whilst Kara & Kane were delighted at being able to speak to them so openly about their real lives and how wonderful it had been to meet their true birthfather Richard.

The twins were also very grateful for all the warm hospitality they had both received since they arrived and whilst they would be continuing with their journey when the next full red Moon appeared, they would remember this night and their time at KLOPTON with great fondness.

They all then started saying goodnight to each other, but before they could finish, Sir James said that he had something very important he must talk to them about the following morning.

He therefore needed to meet up with them all again straight after an early breakfast, which they all acknowledged and then retired to their rooms wondering what it was he had to tell them.

Clopton Manor House across the garden lake

79

Chapter 9 : **The Black Death**

The following morning the twins were woken up by not only a glorious sunrise beaming through their bedroom drapes, but also by a loud commotion emanating from the main courtyard below.

They both got dressed as quickly as they could and after going downstairs to grab themselves a drink from the kitchen, went over to the front entrance to see what was going on.

Upon opening the main door, they were taken aback to see a few dozen soldiers in armour, jostling around the Manor House yard amongst some tables set up for them with food and drink, which they devoured nearly as quick as the servants could keep them replenished.

Meanwhile, another group of stable lads and farm hands were busy running around feeding and grooming all of the soldiers horses.

After a couple of minutes simply watching this frenetic spectacle, the twins decided to step out into the courtyard to become part of the experience, whereupon Richard spotted them and shouted for them to come and join him.

As they headed over in his direction, they could see that he was talking to a knight who was splendidly dressed in highly polished armour and clearly the person in charge of all the soldiers.

They both became a bit apprehensive as they approached this impressively built large man, until Richard introduced him as Sir Stephen, son of Sir James, after which they felt much more at ease since they were related, albeit quite distantly.

Sir Stephen was quite handsome in a rugged way, with thick dark brown hair, a square chin carrying a full beard and deep brown eyes.

In spite of his formidable stature however, his voice was relatively calm and polite as he welcomed the twins to KLOPT0N and explained how he had already been told about their arrival.

He then added that unfortunately it was time for him and his men to head off to reinforce the garrison at Warwick Castle, but he would be back in a couple of days when they could have a proper talk, especially about their recent journeys.

Sir Stephen then shook Richard by the hand as he thanked him for the hospitality shown towards his men, before he turned around and in a stern loud voice ordered them all to finish off their food quickly and mount their horses in readiness to leave.

A few minutes later, the twins stood there at the front of the Manor House watching with Richard as they all rode off, after which Sir James came to the door and asked them to come inside as there was a significant matter they needed to discuss urgently.

Once in the drawing room where Lady Susan was already waiting, Sir James asked everyone else to sit down too, as he had some very grave news he needed to tell them from his son Sir Stephen about a deadly danger they would all soon be facing.

Turning first to the twins, Sir James said, "I am sorry that you have chosen to visit us at this time, although had you known the actual year you were traveling to then you probably would not have come".
Kane & Kara both looked very puzzled by what he had just said.

Sir James continued, "As Richard mentioned to you when you first reached us here in KLOPTON, the year was 1347.
Since then however, time has moved on and whilst we would have normally been delighted for you to stay with us as long as you could, you have arrived just as a great plaque has reached the coastal towns of England from across Europe".

The twins looked over at each other, as suddenly the significance of the year 1348 dawned upon them, especially since they had read all about this in their 20th Century history books and reacting first, Kara said out loudly, "The Black Death!".
"Yes" said Sir James, "we have heard it called that before and over the next few weeks or maybe longer, we know this terrible disease will spread upwards across England until it impacts on the people of Stratford-upon-Avon and also KLOPTON".

They all went quiet and listened intensely as Sir James further explained that Sir Stephen and his soldiers had been sent from the south east of England to help strengthen the Warwickshire garrison in the event of civil unrest breaking out once the plague arrived and people started dying.

Everyone in KLOPTON needed to take immediate steps to start protecting the estate and all those living there by becoming much more self-sufficient, with future travel to Stratford-upon-Avon being strictly restricted for essential items only, whilst no physical contact should be made with the residents of the town during any such journeys.
New horseback patrols were to be introduced and everyone told to be more vigilant to ensure that no strangers entered the grounds, especially once the plague had reached the edge of Warwickshire.

All the estate fences were to be made stronger and the outer field gates locked, with all the cattle and other livestock brought within the reinforced inner estate boundaries.
Furthermore, all crops and other supplies on the estate including those around the stables, would be guarded, with anyone caught stealing food

being thrown off the estate or even locked up in the nearby prison at Warwick Castle.

Basic rationing would be introduced initially, but this could increase further once the full impact of the plague as it spread across Warwickshire and Stratford-upon-Avon was known.

Turning back to look at the twins, Sir James told them that the plague should not actually affect them, as they were not born in this KLOPTON time and their bodies should therefore be immune to the disease.

However, many other people across the area would become infected and as those people got very distressed and looked for answers as to why their families were dying, they would soon want someone to blame.

As you are both strangers in the town and also have a different skin tone to that usually seen, some of the locals may think you are carrying the plague and this could be the catalyst for civil unrest and they would probably want to burn you both alive in the belief that it will stop you from spreading the disease any further, so you will have to be extremely vigilant at all times.

The twins looked at each other rather concerned and their anxious expressions were quickly noticed by Sir James, who straight away tried his best to comfort them.

He knew that Richard had already organised swords for each of them and that he was training them in their use, not only for self-defence but also to cover aggressive combat scenarios.

Sir James reminded them of how impressed Richard was with the skills they had learnt so far and that they were to always carry their swords around with them wherever they went.

Kara however, must also keep hers hidden underneath the full length dress she wore when outside walking or horse riding in public areas.

Additionally, he re-iterated what Richard had said before, which was if anyone threatened them then Kane must display his 'K' signet ring, whilst also stating that they were both relatives of Sir James Klopton, who was close friends with King Edward III of England.

Any aggressive action taken against either of you or injury caused would therefore result in the most dire of consequences against the perpetrator and you should therefore be left in peace.

Unfortunately, at that time, no-one knew the date when the next red Moon would appear again and therefore Sir James told them that they were both welcome to stay on the KLOPTON estate as long as they needed to.

They should be quite safe there until the plague had gone or else the next lunar eclipse occurred and they could then continue on their journey

In the meantime, Sir Stephen was there to help protect KLOPT0N and would also assist looking after the twins.

He will therefore be pleased to let you accompany him during his visits to both Warwick and Kenilworth Castles if you wish, which offer they both told Sir James they would be delighted to accept.

The next few months passed by quickly and as the plague started to spread across many parts of Warwickshire, Kane & Kara's horseback journeys with Sir Stephen became restricted to only essential visits.

During one of their visits to Kenilworth Castle however, Sir Stephen introduced the twins to a young soldier named Edmund to look after them for about an hour, whilst he had some important troop matters to deal with.

Kane & Kara quickly realised that Edmund was knowledgeable about some private KLOPT0N family matters and instead of discussing the castle's history with them as they had presumed, he was much more inquisitive about the real time era the twins had come from and their journeys.

They both felt very uncomfortable however, about answering his questions regarding their real lives, especially as Richard had quite rightly told them not to discuss any such matters with anyone else due to the significant dangers this could cause.

Edmund sensed the twins' hesitation, but told them not to worry about talking to him, as he was in fact Sir Stephen's son and knew the real truth about KLOPT0N from his father.

Kara was not convinced by Edmund's story however, as Sir Stephen had previously told them both that his wife Christine had died many years ago and that he had never remarried, plus he never mentioned having a son.

Edmund answered this by explaining that he never knew his mother because she died giving birth to him and that even now his father still blamed him for her death, although he would occasionally speak to him and also helped him enlist as a soldier with the garrison based at Kenilworth Castle.

Neither of the twins were still certain if Edmund was actually telling the truth, especially as he bore little facial resemblance to Sir Stephen, although this may have been because he did not have a beard and also had lighter coloured hair.

They both decided that the best way to verify what he was saying was to see his birthmark, whereupon Edmund rolled up his sleeve and there underneath his arm was the deep brown hexagon inherited by all children born of the original KLOPT0N bloodline.

About an hour later Sir Stephen rejoined them and with a knowing look said that he hoped they had all introduced themselves to each other properly, to which they all smiled back and nodded in agreement.

Sir Stephen then said that he had another surprise for them and turned around to beckon forward a family of four, who were all standing just a short distance behind him.
Once they had walked over to join them, Sir Stephen introduced the family to everyone.
They comprised Sir Frederick & Lady Khloe plus their teenage children Kathryn & Ryan, all of the House of KLOPTON.

Kara, being forthright as usual could not contain herself and before Sir Stephen was able to continue, she responded by introducing herself and Kane as also being of the House of KLOPTON, and that they were delighted to meet Sir James & Lady Susan's family who they had heard so much about.

After exchanging a few further words, Sir Stephen then introduced Edmund to the rest of the family, whom he greeted with a military salute and welcomed them all to Kenilworth Castle.
Sir Stephen explained that Sir Frederick's family had arrived the day before from London with some soldiers and it was now his responsibility to escort them to KLOPTON, where they would also be staying in the Manor House.

Within a short time everyone was ready, with Kara joining Lady Khloe and the children in the coach so they could talk to each other on the way, whilst Sir Frederick rode on horseback alongside Kane.
Sir Stephen led them all out of the castle, with half his troops to the front and the rest including Edmund to the rear, in order to help ensure that the family were protected during their journey to Stratford-upon-Avon.
They quickly arrived at the Kenilworth market place, where Sir Stephen told the family to remain with some of his troops, whilst the others went with him to collect the fresh vegetables and other supplies they had already organised to take back with them.

After only a few minutes however, a lot of voices were unexpectedly heard coming from the main street towards them and after they turned to look what was happening, they saw a large crowd heading in their direction, with many of the men brandishing sticks and shouting aggressively.
These men quickly reached the coach with the family inside and although the soldiers stood in line with their swords and shields to guard them, the crowd seem undeterred by their presence and pushed forward trying to reach them.

Kane and Sir Frederick were not sure how best to try and help handle this situation, but thankfully before matters got any more out of control, Sir Stephen had returned with his soldiers and charged straight at the crowd with their swords to disperse them.

As some of the attackers fell injured onto the ground, the others ran off as fast as they could in different directions to escape the soldiers swords, but Sir Stephen decided not to give chase and let them go.

Suddenly however, Lady Khloe and Kara started screaming out Ryan's name from inside their coach, as he had disappeared during the fracas.

Upon hearing the sheer distress in the two women's voices, Sir Stephen immediately galloped back towards the coach and once there, both ladies stepped outside to tell him that Ryan had gone missing.

Sir Frederick and Kane were also there with them and they agreed that Ryan must have got so scared during the fighting that he climbed out of the coach door on the opposite side to where they were standing and ran off unnoticed, presumably to find somewhere safe to hide down one of the side streets.

Sir Stephen however, was not convinced that this was what actually happened and instead he considered it more likely that the main crowd attacked one side of the coach to create a diversion, whilst on the other side some other men approached and abducted Ryan.

Either way, Ryan had gone missing and they had to find him quickly before he came to any harm.

Sir Stephen immediately sent Edmund back to the castle to get some reinforcements to help, whilst half of his troops remained with the coach to guard the rest of the family and the other half spread out along the streets to try and locate the boy.

Kane and Sir Frederick also wanted to help find Ryan, but Sir Stephen would not let them and instead insisted that they stay with the coach and help his soldiers protect the women.

Within a couple of minutes however, Sir Frederick saw smoke rising up above some of the houses in the distance on the edge of the town and immediately showed this to Kane, who fearing the worse told him to stay with the three women in the coach, whilst he mounted his horse and rode over to where Sir Stephen was still organising the search.

Upon seeing Kane approach, Sir Stephen shouted at him to return to the coach, but instead Kane pointed over to the fire in the distance and straight away drew his sword before heading off at a gallop in the direction of the smoke, calling out that he was going to save Ryan.

Immediately realising what dreadful deed might be taking place, Sir Stephen instantly ordered his remaining troops to mount up and with their swords raised, follow him and Kane as quickly as they could.

85

Less than a minute later, Kane arrived at where the smoke was and to his horror he saw Ryan tied to a wooden stake in the centre of the fire, with the poor boy screaming out in agony as the locals shouted "death to anyone who has the plaque".

Kane raised his sword and tried to push his horse forward through the raucous crowd, but there were too many of them and they quickly managed to grab his reins and stop him from going any further.

They then dragged him off his horse and upon noticing his different skin tone, started yelling that he too had the plaque and they were going to also burn him to death.

Thankfully, at that moment however, Sir Stephen arrived and realising what was happening, ordered his soldiers to charge forward with him.

They immediately all rode straight into the crowd, where they cut down several of the men with their swords and maimed many others, whilst the rest of them started to run off down the streets in fear for their lives.

Kane laid on the ground quite badly bruised and shaken for a few moments as his attackers fled, but soon saw Sir Stephen dismount and come towards him.

As he got closer, Kane pointed over to the fire and frantically shouted out that Ryan was still tied to the wooden stake, whereupon he picked himself up and started to run over to try and rescue the boy.

Before he could get very far however, Sir Stephen grabbed hold of his arm and told him to stop as it was too late to save him.

Tragically, Ryan was already dead.

They both just stood there looking at the fire whilst the flames glowed even redder and watched on as the final remains of Ryan's burning body turned to ashes in front of their eyes.

With sheer sadness etched across their faces, they both knelt down together on the ground and each said a personal prayer for their young relative.

During this moment of grieving, some of the remaining wounded men started to try and slip away, but upon seeing this Sir Stephen immediately stood up and ordered his soldiers to arrest them.

They quickly managed to round most of them up and after tying their hands firmly behind their backs, dragged them over to face their judgement.

At that moment however, the sound of horses could be heard galloping towards them and upon turning around, Sir Stephen saw a troop of soldiers had arrived from the castle.

Edmund was riding at the front next to the lieutenant in charge, who upon seeing Sir Stephen asked him what assistance they could provide.

He replied by saying that he would be taking responsibility for dealing with this despicable matter and in doing implement the King's rule of law, but first of all he needed to know that his family were safe inside their coach, to which the lieutenant replied they were being well guarded by his soldiers.

Upon hearing this, he requested that they fetch Sir Frederick to join them, but not to bring any of the women as they were to remain inside the coach until he advised otherwise.

Additionally, Sir Stephen instructed the lieutenant to dispatch the rest of his soldiers to help round up the remaining injured men involved in the attack on his nephew and to bring them over to join those who they had previously captured.

A few minutes later Sir Frederick arrived and Sir Stephen took him to one side whilst he told him the tragic news about what had happened to Ryan.

Sir Frederick was deeply distraught and extremely angry as he demanded justice be done to those cowards that carried out such a barbaric act against his son, who was just a defenceless young boy.

Sir Stephen assured him that justice would be carried out and shortly afterwards another group of injured men were dragged in front of them by the soldiers, to join the other severely wounded ones already held.

Sir Stephen asked Edmund to watch over the men, whilst he and Sir Frederick walked over to talk to the lieutenant to discuss what to do.

It was agreed that the ring-leaders would be hanged from a large tree in the street as some rope was quickly organised and tied to one of its main branches.

Meanwhile, the troops rounded up some of the local town's people and made them come to watch the men being hung, whereupon it soon became apparent that some of their families were amongst them and started screaming to let their men go.

The lieutenant quickly ordered his soldiers to draw their swords and then shouted to all the people

"Be quiet or you too will join your murdering relatives".

Sir Stephen then took control of the situation and in a very powerful commanding voice pronounced to all those present

"I am Sir Stephen Klopton and a Knight to King Edward III.

My father is Sir James Klopton, who is also a good friend of the King.

The young boy who you murdered in such a barbaric manner was my nephew Ryan Klopton, who was also the son of the gentleman standing next to me, Sir Frederick Klopton.

Hear me well, this atrocious deed will not go unpunished and I demand to know who the main perpetrators were of such a callous act?"

87

Upon hearing this, the crowd went very quiet, but after a short period without any response, Sir Stephen continued

"Unless someone tells me now who carried out this unforgivable act, I will have all of the men standing in front of you hung until they are dead and the soldiers will not only burn their bodies, but also their houses".

Suddenly, a woman stepped forward crying hysterically and fell to her knees bowing, before saying

"Please Sir knight I beg you for forgiveness for my husband who is standing at the end of the line, as he was not one of the attackers, but someone who simply got caught up in the crowd.

We were all told that the young boy carried the plague and there was nothing my husband could have done to save him from the burning fire".

Sir Stephen responded to the woman in a very stern voice

"Your excuse for your husband's act is pathetic and I will hang him now unless you tell me who the men were that tied my nephew to the stake and set fire to him".

Hardly daring to look up, the woman who was clearly shaking, pointed over to two of the men in the line, whereupon Sir Stephen gestured to the soldiers to bring them both forward to face him.

They were quickly dragged over and thrown to the ground, where they began begging for their lives, but he was having none of it and forcefully demanded

"Are you the men who took the boy from the coach in the town and then burnt him alive on this fire?"

One of the men responded straight away

"I was told by this man next to me that the boy had the plague and I only helped him in order to protect my family and everyone else".

The other man instantly replied

 "No, it was the other man who said the boy had the plague and it was him who grabbed the boy and put him on the fire".

"Enough!" shouted Sir Stephen at the two men, before he turned to face both Sir Frederick and the lieutenant, and after a brief discussion they all nodded their heads in agreement.

Sir Stephen spoke out again so everyone present could hear his words

"Both of you men have admitted to being complicit in the brutal death of an innocent young boy and by the authority vested in me as a Knight of the Realm appointed by our King, I hereby sentence you to immediate death by hanging".

The two men tried to protest, whereupon Sir Stephen firmly told them

"Be quiet or your families will also be hung with you and your houses burnt down".

They both went silent and bowed their heads, knowing that their fates had been decided.

The lieutenant ordered his soldiers to take the men over to the tree where a second rope was added and a noose wrapped around each of the men's necks.

The soldiers then pulled the two ropes tight and awaited their orders, whereupon the lieutenant nodded his approval and without any further delay, Sir Stephen gave the command for the soldiers to carry out the executions.

Once the men had been hung, Sir Stephen thanked the lieutenant for his help and left him to deal with the corpses and to escort the other attackers back with him to the prison at Kenilworth Castle, where they would stand trial for their part in Ryan's murder.

The soldiers also moved to disperse the crowd who disappeared quickly, clearly being fearful of any more reprisal hangings for the boy's death.

Sir Frederick then moved over to join Sir Stephen and asked that he accompany him to where Ryan had been burnt alive, in order to collect some of his son's ashes before he rejoined his wife and daughter.

Upon seeing the anguish on his face, Sir Stephen asked Edmund to find a suitable container for this purpose, whilst he ordered his soldiers to surround the still smouldering fire perimeter in order to provide Sir Frederick with a degree of privacy.

Edmund soon returned with a small hand-made ornate wooden box from one of the shops and handed it to Sir Frederick, who thanked him.

Sir Frederick then drew his sword and with it he carefully lifted up some of the red glowing embers from the base of the fire where Ryan had been standing, before placing these inside the box and closing the lid in order that they would fully extinguish.

He then offered a quiet personal prayer over Ryan's ashes inside the box, before he returned his sword back into its sheaf and said that it was now time for him to somehow tell his family the tragic news.

They remounted their horses and Sir Stephen said goodbye to Edmund and also the lieutenant, who would both be returning to Kenilworth Castle with their troops.

He then beckoned over to Kane to join him and together they rode off slowly in front of Sir Frederick on the short journey back to the coach, followed by their soldiers riding behind.

Upon reaching the coach, Kane immediately fetched Kara and once she was outside, Sir Frederick climbed inside to be alone with his wife and daughter whilst he told them the traumatic news about Ryan.

A long few minutes passed before the crying from inside the coach stopped and Sir Frederick looked very forlorn as he stepped out to tell Sir Stephen that it was time for them to return to KLOPTON House so Lady Khloe and Kathryn could be comforted further by Sir James & Lady Susan.

Kara could hardly believe what had just happened to Ryan and she decided that she would ride with Kane and Sir Stephen on horseback instead of inside the coach, so Sir Frederick would have some private time with his family to try and come to terms with their grief.

It was a very solemn journey back to KLOPTON and upon their arrival, Sir Stephen helped his sister Lady Khloe out of the coach to give her a loving brotherly embrace, before fetching Kathryn to also join them.
Sir James then appeared at the Manor House front door to greet them, but immediately sensed something was wrong and after talking with both Sir Stephen and Sir Frederick, he took all of the immediate family inside without any further delay.

Kane & Kara however, remained outside not quite sure what to do, but soon Sir Stephen reappeared.
He told them it would probably be best if they both went upstairs for the rest of the afternoon and to have an early evening meal delivered to their rooms later on by the servants.
The following morning, once the initial trauma of the tragedy should have eased slightly, they would then all speak together further on this very distressing matter.
In the meantime however, Sir James had instructed that none of them were to walk around outside on the estate until extra soldiers had arrived and more security was put in place.

The twins agreed to comply without hesitation to both Sir James and Sir Stephen's requests and after offering their sincerest condolences on Ryan's death to the whole family, they started heading off through the front door to their rooms.
Sir Stephen simply nodded his acknowledgement to their kind statement, before walking back inside behind them, where he entered the sitting room to rejoin St James and the rest of the family.

Chapter 10 : **Long Farewell**

A year had passed since Ryan's death, but the plague was still prevalent and tens of thousands of people across England had died, including many from around Warwickshire.
The whole of the KLOPT0N estate was constantly guarded by some of Sir Stephen's soldiers, who with the Manor House staff and farm workers remained on site in extra temporary wooden buildings erected close to the stables and animal pens.

The estate had now become virtually self-sufficient, with any other essential goods ordered by letter and their delivery only accepted from well known suppliers in the town.
Even then, all items including any food supplies, were left with the soldiers at the entrance to the estate's long driveway after all their packaging had been removed and disposed of.
The contents would then be brought up to the kitchen staff where they were either wiped over or washed in the stream, before being allowed inside the Manor House.

One advantage of having visitors from a future time period however, was that the family had a much greater understanding of how diseases spread and the precautions they should take to help prevent this.
Even Sir James did not leave the KLOPT0N estate, but Sir Stephen had to go out as his military duties required him to visit both Warwick and Kenilworth Castles, to assist in ensuring that public order was being maintained as much as possible in the local towns and villages.
Sir Stephen would always be accompanied by at least four soldiers due to the continuing civil unrest, but he also used these trips to exchange both official and private letters to help reduce any unnecessary travel or direct personal contact.

The official military communiques would always be sealed, but many were also shared with Sir James due to him being one of the prominent land owners in the area and a friend of King Edward III.
These documents mainly included up to date information on how virulent the plague was and whether there was any sign that it might be abating, but they also contained details on any significant troop fatalities across England so the King's troops could be moved if necessary to provide extra cover in any essential areas.

The more private letters mainly exchanged news on the health of the various family members and close friends, plus any personal items of gossip on the children's education and other activities during those difficult times.

After all his days travelling around parts of Warwickshire, Sir Stephen would always go for a swim in the KLOPTON lake when he got back, whilst his clothing would also be scrubbed in an effort to ensure that he did not carry any of the plague virus back with him.

Only when everything was cleaned would he return to his personal living accommodation and then meet with Sir James to deliver his letters and discuss what was happening in the nearby towns and castles he had just visited.

Kara & Kane continued living in the Manor House and although the atmosphere had become much more cordial, they both believed that deep down some of the family still partly blamed their presence in that time period for Ryan's unnecessary death.

Everyone knew however, that Kara & Kane could not continue with their journey until the next full red Moon appeared and whilst waiting for such an eclipse to occur, Sir Frederick & Lady Khloe had reached a decision to try and help safeguard Kathryn from the plague.

With Sir Stephen now back in KLOPTON, a meeting was called with Kara & Kane to discuss important family matters and the twins were very concerned what this was going to be about.

They all met up promptly that evening at 7.00 in the dining room as instructed and after everyone had engaged in polite conversation for a short while, they were soon invited to sit down around the table as it was time for the servants to serve their food.

About an hour later they finished eating their meal, but everyone remained seated as Sir James quickly took charge of matters and told the servants to leave the room.

Then, in a sombre voice he started the proceedings by reminding the family that it had been a year since Sir Frederick & Lady Khloe tragically lost Ryan and he asked for everyone to bow their heads in silence for a private minute of reflection, after which he would read out an appropriate prayer of remembrance.

Once over, this poignant and very personal memorial to Ryan brought tears to all the ladies eyes, whilst from the men's distraught facial expressions it was obvious that they too found it difficult to contain the raw emotions still felt by the whole family towards the young boy's brutal death.

Sir James then spoke again and explained that with Ryan gone forever, neither Sir Frederick nor Lady Khloe wanted to lose Kathryn too and as she had now turned sixteen years of age, they had very reluctantly agreed that she should travel through the cavern's red glowing waters next time the full Moon shone red in the evening sky over KLOPTON.

By taking this journey, Kathryn would be able to escape the plague which threatened to kill all of them, apart from the twins who were of a different time period.

She would, of course, also be safe from any barbaric attack similar to that perpetrated on Ryan.

But, Sir James added, there was a problem with this proposal, which was that neither of Kathryn's parents would be accompanying her across the void of time and after this dramatic statement, he asked Sir Frederick to continue.

Sir Frederick looked at his wife and after taking hold of her hand, he explained to all the family that he was not born of the KLOPTON bloodline and he would therefore never be able to make the journey to another time through the cavern on the night of a red Moon.

He then stopped talking to allow his wife to continue, but before she would start, she reached over to take hold of Kathryn's hand who was also sitting next to her and gave her a warm smile.

Lady Khloe then said how she loved both her husband and daughter as much as each other, but with Sir Frederick still recovering from a very bad horse riding accident, she would not leave him on his own.

Kathryn however, had grown into a very independent young girl over the past year since Ryan died and she had also learnt how to look after herself, especially with all the help and encouragement she got from Kara & Kane.

They had all agreed therefore, that they wanted the twins to take Kathryn with them through the cavern red waters and to let her join them as they continued onwards through their next journeys in KLOPTON time.

The twins looked at each other and were both a bit overwhelmed by the significant responsibilities of this request, so much so Kane spoke first before Kara had the chance to.

He asked if Sir Stephen could also accompany them to help look after Kathryn, since he was a much more formidable swordsman than he was and they did not know what new dangers they may be facing next.

Sir Stephen answered by explaining that whilst it would have been a great honour to accept the position of guardian for his niece, his primary duties were not only to the other members of the KLOPTON family, but also to King Edward III and he could not abandon his sworn allegiance to either of them.

Furthermore, he knew that both the twins had enhanced their sword skills significantly since their arrival on Sir James' estate and that they were also very intelligent, which fact was no doubt helped by the extraordinary knowledge they brought with them from their different timeline.

Indeed, he had already discussed Kathryn's guardianship in some depth with the rest of the family and everyone agreed that the two of them would be the best choice to take good care of her.

Upon hearing Sir Stephen say all of this, Kara had no more doubts about accepting this responsibility being asked of them both and looked over at Kane, who with a reassuring smile nodded his approval too.

Kara then stood up and walked around the dining table towards Kathryn, where upon coming close to each other, both girls put out their arms and gave each other a big hug, prompting everyone in the room to start applauding.

Kane also moved over to join them and said how deeply honoured both he and Kara would be to be Kathryn's guardians, even though they were all of a similar age.

Additionally, they would do everything in their power to look after Kathryn until the day she was able to return back to this time period and rejoin her parents after the plague had gone.

The atmosphere in the room had now changed completely as the whole family were totally at ease with each other again for the first time since Ryan's death.

The following morning after breakfast, Kane & Kara met up with Lady Khloe and Kathryn in the lounge to discuss the passageway in the red cavern and the glowing waters Kathryn would encounter on the night of the full red Moon, as neither mother nor daughter had explored these wonders or undertaken such a journey before.

After explaining everything they could, including the significance of the hexagonal birthmarks under their arms and why those the twins had were a bright red colour compared to the deep brown ones both Lady Khloe and Kathryn had, it was agreed that all of them would visit the passageway that afternoon so Kathryn in particular, would have a much better idea of what to expect when the next full lunar eclipse appeared.

Over the next few months everyone on the estate tried to continue with their lives as usual, although the plague had still not subsided and the increased public disorder in the surrounding towns was keeping Sir Stephen's soldiers and the castle troops very busy.

Then early one September morning, as the clouds on the horizon turned shades of red and Kara gazed out of her bedroom window over the hills to watch the glorious autumnal sunrise unfolding, she suddenly noticed that the crystals in her 'K' pendant were also starting to glow bright red.

Kara instantly started to head off out of her door, when she realised that she was only wearing a thin night gown and so grabbed whatever clothes she could to get dressed in quickly, but by the time she got to Kane's room he had already left.

She then remembered they had previously decided that when the crystals shone red, they would meet up in the dining room where the wooden KLOPTON clock was and after virtually jumping down half the hallway staircase in her excitement, Kara ran into the room where Kane was waiting for her.

Kara was overcome when she saw him and in a clearly emotional voice shouted out

"It's happened at last!".

Kane reached out and took his sister in his arms as he tried to calm her down and then reminded her that they had to stay there until everyone else had also joined them.

Sir James was the first to enter the dining room and upon seeing the twins together, he greeted them both in his usual formal voice whilst also shaking Kane by the hand.

He then advised that Lady Susan had gone to find the other family members, since none of them possessed a KLOPTON ring and they would therefore not know that the red Moon was appearing overhead that afternoon.

Unfortunately, Sir Stephen would not be able to get back to the estate before they set off that evening, as he was away helping organise troop placements and would be staying elsewhere all of that week.

Thankfully however, he had left a message for them in case he was absent when they left, which was that he wished them both a safe journey and hoped they managed to fulfil their destiny.

Kane was just about to respond with a kind message of thanks for Sir Stephen from both of them, when they heard voices just outside the door as Lady Susan walked in, followed by Sir Frederick, Lady Khloe and Kathryn.

After a brief interlude, Sir James took charge of proceedings again and although everything had been discussed in some depth several times before, he reiterated rather formally what had previously been agreed between all of them.

The three travellers would say their goodbyes that morning to all those friends they had come to know on the estate, but to avoid raising any suspicions they would each tell the same agreed story that they were leaving KLOPTON in order to stay on Sir James' other country estate in Suffolk.

They would then get changed into the more appropriate travel clothing already arranged for them in their bedrooms, whilst they would also take their original clothes with them to hide in the cavern in case they needed these at some future date during their travels.

Afterwards at noon, the whole family would have a final farewell lunch together in the dining room, followed by some spare time to say any remaining personal farewells.

The three of them would then make their way up to the rock face entrance to wait for the full red Moon from the lunar eclipse to glow and the passageway crystals to also shine bright red.

Everyone acknowledged what Sir James had just said, but the twins were fully aware that one significant matter had not yet been discussed, this being the red glowing letter 'L' which the dial on the wooden clock was pointing at.

Kara spoke first and asked if anyone knew what time period this letter referred to, but after everyone had finished shaking their heads, Sir James said that he had hoped the twins would know the answer to this question.

Kara looked over to Kane, who said that they were both uncertain, but one thing they had noticed so far was that each of the two letters from the word KLOPTON they encountered, referred to the name of an era in time.

If this was correct, then from their knowledge of English history, they could be about to travel over one hundred years into the future to the 15th Century, but they could say no more about this era for the fear of possibly effecting the future they leave behind.

Sir James responded by stating that he fully understood their answer and that everyone should now depart to deal with the tasks they needed to undertake in the last few hours still available to them.

Kane & Kara were the first to leave the room, as they both had one very difficult meeting to attend which they did not really want to, but they knew they had to say a poignant goodbye to their birthfather.

The twins found Richard sitting alone quietly in the drawing room and as they entered the room, he looked up at them both with great sadness etched across his face.

Before they could speak however, he said that he knew why they were there, as he too had seen the crystals on the clock dials glow red that morning and therefore realised it was time for them to continue on their long journey.

Richard stood up and as he opened his arms to hold them both for one last time, Kara went over first to gave him a big hug and a kiss on the cheek.

Kane quickly joined them and it was nearly a minute before Richard gently pulled away, as a few tears began running down his face and he said that he knew this day would have to come.

Kara then started crying too and although Kane was trying to contain himself, his sad face clearly showed the sheer anguish of this moment.

Kane then somehow managed to compose himself again enough to ask Richard if he had any words he would like them to pass onto Katrina when next they saw her, to which he very movingly replied,

"Please tell your mother that it was the most wonderful part of my life to have known her and to have also been able to spend some time with our two wonderful children.

I wish her great happiness and I hope that one day we may even get the chance to meet each other again, should the opportunity ever arise.

Most importantly though, you must also let Katrina know that I will always love her".

After Richard finished speaking, Kara was in an emotional meltdown as she moved over to hold her father tightly once again and confirmed that she would make sure her mother got his message.

The time had then come for them to say their final goodbyes to each other, knowing that once they had all left that room to go their separate ways, they may never meet again.

Kara however, was not prepared to accept such a scenario and lifted her left hand up to show Richard that she was still wearing Rosemarie's ring and to tell him that she wished to borrow it until her and Kane had finished their journey together.

On that day, they would then re-visit him again and only then would she return the ring to him as she had promised, so he therefore had no choice but to be there waiting for them!

A huge smile came over Richard's face as he told Kara she could keep the ring as long as she needed it and that he would still be there when they both came back, whereupon he slowly walked out of the room and was gone.

The rest of the morning went very quickly and after lunch, which Richard did not attend, Sir Frederick & Lady Khloe said their equally moving farewells to their daughter Kathryn, as they had already agreed it would be too emotional for them to accompany her to the crystal passageway that afternoon.

Sir James & Lady Susan then said their fondest goodbyes too and after that the trio left the Manor House towards the concealed rock face crevice entrance in the Oat Hill woodland.

They would then wait there amongst the overgrowth until dusk and for the red lunar eclipse to fully appear, before setting off again on the next part of their journey across KLOPT0N time.

The rose-pink crystal hillside cavern

Part 4

HOUSE OF CLOPTON
- 20th Century -

Chapter 11 : **Brief Reunions**

Meanwhile forward in the 20th Century, Katrina & Tarak were both really missing the twins and worked tirelessly keeping themselves busy in the field War hospital, as they tried to take their minds off the dangers Kara & Kane might be facing during their journey through KLOPT0N time.

Neither of Katrina's parents Kathleen & Andrew were particularly well and in order to look after them both, they came to stay with her and Tarak in their Manor House apartment, sleeping in the twins' bedrooms whilst they were away.
Her mother was initially very unsure about coming back to live at Clopton after her previous time there, but she was pleased to be staying with her daughter so they could catch up on the many years they had lived apart.
They would also be close to the field hospital where they could get better medical care, especially for Andrew, who's health was steadily deteriorating.

Kathleen had visited KLOPT0N time herself after she turned sixteen, so Katrina and her had even more to talk about, including when the twins might next get the chance to visit them.
Both mother and daughter checked the wooden clock every day just waiting for the rose pink crystals to change colour, but the months went by and nothing happened.

It was over a year later in September that the letter 'L' hexagon crystals on the clock started glowing bright red and as soon as Katrina saw this, she went off to find Tarak in the field hospital, where he was busy working hard as usual.
They both agreed to finish off all their day's tasks late that afternoon and then after taking an early tea, walked over to the Oat Hill woodland where they squeezed through the narrow crevice rock face entrance.

Once inside, Katrina made her way up to the edge of the red glowing stream to wait and see if the twins managed to open the underwater passage for her, whilst Tarak only followed her part of the way since the red waters were very dangerous for him.

It was more than an hour later before Katrina suddenly heard a loud thud within the rock wall, but was this coming from inside their red stream section and was it the twins who caused it?

She looked over to where Tarak was standing and they both waited to see what happened next, but after a couple of minutes the water level had still not changed and Katrina realised that this noise must have been from another passage being created to allow someone else access to the main cavern.

Another ten minutes passed by before a second loud thud was heard, which they knew must have come from the same gap closing again and whoever it was should hopefully soon be opening up a different passage to their next destination.

The wait was agonising, but there was then a third loud thud which sounded much closer and as Katrina intensely watched the red stream level in front of her, it started to rise and flow faster, prompting her to shout over to Tarak

"Our underwater passage has just been opened up, but do not worry as I will be back soon!".

Then, without any hesitation, Katrina took a deep breath before diving off the rocks into the stream and she was gone, whilst Tarak could only watch on from a distance and hope for her safe return.

The strong underwater current helped pull her along quickly through the passage gap in the rock wall and in less than a couple of minutes, she had resurfaced inside the bright red glowing crystal cavern.

Katrina had only just started to wade out of the water however, when she saw someone coming towards her and instantly realised that it was Kara, who was running so fast that upon reaching her mother she slipped and dragged them both into the shallow red water together.

The two of them just sat down on the wet cavern floor for a few moments next to each other laughing out loudly, until Kane arrived and helped them both to stand up again, whereupon all three of them had a long emotional embrace.

Then, with so much to talk about but so little time in which to do so, the conversation between them all became a bit frantic, until Katrina paused as she noticed someone else standing and watching them from nearby in the cavern.

Not recognising who this girl was, Katrina asked her siblings, whereupon Kara told her she was Sir James Klopton's grand-daughter Kathryn Klopton, who was travelling with them to escape the Black Death plague from the 14th Century where they had just been.

All three of them walked over to join Kathryn, with Kara going up ahead first so she would not feel uncomfortable at meeting their mother for the first time, especially since Kathryn had just left her own parents behind so she could travel through the cavern waters with the twins.

Once they were all together, Katrina became the perfect 'mother hen' as she listened warmly to Kathryn whilst she talked all about herself, her parents and how much they trusted Kara & Kane to be her guardians during their journey through KLOPT0N time together.
Sadly, the night was passing by far too quickly and before long Katrina knew she had to return to Tarak in her 20th Century timeline, whilst the three teenagers continued on to their next destination.

It was agreed between the twins, that Kara would walk back over with their mother to where she had to enter the stream, as before she set off Kara had something very important and personal to tell her.
Meanwhile, Kane would remain with Kathryn near to the seven hexagonal device, so he could lock the 'K' key once Katrina had swam back through the underwater passage again.

After an emotional farewell to her son, Katrina went slowly back across the cavern floor with her daughter, who told her how they had both met their birthfather Richard in KLOPT0N time during their journey to the 14th Century and that he was keeping well.
This news really pleased Katrina as she had not known if he was still alive, especially after the number of years it had been since they last saw each other, whereupon her voice went quieter as she hesitantly asked if Richard had sent her any message.

Kara took hold of her mother's hands and after a few moments carefully told her exactly what Richard had said to her that morning before they left KLOPT0N.
Upon hearing his words however, Katrina could not contain her emotions anymore and tears started rolling down her cheeks again for the third time that night.

It took a couple of minutes for Katrina to compose herself and after giving Kara one final farewell kiss on the cheek, said that she would be waiting for the day when both her twins would be able to return home so they could all become a family again.

Katrina then released Kara from her hold and turned away to wade out into the deeper cavern water, where she quickly found the current that would help her swim back through the gap and up to the surface passageway.

As soon as she was chest deep, Katrina turned around again for one last glimpse over at the twins, before taking a deep breath and diving into the stream water, where she soon reached the underwater gap in the rock wall.

When she was just about to enter through this passage however, Katrina was suddenly startled by a man swimming up close alongside her, who upon realising that she had just seen him, simply smiled at her and turned around to swim back in the opposite direction towards the cavern again.

Frustratingly, Katrina could do nothing about this, as she was pulled through the gap by the underwater current and then had to swim back up to the stream surface, where she recovered for a short while as she took a few calming breaths.

Upon climbing out over the rocks on to the passageway, she was welcomed back by Tarak who despite the danger had walked further up the passageway and took hold of her in his arms to greet her with a loving kiss.

Katrina just stood there in that moment, quite silent and lost in her thoughts, but after subsequently taking back control of her very mixed emotions, turned to tell Tarak about the man she had seen swimming in the stream water close to her.

Before she could do so however, they both heard a fourth loud thud and knew that the rock wall passage had been closed, which it would remain so until the next full lunar eclipse.

This noise reminded Katrina that the man must be someone born of the KLOPT0N ancestral bloodline, as without the family birthmark he would not have been able to pass through the red waters safely during the period of the red lunar eclipse, but who he was, she did not know.

Furthermore, since Tarak had been watching the 20th Century stream for the whole time the underwater gap was opened with the 'K' key, but did not see anyone, then the man must have entered the cavern with Kara & Kane when they used the 'P' key and therefore followed them from the 14th Century.

The fact that no one mentioned this man to Katrina when she was with them and he was swimming under the water with her when he should not be, clearly showed he was hiding because he was not supposed to be there.

Unfortunately, there was no longer any way for Katrina to get a message to Kara & Kane to warn them about this man and she could only hope instead that he meant them no harm.

It was now time for Katrina & Tarak to make their way back to the Manor House and as they re-appeared from within the hidden rock face, the clear evening sky was still lit up by the bright red glow reflecting from the full Moon eclipse.

After they covered the crevice gap back over with some bushes and thick overgrowth, they walked slowly down the hillside as Katrina told her husband what else happened in the cavern, although she decided not to mention the message sent to her by Richard, apart from that Kara had told her he was still alive.

Katrina also knew that her parents would be very anxious for some news about their grand-children, but they decided that this would have to wait until the morning as she and Tarak went straight into their room to get some sleep after what had been quite a traumatic time.

The next day after breakfast, all four of them sat down together in the lounge to talk about the night before and in particular who the mysterious KLOPT0N descendant might be that had followed the twins through the stream waters.

Whilst Katrina & Tarak had no idea, Kathleen got very emotional and leant over to whisper in her husband's ear
"You don't think it could be .... ",
but before she finished the sentence, Andrew interrupted in a very gentle voice to tell her she should not get upset when it was impossible to know.

Upon hearing his words however, Kathleen could not contain herself any further and looking directly at Katrina she said out loudly with deep emotion in her voice, "It must be Graham!".

Katrina was taken aback by her mother's reaction and immediately asked who Graham was, although she certainly did not expect to get the answer she was given.

Kathleen took hold of her husband's hand, before reminding Katrina of their previous conversation about her own journey years earlier through the crystal cavern during a full lunar eclipse.

What she had never told Katrina before however, was that whilst in KLOPT0N time she met and married a wealthy farmer called Harold Clifford, with whom she had a son called Graham, who would therefore be her half-brother.

Sadly after only a few years, Harold became paranoid about Graham's future because of his hexagonal birthmark and was convinced that she would take his son away from him, especially since he would not be able to go with them both through the red cavern waters.

From then onwards, Harold kept Kathleen watched at all times and would only allow her to be with Graham when there were at least two maids present.

103

The situation became very distressing, but when she complained to Harold he became very aggressive towards her, so much so that she began to be afraid of him, especially when he took a lover to keep him company in her forced absence.

Thankfully, the next red lunar eclipse appeared before matters got too unbearable and she managed to escape from the farm house late that evening before anyone realised she had gone.
Graham however, was under the constant supervision of Harold's maids and Kathleen knew she had no other option but to leave him behind if she ever wanted her life back.

Once outside, she quickly made her way over the fields to the cavern entrance and although she was distraught at not being able to say goodbye to her son, she knew that Graham would be well looked after by his father.
Ever since then, Kathleen never risked returning to KLOPTON to try and see him again, but she had of course since then fallen in love with Andrew and together they had their wonderful daughter, who was so much more than either of them could ever have hoped for.

Katrina stood up and walked over to join them both as Andrew tried to console Kathleen whilst tears rolled down her cheeks and Katrina said for her mother not to be so upset.
She also told Kathleen that she would try and get a message to the twins during the next lunar eclipse, to find out if they had ever met either Harold or Graham during their travels in KLOPTON time and if the half-brother she had never known was still alive

This would all have to wait for another day however, as the four of them had seen the crystals in the letter 'L' on the clock glow bright red the previous night and knew that the three teenagers would by now have entered the 15th Century during the era of the House of Lancaster.
What no-one knew of course was the actual year they arrived, nor what dangers they might encounter during their stay.

Katrina also had no realistic idea as to when Kara & Kane would finally return back home to stay with her again in Clopton, although listening to Kathleen reminded her of an old story about their ancestors, which her mother had told her before she left for Ireland and the twins were born.

Apparently, KLOPTON legend told of a prophecy only known through generations since long gone, part of which was still inscribed on each of the KLOPTON keys, but also recorded more fully on a special scroll locked away within the large crystal cavern.

Whilst Katrina had read the few cryptic words etched on each of the two keys she once held, neither her mother nor any of their family still living had ever read all of the seven texts or the scroll parchment.

Kathleen therefore believed that their ancestors never discovered the full meaning hidden within the various inscriptions and that it was Kane & Kara's destiny to do so, as they were the only known twins of the true bloodline to have been conceived in KLOPTON time, but subsequently born across the void in another era.

Furthermore, the legend said that until the prophecy was revealed, the teenagers of KLOPTON blood would forever continue to be drawn through time to undertake the journey their ancestors failed to complete.

Everyone in the room looked at each other as they suspected at least part of what Kathleen said was true, but they also wondered if Kane & Kara were the ones who would at long last uncover the ancestral secrets and in doing so fulfil its destiny together.

. . . .

Meanwhile, back in the cavern the previous night, the twins had seen their mother turn around for one final glimpse in their direction, before she dived back into the red stream water to return home.

Several minutes later, Kane used the 'K' key to lock the underwater gap in the rock wall and after hearing a loud thud, they knew that this passage to the 20th Century was closed again.

Having already locked the 'P' key back in its hole to close the 14th Century passage with after they had swam through it to the cavern, the only key hole on the panel to remain empty was the one for the 'O' symbol.

The other hexagon on the panel device to still be glowing red was that for the 'L' key, which the twins had already surmised would open a passage to the 15th Century and it was now time for them to find out if they were right.

Kane took a firm grip of the 'L' stud in order to turn and remove it, after which they heard a loud thud and knew that a new underwater passage had just been opened.

All three of them stood there for one last look at the numerous red glowing lights flickering around the cavern walls and ceiling, as Kathryn commented how these made some of the dark shadows hidden amongst the jagged rock crevices, seem almost alive.

Kara then fastened both the 'K' and 'L' pendant keys onto the silver chain around her neck and once secure, they all walked off slowly together in the direction of the stream as the water level started to rise.

105

After Kathryn's first swim through the red glowing water to enter the cavern, her hexagonal birthmark had changed from brown to bright red and soon all three of them had waded in far enough to now take a deep breath and dive off into the new underwater current.

Kara led the way with Kathryn next, followed by Kane last and they all soon reached the gap in the rock wall, before continuing to swim upwards with the current to the stream surface.

Once above the water, Kane waited for the two girls to climb out over the rocks in front of him to ensure they made it safely, before joining them on the side of the passageway where they all sat down for a welcome rest.

. . . .

Back inside the cavern and unknown to any of them, someone else born of the original KLOPT0N bloodline had managed to follow them through the red stream from the 14th Century, where the twins had been staying.

This man had been hiding in the shadows all the time they were there, watching everything they were doing and now the three of them had swam off in the underwater stream, just as he had seen another woman do a short time earlier, he walked over to the seven hexagon device to take a closer look at it.

He saw that only the 'L' hexagon was glowing red, but its key was missing and he immediately realised that he had better leave through the same underwater passage before it too was closed, or else he would became trapped inside the cavern.

He quickly walked over to the stream and dived in, but before he had reached the gap he heard a loud thud and started to swim even faster.

Thankfully, he managed to get through the hole before it shut to and then swam upwards with the strong current to the surface, where he stopped to exhale and start breathing again.

Whilst recovering, he heard some people talking close by and so decided to remain out of sight beside the stream edge next to the rocks, until they had gone.

Chapter 12 : **The New Maharaja**

The Great War was becoming ever more brutal with hundreds of thousands of soldiers dying across all the continents, including those from the Indian armies fighting with honour and valour alongside other allies of the British Empire.

One early spring morning, an Indian army officer arrived in full military uniform at the Clopton Manor House, to inform Tarak that his royal uncle had been killed in India.
The family's coastal palace had been bombarded from the sea by the German navy and his father was now the new provincial Maharaja in his uncle's place.
The officer then gave Tarak a secure military communication package, inside which was a private letter on ivory coloured rice paper bearing his father's royal seal and whilst the officer sat down for a rest, Tarak went off for a walk away from the field hospital to find a quiet place where he could read this without being disturbed.

The hand written letter briefly explained how the war in India was going, plus more details about how the German battleship had inflicted significant damage on the palace during its surprise attack that killed his uncle and some of the other senior officers discussing the war with him that day.

Due to the sensitive nature which any further information on the current war situation might provide if the letter was to fall into the wrong hands, his father then wrote instead about how Tarak's mother and siblings were struggling to cope with the everyday problems they were facing.
After a couple of more pages, he finished the letter by telling Tarak that it was now time for him to return back home to India to accept his royal position and also the responsibilities he had to his family, subjects and country of birth.

Tarak sat there for a while, before slowly getting up again and walking the long way back across the Clopton hills to the field hospital, so giving him even more time to try and clear his head.
He had a very difficult decision to make and no-one to discuss it with.

Both Kane & Kara were still away travelling in KLOPT0N time and he suspected that they would have probably already met their real birth father Richard by then.
Tarak however, had no children of his own, because Katrina had a very difficult childbirth during which she nearly died and thereafter was unable to become pregnant again.

107

After another hour of further soul searching, Tarak knew that he had no other choice but to return back to India and help his people, but he also knew he could not tell Katrina to her face of this momentous decision, because if he did he would never be able to leave her.

So instead Tarak waited for her to go out on an hospital errand into Stratford-upon-Avon, before he quickly packed a couple of travel bags.

He then sat down to write her a lengthy letter trying to explain why he had to go back to India on his own, but also to say how much he still loved her and always would.

Without waiting any longer to ensure that Katrina did not return before he had chance to depart, Tarak handed his letter over to the matron and very briefly explained its contents, before with sheer anguish etched across his face he said a very sombre farewell.

After walking outside, he climbed into the military vehicle that was still waiting for him and there was no changing his mind now.

He then took one last look over at the Manor House as the Indian officer drove off down the driveway for their long journey to the docks and a military ship leaving England that evening.

Katrina returned back to Clopton House a couple of hours later, but being unable to find Tarak she went to the matron's field hospital office instead, who told her how he had urgently driven off with an Indian army officer that afternoon.

The matron then handed Katrina the letter which Tarak had left for her.

They both walked silently across the courtyard into the Manor House sitting room and after shutting the door behind them for privacy, sat down on separate chairs as Katrina began reading the several pages of very moving text Tarak had written her.

Once she had finished it all, she looked over at the matron and with tears rolling down her face, started to cry uncontrollably.

Katrina was heartbroken.

The second true love of life was also now gone and she knew that it was very unlikely she would ever see either Tarak or Richard again.

Katrina then started muttering something about when the twins might return home, which the matron did not understand, before Katrina became so overcome with emotion that she collapsed onto the floor and the matron rushed over to try and comfort her.

. . . .

It took more than a couple of weeks before Tarak arrived back in India and once he reached his father's provincial palace he was met by his parents, who were both overjoyed at seeing him again.

That evening, they all sat down together for a small formal banquet with some musical entertainment, where the rest of the family also joined them to celebrate his homecoming.

After the main meal was finished however, Tarak's father had another surprise for his son as he introduced him to a young Hindu bride who had been specially chosen for him to marry, so they could have children together.

One of Tarak's royal responsibilities was to continue the family blood line and when a boy was born, their son would become the next provincial Maharaja in succession.

In that part of India, Hindu men of royal birth were allowed to have two wives and Tarak therefore reluctantly agreed to his father's request, whilst also knowing that he would probably never see either Katrina or the twins ever again.

Tarak was quickly appointed as a senior lieutenant in the Indian army and after several weeks of intensive officer training including battlefield scenarios, he started to lead his own troops on many campaigns.

Later that year however, he was brutally killed during an ambush whilst fighting with his soldiers along the North West Frontier near Afghanistan, after he and his men got separated from one of the main battalion groups.

A short time later after his Indian funeral cremation, a formal military communique of condolence was sent to Katrina in England to inform her of Tarak's tragic, but highly distinguished death.

Not knowing what this letter was about when it arrived however, but recognising that it had come from India, Katrina was all by herself in her room when she opened it.

After reading the distressing content she was overcome with grief, as she also realised that she was now all alone, with both of her parents having died within a week of each other only a few months earlier and Kara & Kane still away travelling in KLOPTON time.

With no one else to turn too and totally distraught, Katrina slowly made her way upstairs to the small private chapel in the Manor House to pray for them all, but especially for her twins eventual safe return.

After an hour of trying to find solace through God, Katrina lay down on one of the small chapel benches, where with no more tears to weep and physically exhausted, she fell into a restless sleep.

Winter snowfall over Clopton Park estate

HOUSE OF LANCASTER
- 15th Century -

Chapter 13 : **A Winter's Tale**

After their short rest, Kane, Kara and Kathryn all stood up again and walked slowly along the illuminated passageway, as they followed the red glowing lights that were still shining all the way to the narrow crevice gap in the rock face.

Once at the end, Kane made his way outside first, where he found the exit to be heavily overgrown with numerous large bushes which were difficult to push past, especially the thick gorse that was covered with hundreds of sharp thorns protruding from its stems.

Kane withdrew his sword to chop a small pathway for him to walk through, whilst trying not to disturb the flora too much so he did not leave the crevice gap exposed after they left.

Fortuitously, Kane soon discovered amongst the gorse a variety of green leafy bushes that did not need to be cut back as much and after taking several more steps, he also found some tall wild grasses which also helped provide extra cover.

As he now looked across at what he assumed was the Oat Hill woodland running along one edge of the ridge and furrowed sloping fields, he stood quite still and silent for a couple of minutes, whilst he listened intensely for the sound of anybody else nearby.

He also watched to see if in the fading red light of the setting Moon, there was anyone moving around in the fields fronting the buildings in the distance, the main one of which he assumed was the Manor House.

Then suddenly from somewhere behind him, Kane heard the sound of a twig snap and instinctively spun around with his sword in his hand ready for combat, when he saw that it was the two girls who had followed him out of the passageway instead of waiting there for his return, as he had told them to.

Kara, upon seeing her brother so startled could not help but grin slightly, but then realising from his expression that he was not very amused she apologised for her usual impatience, to which he quipped that he should have known better and with a sarcastic sigh, returned his sword into its sheath.

All three of them then just stood there together for a few moments looking out over the Moon lit hills towards the woodlands up ahead, before Kara asked if either of the others had noticed that the fields appeared to be glowing a redder than usual, particularly compared to when they left KLOPT0N only a few hours earlier.

From her voice, Kane realised that his sister was shivering and looking over at Kathryn, he saw that she too was doing the same.

It then occurred to him that it was actually a bitterly cold night and as his high adrenaline levels started to lower, he also started to feel the cold for the first time as the breath he exhaled turned into a fine mist.

Kane leant downwards and reached out to feel the ground below him, but instead of touching grass as he had originally expected after he stepped out through the crevice into the wet overgrowth, he realised that everything around him including his boots were covered in a layer of white snow.

This snowfall obviously explained why the red glowing light from the Moon was reflecting brighter off the ground compared to when it was just lighting up fields of grass, but what he did not understand was why when they left KLOPT0N a few hours earlier it was Summer and now they had arrived on the same night it was evidently Winter.

This conundrum however, would have to wait for another time, as all three of them were still soaking wet from swimming through the red cavern waters and they clearly needed to get somewhere dry and warm as soon as possible, if they were not going to catch colds.

Kane returned straight away to the crevice entrance and pulled as many bushes as he could back into place whilst also covering the surrounding ground with some of the leaves and flora he had removed earlier.

It was not possible however, for him to hide all of their footprints as these were clearly visible in the snow, but for now they would have to leave things as they were and hope that it either melted later that day or there was another snowfall.

Fortunately though, there was no evidence of any other footprints in the vicinity and from the thickness of the overgrowth, it certainly appeared that no one else had recently been near that part of the rock face.

Without any further delay, Kane told the girls that they must walk in a singe line behind one another and also step in each others footprints, so there would be only one set of tracks visible.

Kane went ahead first, with Kara at the rear to keep a watchful eye over Kathryn, who was clearly the most hesitant of them in the snow.

They headed off down the hill towards the dip they could see between the two nearest fields, as they assumed this was where the stream would be and lead them to the Manor House.

After a difficult walk due to the numerous deep snow drifts covering the uneven ground, they eventually reached the edge of some trees.

From here they could see light shining out of several of the buildings windows a short distance up ahead of them and also some smoke rising from their chimney tops.

They stopped for a moment and turned around to look up at the night sky behind them, where they saw that the Earth's shadow had started to cover the bright Moon and cause it's red glow to fade, although along the distant horizon the starlit sky over the hills was still an eerie colour.

It was then that Kane realised he could not get the bearings he needed in order to find their way back to the crevice entrance they had just left, due to everything around them being covered in snow.

Whilst the night-time stars up in the sky would usually help in such circumstances, they were not much use when it was cloudy, so he took out the compass he still had in his pocket instead.

Using its north point, he then quickly worked out the direction they would have to travel to get there again when they left the Manor House in the future.

As Kane looked back up towards the hills however, he suddenly noticed in the distance a dark figure of someone appear from where they had just arrived a short time earlier.

This unrecognisable person began moving across the front of the rock face and then in the same direction as they had all just walked.

Turning quickly towards the girls, Kane told them to remain still and quiet, as he pointed over towards the mysterious shadow whilst it flickered in the fading light of the Moon over the snow covered hillside.

Kara gasped as she saw the person's outline too, but in a surprisingly calm voice then simply said that this must be someone following them, to which both Kane and Kathryn nodded their heads in agreement.

They all stood motionless for what seemed like an eternity, whilst they watched the dark figure continue slowly in the same direction, on what appeared to be a relentless path across the fields towards them.

Kane then spoke slightly louder which startled the girls, but he told them they should now leave that place before whoever it was got too close.

He also said that it would be best if they did not lead their pursuer in the same direction as they were going towards the Manor House, and even though they were still wet and very cold, they both reluctantly agreed.

They all turned around and set off quickly in single file again, but this time they walked haphazardly through the woodland trees where there was virtually no snow on the ground and also much less light, so hoping that their tracks would not be as visible as they would be if they continued across the snow covered field instead.

It wasn't long before they reached the Manor House lake and gardens, but as they approached the courtyard Kane suddenly stopped still and signalled for both Kara and Kathryn to do the same.

Up ahead of them he was alarmed to see soldiers standing sentry at the front door, whilst on the land to the other side of the main buildings were about a dozen military style tents guarded by soldiers, who were clearly trying to keep themselves warm by staying close to the log fires.

After trying to assess the situation from the soldiers' uniforms and insignia, Kane turned towards the girls and said that unfortunately he didn't know if these soldiers were loyal to the KLOPTON family or not.

Indeed, their ancestors in time, may have had to temporarily move elsewhere and the estate was therefore currently occupied by other forces, who might not be very welcoming towards them.

Unfortunately however, being acutely aware of how cold both girls were, Kane knew they needed to find a warm place to shelter, plus some dry clothes and hot food if they were going to survive this bad weather.

They therefore had no real alternative but to proceed up to the Manor House front door as originally planned and hope for the best.

Initially however, none of them should mention who they really were and instead, the story they tell would be changed so they all had the same family surname of 'Greenway'.

Once they had then determined the soldiers reaction, they could decide what further information they would disclose to them next.

Kara agreed with this and although Kathryn was not sure what she should now be saying, she was shivering far too much to speak and so simply nodded to them both by way of agreement.

Kane decided that they should walk up to the front door together, since the sentries would feel less threatened upon seeing two women, but he should be the one to speak to them first.

They then all stepped out from under the cover of the trees where they had been hiding and set off across the courtyard, which was only dimly lit by the early morning night sky as the Moon had now disappeared behind some thick low laying clouds on the horizon.

As they approached the Manor House however, they were soon spotted by the sentries who drew their swords and ordered them to stop and identify themselves.

Kane spoke first as the three of them had agreed and introduced themselves as brother and sisters of the House of Greenway, who had been attacked by robbers whilst on the way from their home in Suffolk to visit other family in Chester.

Their horses were stolen and they only escaped by jumping in a nearby river, which is why they were so wet and cold.

They then made their way across some fields and upon seeing the smoke from the chimneys and lights in the windows, they were hoping to find temporary refuge somewhere dry and warm.

One of the sentries told them to follow him over to where the tents and fires were and once they got closer they were glad to feel the warmth from the flames, as a couple more soldiers also came over to join them. In the brighter light, the soldiers realised that the three of them were only teenagers and that two of them were girls, but all of them looked quite dishevelled and were clearly shivering from the cold, as the sentry told one of the soldiers what Kane had just told him.

The soldier then went over to the largest tent and within a few minutes returned with another soldier, who was clearly higher ranked than him. This officer said how sorry he was to hear of the attack on them all and after dawn he would send out some soldiers to see if they could track down the robbers.
In the meantime however, they had no space available within their tents to accommodate two young ladies and if they would instead accompany him over to the Manor House, he would ask the servant of Sir John Klopton the owner, if there were any spare rooms available for a few hours so they could at least get dry.

Upon hearing that the main house was occupied by one of their distant KLOPTON relatives resulted in all three of them letting out a big sigh of relief, as they now knew they were safe.
Their evident over reaction prompted the solider to ask if something was wrong, but before answering the question Kane removed his right hand glove to reveal the 'K' signet ring of the KLOPTON family, which he was wearing on his middle finger.
He then said that Sir John Klopton was their uncle, but that they had not disclosed this before as they were unaware if the soldiers were there to protect him or instead were his enemies who had taken over the estate.

The soldier offered his apologies for not knowing about their imminent arrival and took them without delay to the Manor House.
Once there, Kane saw that the red & black KLOPTON crest was above the front door, as it was the last time they had journeyed there in time.
Meanwhile, the soldier gestured to one of the sentries, who banged on the door to attract the attention of someone inside, even though it was very early in the morning and most people would still be asleep.

Thankfully, it did not take too long before they heard footsteps from inside and as the front door opened, they were greeted by a servant who turned to the soldier and asked how he could help?

After a brief introduction during which Kane showed his 'K' signet ring again, the solider asked for the family to be let into the Manor House as they were all shivering outside in the cold and needed to to get warm.

The servant quickly let them through the door and into the main entrance hallway, where Kane and the girls noticed that this part of the house had not changed much from what they had recently left behind, apart from the number of unrecognisable portraits hanging on the walls.

Kara could no longer stand the suspense however and turning towards the servant, told him that she had lost track of time due to their long journey and asked if he would please remind her of the date?

Whilst looking slightly surprised by her question, the servant answered that it was the 3rd January, to which reply Kara became agitated as she said that she also wanted to know what year it was?

Upon hearing Kara's rather surprising further request, the soldier interjected and told her that it was the year 1459, to which reply Kane then spoke before Kara had chance to say anything else.

He explained to the soldier and servant that his sisters were both distressed and extremely tired after the difficult couple of days travelling they had just undertaken.

They would therefore be very grateful for some dry garments to wear and warm beds to lay in, as they all needed to get some sleep for now and then later that morning, would discuss matters with Sir John after the Sun had risen.

Without further delay, the servant told them all to follow him upstairs where a couple of bedrooms were available for them to use, whilst the solider said his farewells and went back outside to his military tent.

Once inside their respective rooms, all three of them got changed into the clean night-time garments provided and after some hot drinks to help them warm up, they soon fell asleep.

Unfortunately however, their slumber only lasted for a few hours as the cockerel from the estate farmyard crowed upon the rising of the morning Sun and woke them all up again!

A short time later, one of the maids gently tapped on both bedroom doors to deliver their dry clothes which had been cleaned that morning.

She also told them that their breakfast would be served in thirty minutes and Sir John was looking forward to meeting them in the dining room.

After hearing this, Kane got dressed quickly and went straight over to the girls' room to knock a couple of times on their door, before saying that he was waiting outside for them both in the corridor.

Within a few seconds Kara called for Kane to come inside, where he saw her sitting on a bedside chair staring at the 'L' pendant key she was wearing on the silver chain around her neck.

116

Upon seeing her brother enter, Kara lifted up the underneath of the key close to her eyes to re-check the two-part inscription engraved in a medieval font on either side of the longest silver stem, which she had been studying earlier.

Kara then looked upwards and told Kane that the text read

'only the living ... will display mark'

She then took the 'L' pendant off the silver chain around her neck and passed it over to him, so he too could have a look at the text close up.

After a few seconds Kane nodded his agreement and they both decided that this phrase must refer to the hexagonal birth mark seen underneath the right arm of every true KLOPTON family descendant.

They also noticed that once again there was an unusual shaped object etched onto both sides of the longest stem end, which on the 'L' key looked like the letter 't' fixed alongside the number '2'.
Kane however, recognised this object from when he studied astronomy at school in Cork and told Kara that it was an ancient symbol identified with the planet Saturn.

Additionally, he now remembered that it was also whilst at school he saw the unusual shaped object etched onto the 'P' key stem and it too was an ancient symbol, but one identified with the planet Venus.

They had both already assumed that the crescent shaped object etched onto the stem of the 'K' key Kara wore around her neck was identified with the Moon, and Kane now realised that this must be correct as it too was an ancient symbol detailed in the same astronomy book.

Whilst Kara was impressed by her brother's knowledge of the planets he gained at school, she wanted to know what this all meant.
Unfortunately however, Kane did not yet have the answer to such an intriguing question and instead he expected that they would have to wait until they had undertaken all their journeys in time to discover this.

Kane did however, continue to tell Kara about some other possible relevant information which he had read during his astronomical studies.
It was recorded in various old documents, that people used to believe the Earth was at the centre of the Universe, whilst the Sun, Mercury, Venus, Moon, Mars, Jupiter and Saturn all travelled in circles around it.
Collectively, these seven rotating celestial bodies were known as the 'Seven Classical Planets', being the only physical objects that could be seen and identified with the naked eye from Earth at that time.
Each of them were designated by a different ancient symbol, such as those they had found etched onto a stem of the three KLOPTON keys.

It was not until many centuries later however, that scientists realised that the Sun was at the centre of our solar system around which the Earth and all the other planets travelled, including Uranus and Neptune which were subsequently discovered through the use of the telescope.

Additionally, neither the Sun nor Moon were any longer referred to as planets, although each for quite different reasons.

Kara was just about to ask Kane another question, when there was a knock on the bedroom door and a servant announced their breakfast was ready, with Sir John waiting for them all to join him downstairs.

Both of the twins were very hungry and Kara quickly stood up from her chair to go to the other inner bedroom and fetch Kathryn too, who eagerly followed her.

As the three of them reached the dining room, another servant appeared at the door and asked each of them to confirm their name, after which he told them to follow him into the room.

Once inside, he introduced them in turn to Sir John Klopton and his wife Lady Agnes, who both stood up to greet their guests.

After completing the welcoming formalities, Sir John said they should all start their breakfast straight away as the three of them must be hungry.

He then beckoned over the servants who were standing quietly waiting for their instructions, to begin serving everyone their food.

As they keenly ate up all of the various courses, they talked about the changes to the present day KLOPTON estate and in particular the updated Manor House decor since their last stay there.

Kara and Kathryn were also both interested in the latest ladies fashions of the time, which Lady Agnes was only too pleased to discuss with them as she was delighted to have some new female company.

After they had all finished eating, the three teenagers felt much better and also a lot more relaxed than when they first arrived.

The servants then left the dining room, closing the door behind them and as soon as the family members were on their own, Sir John turned to Kane and asked him if there was anything else he could show him apart from the 'K' signet ring, to prove his genuine KLOPTON lineage.

Kane knew exactly what Sir John was seeking and instantly stood up from his chair, where he removed his jacket and rolled up the right sleeve of his shirt to expose his arm.

Sir John then got up and walked over to join Kane, who lifted his arm upward to let him see the red hexagonal KLOPTON birthmark concealed underneath.

Meanwhile, despite not having been asked to do so, both Kara and Kathryn turned back the blouse sleeves covering their right arms to also reveal their red hexagons.

After examining all three of these marks, Sir John rolled up his own shirt sleeve and showed them that he too bore the same House of KLOPTON hexagonal red birthmark.

He apologised for doubting them, but explained that he had never met another direct KLOPTON descendant before and therefore wondered if any others did still exist.

It was only at the age of eighteen during the full red Moon, that he decided to enter the red glowing water beside the crystal passageway.

Once inside the stream, he was pulled along with the strong underwater current into the magnificent illuminated cavern, but he only stayed a short time before returning back the way he came and never returned.

Sir John then went on to talk about his three sons, the eldest named Sir Thomas was a scholar who spent most of his time in Oxford, whilst his second son Sir Hugh was a merchant who worked mainly in London.

There was then a great sadness in his voice, which became very melancholy as he started to tell them about his youngest son, who was also named John.

He had decided to swim through the glowing red stream waters and into the cavern on the night of the red Moon when he was only sixteen, as he did not want to fight in the bloody war that was then being waged.

Sir John continued to explain that it was now over three years since his son left but never returned and he wondered if any of them had either met or heard of him during their KLOPTON journeys?

All three of them looked at each other, but shook their heads and Kane replied that unfortunately none of them had.

The previous night however, when they first arrived in this KLOPTON era, Kane told Sir John how all three of them did see a man come out of the rock face crevice behind them, a short time after they had left.

He then followed them across the fields towards the Manor House, before disappearing somewhere on the other side of the trees once we had entered the main courtyard.

None of us recognised who this man was though, as it was still dark and he was quite some distance away, but if he too had come through the cavern waters as we did, then he must also be from the KLOPTON bloodline and have the same red hexagonal birthmark.

Upon hearing this unexpected news, Sir John stood up out of his chair and after opening the dining room door, ordered one of his servants to go outside immediately and fetch the duty officer.

He then turned back towards Kane and said that he would organise his soldiers to undertake a thorough search of the entire estate straight away to find this man, especially as he could still be laying injured somewhere in the snow.

Furthermore, there was always the possibility that this KLOPTON family member could be their missing son John, but either way they had to try and find out who and where he was, as quickly as they could.

Kane remembered the footprints they had left in the snow only a few hours earlier and he was concerned that when the soldiers were outside searching for this man, they would follow their tracks back to the crevice passageway entrance and possibly go inside.
Sir John told him that he need not worry about this as it had snowed again that morning and all their footprints across the fields would be covered over by now.
A couple of minutes later the officer turned up at the door, whereupon Sir John left the dining room to give him his orders.

He returned shortly afterwards, but instead of remaining where they were, Sir John invited the three of them to follow him and Lady Agnes into the sitting room, as it had a larger log fire and they would be able to discuss their family matters in much greater comfort.
Upon entering the other room, the three of them straight away noticed that the old wooden KLOPTON clock was standing on the mantelpiece above this fireplace instead of in the dining room, whilst this room had also been refurbished since their last stay in the Manor House.
Sir John politely directed them over to their armchairs and whilst they all sat down, he told the servant that they were not to be disturbed.

He then began by confirming that the year was 1459 as his servant had advised them when they first arrived and that England had been ruled by King Henry VI from the House of Lancaster since 1422.
Four years ago however, war broke out after Sir Richard York, 3rd Duke of the House of York, made his claim to the English throne.
At that time, the area of Warwickshire which included KLOPTON, was controlled by Sir Richard Neville, 16th Earl of the House of Warwick, a very wealthy nobleman and powerful military leader, who together with his father also named Sir Richard Neville, but 5th Earl of the House of Salisbury, supported the Yorkists in their fight against the Lancastrians.

Together, the three Houses won a decisive battle on **22 May 1455** at the **Battle of St Albans** in Hertfordshire where they captured King Henry, after which Sir Richard of York became Lord Protector of England for a number of years.

Sir John made it clear that whilst he supported the Earl of Warwick and would provide him with whatever help he could, including allowing his soldiers to stay overnight on the estate, he had to always be wary of the nearby Kenilworth Castle owned by the King, as KLOPTON could not defend itself if it was attacked by Lancastrian soldiers stationed there.

Kane & Kara in particular were alarmed to hear that they had journeyed across the void of time, only to arrive when England was in the middle of a brutal war with itself.

Having both studied history at school when they lived in the 20th Century, they were aware that several battles had taken place during the era of the House of Lancaster and that this period of time was known as 'The Wars of the Roses', whilst also identified by the KLOPT0N letter 'L'.

In the circumstances, the twins realised that if they ever disclosed any knowledge they possessed of this era to anyone involved, including to Sir John & Lady Agnes, this could potentially impact significantly on aspects of the wars and even on history itself.

They therefore knew that they could also not risk telling either of them the truth about when and where they were really from, even though events that actually occurred in this period of KLOPT0N time might be different to those recorded as having happened in their future.

Sir John then turned the conversation to family matters as he asked,
"I understand from my servant that you told him all three of you were siblings. Is this true?".
Kane replied,
"No, this is not true and we apologise for misleading you, but we did not know when we arrived here who was living in the Manor House and whether or not we would be safe".
"I fully understand your reasons and please continue" said Sir John.

Kane then explained.
"Kara and I are actually twins and we will be 18 years old in February.
Our father was Richard Greenway, who lived on the KLOPT0N Estate over one hundred years ago when it was owned by Sir James Klopton.

Katrina Klopton was our mother, but sadly she became very poorly after giving birth to us both.
In the hope of saving her life sometime in the near future however, she reluctantly decided to journey through the red cavern waters on the night of the full red Moon without us.
Distressingly, we have never heard from her since and the main reason for our also travelling through KLOPT0N time is to try and find her".

Upon hearing this story, Lady Agnes spoke
"Sir John and I are very sorry to hear of your mother's continued absence and we hope that you will find each other one day soon".
"Thank you for your kind words" said Kara, whilst Kane smiled and nodded his acknowledgment.

Kathryn then joined the conversation with her own brief family story.
"My parents were Sir Frederick & Lady Khloe Klopton, with my mother being the daughter of Sir James and I am sixteen years old.
I have travelled through time with Kara & Kane to escape the Black Death which was crossing England from Europe in the 14th Century when we left".

Sir John was taken aback by what he had just heard and his voice sounded very concerned as he asked them all,
"Is there any possibility that any of you have either caught this deadly disease or else are carrying it here with you?".
Kane instantly replied reassuringly,
"Categorically not and you needn't worry yourselves about this, as the plaque had not reached Warwickshire nor KLOPTON by the time we left, just as Kathryn has said".
"We are obviously very pleased to hear this" Sir John added.

He then continued to say,
"You are all welcome to stay in the Manor House for as long as it takes the next full red Moon to appear, although it will be necessary for Kara and Kathryn to share a bedroom, as our two sons return back home from time to time and we do not have enough rooms for everyone".
"We fully understand and are very grateful" said Kara,
whilst Kathryn also added
"Yes, that will be just fine and thank you again for your hospitality".

Lady Agnes was next to speak.
"It will be lovely having you all to stay with us and tomorrow after you have rested a bit more, I will be delighted to take the two young ladies to Stratford-upon-Avon with me, where I will treat you to some new clothes to replace the old ones you are wearing".
Both Kara and Kathryn excitedly replied,
"Yes please, that would be wonderful thank you!",
to which Lady Agnes gave them both a big smile.

Sir John then changed the topic and turned back to Kane to ask him
"Have you ever been into the future during your many journeys or alternatively met someone else from KLOPTON who has?",
to which Kane replied,
"This time period we are here with you now, is the furthest into the future we have ever been, although we do not yet know what our next destination will be. Is there any particular reason why you are asking?".
"No" Sir John said, before quickly adding,
"Although, I must admit I was hoping that you might have been, since if you had then any information you gained could have assisted us in the ongoing war against the Lancastrians".

"Yes, I understand" said Kane "and if we had, then we certainly would have tried to help you, but unfortunately we cannot on this occasion".
"Thank you anyway" replied Sir John.

The rest of the afternoon was primarily spent discussing the family dynasty, with Sir John & Lady Agnes able to trace their ancestors as far back as Sir James & Lady Susan Klopton, which included Kathryn and her parents Sir Frederick & Lady Khloe Klopton.
They could not however, find any trace of Kara & Kane nor their parents Richard & Katrina Klopton, although Sir John had heard of a family lineage in Suffolk where the twins said they were from and he therefore appeared content to accept their story.

Kane then changed the subject and asked Sir John if he would tell him more about the history of their time, whereupon the girls and Lady Agnes decided to talk about other topics instead until their evening meal was completely finished, after which they all retired to their rooms for a good night's sleep.

Clear sky and snow on Clopton hills

Chapter 14 : **Close Encounters**

During their first weeks exploring the 15th Century KLOPT0N estate it soon became apparent that not much had really changed, with only certain parts of the Manor House and decor having been updated since they were last there, whilst the outside grounds including the workers buildings and servants accommodation remained virtually untouched.

The stables however, had been noticeably improved due presumably to the increased number of pedigree horses being looked after and the twins always enjoyed taking them out for a ride as often as they could.
The kitchen gardens too were better stocked with a greater variety of fruit trees and vegetables, plus additional poultry and livestock to help make the estate more self-sufficient.
Meanwhile, some picturesque floral landscaping with a couple of ornate screened seating areas had been added around the lake, which all three of them found to be ideal when they needed somewhere they could rest and talk privately.

Occasionally, when there was just minimal snow on the estate, the twins would take Kathryn for a ride with them over the fields and past the stream to the Oat Hill woodland, nearby where the hidden crevice gap in the rock face was located.
None of them would venture too close however, so not to disturb the overgrowth nor cut up the ground outside the entrance whilst it was so soft under foot.

Although they were always relieved that there was no sign of anyone having been through the passageway opening, they were still very concerned that no trace had yet been found of the man who followed them that morning when they first arrived.
Furthermore, until he was identified they all had to remain vigilant, especially since they had no idea what his intentions were.

Sir John & Lady Agnes soon provided the three of them with a new wardrobe of clothes to replace the old fashioned garments they were originally wearing and they now all looked to be every bit a full part of the wealthy aristocratic KLOPT0N family they were born into.

The two girls were especially delighted with their elegant full-length hand-embroidered dresses and styled winter overcoats, which Lady Agnes had helped them choose when she took them shopping in town.
Kathryn had never even imagined such wonderful designs before, having come from the 14th Century and she was initially overwhelmed by the whole experience.

Kara enjoyed wearing her new outfits too, as although old fashioned in style for her, they were beautifully crafted for the era they were now in.
She also wished that she could take a picture of herself as a memento of how glamorous she looked, but sadly knew this wasn't possible as the camera would not be invented until the 19th Century!

Meanwhile, Kane's new wardrobe included hand-stitched shirts with silk cravats, smart black suits and matching full length overcoat, all of which made him look very much the aristocratic gentleman he now was.
He sometimes still preferred however, to wear the more casual walking and riding clothes Sir John's manservant had also sourced for him.

Both of the twins were also provided with new swords, the design and construction of which had changed over the last century since they were given the old ones they brought with them.
As soon as they got these, they were both delighted with their better balance and quickly set about fighting against each other as often as they could when no-one else was around.
Unfortunately, ladies were still not expected to be seen wielding a sword in those days, even a smaller sized one like that which Kara preferred to use and was becoming very proficient with.

Kane also obtained a petite dagger for Kathryn to discretely carry on her, as although she was too timid to wield a sword, the twins wanted her to at least have something she could try and defend herself with.
Kara did attempt to teach her some basic fighting moves, but quickly realised that unless Kathryn could brandish the dagger with any conviction, it was unlikely it would ever be an effective deterrent against a potential attacker.
Kara decided that she would therefore have to stay close by Kathryn's side whenever they were away from KLOPTON in order to protect her.

In the meantime, Lady Agnes was delighted to be able to assist with Kathryn's further upbringing and education, thus ensuring that she was properly prepared to take a young lady's place in 15th Century male dominated society.
Although both of the twins also wanted to help, they acknowledged that this might cause some problems due to their different perspective on social situations gained during their previous travels.
Kara's strong feminist opinions in particular, would probably lead Kathryn to sometimes interact inappropriately with other people, especially whilst they all remained in that time period.

During the following weeks the winter weather continued to stay very cold with snow often covering the ground, but the three teenagers kept themselves as busy as they could and also managed to meet most of the other people who lived and worked on the estate.

The implications of getting to know everyone however, was difficult for them to fully process, as they soon realised that some of them were in fact the great grand-children of the friends and workers they had previously known back in the 14th Century, over 100 years earlier!

Thankfully, by the first week of February, the snow had all but cleared and there was great excitement in the House as both Sir Thomas and Sir Hugh were coming to visit KLOPT0N to share in some belated Christmas family celebrations, which had to be postponed due to the bad winter weather being too severe to risk travelling the long distance.

All the servants were kept very busy making sure that everything around the Manor House and gardens would be ready in time, whilst the kitchen staff organised all the food and drink needed for everyone.
Meanwhile, Sir John also ordered in some additional supplies for all the estate workers to share as a thank you for their hard work and loyalty over the previous year.
Furthermore, as it was both Kane & Kara's eighteenth birthday on the 12th, it was also agreed that during the five days they should celebrate their special day too.

Both of Sir John's sons arrived at around midday on the 10th and over most of the next few evenings there were formal lavish banquets with drinks held in the great banqueting hall, which all of the KLOPT0N family members attended.
Meanwhile, during the day they would usually all go out and visit either Stratford-upon-Avon or Warwick town to do some more clothes shopping and enjoy lunch elsewhere for a change.

On the evening of the twins birthday however, a casual hog roast banquet was arranged instead of a formal meal, with entertainment and dancing organised in the adjoining room.
A few other teenagers from amongst the estate staff were also invited to help make the party feel even more special for Kara & Kane.

Sadly however, no matter how much they enjoyed all of the festivities, the whole occasion only made the twins realise how much they missed their own family.
Kathryn also found it very difficult to accept that her parents were no longer with her and that she would probably never see them again, although in reality it had only been a few weeks since she had last been with them both.

After everyone had finished eating, the entertainment and dancing continued until the hallway clock chimed 23.00, upon which they all said their goodnights and began returning to their respective rooms in either the Manor House or the estate outbuildings.

Kara & Kane were both very grateful for their eighteenth birthday party and thanked Sir John & Lady Agnes once again for all their kindness and generosity, including the extra personal gifts they had given each of them to remember their birthday with.

As the twins then got ready to return to their bedrooms, Kara saw that Kathryn was slouched in an armchair with her head in her hands and upon approaching her closer to check if she was alright, realised she was inebriated from the evening party!
After waiting until everyone else had left the room, Kara got Kane to help take Kathryn upstairs as quick as possible to the bedroom they shared, before anyone else in the household also noticed her condition.

Kane left both the girls in their room before returning to his, but ten minutes later there was a knock on his door and when he opened it he found Kara outside smiling as she asked him "Can I come in?",
to which Kane replied "Of course you can, but is there a problem?".
Kara entered the room and after Kane had shut the door behind her, she explained
"I think it would be best if I left Kathryn to sleep in our bedroom by herself tonight as she is very tired and confused, no doubt influenced by the large amount of wine she has just drank which she is not used to".

Kane smiled and upon noticing that Kara had got her bed clothes with her too, he said
"You are welcome to stay in my bedroom tonight and please make yourself at home, but do tell me more".
Kara sat down on the edge of the bed and after Kane had sat down next to her, she initially hesitated for a short while before beginning to explain.
"After you left our room, I started to get changed when suddenly Kathryn came up behind me, put her arms around my waist and then started to kiss the back of my neck.
I pulled myself away from her immediately and upon realising that she had done something wrong, Kathryn burst into tears whilst saying that she was very sorry and asked me not to be angry with her, but she felt so lonely and had no-one else in her life to comfort her".

Kane took a sharp intake of breath as Kara continued.
"I felt really sad for her and so I turned around and reached over to gave her a hug, but before I could say anything else she took my actions the wrong way and leant forward to kiss me again.
This time I took a firm grip of her arms and told her that I could not give her the type of love she was looking for, but that she would meet someone soon who would feel the same way about her.

Upon hearing this however, Kathryn became even more upset, so I laid her down onto the bed still fully clothed, but covered her with a single bedsheet and told her to get some sleep, so we could talk about things again in the morning with clear heads.

I then stayed with her for a few minutes more until she had stopped sobbing, after which I got my own bed clothes and told her that I would come over to stay in your bedroom for the night so she could be alone with her thoughts".

As soon as Kara had finished talking, Kane stood up and wandered around the room very slowly for a short time just thinking, before ending up back where Kara was still sitting waiting patiently for him.

He then spoke to her in a quiet, but more serious tone than usual,

"Kathryn has clearly reached the age when she needs some wiser adult guidance and I think it would be best that you therefore tell Lady Agnes tomorrow about what has happened.

She can then talk to Kathryn in private as the mother figure she is obviously missing and in doing so hopefully help her through this difficult time in her young life, more than either of us two could ever do".

Kara gave him a warm smile and nodded her agreement to this suggestion, whilst Kane without saying another word, sat back down on the bed next to her again.

From the concerned expression on his face however, Kara realised that there was something else Kane wanted to tell her.

For what then seemed like ages, they just simply sat there looking anywhere else in the room rather than at each other, before Kara reached over to hold Kane by the hand and gently asked him

"What is on your mind dear brother?".

After a few moments, Kane looked into Kara's eyes and then with some obvious uncertainty in his voice, began to tell her what it was that was troubling him.

"This is not actually the first time that Kathryn has got confused about her teenage sexuality" said Kane.

"On the previous occasion however, I thought it something I need not tell you about since nothing really happened and it was best left forgotten, but I now know this was the wrong decision".

Kara's facial expression changed as she look on anxiously waiting to hear what Kane was going to say next, as he then continued.

"Back in December when we were having the New Year's party, Kathryn literally bumped into me in the kitchen whilst I was getting some drinks to take back into the banqueting hall for our guests, as all the servants were busy doing other tasks elsewhere.

We both laughed about it and after I joked to Kathryn that we should probably find somewhere else to meet up when we wanted a secret drink together, she replied by saying that we could always take our drinks up to my bedroom.

Then, before I could say anything in response, she moved forward and kissed me on the lips".

Kara gasped at what she had just heard, causing Kane to pause for a moment whilst he took a deep breath before speaking again,

"Kathryn's actions took me totally by surprise and it was several seconds before I fully appreciated the significance of what had just happened, whereupon I backed away from her not knowing what to do.

Kathryn then spoke first and explained how she had always fancied me, before trying to kiss me again, but this time I stopped her before she got another chance.

I told her that I was very sorry, but nothing romantic was ever going to happen between us as I already loved someone else.

After an awkward few moments we both picked up our drinks and swiftly made our way back to the banqueting hall.

Ever since then Kathryn has made no further advances towards me, although occasionally she will ask me who my lover is, to which I just smile back and tell her that it is someone she does not know who lives in town".

By the time Kane had finished speaking he realised that Kara was no longer facing him, but instead she was staring blankly over to the far side of the bedroom with an obvious sadness etched across her face.

Then, after it went quiet for a moment, Kara turned back towards him and rather bluntly asked in a rather subdued voice,

"Who is your secret lover and do I know her?".

Kane felt so deeply upset to hear such anguish in Kara's voice that without any hesitation he took hold of her hands, before replying in the most gentlest voice he could muster,

"Kara, my dearest sister, please look straight at me whilst I answer your question".

After slowly turning her head around to face him, Kane greeted her with the warmest of smiles, before saying,

"You must surely know by now who it is that I love more than anyone else in this World and who I would also without hesitation, willingly give up my life to protect from any harm".

Upon hearing her brother's heartfelt words, Kara's demeanour immediately changed to one of utter joy, as she looked into his eyes for nearly a minute with all the love she could possibly show, after which with a few tears now rolling down her cheeks, she replied,

"Yes my dearest brother, I believe I do know who it is that you love and I also know that this same person loves you just as much and even more if that is possible".

Both twins now stopped talking and instead just sat there on the edge of the bed looking into each other's deep blue eyes, not quite sure what to do next.
Kara reacted first by slowly pulling one her hands away from Kane's loose grip and lifting it upwards to gently caress one side of his face.
Kane instantly responded by doing the same to Kara's face using his free hand, whereupon they both leant forward and after a hesitant initial first kiss, embraced each other passionately in a long embrace.

It wasn't too much later that they both stood up from where they were sitting and whilst still holding hands, slowly moved over to the side of the bed together.
They paused there for a moment for another kiss before shyly getting undressed, after which Kara lay down on the bed first under the blanket, whilst Kane blew all the bedroom night candles out and joined her.

Kara was woken the following morning by the cockerel outside in the farm yard, but as she rolled over from her side of the bed she realised that Kane was no longer there.
She then saw that none of his clothes were on his bedside chair and knew that he had already left the room.
She quickly got dressed and after combing her hair, went over to her own bedroom to see if Kathryn was alright, but instead found her still fast asleep despite the cockerel crow and so decided not to disturb her.

Kane was sitting downstairs in the kitchen eating his breakfast when Kara walked in to join him and as soon as he saw her come into the room, he stood up out of his chair ready to greet her with a kiss.
At that moment however, one of the servants also entered the kitchen and for an instant they both stood motionless, uncertain as to how they were going to welcome each other that morning.
After initially just grinning for a short while, they both agreed to continue with their usual brother-sister quick hug for the time being, although realising that they would need to be careful and hide their true feelings for each other when anyone else was around.

Later that morning, Kara found a few moments to tell Lady Agnes about Kathryn's recent teenage urges and she readily agreed to offer Kathryn the motherly guidance needed for controlling such adolescent desires.
Lady Agnes also told Kara however, that they should all try and find Kathryn a husband before too long, as if a suitable gentleman could not be found before the next full red Moon, then a much more difficult decision about the future direction of her life would have to be made.

The next few days flew by quickly and after Sir Hugh and Sir Thomas had both left the Manor House to return home, the atmosphere around KLOPTON became a lot quieter as everyone caught up on their essential duties, including the replenishment of all the household supplies needed.

As the months continued to pass by, the three of them learnt to adapt to their new lives in the 15th Century and kept themselves busy mainly with daily chores and horse riding, whilst Kathryn became very reliant on both of the twins, but especially Kara with whom she was very close.

Summer soon arrived and there was some great news in the Manor House when a letter arrived for Sir John inviting the KLOPTON family to attend a jousting tournament at Warwick Castle on 24th August, to celebrate Sir Richard Neville's latest return to England from France.
Amongst Sir Richard's many titles he had also been appointed as the Constable of Calais and was responsible for the very large garrison based there, which he not only used to help protect the English coast from the French, but also to further his own strategic ambitions.

The tournament was to be held over three days between eight knights from Sir Richard's troops and another eight of his father's, who also being named Sir Richard Neville would be referred to as 'Salisbury' in the presence of his son, who similarly adopted a designation of 'Warwick' at such times to also help try and avoid any confusion.

Sir John immediately accepted the invitation and dispatched one of his best horse riders back over to Warwick Castle to hand deliver his personal letter of gratitude and acceptance to Sir Richard on behalf of the House of KLOPTON family.

Later that day when they were also told of their invite to the tournament, all three of the teenagers became overwhelmed with excitement about attending such a spectacle, particularly since none of them had ever been to a jousting event like this before.
Indeed, for the next couple of weeks they all hardly stopped talking about anything else!

With such a short time to prepare for their attendance and so much to do however, everyone on the estate was kept extra busy by Sir John.
He meticulously oversaw that everything would be ready for this very special occasion, especially as other aristocratic families and wealthy landowners would also be joining them at the Castle.

The grandest ceremonial KLOPTON black coach was chosen to carry all four of the ladies, including Lady Agnes' personal handmaid Sheila and this therefore needed to be refurbished accordingly.

The red & black coloured crest of the House of KLOPTON was re-embossed on both main side doors, whilst the silver mounted harnesses were polished and new matching crest coloured material drapes made ready for the horses.

In addition, they would all be escorted to Warwick Castle by six of Sir John's most trusted soldiers, four of whom would be riding horseback in full armour as their formal guard, whilst the other two would drive the coach whilst dressed in matching colour braided coachmen outfits.

Unfortunately however, neither Sir Hugh nor Sir Thomas could make it back home to the estate on the tournament dates and so Sir John decided to spoil Kane instead.

He organised for him to wear one of the KLOPTON family suits of highly polished ceremonial armour, similar to the one he would also be wearing for the occasion.

Kane was acutely aware of the great honour Sir John was bestowing on him and he could not wait for the day to arrive.

Not to be outdone however, Lady Agnes took great delight in taking both the girls and her handmaid to visit the most expensive ladies fashion shops in Stratford-upon-Avon, where she bought them all some luxurious new summer outfits with co-ordinating hats.

Needless to say, all four of them looked very elegant and were now even more excited about the forthcoming event, although unsurprisingly Lady Agnes selected the most exquisite and colourful apparel for herself!

An old family Crest in stone

Chapter 15 : **Treacherous Attack**

The date of the tournament soon arrived and the early morning sunrise was announced by the cockerel crowing in the stable yard.
Everyone got up straight away to get dressed but only had a light breakfast, after which Sir John instructed the servants to ensure that the coach and horses were brought around to the main entrance as arranged, so they could ensure that they left on time.

It was a glorious sunny August day, so all four ladies were delighted that their multi-layered fashionable summer outfits were made of light material, especially their corsets which were rather tight fitting in order to suit the high society style of that era.

As soon as everyone was ready, the ladies were all escorted outside with Lady Agnes leading the way, where they were helped into the splendidly dressed coach by two of the servants, although they all had to be careful not to dislodge the rather extravagant hats they were wearing for the occasion.

Four matching pristine black horses draped in the House of KLOPTON colours were harnessed to the front of the coach, whilst two soldiers dressed in formal coachmen's attire sat on top, firmly holding their reins in readiness for them to leave.
Meanwhile, four soldiers wearing full body armour were mounted on their own perfectly groomed black horses as they waited in formation behind the coach for Sir John to join them.

In all the excitement Kara realised that she had not seen Kane since breakfast and as she started to wonder where he had gone, she noticed Sir John appear from around the side of the Manor House riding slowly towards them on top of a thoroughbred white stallion.

He looked almost regal in his glorious suit of highly polished body armour and matching shield, which displayed the KLOPTON colours intertwined with the family crest and glistened in the morning Sun as it shone through the breaks in the thin cloudy sky overhead.
In addition, the letter 'K' hexagonal shaped emblem was prominent on Sir John's co-ordinating helmet and also the handle of the huge steel sword protruding from the red & black coloured leather sheaf at his side.

Meanwhile, his magnificent stallion was partly covered with several pieces of matching polished armour, whilst also draped in the dramatic KLOPTON Coat of Arms, as if they were ready to go to war!

Kara then noticed someone else approaching their coach on a similarly well groomed white steed, who she assumed was another one of Sir John's knights coming to join them at the tournament.
He too wore a suit of highly polished armour, whilst carrying both a shield and sword displaying the House of KLOPT0N red & black crest.
As this rider got closer however, Kara could see his facial features through the open visor on his helmet and instantly recognised that it was Kane, upon which her face lit up at how dashing he was.

With seeing Kara smiling at him through the coach window, Kane rode over to greet her with a huge grin as he asked "How do I look?".
Kara beamed back at him and with a playful tone to her voice replied "Just how I would expect my handsome Prince to appear",
to which Kane responded in an equally light-hearted manner by saying, ".. and you look everything the beautiful Princess you were born to be!".

Then, before either of them could say anything else to each other, Lady Agnes, who in the excitement Kane had forgot was also sitting in the coach, said to them in a firm but gentle voice,
"If you both look over towards Sir John, you will see that he is waiting patiently for Kane to join him so we can all set off and I think you should therefore continue this mutual admiration for one other at another time".

Kane immediately sat upright on his horse as he visibly blushed and in an apologetic voice said to Lady Agnes,
"I am sorry if I have caused any delay and I wish you all a very pleasant journey",
after which he promptly rode over to join Sir John, whilst Kara smiled politely at Lady Agnes who gave her a rather inquisitive look in return.

Sir John then gave a final few instructions to his estate officer who was looking after everything during his absence, before turning around to give the order to leave, whereupon they all set off at a canter through the courtyard gates on the relatively short journey to Warwick Castle.

The time passed by quickly as they all enjoyed the glorious peaceful countryside views and sooner than expected saw the flags on top of the turrets of Warwick Castle fluttering on the horizon through the trees, whereupon they knew they would soon be there.

Suddenly however, as they rounded the next bend in the road, Kane saw up ahead in the distance a dozen or so horsemen galloping down the road towards them.
At the same time Sir John pointed out another man dressed in a shabby suit of armour sitting on his horse at the edge of the nearby woodland, evidently watching what was happening like a wolf would watch its prey.

As the unknown horsemen got gradually closer, Sir John became increasingly concerned as to what their intentions might be and raised his hand to bring their cavalcade to a halt.

Once they had all stopped, he ordered the four soldiers riding to the rear to join him and Kane, whereupon he gave instructions that the six of them would surround the coach in a defensive hexagonal shaped formation.

He then told the two coachmen to not only help guard the coach and ladies inside, but to also ensure that they maintained firm control of the horses' reins at all times.

Sir John rode over to the coach window where he told Lady Agnes and the other ladies to stay inside the coach and not to be afraid.

He then spoke directly to Kara,

"I have been told that you are now very proficient with your sword and I hope you have therefore brought this with you today?".

Despite Kara realising the dangerous situation they clearly appeared to be in, she responded in her usual confident voice and without showing any fear calmly said

"I never go anywhere without my sword Sir John and I have it here with me underneath my jacket",

to which he replied "I am very pleased to hear this".

Sir John then added,

"If any of these horsemen approaching us are hostile, as I believe they may be, I am counting on you Kara to help protect all of the ladies inside the coach".

Without any hesitation, she undid her jacket to reveal her sword and immediately took it out of it's sheath, before replying defiantly,

"Do not worry Sir John, I will protect them all from any harm with my life".

"Thank you" he said, before looking back at his wife and leaning forward through the window to kiss her on the cheek.

Sir John then smiled warmly at Lady Agnes once again, before turning around to rejoin Kane on the road at the front of the coach, where he stopped and withdrew his sword from its sheath before instructing all his men to do the same.

He then gave them their orders.

"If these horsemen now approaching us are hostile, then upon my command it will be the solemn duty of each and every one of you to defend the ladies in the coach with your lives if necessary, do you all understand?".

The men all lifted up their swords in unison and shouted out

"Yes Sir John, we do!".

Upon hearing this, he then added,

"Furthermore, if I am killed, then you will take your orders from Kane if he is still alive, but at all costs you must escape with the ladies in the coach to Warwick Castle at the fastest possible speed, do you understand?".

Again, the men all shouted out together

"Yes Sir John, we do!",

to which he responded with pride in his voice.

"You are all very brave men and it is now time for us all to take our positions with courage in our hearts ready to face these unknown assailants".

Only a short time later the horsemen arrived, all shouting loudly and brandishing their swords menacingly before they suddenly came to a stop on the road a close distance away from the front of the coach, where Sir John and Kane were calmly waiting for them on their horses.

It was immediately obvious from the aggressive stance and ragged appearance of these men that they were a band of outlaws, but before they had chance to say anything Sir John decided to pre-empt the situation by booming out in his strong commanding voice,

"I demand to know what your reason is for stopping and confronting us here today on our journey to Warwick Castle?".

After clearly being initially taken aback for a few moments by Sir John's unexpected forthright attitude, a particularly large and thuggish looking horseman, wearing what was evidently battle damaged chainmail covered in part by pieces of protective plate over his upper body, rode a few extra steps forward from the other riders.

This man then brashly replied,

"We are here to take all of your valuables and if you hand them over to us now we will let all of you leave this place unharmed, but if you do not then you will all die and we will also take your women for our pleasure", to which all of the other horsemen behind him cheered loudly.

Sir John kept himself impeccably calm as he retorted back in a defiant authoritative loud voice,

"You presumably are the leader of this ragged band of foolish outlaws, but you obviously do not know who you are trying to threaten in such a contemptible manner.

I am Sir John Klopton, a close personal friend of Sir Richard Neville Earl of Warwick, his father Sir Richard Neville Earl of Salisbury and also King Henry VI".

He then pointed to the 'K' signet ring he was wearing on his sword hand and also to the black & red KLOPTON crest on the side of the coach and his shield, before continuing.

"If any of you leave this place now the way you have come, then you have my assurance that those of you who do will live.

If however, any of you decide instead to stay and attack any of my family here with me, then you will be brutally slaughtered without any mercy being shown by either myself or my soldiers.

Furthermore, if by chance any of you manage to escape, then you will be tracked down like the cowardly dogs you are and put to death in the most painful way possible inside the Warwick Castle dungeons".

After these strong combative words from Sir John, several of the outlaws started to look nervous and began muttering amongst themselves, until suddenly four of them rode off back down the road as quickly as they could to where they came from.

Upon seeing this, Sir John's men banged their swords repeatedly against their shields and cheered loudly.

During all of this verbal exchange, Kane had been assessing the original fifteen horsemen facing them to decide which of them were probably trained swordsmen and which were simply thugs, in order for him to prepare a battle strategy.

With only eleven of the horseman now left however, the odds were much better stacked and he moved over closer to Sir John to tell him his plan, to which Sir John nodded his agreement.

Even though Kane was not a knight, he looked every bit the part in his splendid KLOPTON armour and none of the outlaws knew otherwise, so he decided to make use of this to his advantage and confidently rode a few steps forward whilst brandishing his sword, before shouting out aggressively,

"It is now time for those of you who are still here to make up your minds as I have a jousting tournament to take part in at Warwick Castle in a couple of hours, so either get out of our way or prepare to die.

The decision is yours".

In the coach Kara gasped as she heard what Kane had just said and Lady Agnes took hold of her by the hand to help comfort her.

The outlaws responded to Kane's demand by closing ranks around their leader and after a further brief discussion between them ended, they parted again, but it was evident as they all turned to face them again that they were not going to leave.

Over half of them started to move slowly forward to surround Sir John's soldiers defending the coach and Kane knew that these were probably the more experienced swordsmen amongst them.

Meanwhile, their leader stayed where he was in front Sir John and Kane, with the other remaining outlaws on horseback behind him.

137

His tactics appeared quite clear to Kane who kept a watchful eye on what he was doing, as it had already been agreed with Sir John that he would be the one to fight the leader first, since if Kane could kill him then the others would probably ride off.

Suddenly, the outlaw leader shouted out "Attack!" and immediately his men rode forward together whilst swinging their swords, as the anticipated fight around Sir John's perimeter defence of the coach was now about to begin.

Within only a short time the sound of swords clashing could be heard, which was soon followed by some screams of agonising pain as various limbs were chopped off and some outlaws fell to the ground severely wounded, with fatal blows subsequently landed on those still alive.

Sir John was a very good swordsman and without hesitation he took on two of the outlaws at once, whilst Kane quickly caught up and confronted the leader as he approached the coach with the clear intent of attacking the coachmen assigned to protect it.

Kane's duel proved very difficult for him as it was soon evident his opponent was a strong swordsman and although Kane was fitter and more agile, he was grateful for his armour which had so far protected him from any serious injury.

Meanwhile, one of the outlaws managed to pull open the door on the side of the coach where Kara was sitting and then started to reach inside to try and grab hold of the silver chain and KLOPTON pendants around her neck.
Unfortunately for him however, Kara had prepared for such an attack and in anticipation previously placed her sword out of view behind her back, ready to defend herself.

Her heart started to beat faster as she waited anxiously for the outlaw's next move, but as soon as he leant closer towards her, she immediately stood up and without any fear swung her sword around in her hand before the man had the chance to defend himself, slicing him with one thrust straight through his throat.

After pausing for a few moments to make sure that he was dead, Kara lifted up her foot and forcibly kicked her attacker's blood covered corpse back out of the coach onto the ground below, before slamming the coach door to behind him.
"Very well done Kara" said Lady Agnes, with immense admiration in her voice, as she passed Kara a clean handkerchief to help her dab away some of the outlaw's blood that had splashed over her.

Before Kara had time to compose herself after this attack however, she and Lady Agnes suddenly heard Kathryn and Sheila start to scream from behind them inside the coach.

As they both turned around to see what was happening, another outlaw had opened the door on the opposite side of the coach and was trying to drag Kathryn outside.
Lady Agnes immediately took a firm hold of Sheila and pulled her tightly towards her, whilst Kara clambered over the coach seat as quickly as she could to try and grab Kathryn, but she was too late!

The attacker had already got a strong grip on Kathryn and also taken her dagger, before with one final tug he pulled her through the coach door onto the ground.
He quickly shut the door again in order to keep Kara inside with her sword, before then tying a piece of rope around the door handle to stop her from opening it again.

Kara was distraught and even more so when through the coach window she could only watch on horrified as the outlaw climbed on top of Kathryn and started to rip her clothes off whilst brutally groping her, as she cried out hysterically.
Kara screamed at the man to leave Kathryn alone or she would kill him, but he simply ignored her and none of the soldiers could help neither as they were all fighting ferociously against the other outlaws.
With the situation looking seemingly lost, Kara vowed to stay inside the coach to help protect Lady Agnes and Sheila who were both clearly very frightened, rather than let them too be molested by the outlaws.

Suddenly, they all heard the sound of a trumpet being blown from somewhere not too far away down the road behind them.
Everyone fighting outside the coach was also clearly distracted by the trumpet noise and a slight lull quickly followed as the sound of galloping horses and men shouting could be heard approaching rapidly along the road towards the rear of the coach.

Not knowing who these horsemen might be, Kara feared for the worse and thought they were probably more outlaws coming to help the others in their fight.
She looked around outside to find out where Kane was, only to see that he was still battling hard in his duel against the large outlaw thug.
A profound sadness became etched across her face as Kara watched Kane fighting valiantly, but realised that this might be the last time she would ever see her brother alive again.

Thankfully however, Kara was wrong and her face lit up when through the coach window she saw that these new horsemen were knights in full armour and holding wooden lances, who Lady Agnes recognised were all displaying the red, white & blue crest of the House of Salisbury on their shields.

Within a very short time these knights joined the fight and without any hesitation charged directly at the outlaws, who by then were already backing away and instead trying to ride off along the road they had originally come from.
Unfortunately for the outlaws however, the knights were far too fast for them and one by one they unseated them from their horses with their lances, including the outlaw leader who had not yet been able to retreat from his fight with Kane.

The knights, with some help from Sir John's soldiers, then attacked the outlaws still fighting on the ground with their swords and tied up those who yielded, whilst slaying any who still continued to fight on.
Kane shouted out to the knights that the outlaw he was fighting with was their leader and they should try to take him alive, whereupon two of the knights joined Kane and together they soon overpowered the man before tying him up with the other captured outlaws.

Elsewhere, one of the other knights had seen Kathryn being attacked in the grass near to the coach and as soon as he caught up with the outlaw who had been doing this deplorable deed before now trying to flee, the knight showed no mercy and hacked him into pieces so he would die an agonising death.

He then quickly returned to where Kathryn was sobbing uncontrollably on the ground, as she tightly held onto her torn clothes to cover herself.
After dismounting, the knight slowly knelt down next to her before removing his helmet and in a gentle voice told her,
"Young maiden, you are now safe and I have killed the vile worthless wretch who so cruelly attacked you".
Kathryn opened her eyes and upon seeing the handsome young knight looking at her with such a caring smile, she flung her arms around his neck and grabbed hold of him tightly, whereupon he lifted her up out of the grass and laid her into his arms so she would be more comfortable.

She slowly managed to stop crying, but was still shaking from her ordeal as she spoke
"Thank you for saving my life Sir knight, I am so very grateful".
"It was my pleasure to have been able to assist you" replied the knight "and if I can help you any further please let me know".
Kathryn replied "Will you please just hold me for a few moments longer whilst I try and compose myself?".

"I will be delighted to hold you for as long as you need young maiden, especially if you tell me your name" said the knight.
"My name is Kathryn" she softly replied,
before asking him "May I also know what you are called Sir knight?",
to which he answered "My name is James".

Upon hearing the young knight's name, Kathryn shed a few more tears as she told him
"My grandfather was also called James and you honour his memory with your great valour",
to which he replied in an even gentler voice than he had before.
"It is you who has shown the greatest courage here today after the barbaric ordeal you have just suffered and you are a credit to both yourself and also your grandfather, who no doubt loved you dearly".
Kathryn looked straight into Sir James's deep blue eyes and could hardly contain her immediate feelings for him and his wonderful words, as she hugged him even tighter.

In the meantime both Sir John and Kane thanked Sir Richard and all his knights for their help in defeating the outlaws, before then returning to the coach to check on the ladies and their soldiers.
Kara was already opening the coach door as they approached and upon seeing Kane she jumped out and ran as fast as she could towards him, with tears of joy in her eyes.

Upon seeing her, Kane immediately dismounted from his horse and the pair of them were soon hugging each other in a long embrace, until Kara was first to ask
"Are you injured at all?", to which Kane replied
"I have a few cuts and bruises, but otherwise I am fine thanks.
How about you though, I was so worried?".
Kara responded with clear relief in her voice,
"I am also okay thank you and I even managed to kill an outlaw who tried to attack us in the coach.
Kathryn however, was dragged outside by another one of the outlaws and we must go and see how she is".

After a quick kiss on each others cheek, they both released their hold and swiftly walked around to the other side of the coach, where they saw the knight holding Kathryn in his arms trying to console her.
Kane for was the first to speak,
"Thank you Sir knight for taking care of my cousin. Is she alright?"
"I think so" replied the knight, "although she is still very distressed and her clothes have been ripped by the outlaw who attacked her, but he is now dead", upon which the knight pointed over to the body laying in pieces on the ground.

Kara then spoke to the knight.

"Kathryn is my cousin too and I am also very grateful to you for saving her from the savage ordeal she endured at the hands of the outlaw.

May I know who you are Sir knight?".

"I am Sir James" he replied, before continuing,

"The other knights and I are all on our way with Sir Richard Neville the Earl of Salisbury, to take part in a jousting tournament starting later today at Warwick Castle".

"We too are also attending the same tournament" said Kane, "but not taking part, as we are personal guests of Sir Richard Neville's son the Earl of Warwick.

We are all from the House of KLOPTON and are travelling from Stratford-upon-Avon with our Uncle Sir John and his wife Lady Agnes, before we got attacked by this band of outlaws".

Kara then spoke again to Sir James

"Please may I ask you to carry Kathryn back over to the KLOPTON coach so I may help comfort her and also tidy up her clothes before we continue on our journey to Warwick Castle".

"Of course I will" Sir James politely replied and he promptly walked over to where Lady Agnes and Sheila were sitting inside the coach, both still visibly shaken from the whole ordeal.

Once outside the coach, Kane opened the door as Sir James lifted Kathryn upwards and tried to place her inside, but instead she clung on to him even more tightly and would not let go.

Kara then joined them and together they slowly managed to coax her onto the seat inside where she finally let go of Sir James, after which Kara climbed in behind her and closed the door.

Sir James bid his farewell and was just about to return to his horse, when Kathryn leant through the coach window and said to him softly,

"Thank you so very much again for your bravery and kindness today Sir James.

Will I ever get the chance to see you again when I have recovered from my ordeal?".

Smiling warmly back at her, the knight replied

"Yes Kathryn, you will and probably much sooner than you might have thought.

I am taking part in the tournament at Warwick Castle over the next three days and so you should be able to see me take part in the jousting".

At that moment Lady Agnes made a discreet cough and as Sir James looked over in her direction, she said to him in a very polite voice,

"Sir James, my whole family is very grateful for your brave actions here today, but we must now be on our way to Warwick Castle and you should probably also be rejoining Sir Richard and the other knights".

"Of course your Ladyship" he replied with all due reverence, before remounting his horse and riding off to rejoin the other knights who were still strapping all the dead bodies and wounded outlaws to their horses with rope in readiness for the remaining short journey to Warwick Castle.

Sadly however, three of Sir John's soldiers had been killed during the fighting and they too were to be taken with them for now to Warwick, but then returned to KLOPT0N House afterwards for a proper burial.

Meanwhile, Sir John was talking to Sir Richard about the other shabbily dressed knight he had seen on the edge of the woodland at the same time as the outlaws were riding along the road towards them, but who had since disappeared amongst the trees.
They both agreed that he was probably the man who organised the attack on Sir John's cavalcade and Sir Richard said that all the prisoners would be tortured in the castle dungeons before they were executed, in order to find out who he was.

Sir Richard's wife Lady Alice and her handmaid Julia had also travelled to the tournament with the House of Salisbury cavalcade and some of the knights closely guarded the ladies, as they sat patiently inside their ornate coach blazoned with the family colours and Coat of Arms, waiting to proceed on their way again.
Sir John knew the Salisbury family very well and Sir Richard was only too willing to offer them all an escort to Warwick Castle for the tournament, which he graciously accepted.

Before departing however, Sir Richard ordered two of his knights to set off up ahead of them to let his son know what had happened and to request that some soldiers with hunting dogs be sent out into the surrounding woodlands to see if they could find any trace of any of the outlaws who managed to escape.

Similarly, Sir John instructed two of his soldiers to return to KLOPT0N immediately to arrange extra protection for the estate in his absence, before coming back two days later with some more soldiers to accompany them all back to Stratford-upon-Avon again.

Within a few more minutes everything was organised and they all set off together in one cavalcade with Sir Richard and Sir John leading the way at the front, whilst the two coaches were surrounded front and back by the knights and soldiers.

Jousting tournament at Warwick Castle

HOUSE OF LANCASTER
- 15th Century -

Chapter 16 : **Warwick Castle**

The remaining part of the journey to Warwick was relatively short, but it felt like a lifetime as the ladies all sat in virtual silence after their ordeal.
Once their coach had passed by all of the buildings in the main town and reached the long driveway to the Warwick Castle entrance, Sir Richard ordered for the whole cavalcade to come to a standstill.
Although Kane & Kara had visited Warwick a few times before, this was the first time they had been up so close to this magnificent medieval castle and they both watched fascinated by the spectacle unfolding in front of their eyes.

As soon as they were all stationary, one of Sir Richard's soldiers rode forward several more horse lengths whilst holding aloft a large flag fastened to the top of his lance which displayed the House of Salisbury coat of arms, where he was quickly joined by one of Sir John's soldiers similarly carrying the House of KLOPT0N colours.

Once they had stopped next to each other, both soldiers announced their arrival by blowing their trumpets in turn for almost a minute, before turning around to rejoin the rest of the procession.
After a short wait, a number of individual trumpet responses were then heard coming from somewhere within the castle walls, as the huge wooden drawbridge was slowly lowered across the moat and the large metal portcullis raised up behind it.

When the Gatehouse was cleared, a loud voice shouted out the order to proceed and immediately dozens of soldiers marched out of Warwick Castle in unison across the open drawbridge, where they all lined up in formation adjacent to the moat on either side of the driveway facing the cavalcade.

After all the soldiers were standing to attention, the trumpets from the castle stopped, whereupon Sir Richard with one of his knights and also Sir John with Kane, all rode forward together several lengths whilst displaying their respective coat of arms again, before coming to a stop and dismounting.
They then stood still and patiently waited for the next part of the formal pageantry to begin.

Everything around them went quiet for about a minute, with the only sound to be heard being that of the wildlife in the surrounding fields, until dramatically this tranquil scene was abruptly interrupted by a barrage of cannon fire coming from around the castle ramparts.

This thunderous noise not only startled most of the entourage in the cavalcade, but also caused numerous flocks of birds to take flight in the sky for a few moments, where together their large number managed to block out some of the morning Sun.

Soon afterwards there now began a chorus of beating drums and further trumpets, followed by the additional sound of horses hooves getting louder and louder.

Suddenly, dozens of knights and soldiers came galloping out through the castle Gatehouse across the drawbridge towards them, most of whom carried flags displaying the House of Warwick coat of arms.

Once outside the castle inner wall and on the driveway past the foot soldiers, the horse soldiers gradually peeled off one by one to create a line along both grass verges, where they came to a halt side by side facing each other.

In the meantime, the knights continued riding forward a bit further towards the Salisbury and KLOPTON coaches, where they stopped in a semi-circle formation in front of Sir Richard and Sir John, before dismounting.

At this juncture, the horse soldiers further down the driveway waived their flags from side to side for a few moments and upon seeing this signal, the trumpets and drums inside Warwick Castle ceased.

Sir Richard and Sir John then started walking over towards the knights, where they quickly saw that it was Sir Richard's son the Earl of Warwick standing at the front of his men waiting to greet them.

Following on from a warm embrace between father and son, Sir John stepped forward and also shook Sir Warwick's hand.

Their subsequent conversation out on the castle driveway took longer than would have normally been expected, but then a lot had happened that morning which Sir Warwick needed to be told about before they could proceed any further.

As soon as they had finished talking, both Sir Salisbury and Sir Warwick beckoned over one of their knights each to join them and some lengthy instructions were given.

They then all remounted their horses, after which the flags were waived again by the soldiers and another fanfare of trumpets and drums started sounding from amongst the castle walls.

146

The whole cavalcade set-off in procession back down the driveway and through the Gatehouse into the main courtyard, followed by all the knights and soldiers.

Meanwhile, the three men of Sir John's who had been killed during the fighting with the outlaws, were draped in the House of KLOPTON colours and given a guard of honour.

Their bodies were then taken directly to the castle chapel to be cleansed, re-dressed in funeral robes and placed in wooden coffins until the tournament was over, whereupon they would be taken back to Stratford-upon-Avon for a formal burial.

In the meantime, some of Sir Warwick's soldiers had been given the responsibility of dealing with the prisoners and took them into the castle through the smaller north west entrance, so they would not be any part of the main cavalcade.

Once inside the walls, the five outlaws still alive were dragged off their horses onto the ground and thrown down the stone steps in Caesar's Tower, before being locked up in the dungeons for subsequent brutal torture and interrogation.

Meanwhile, any garments remaining intact on the dead outlaws' bodies were removed for distributing to the town's poor later that day.

Their worthless carcasses however, were abruptly disposed of into the castle's waste pits on the outside of the southern wall, where they would be devoured by the many ravenous animals roaming around, with any other remains picked off their bones by the wild birds.

As the cavalcade approached the outside entrance steps leading up to the reception rooms inside Warwick Castle, Sir Warwick's wife Lady Anne stood there waiting with their two young daughters, Isabel who was eight and Anne who was only three, to meet everyone.

She gently held her eldest girl by the hand as she was very excited to be wearing such a beautiful dress and had been practising all day to curtsy properly as she greeted the guests.

The youngest girl however, was clearly overawed by the occasion and therefore closely looked after by one of her most trusted handmaids.

Several other handmaids were also on hand to help any of the other ladies once they had all alighted from their coaches.

In addition, a dozen squires stood close by to attend to the knights after they dismounted from their horses, whilst a further two dozen servants waited in a line around the perimeter of the courtyard ready to assist the soldiers and provide everyone with refreshments.

Sir Warwick and Sir Salisbury jointly brought the cavalcade to a halt and at the same time as it came to a stop, all the drums and trumpets around the castle walls immediately went quiet.

After dismounting their horses, both father and son went straight over to greet Lady Anne and the two girls, before walking back over to the Salisbury coach where the door was open and Lady Alice already waiting to receive them.

After the family hugs and smiles all around had finished, Jane walked over to join them and took the young girls with her to the Great Hall.

The two men and their wives then walked over to join Sir John & Lady Agnes who were both waiting outside the KLOPTON coach and as everyone already knew each other, the greetings were quite brief.

The conversation therefore quickly turned around to the topic of the outlaws who attacked them earlier that morning and Sir John beckoned Kane over to join them.

He had never met Lady Anne before and after a short introduction during which she asked about the extent of his injuries, she also expressed her greatest sympathy for the dreadful ordeal both Kara and Kathryn had just endured.

After thanking Lady Anne for her kind words, Kane explained how Kathryn was his niece and being a gentle mannered girl, was very distressed by the appalling attack on her person.

She ideally needed somewhere private to have a relaxing bathe and get changed into a different new frock she had brought with her.

His sister Kara however, was slightly older and much stronger in character, but she too would greatly appreciate the opportunity for a wash to remove all of the blood from the outlaw she had just killed whilst defending Lady Agnes in the KLOPTON coach.

Luckily, she too had brought another new dress to wear.

Lady Anne confirmed that she would get this organised immediately, when all of a sudden they heard a slight commotion behind them.

Turning around, they saw that Kara was standing on the ground holding a tearful Kathryn by her hand, as she tried to coax her out of the coach.

Meanwhile, Sheila was still inside the back of the coach also trying to encourage Kathryn to leave down the steps in front of her.

Upon seeing this upsetting scene, Lady Agnes went over to provide her assistance too and gradually between the three of them, they managed to get Kathryn outside and into the courtyard.

By this time Lady Anne had also joined them with two of her handmaids and in her gentlest voice offered Kathryn whatever help she needed.

Lady Agnes, who herself was also still shaken from what had happened that morning, thanked Lady Anne once again for all her kindness and asked if the four of them could now retire to their rooms for the next hour to freshen up and rest before the tournament began.

Sir John and Kane would also be accompanying them up to their rooms, but they both still needed their various injuries attending to and Lady Anne straight away summoned the castle doctor, plus a couple of extra servants, to join them.

She also ordered that some light food and drinks be sent over from the kitchen to everyone's room immediately.

The five KLOPTON family members plus Sheila, all then followed the servants across the courtyard to where their private rooms were already waiting for them in Guy's Tower, whilst Lady Anne went back inside the Great Hall with Lady Alice and their handmaids to ensure that everything was in place for that evening's banquet.

At that time, those of Sir Warwick's soldiers still in the courtyard were ordered to finish off their drinks and stand to attention.

They were then marched off to their temporary tented barracks erected close to the outside of Warwick Castle's northern walls, where they would help maintain guard over the gated entrances and jousting arena.

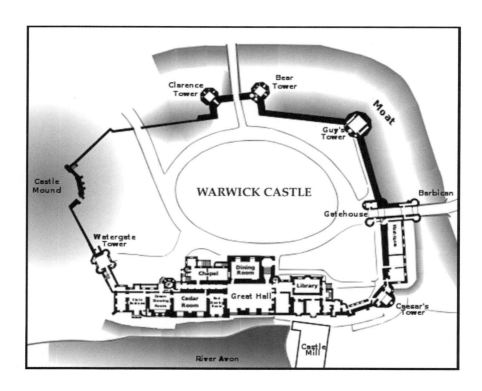

HOUSE OF WARWICK   *versus*   **HOUSE OF SALISBURY**

Sir Warwick and his father were next to mount their horses before setting-off through the same side gate where the soldiers had gone.

They then rode down to the adjacent main field where the jousting arena and tiered wooden seating had been built for the duration of the tournament.

Both sets of eight knights carried their respective House colours as they followed along the same route until they too entered the centre of the arena, where they separated into their two different groups directly behind either Sir Warwick to the south or Sir Salisbury to the north, before coming to a standstill opposite each other.

In-keeping with such tournaments, each House appointed an independent lieutenant to oversee the honour and integrity of all the various jousts, and these two men rode forward together to meet the waiting knights.

After they had introduced themselves, the lieutenants reminded all the knights of the rules of chivalry that must be adhered to in accordance with their sworn oath to the King and Realm, or else they would forever face disgrace and dishonour.

"We do!" was the fervent reply bellowed out by all sixteen knights together as they held their swords up in the air, before lowering them back down again to bang repeatedly on their shields for a few moments.

Both father and son then drew their swords from their sheafs in order to join in with their men, before shouting out together

"May the boldest knight be the victor!",

which announcement drew another rousing cheer in response.

As the time had now past noon, the lieutenants needed to move proceedings along and gave further instructions for all the knights to get themselves ready for a prompt 2.00 afternoon start.

Sir Warwick's knights' quarters for the three days of the tournament were in several large tents erected on the northern edge of the arena, whilst Sir Salisbury's knights were located in identical tents built for them on the southern side.

Two dozen horses for both sets of knights to chose from were tethered inside the fenced paddocks situated near their tents, whilst an equal number of squires were on-hand to help both Houses throughout the tournament.

Further servants were also available to fetch refreshments and deal with any other requirements, whilst two medical tents with suitable personnel were ready to attend any knights who sustained an injury.

Finally, after the day's jousting had finished, there would be a welcoming banquet in the Great Hall starting at 6.30 that evening, so all the knights were to be suitably dressed and presentable by that time.

On that note, both Sir Warwick and Sir Salisbury bid farewell to the two lieutenants and each rode off with their men to their respective tents.

Meanwhile, back inside the castle as it approached 1.00, Kathryn was woken up by Kara in order for her to get ready in time to watch the jousting.

Thankfully, all four ladies were feeling much better after their short rest and it didn't take long for them to get dressed into their splendid new outfits they had brought with them.

After the trauma of that morning, the mood amongst the ladies soon became more relaxed as they chatted away in excited anticipation of the tournament, before heading off downstairs to the tower entrance where Sir John and Kane were stood outside waiting.

Upon appearing though the tower door, Sir John greeted all four of them with a warm smile, before taking both his wife and Kara over to the KLOPTON coach, whilst Kane escorted Kathryn and Sheila just behind.

Once all the ladies were seated inside, Sir John and Kane mounted their white steeds and after instructions to the coachmen, they all set-off on the short journey through the west gate to the tournament field.

A couple of minutes later they arrived in the centre of the noisy and crowded arena, where the ladies alighted and were quickly escorted by one of the lieutenants up to the cushioned seats along the raised middle row of the main wooden stand.

Lady Anne was already seated in the centre of this row with Lady Alice on her left-hand side and upon seeing Lady Agnes she instantly invited her to sit on her other side, whilst Sheila joined the other handmaids Jane and Julia at the very end of the row.

Kane, Kara and Kathryn meanwhile sat down together on the right-hand side of Lady Agnes.

151

Sir John however, was escorted up a few more steps to a lavishly dressed grand wooden pavilion built on it's own platform, directly above where all the ladies were now sitting.

He sat down on one of the three large leather covered ornate chairs specifically put in this enclosure and then waited for Sir Warwick and Sir Salisbury to join him.

Affixed to the top beam and along the edges of the pavilion canopy were several wooden posts, on which banners for each of the three Houses were being flown to confirm their presence at the tournament.

The remaining rows of tiered wooden seating along that same side of the arena were full of other aristocratic families and wealthy dignitaries from around Warwickshire.

Directly facing them on the opposite side of the central jousting barrier were several rows of plain wooden benches filled by dozens of local townspeople, whilst hundreds more stood behind them waiting to enjoy the spectacle as it unfolded.

Sir Warwick's soldiers maintained a very visible presence along the whole perimeter of the field to provide security and also make sure that none of the noisy crowd got out of control, whilst groups of jugglers, acrobats and minstrels moved around the arena keeping everyone entertained.

Kane & Kara shuffled up a bit closer to each other as they felt the tension of the occasion build and eagerly waited on the edge of their seats for the tournament to start.

Suddenly, individual blasts were heard coming from the top of the castle walls as two cannons were fired into the neighbouring empty field, to signal it was 2.00 and time to begin.

Instantly, everyone in the large raucous crowd started cheering loudly, whilst those seated in the main stand clapped politely instead.

This continued for a couple of minutes, until the two lieutenants stood up from their chairs and a solitary trumpet was blown to signify that everyone be silent.

As both men then walked forward into the arena they were joined by two squires, each of whom carried a banner for either the House of Warwick or the House of Salisbury.

The lieutenants kept themselves several feet apart from each other before coming to a stop in front of the pavilion stand, where they ordered everyone in the arena to stand as they all greeted their distinguished hosts for the tournament,

"Sir Richard Neville 16th Earl of Warwick and his father Sir Richard Neville 5th Earl of Salisbury".

As soon as they had finished announcing them, both squires waived their banners aloft and a fanfare of trumpets began almost immediately from amongst the castle's ramparts, which was quickly followed by the beating of drums and even more loud cheering from the crowds.

A few moments later Sir Warwick rode into the arena from the northern side of the castle followed by his eight knights, whilst Sir Salisbury came in from the southern edge with his eight knights also riding closely behind him.

Father and son were both impeccably dressed in glistening suits of battle armour and rode upon magnificent thoroughbred black stallions draped in their respective House colours.

They all came to a standstill in front of their respective lieutenants, where the two Earls quickly dismounted before walking over towards each other and removing their gauntlets.

Upon meeting each other they reached out and shook hands as a symbolic, although genuine act of friendship, after which they raised their arms upwards together into the air for all to see.

In unison, they then shouted out at the top of their voices so everyone could hear them both.

"You are all most welcome here over the next three days to share this special jousting tournament between the House of Warwick and the House of Salisbury".

This very publicly staged greeting prompted all the soldiers and knights to start banging swords against their shields repetitively, whilst joining in with all the cheering that was reaching a crescendo from every section of the arena.

The sheer pageantry and atmosphere of the occasion was nothing like either of the twins had ever experienced before in their lives and instinctively, as if to re-assure themselves that it was in fact real, they took hold of each other by the hand and gave a gentle squeeze.

The enthusiastic reception continued for a few more minutes as father and son separated from each other and slowly walked up the wooden steps on either side of the pavilion platform, where they both came together again to acknowledge the ongoing applause from the crowd.

After a short while both lieutenants ordered that a solitary trumpet be blown to signal everyone be quiet again and as soon as the noise ceased, Sir Warwick made a short speech of welcome to his father and Sir Salisbury responded to thank his son for his wonderful hospitality.

Both Earls then removed their swords from their sheaths and pointed them upwards, before shouting out so everyone would hear them say,
"Long live our Sovereign Henry VI of England.
God save the King".

Immediately, another chorus of trumpets and drums sounded out from within the castle walls and as the knights and soldiers held their swords up aloft, everyone repeated the same words of loyalty to their King as loudly as they could.

After the noise slowly abated, both Sir Warwick and Sir Salisbury removed their helmets and turned around to shake hands with Sir John who was standing behind them.

Each of them then sat down on one of the three grand wooden chairs with Sir Warwick in the middle, upon which everywhere went silent and the lieutenants stepped forward again to take control of proceedings.

They first summoned the two squires holding the House banners to lead both groups of knights with their horses over to the front of the main pavilion, where they created two lines next to each other in formation facing the stand.

Each knight carried a shield displaying their respective coat of arms with matching colour plumage on the top of their helmet and all of them looked very impressive in their glistening armour.

One of the lieutenants then introduced the Earl of Warwick to a chorus of cheers, before he welcomed all of the knights to Warwick Castle.

He then reminded them all and everyone present that the jousts would be fought with hollowed wooden lances since it was not the intention for anyone to be seriously injured during the tournament and that there would be no dishonour whatsoever in any knight having to yield to his opponent over the next three days.

The other lieutenant then introduced the Earl of Salisbury to an equally noisy cheer, after which he reaffirmed the rules of engagement and reminded all the knights to honour their oath of chivalry.

Finally, the two Earls shouted out together for the whole crowd to hear, "May the boldest knight be the victor!",

which statement prompted one of the noisiest responses so far.

Both sets of knights were then slowly led off by their respective squires to their tents at the opposite ends of the arena before dismounting, except for one knight from each House who had remained behind facing the front of the main stand.

Upon a previously agreed signal, the two knights introduced themselves to all those seated in the main stand, after which their names were repeated out loudly by the lieutenants so everyone else in the arena would also know who they were.

The two knights then hit their lances against each others to signify their forthcoming contest, before both riding off to their ends of the arena in readiness for their joust.

A short while later after a signal was given by each knight's squire, both lieutenants ordered a series of two trumpet blows and with a huge cheer of encouragement from the crowd, the knights charged forward towards each other down the middle of the arena with their lances pointing over the central barrier that stood between them.

This first charge ended in a draw as neither knight could dislodge the other and so they turned around at the opposite ends of the arena and after another two trumpet blows, charged at each other again.

This time the Salisbury knight hit his opponent on his right shoulder with his lance, which sent him spinning out of his saddle and onto the ground with a heavy thud.

The Warwick knight did not move and a squire ran forward to see if he was alright, but realising that he was unconscious, yielded defeat on the knight's behalf.

The squire then summoned some help to carry the knight back to the Warwick tent, whilst his horse was returned to its paddock.

The trumpet was then blown and a single Salisbury flag raised on a post on the south side of the main stand to signify the victory, whereupon everyone in the main stand, especially Sir Salisbury, stood up to loudly applaud the knight.

The partisan crowd were understandably less enthusiastic about the Salisbury win and only gave the knight a brief cheer as he rode pass them to his tent with his lance pointing upwards to acknowledge his win.

After a short pause, the same sequence of events was repeated by two different knights on each occasion, until after five completed jousts with the score at three victories to Salisbury and only two for Warwick, it was now Sir James' turn to fight.

Upon announcing his name in front of the main stand where Kathryn was sitting she could hardly contain herself, but Kara took her by the hand and whispered for her to calm down as she knew what was coming next.

From behind them, Sir John stood up and spoke loudly so everyone would hear him.

"Before the next joust begins, I would like to personally thank Sir James on behalf of the House of KLOPTON family, for saving my niece Kathryn this morning from a vicious attack by a cowardly outlaw".

Sir James nodded his head in acknowledgement and modestly replied "It was my honour to be able to help your delightful niece and upon seeing her sitting in front of me now smiling after such an horrendous ordeal, is reward enough".

Upon hearing his comments Kathryn blushed, before lowering her head slightly to look away for a moment.

Meanwhile Sir John spoke again,

"Well said Sir James, as a truly honourable knight would and on behalf of Kathryn I know she too would like to thank you for your brave deed".

Sir James looked over to where she was sitting and saw that her eyes were now fixed on his again, as Sir John asked him,

"With your permission Sir James, Kathryn would like to express her gratitude by tying her personally initialled silk handkerchief onto your lance and in doing so wish you every good fortune in all your jousts throughout the tournament".

Sir James replied "I gratefully accept with all humility this gracious gift from such a beautiful young maiden" and slowly rode forward on his horse towards Kathryn, where they both smiled at each other before he carefully lowered the tip of his lance into her hands.

After the white handkerchief had been fastened on tightly, Sir James thanked her as he bowed his head, before turning to join his opponent.

Both knights were then instructed by the lieutenants to accompany the squires back to their respective ends of the arena in readiness for their joust to begin.

Kathryn could hardly contain herself as she waited anxiously for the trumpets to be blown and once they were, she reached out to hold Kara's hand tightly whilst she watched on in trepidation as the two knights charged towards each other at a gallop.

Each lance struck its target with a thud and although both knights slightly buckled in their saddles, neither were dislodged from their horse and continued on to the opposite ends of the arena to turn around.

Kara had little time to calm her cousin down before the next charge began and soon the knights were colliding with each other again, although this time it was to the sound of a breaking lance.

Kathryn took a deep breath and looked away thinking that Sir James had been injured, but it was his opponent who had been unseated and Kara quickly dispelled her fears, which brought a tear of joy to her face as she began clapping as loudly as she could.

Sir James lowered the visor on his helmet and smiled up at Kathryn who beamed back at him, whereupon as the victor of this joust, he rode off to rejoin the other Salisbury knights.

After the remaining two jousts of the first round were completed, the score was five jousts to the House of Salisbury and three to the House of Warwick.

The lieutenants announced a short fifteen minute break, whilst drinks were replenished and the next round of jousts organised.

The time quickly passed and everything was soon ready for the second round to start, whereupon the next two knights rode into the arena and the tournament continued again.

One by one, each remaining joust for that day followed and at the end of the second round the overall score had been brought level to eight jousts each as the House of Warwick had been victorious this time winning five jousts to three, with Kathryn being especially happy as Sir James had won his second joust too.

The lieutenants then ordered that the squires blow their trumpets three times to end proceedings for the first day, after which they declared, "The time is now 4.30 and the tournament is over for today.

The jousting will start again tomorrow morning at 10.00 and everyone wishing to join us will be most welcome by your hosts Sir Richard Neville, Earl of Warwick and his father Sir Richard Neville, Earl of Salisbury.
Access to the castle grounds will be permitted from 9.30 and you are requested to arrive in time for a prompt start".
The end of this announcement was followed by a single cannon blast from the castle walls, which brought one final loud cheer and some noisy applause from the crowd as everyone started to leave.
Meanwhile, the knights briefly returned to their tents to freshen up, whilst the squires stayed to look after the tournament horses.

The three individual House coaches had arrived to collect the family groups from the arena and take them back along the driveway to the castle courtyard, whilst the men mounted their horses to lead the way.

As soon as they were all outside on the castle entrance steps, they went inside and gathered together along one of the main corridor walls leading to the Great Hall, where the evening's banquet was being held.
They then stood in a line next to each other to formally greet all their guests, with Sir Warwick & Lady Anne plus their eldest daughter first to receive, followed by Sir Salisbury & Lady Alice, and finally Sir John & Lady Agnes with their family.

Both lieutenants soon arrived and upon seeing that the families had already organised themselves, one of them immediately ensured that the servants were also in place to escort all of the guests up the outside steps to the entrance corridor.
Once there, the formal invitations would then be passed over to him so he could announce everyone by name to their hosts.

Meanwhile, the other lieutenant would meet the guests at the far end of the line, where they would be handed drinks and taken to their seats by the servants, whilst groups of minstrels would provide background music to keep them all entertained as they waited.

After all the final dignitaries had been introduced, it was then time for them to welcome the sixteen knights, who were still dressed in their armour but without their gauntlets, swords and helmets so not to look too intimidating to everyone else at the banquet.

The House of Warwick knights were first in line and Kathryn could hardly contain herself knowing that it would soon be the House of Salisbury knights next and she would meet Sir James again, but she was unsure what to say to him.
It was obvious to Kara that Kathryn was very nervous and she tried to keep her calm, especially when they both heard his name announced at the front of the receiving line.

As Sir James approached Kathryn she saw that he had fastened her initialled handkerchief from his lance onto a buckle on his armour sleeve instead and her face lit up with joy.
Upon reaching her he bowed his head as she curtsied, after which he said
"It is wonderful to see you again Kathryn and I am delighted that you are looking so well",
to which she replied with a huge smile on her face,
"It is all due to you and I will forever be grateful for you saving my honour today".

Sir James smiled back and then carefully took hold of her right hand as he lifted it up towards him and gently placed a single kiss on the back.
Kathryn looked into his eyes as she uncontrollably blushed, before shyly saying
"Thank you for the great kindness you have shown towards me",
to which he replied
"It is with my upmost respect for you Kathryn and although I must now move along the receiving line, I do hope that we get the chance to talk again this evening before the banquet finishes".
Just before he then walked forward to meet Kara who was next in line, Kathryn replied, "... and so do I, Sir James".

Once all the guests and knights were seated, the first lieutenant entered the Great Hall and politely requested that they all be silent.
The talking quickly stopped and the minstrels also finished playing, as he then asked everyone to be upstanding to receive their hosts.

The second lieutenant then stepped forward and announced each of the three Houses in turn, starting with Sir Richard Neville & Lady Alice of the House of Salisbury, who walked in to a round of loud applause.
Sir John & Lady Agnes of the House of KLOPT0N were welcomed next, as the applause continued unabated.

Finally, their hosts Sir Richard Neville & Lady Anne of the House of Warwick were introduced and received by far the loudest applause, plus some additional spontaneous cheering from all of their knights, before taking their places at the centre of the top table.

The lieutenant then requested for everyone to be quiet again in order for him to say grace, after which Sir Warwick & Lady Anne sat down first, followed by the rest of the top table and finally by all the guests.

This prompted dozens of servants to appear with platters of sumptuous hot and cold food, which they took to the top table first in order for it occupants to be served straight away, whilst more platters followed straight afterwards for all the other tables and guests.

This extravagant banquet continued over several more courses including a colourful array of fruit and other delicacies not often seen outside of London, all of which was accompanied by a choice of excellent wines or mead.

Meanwhile the jesters, jugglers and minstrels provided continuous entertainment throughout the Great Hall which helped maintain a bustling atmosphere full of noise and enjoyment for all.

It took nearly two hours for everyone to finish eating their meal, whereupon the lieutenant dispersed the jesters and jugglers, before signalling for the minstrels to pause for a sort break as he announced that the dancing for the evening was now to begin.

Upon hearing this, Sir Warwick and his wife stood up and made their way to the centre of the room, where they were quickly followed by Sir Salisbury and Sir John together with their wives.

They decided to do the traditional 'circle dance' first, although for this they ideally needed at least eight people to create a large enough circle on the floor space and so Sir James beckoned Kane & Kara over to join them.

The twins looked at each other with a hesitant smile, as although they had been practising various 15th Century dances since they were told about the banquet, this was only three weeks earlier and they were both therefore understandably a little bit nervous!

Gamely however, they both stood up and Kane took Kara by the hand as they walked over to join the others, where everyone formed a large circle and as soon as they were ready, the lieutenant instructed the minstrels to start playing again.

The dance seemed to last for ages, but it was quite a repetitive routine danced at a relatively slow tempo and whilst this suited the twins as it helped them keep up with the other couples, they were taken by surprise when the dance ended quite abruptly as the minstrels stopped playing and the guests started applauding.

159

The eight of them then separated back into their pairs, whereupon the men bowed and the ladies curtsied to each other, before they were all led off the dance floor by Sir Warwick to return to their top table chairs.

It was now the chance for all the other guests to dance, but with nearly 100 people at the banquet the lieutenant took charge of organising proceedings again in order to avoid a crush.
He invited a few guests at a time from each table onto the dance floor, where he organised them all into two circles of five couples each.
Sir James was not going to waste this opportunity however and quickly asked the lieutenant to hold two spaces for him whilst he went to fetch his intended partner from the top table.

He then walked over to where Sir John was sitting and after bowing his head in greeting, he politely asked
"May I have your permission Sir John to ask your niece Kathryn for the next dance, if she will agree of course?".
A broad smile immediately came over Sir John's face as he glanced towards Kathryn, who having overhead their conversion nodded back to him excitedly, whereupon he replied
"You have my permission Sir James".

Upon hearing this, the knight took a few steps over to where Kathryn was sitting, but before he had the chance to ask her, she could not contain herself as she looked into his eyes and said
"Yes Sir James, I would be delighted to dance with you",
whereupon he gently took hold of her hand and slowly escorted her with him to the dance floor.

Once all twenty guests were organised into two circles, the lieutenant instructed the minstrels to start playing again, upon which Sir James and Kathryn joined in the dancing enthusiastically, whilst Sir John & Lady Agnes spoke to Kane & Kara briefly to discuss their opinion on the clearly infatuated couple.
They all acknowledged that the two of them could be ideal for each other, although if they were to enter into a formal relationship then social etiquette must prevail and with Kathryn's seventeenth birthday being in November, any betrothal and eventual marriage should be after that date.

Furthermore, during any approved courtship, Kathryn would need a chaperone and if Kara agreed, she would be the ideal person for such a role, to which she nodded her agreement but with a slightly bewildered smile, as such a ritual requirement was rarely practised anymore where her and Kane came from.

Another more serious matter to discuss however, was that Kathryn could never tell anyone the truth about her real family history, so the story of her KLOPTON lineage which they decided upon would have to be the version of her life forever, to protect the ancestral secret.

After much discussion, they all agreed that her parents' names would remain as Sir Frederick & Lady Khloe Klopton, who lived in their family residence in Suffolk, until they died there with her only brother Ryan in a house fire last December.
Thankfully, Kathryn was out of the house at the time with Kara, who had stayed there for a few days helping celebrate her recent birthday.
After the tragedy, she took Kathryn under her guardianship and brought her back to KLOPTON with her at the beginning of January, in order to stay with her uncle Sir John and the rest of his family whilst she finished her education.

Meanwhile, the dancing continued throughout the evening and as Sir James & Kathryn spent more time together, it was obvious that they were besotted by each other, so much so that both of them expressed the desire to see each other again after the tournament had finished.

Before the banquet came to a close therefore, Sir John met up with Sir Salisbury to discuss this matter and was surprised to find out that Sir James was in fact his bastard son, who's mother had subsequently died after a difficult childbirth, when he was only one year old.
Sir Salisbury immediately decided that James would live in the family house and over the years he became one of his best squires, so much so that when he was sixteen he became a soldier and was then legitimised with the Salisbury name, so gaining a total of eleven brothers and sisters.
Two years later on his eighteenth birthday he was knighted and was now one of Sir Salisbury's bravest and most trusted knights.

They both agreed that the pair would be a very good match and if they wanted to get betrothed then the wedding should be held towards the end of the year, being a respectable length of time for them to get to know each other properly.

The evening's formal festivities came to a close at 10.00 and after all the guests had said their farewells and left, it was time for everyone to go to their rooms in readiness for the next day of the tournament.
Kathryn however, was so excited after meeting Sir James again and especially having danced with him, that it took nearly an hour of talking with Kara before she became so exhausted that she could no longer stay awake and fell to sleep.

Chapter 18 : **Revenge and Victory** - 25th August 1459

The following morning at 7.30, a solitary trumpet was blown in the castle courtyard to signify that breakfast was being served in the dining room.

Sir John and Kane were already up and went straight over to the main castle to get something to eat, before any of the ladies were dressed.

Just as they had finished their first course however, one of the lieutenants came into the room and asked them to accompany him to meet Sir Warwick in Caesar's Tower, where the captured outlaws were imprisoned.

They both got up and quickly set off into the courtyard, where a couple of soldiers were guarding the solid wooden doors to the dungeons.

The lieutenant led them inside down the stone steps until they reached the damp cells holding the outlaws, whereupon Sir Warwick saw them approach and stepped out of the shadows to greet them.

After all walking over to where the outlaw leader was tied down on a huge wooden rack, it was immediately obvious he had been brutally tortured during his questioning; not that he got any sympathy from his captors for the severe wounds inflicted on him.

Sir Warwick stood with his hands clasped as he spoke first.

"This outlaw, after a lot of persuasion, told my interrogators that he and his men were paid two silver coins each by an unknown soldier, who apparently wanted your family killed so he could recover various family jewellery which belonged to him.

This soldier called himself Sir Edmund Klopton and claimed that his grandparents were the true heirs to the KLOPTON estate.

He also insisted that his inheritance had been stolen from him by your descendants and that this was the only reason you now lived in the Manor House".

Sir John responded with anger in his voice,

"This is an absolute lie, as none of my family or relatives have a son named Edmund and his story must have been concocted to justify the attack on us.

We must find this man as soon as we can however and in the meantime increase security around the KLOPTON estate, whilst also send a message to both my sons and warn them of this threat to their lives.

Thank you for your help Sir Warwick and as we no longer need these cowardly outlaws, will you have them hung in front of the crowd before the tournament re-starts and so deter anyone else from future attacks on my family".

Sir Warwick agreed to organise this straight away and instructed his guards to make arrangements for the hangings to take place in the arena that morning.

He then turned back towards Sir John and said,

"Please return to finish your breakfast as you have been away for some time and your family will no doubt be wondering where you are.

Also, if you let me have your letters for both Thomas and Hugh, I will arrange for them to be dispatched immediately".

After thanking Sir Warwick, they both made their way back up the tower steps and as soon as they were outside in the courtyard where they could not be overheard, Kane asked Sir John to stop for a moment as he had something very important to tell him.

"I think I know who Edmund Klopton is" said Kane.

Sir John looked astonished by this statement, but before he had chance to ask for an explanation, Kane continued.

"Your ancestor Sir James Klopton, who Kara and I stayed with in the 14th Century, had a son named Sir Stephen Klopton, who in turn had a son called Edmund.

However, the boy was not christened with the Klopton surname as his mother died in agony giving birth.

Sir Stephen never got over the sadness of his wife's death and disowned Edmund from his family forever.

I know Edmund's hereditary lineage to be true however, as I met him during his timeline when he was much older and also saw his hexagonal KLOPTON birthmark underneath his right arm.

Whilst I will only know for definite that he is the man we are seeking when I meet him again, if I am right then Edmund will no doubt also be the person who followed Kara and I out of the rock face entrance when we first arrived here in KLOPTON on the night of the red Moon.

However, none of us can disclose our family's history about Edmund to either Sir Warwick or Sir Salisbury".

After Kane had finished, Sir John said

"If you are correct, then we must indeed ensure that the secret of KLOPTON is kept safe and I will arrange for some of my most trusted soldiers to be posted outside the crevice entrance when the next full lunar eclipse appears".

They then continued walking back over to the dining room, where the ladies had already finished their breakfast and were waiting for them.

As they only had a short time left in which to eat their final course, Sir John said he would explain matters later and meet them in the courtyard to accompany their coach to the tournament arena.

163

They soon all arrived at the main stand and started taking their seats, when they saw the five remaining outlaws who attacked them, being brought into the arena inside a locked metal cage carried on top of an old cart, accompanied by a dozen armed soldiers.

The carthorses were brought to a halt by the lieutenant in front of the large wooden gallows erected previously.
This structure comprised of five hanging nooses fastened to individual large sacks, each of which stood on top of separate trap doors built into the raised platform.

The soldiers dismounted and together pushed the cage off the cart to the floor, with the outlaws still inside wearing just a few blood stained rags and their hands tightly tied behind their backs.
The cage padlock was then removed and they were all dragged out onto the ground and taken up the wooden steps one at a time onto the gallows platform.

Once there, they were each stood on top of a trap door with a noose fastened around their neck, whilst the rope at the other end was pulled taut by the counterweight of a heavy sack full of rocks.
At this stage, one of the lieutenant's signalled over to Sir Warwick who acknowledged him, after which two subsequent cannon blasts were heard from the castle walls and the second day of the tournament was about to begin.

Before it could start however, there was the issue of the outlaws to be dealt with and after a single trumpet blow, the other lieutenant asked that everyone be upstanding to welcome Sir John Klopton, whereupon both Sir Warwick and Sir Salisbury stood up first to lead the applause.
Once Sir John had reached the front of the pavilion, he raised his right arm upwards in acknowledgement, as he waited with a stern look on his face for the noise to quieten down before he spoke,

"I have some very distressing news to share with all of you today regarding the outlaws tied to the gallows in the arena.
Yesterday morning, several members of my family were travelling to the tournament when we were attacked by these cowards.
Indeed, had it not been for the bravery of Sir Salisbury and his knights who helped us defeat these thugs, then we would have all been killed, as were three of my most loyal soldiers who fought by our side".

Sir John paused for a moment in remembrance of his men, after which he turned around to once again thank Sir Salisbury as a section of the crowd started yelling "Death to the cowards!" and "Hang them all!".

164

The atmosphere around that part of the arena soon began to deteriorate as a mob picked up some stones off the ground and made their way over to throw these at the outlaws.

Sir Warwick quickly spotted this and immediately ordered his soldiers to create a physical barrier in-between the raucous crowd gathered in front of the gallows.

He then gave a signal to his lieutenant for the trumpet to be blown, whereupon in a loud and commanding voice Sir Warwick said,

"People of Warwick and all other guests with us here today, whilst I fully appreciate your anger towards these murdering outlaws, you must not let your strong emotions spoil this joyous tournament.

Please put down the stones you are carrying and return to your places immediately, so we may continue the jousting without any further delay".

This authoritative speech had its desired effect, as the rowdy section of crowd stopped their aggressive behaviour and dropped their ammunition back onto the ground.

Upon seeing this, the soldiers created a gap in their line surrounding the crowd so they could return to the other side of the arena, although several of the soldiers accompanied them to ensure there wouldn't be any more over-zealous behaviour.

With this potential problem resolved, Sir Warwick turned to Sir John and they both agreed that it was now best to get the hangings over with as soon as possible, whereupon instructions were given to the lieutenant who signalled to his counterpart overseeing the gallows that they were to begin when ready.

The executioner's first job was to double-check with the soldiers that everything was in place, whereupon he put his black hood on to cover his face and walked over to where the outlaws were standing.

After making sure that each of the nooses were fastened tightly around their necks, he opened each of the trap doors in turn, which immediately caused the heavy sacks to fall through the platform floor and in doing so, yank the outlaws' bodies up into the air.

If the men were lucky their necks would snap instantly, but if not then they would flounder around in the air in agony until they had choked to death.

Once all the outlaws bodies had stopped moving and also been stabbed through with the executioner's sword to ensure they were dead, the crowd let out a huge cheer as the bodies were cut down and thrown back into the cart for immediate disposal on the wild animal waste pits.

It was now time for the jousting to begin and a trumpet was blown to announce Sir Warwick as he stood up to formally welcome everyone to the tournament.

Next, with significantly less pageantry than the day before due to proceedings running behind schedule, the knights from both Houses bowed to the dignitaries in the main pavilion before riding off to their respective sides of the arena.

Two opposing knights initially remained behind and after introducing themselves by name to everyone, they too followed the others to get themselves ready for the first joust.

During the second day, the remaining six rounds of eight jousts each were to be held, including a break for a light lunch around mid-day.

At the end of the afternoon, every knight from both Houses would have individually fought all of their opponents.

The winners of the jousting would be the House and also the single knight who gained the most wins.

The whole day went by smoothly, without any further incident nor any knight being significantly injured and later that afternoon a trumpet was sounded to signify the end of the jousting competition.

One of the lieutenants then announced that Sir John Klopton would be declaring the overall results so far and everyone instantly cheered as he stood up at the front of the main pavilion.

Sir John was in a much more buoyant mood than he had been that morning, as he addressed the crowd in a rousing voice,

"It gives me the greatest pleasure to introduce you all to the winning knights from the jousting section".

He picked up the silver etched tankard from the table behind him and held it up in the air for all the crowds to see, after which he explained to everyone,

"This silver tankard is to be awarded to the individual knight who won the most jousts over the past two days, with six victories and two draws. I am delighted to tell you all that the jousting champion for this year's tournament is .... Sir Robert, who is one of the knights from the House of Salisbury".

A huge cheer erupted as Sir Salisbury stood up to join the acclamation from the crowd, whilst the winning knight dismounted from his horse and made his way up the steps to the pavilion to collect his prize.

After Sir Robert had received the silver tankard from Sir John and held it aloft in celebration, all seven of the other Salisbury knights drew their swords out of their sheafs and repeatedly banged them against their shields as loud as they could, whilst shouting "Victory!" to acknowledge their fellow knight's win.

166

Not to be outdone however, and in a magnanimous act of chivalry to a competitor knight, Sir Warwick's eight knights also started banging against their shields too as they joined in the cheering for Sir Robert.

Once all the noise had quietened down and Sir Robert returned to join his fellow knights, Sir John held up another silver etched goblet for the crowd to see, before explaining,
"This silver goblet is one of eight to be awarded to each of the knights who won the most jousts on behalf of their House over the past two days, with twenty-eight victories and twelve draws in total from out of the sixty-four fights that took place.
It is my privilege to tell you that the winning group of knights for this year's jousting is ... the House of Warwick".

The reaction from the very partisan crowd and guests was overwhelming as the whole arena erupted into a raucous crescendo of cheering and clapping, especially when Sir Salisbury also stood up to applaud the win and shake his son by the hand.
As the Warwick knights dismounted their horses in readiness to walk up the steps to the pavilion, all of the Salisbury knights reciprocated their opponents earlier chivalrous act by banging their swords against their shields and also shouting "Victory!".
The noise continued unabated as each knight in turn collected their individual silver goblet from Sir John, until all eight of them lifted these above their heads at the same time and one tremendous final cheer reverberated around the arena.

Sir Warwick then took charge of the remainder of the proceedings from Sir John and signalled for the trumpets to be blown three times to signal the end of the day's activities.
After the crowd had calmed down, one of the lieutenants spoke out loud enough for everyone to hear him announce,

"The tournament is over for the day and will start again tomorrow at 10.00, when you are all invited to witness a series of individual sword duels between the two Houses' knights.
Access to the castle grounds will be permitted at the usual time, whilst the fighting will finish around 1.00 mid-day.
Please be upstanding to acknowledge your host Sir Richard Neville, Earl of Warwick, his father the Earl of Salisbury and also their distinguished guests as they leave the arena".

The end of the announcement was followed by a single cannon blast from the castle walls and a loud cheer from the crowd.
The coaches then started arriving to take all of the evening's banquet guests to the main courtyard, from where they would alight onto the outside steps and enter the hallway corridor.

Once everyone had been ushered through into the Great Hall and sat down at the dining tables waiting for their meals to begin, a couple of dozen servants appeared to start serving another extravagant choice of succulent food courses and excellent drinks for them to enjoy.

Meanwhile, they were all entertained throughout the meal by groups of minstrels, plus an array of colourfully dressed clowns and acrobats.

It was just after the clock chimed 8.00 that they all finished the main meal and the lieutenant announced the dancing was about to begin, with the first dance of the evening to be performed again by Sir Warwick and the same top table guests as the night before, although this time they would be doing a line dance instead.

Upon hearing this, Kara & Kane looked at each other with some trepidation, but soon consoled themselves with the fact they had managed to complete the circle dance the night before.

Thankfully, both of the twins kept up with the rest of their dancing partners throughout most of the line dance routine and although they made a few errors, no one seemed to have noticed as they were applauded off the dance floor back to their chairs.

Once they were seated again, the lieutenant stepped forward to announce the following changes,

"I am delighted to advise you all of a new sequence for the dancing this evening, in order that we may acknowledge all of the knights' jousting skills we have witnessed throughout the tournament so far.

I would initially welcome the eight knights, who on behalf of the House of Warwick won the most number of jousts over the past two days, to be the first guests to graciously ask any of the ladies inside the Great Hall this evening to accompany them onto the floor for at the next dance".

All eight knights stood up eagerly to walk around the room, but with not many single young ladies present that evening, one of the more handsome knights bravely made his way over to the top table where he went up to Kathryn and politely asked her,

"Young maiden, would you do me the greatest honour and join me for the next dance?".

Unfortunately, this knight had chosen the wrong girl to ask, as Kathryn instantly replied,

"Thank you for asking me Sir knight, but my hand and heart are only for one other knight here this evening and I must therefore decline your kind invitation".

After a gracious bow of his head the knight stepped away, but he was not going to be deterred at finding himself a dance partner that easily and so instead turned towards Kara, who gave him a rather quizzical look .

Without hesitating however, the knight repeated the same question he had just asked Kathryn before, which instinctively prompted Kara to look over at Kane sitting next to her, but he clearly seemed uncertain as to whether or not he should say anything in reply.

With nothing forthcoming from her brother, Kara returned her line of view to the knight in front of her, but instead of directly answering his question she boldly asked him,
"If you tell me your name Sir knight, then I will decide whether to accept your offer or not?",
which response initially took him by surprise, before he regained his composure and with a smile simply said "William".
Kara looked back at him and in a firm voice replied,
"That is a good name Sir William, so yes I will dance with you",
although without taking hold of his outreached hand, she stood up and walked in front of him to the dance floor.

After the dancing had started, Kara could see that Kane was no longer smiling and also trying to avoid looking directly back at her as she danced around the Great Hall in front of him.
Kara felt very guilty that she had accepted Sir William's invitation and instantly started keeping her distance from her new dance partner as much as she could, whilst anxiously waiting for the line dance to end so she could sit down next to Kane again.

As soon as the dancing finished, Kara made a quick curtsy and after a simple "Thank you", she abruptly turned her back on Sir William and returned to her chair.
Once she had sat down, Kara straight away took hold of Kane's hand nearest to hers under the table and looked him in the eyes as she whispered in her gentlest voice,
"I am so sorry if I upset you, but I never meant to and you should know by now that it is only you who I love".

Kane's face lit up instantly, but before he could reply, Sir William arrived at their table appearing quite forlorn and as Kara looked up at him he gently said to her
"Thank you for our dance Lady Kara, but you seemed to be upset when we finished and I wish to most humbly apologise if I have in any way offended you?".

Kara suddenly realised how unintentionally impolite she had been to the young knight and replied with a kindness in her voice,
"Sir William, it is I who should apologise to you if I seemed abrupt, as you were an exemplary partner throughout the dancing, but unfortunately I suddenly felt light-headed and needed to return to my chair to sit down and get a glass of water".

Upon hearing this, a sense of evident relief came across the knight's face as he responded,

"There is absolutely no need for you to apologise for feeling unwell Lady Kara and I trust that you are better very soon so we may have time this evening for another dance?".

"We shall have to wait and see Sir William" said Kara with a cryptic smile, "but if not, then I thank you once again for our dance", to which the knight bowed his head in acknowledgement and returned to his table to join the other Warwick knights.

Once everyone was seated again, the lieutenant made his next announcement,

"It is now the turn of the eight knights representing The House of Salisbury to invite the ladies to partner them on the dance floor, but as it was Sir Robert who won the most jousts of any other knight over the past two days, he will have the honour as the tournament champion to ask first".

Sir Robert stood up to a loud cheer from all of his fellow seven knights, but having already realised that both of the House of KLOPTON young ladies were spoken for, he walked around the rest of the tables instead.

He soon spotted some guests who had brought their pretty daughter with them and upon approaching her, Sir Robert asked the young maiden for the next dance.

She eagerly accepted the knight's request, upon which he took her by the hand and accompanied her to the centre of the room, where they waited for the rest to join them.

Upon seeing this, the remaining Salisbury knights stood up and Sir James immediately walked straight over as quickly and dignified as he could to where Kathryn was sitting, in order to ensure that he got there before any of the other knights did.

He need not have concerned himself however, as before he had time to speak, Kathryn held out her hand to greet him and without blushing this time, looked straight into his eyes as she warmly told him,

"It is very kind of you to rush over to fetch me Sir James, but I can assure you that I will only hold my hand out for you, being the only one I will ever want to dance with again".

Sir James beamed back at Kathryn and took her by the hand as he escorted her onto the dance floor, where they stood joyfully chatting to each other whilst they waited for all the other Salisbury knights and their respective partners to join them.

The pairings were soon complete and once on the dance floor, the dancing began again and continued throughout the evening as all the other guests took it in turns to also take part.

The evening came to a close again at 10.00 as the minstrels finished playing and everyone else said their farewells as they started leaving the castle.

It was also time for the Klopton family to retire to their rooms as it had been a long day for all of them.

Sir James & Kathryn reluctantly said goodnight to each other, whereupon Kane & Kara escorted her back across the courtyard to Guy's Tower where their accommodation was, whilst Sir James went to join his fellow Salisbury knights in their arena tents.

Thankfully for Kara, Kathryn was very tired and so they all went to their separate rooms straight away to get some sleep in readiness for the final day of the tournament and also their coach journey back to KLOPTON.

Ten minutes later Kane heard a gentle knock on his door and upon opening it he found Kara standing outside with a smile on her face.

Upon seeing each other, she immediately whispered for him to come with her as quickly as he could before anyone saw them.

Uncertain as to what the problem was, Kane swiftly put his shirt and breeches back on in haste over the top of his nightgown, after which Kara led him back along the corridor to her room as stealthily as she could.

Once they were both inside, Kara shut her door quietly behind them and before Kane could say anything, she flung her ams around him and looked deep into his eyes as she said,

"I could not sleep without telling you again how sorry I am for having danced with someone else this evening and also how much my dearest brother, it is only you that I truly love".

She then kissed him passionately and Kane was overjoyed to be able to fully reciprocate.

After a long embrace, they blew out the candles and stayed together in Kara's room for the rest of the night, in each others arms.

Chapter 19 : **Unexpected Challenge** - 26th August 1459

Kane was up early in Guy's Tower that morning and quickly left Kara's room to return to his own before anyone else awoke and saw them together.
Not long afterwards a solitary trumpet was blown in the castle to announce breakfast was being served and as he heard Sir John leave for the dining room, Kane promptly stepped out of his bedroom door to accompany him across the courtyard.

After they had finished eating, Sir James also arrived in the dining room having already had his meal in the arena tent with the other knights, before he made his way up to the castle to speak to them both once they were ready.

Seeing that their breakfast plates had been cleared, Sir James instantly walked over to where they were sitting and after a bow of his head, he politely asked,
"May I join you both at your table for a few minutes this morning, as I have something very important I need to ask about before the sword fighting tournament begins?".
They nodded in agreement and beckoned him to sit down with them, after which he took a deep breath and continued.

"I understand from Kathryn that both of her parents died tragically last year and that whilst Kane is her cousin and guardian, she is also the ward of Sir John who is her uncle.
In the circumstances, I thought it proper that I should ask you both if I may have your permission to start formally courting Kathryn, with the most honourable intention of hoping to marry her at the beginning of next year when she is seventeen?".

Sir John was the first to reply and asked,
"How do both Kathryn and Sir Salisbury feel about this?"
to which Sir James responded with a broad smile on his face,

"Kathryn and I have spoken about continuing to see each other after the tournament has finished, but I have not been presumptuous enough to suggest a marriage proposal with her yet, as I believe such matters would be more fitting after we have spent longer together and she is of the appropriate age.

I have also spoken to my father who is very impressed with Kathryn and subject to your permission, has expressed his delight with such an arrangement".

Sir John looked towards Kane and after they had both nodded to each other they also smiled, as he said

"We too are both delighted to confirm our approval to this arrangement, although until Kathryn is seventeen and a formal engagement agreed, her cousin Kara will have to act as her chaperone whenever the two of you are together".

Sir James could hardly contain his joy as he reached out to firmly shake Sir John by his hand, before replying back to them both,

"Thank you for granting me such a wonderful honour and I assure you that I will always treat Kathryn with the upmost respect and protect her with my life".

He then also shook Kane by the hand, who responded by adding,

"On behalf of the whole KLOPTON family, we would like to wish you and Kathryn all our very best for a long and happy lifetime together.

Furthermore, once the tournament has finished, we will arrange when and where you may both next meet so a time has been agreed before we all set off on our separate journey's home.

For now however, it must be time for you to return to the arena to prepare yourself for this morning's sword fights with the other knights".

Sir James bowed his head and after saying thank you again, turned around enthusiastically as he left the dining room for the courtyard, where he mounted his horse and rode off back to the Salisbury tent.

As Sir John and Kane remained there talking, all four ladies walked in and after they had sat down at the table with them, they were told about what had just been discussed with Sir James, whereupon Kathryn became so overjoyed that Kara had difficulty trying to clam her down.

Before anything else could be said however, a squire rushed up to their table and spoke,

"Please forgive me for disturbing you and your family Sir John, but twenty soldiers have just arrived from KLOPTON in the courtyard to escort you and your coach back home after the tournament has finished.

They are also accompanied by a large black carriage which has been sent to collect your three dead soldiers and their coffins from the chapel, for which the priest requests your instructions".

Sir John stood up immediately and replied to the squire,

"Thank you for the message and I will follow you to the courtyard straight away", upon which he turned to his wife and the other three ladies, before saying,

"Please excuse us whilst you have your breakfast, as Kane and I have already eaten ours and we are both urgently needed to attend to this very important matter instead.

We will then meet the four of you outside Guy's Tower in sufficient time to accompany you down to the arena for a prompt start".

When they were outside in the courtyard they found Sir Warwick waiting for them and after a short discussion everything was arranged for a castle guard of honour to accompany Sir John's soldiers as they carried the coffins from the chapel to the carriage, once the tournament had finished.

Sir John introduced his officer in charge of the KLOPTON soldiers and it was agreed that three of them would stand as an honorary guard in front of the coffins where the dead soldiers presently lay, whilst two others would stay with the carriage and horses in the courtyard.
Meanwhile, the remaining fifteen soldiers would watch the sword fights in the tournament arena, with five of them changing places every hour so they could all pay their personal respects to their colleagues in turn.

With everything agreed, Sir Warwick passed matters over to one of his officers and then with time pressing he set-off to the arena, whilst Sir John and Kane rejoined the ladies waiting in the coach to escort them to the main stand.

Shortly after everyone had sat down, two cannons were fired from the castle walls to announce it was time to start the final day's tournament.
This was followed by a single blow from a trumpet, whereupon after brief statements by both Sir Warwick and his father, the lieutenants once again welcomed all sixteen knights from the two Houses.

He explained to everyone that instead of jousting that morning, there would be a series of sword duels in-between all the knights whilst riding on horseback, until an eventual winner was crowned.
As these exhibition fights were for displaying the knights' prowess only, the metal swords would all be blunt-edged to prevent any serious injury.
In the event of a duel ending in a tie however, the winning knight would be decided by a majority verdict from between the three Sirs.

Similar to the jousting routines over the previous two days, fourteen of the knights would ride back to their respective tents and wait there to watch the upcoming sword fights, as they prepared for their own duels.

Meanwhile, the two remaining knights were introduced by name to everyone in front of the main stand and after they had struck their swords against their shields to signify their forthcoming duel, a huge cheer rose up from the crowd.
Both knights turned around and rode their horses slowly through the gap in the side of a low wooden walled circular enclosure.

Once both inside this purpose built circular shaped fighting arena, they separated onto its opposite sides where they looked towards each other and waited for the signal for their duel to start.

In the meantime, a couple of squires began closing the thick gap behind them with heavy wooden blocks until the circle's perimeter was fully complete.

The lieutenants then instructed for the trumpet to be blown twice, whereupon the knights closed their helmet visors and raised their swords in the air to show that their fight had begun.

Initially, they both trotted slowly in a clockwise direction around the opposite inside edges of the arena, until picking up pace steadily as each of them prepared for their first moves.

Suddenly, both knights turned their horses to face the centre of the arena at the same time, as if instinctively revealing their opponent's intentions, and with a quick increase in speed they both rode forward with their swords pointed directly at each other.

The noise of their weapons clashing as they struck each other's armour and shield was very loud, with neither knight giving any quarter.

As the fierce sword fight continued unabated both horses appeared to become distressed and following-on from a particularly vicious attack, one knight ended up leaning so far out of his saddle that he caused his horse to rear up and throw him heavily to the ground.

The remaining mounted knight watched as his fallen opponent struggled to lift himself up off his knees, whereupon the lieutenant ordered for the trumpet to be blown and to the evident joy of Sir Warwick who jumped out of his chair in celebration, the duel was awarded to the knight from his House.

During the next two hours a further thirteen duels took place between the various knights over three decreasing rounds of eight, four and two fights, until only the final duel was left, which rather fortuitously for the tournament was between a knight from each House, with Sir Stephen on behalf of Warwick and Sir Mathew representing Salisbury.

Sadly for Kathryn, Sir James had been defeated during the penultimate round after a gruelling and at times vicious sword fight against the Warwick champion, but there was certainly no disgrace in his defeat.

Sir James was clearly disappointed however, as he left the arena to return to the Salisbury tent, until he saw Kathryn standing up in the main stand loudly applauding him as he slowly rode past.

This prompted him to pause briefly in front of her and bow his head, after which he held aloft the silk handkerchief she had given him as he smiled to acknowledge his grateful appreciation of all her support.

Following-on from a short rest-break for the final two knights who had already been involved in three duels that morning, the final fight was ready to begin and the lieutenants signalled for the trumpet to be blown. Unsurprisingly, this was a hard fought contest between two of the best knights who were both determined to win not only for themselves, but also the honour of their respective Houses.

The fight lasted for over five minutes without a clear victor, prompting the decision by both Sir Warwick and Sir Salisbury to bring it to an end.

Both knights were so engrossed in their duel however, that when the trumpet was blown they were uncertain where the noise came from and decided to continue fighting instead.

Realising that this might happen, the lieutenants were already mounted on their horses and as they bravely rode into the circular arena together to relay their instructions directly to both knights and separate them, the trumpet was blown again.

Upon now receiving their clear orders to stop fighting, both knights guardedly backed away from each other on their horses, until they felt far enough apart to replace their swords in their sheafs.

They then rode over next to the two lieutenants, where all four of them looked towards the main stand to await further instructions.

With the duel over, Sir Warwick stood up and invited both knights to dismount and join him on the platform with Sir Salisbury.

Meanwhile, the other fourteen knights from both Houses were told to ride over and form two separate lines on either side of the lieutenants still waiting inside the circular arena.

Sir Salisbury then stood up next to his son and together they announced that Sir John, as third judge for the tournament, would now proclaim the winner of the duelling contest.

A loud cheer went up from around the arena as both sets of knights arrived and took their place in front of the main stand, whilst the two final knights also reached the pavilion platform to join Sir John and everyone saluted.

After a short while the lieutenant signalled for quiet as Sir John, with each knight standing on either side of him, spoke to the crowds,

"You have all just witnessed these two knights fighting a series of duels for the honour of becoming the tournament sword champion, but neither were defeated and the winner is therefore to be chosen instead by myself, Sir Warwick and Sir Salisbury.

We have all agreed after much discussion, that the result is ... a Draw!, meaning that both Sir Stephen for the House of Warwick and Sir Matthew for the House of Salisbury are our tournament champions".

At this juncture, Sir John then presented each of the two knights with a sliver tankard and the arena erupted into further applause as both of them were held up in one hand and their opponents hand in the other.

Once the sound had abated, Sir John continued,
"I know that everyone who attended the tournament over the past three days will have thoroughly enjoyed this marvellous spectacle and also appreciated the generous hospitality of our wonderful host Sir Richard Neville, 16th Earl of Warwick.

In addition, we must also thank his father Sir Richard Neville, 5th Earl of Salisbury for his participation in this splendid occasion too, whilst not forgetting each and every one of the sixteen brave knights from both Houses who have fought with such skill and valour for your pleasure".

After another chorus of over-exuberant noise followed from the crowd, the trumpet was blown once again for quiet and Sir John withdrew to allow Sir Warwick to stand up and issue an unexpected invitation,
"Thank you everyone for joining us here at Warwick Castle for this tournament, but before we finish today there is still one time-honoured chivalrous act we must respect and which it is my privilege to now announce on behalf of all the victorious knights.

I hereby declare to anyone present amongst us who has not yet fought over the past three days, the opportunity to challenge any of our tournament champions to a duel and thereby win a purse of twenty-five silver coins.
My lieutenant will now have the trumpet blown three times, but if after the last one has finished and no challenger come forward, then this invitation will lapse and the tournament finally come to an end".

The crowd went quiet after the first blow of the trumpet whilst they waited to see if there would be any response, but after a minute no-one came forward.
A second blow of the trumpet then echoed over the arena as everyone held their breath and went even quieter, but the time passed by again.
The lieutenant then signalled for a third blow and as the trumpet was lifted up ready for a final time, someone hidden within the crowd shouted out in a very loud voice,
"I accept the invitation and hereby challenge the tournament champion to a duel".

Sir Warwick was initially taken by surprise for a few seconds as he looked over in the direction from where the challenger's voice seemed to come, but then with a booming voice demanded,
"Whoever has issued this challenge must present himself to me now!".

Within a few moments, a section of the crowd started to separate and create a gap through which they let the challenger pass.

All eyes were transfixed as the knight rode forward on an immaculate black stallion into the arena and slowly onwards to the front of the main stage.

The knight was fully suited in polished black armour whilst carrying a black lance and shield, all of which displayed the black & red crest of the House of KLOPTON.

Sir John was clearly shocked by what he saw and immediately stood up from his chair before walking over to the front of the pavilion to join Sir Warwick, from where he could see that his wife was also staring at the knight on his horse in front of them.

After regaining his composure, Sir John shouted out

"Sir knight, identify yourself and explain why you are wearing the colours of the House of KLOPTON!"

The knight responded by pulling his sword from its sheaf and raising it above his head to show that it too bore the KLOPTON crest.

He then lifted the visor on his helmet to reveal his face, before turning to look up directly at Sir John and say out loudly,

"Father, do you not recognise your own son?".

Before he could answer, Lady Agnes stood up and with a quiver in her voice replied

"Is that really you John?",

to which the knight responded

"Yes mother, I am indeed your son John and it is good to see both you and father again after all the years that have passed since I left home to explore other lands".

Upon hearing this, Lady Agnes became overwhelmed with emotion as tears began to roll down her cheeks, whereupon Sir John spoke again,

"It is also wonderful to see you my son, but when did you return to KLOPTON and why have you issued a challenge to fight the tournament champion this day?".

After a short pause, John replied

"I returned home in January at the beginning of the year to help try protect you both from your distant nephew Edmund, who wants to kill our family in order to try and inherit the KLOPTON estate for himself.

I had followed Edmund since then, until I lost track of him two days ago after confronting him in some nearby woods upon discovering the vicious attack he had organised against you whilst you were on your journey here to Warwick Castle.

At that time however, I did not realise the large number of outlaws Edmund had recruited and had it not been for Sir Salisbury's timely intervention, you may have all died.

In the circumstances, I want the chance to prove myself still worthy to be called your son and also wear the family KLOPTON armour with honour, by fighting a duel against the tournament champion".

Sir John did not reply, but instead turned to discuss the matter with Sir Warwick and Sir Salisbury, after which all three of them sat back down and the lieutenant stepped forward instead to take over proceedings.

He began with the necessary announcements for the crowds to hear, "The younger Knight John of the House of KLOPTON, has accepted the challenge to fight the tournament champion of which there are two, but as the jousting arena has been dismantled and replaced by the sword fighting arena, then the challenger must choose either Sir Stephen from the House of Warwick or Sir Mathew from the House of Salisbury".

Before replying, John lowered his lance and passed it over to one of the squires in the arena to hold, after which he raised his sword again in the air and then with a formidable voice shouted out clearly for everyone to hear him say,

"I will gladly fight both of these knights in separate duels!"

which bold statement brought a huge cheer from the crowd, especially when each knight held their sword aloft and shouted back together "We agree!".

The two lieutenants looked across at each other, not quite sure how next best to proceed, until everyone in the pavilion nodded their agreement and it was decided that the two knights would draw lots to see who would fight John first.

Sir Mathew was selected and he immediately rode forward to join John in front of the main stand, whereupon as soon as everyone else had emptied the circular arena, the lieutenant introduced both men to the crowd before turning around and leading them back inside the rim.

Their lethal sharp swords were then exchanged for blunt metal weapons as per the original duels between the two House's knights and once the arena low perimeter wall had been enclosed again, the trumpet was blown for the fight to begin.

The two knights started off in the usual manner for such a duel until they turned to confront each other, where John waited for Sir Mathew to ride up close by his side.

Whilst defending against his attacker with his sword, John suddenly swung his body low enough down on the side of his horse to grab his opponent's saddle strap and yank it hard enough to unsteady him.

Sir Mathew was taken aback by such an unexpected tactic, but before he could correct himself John had pulled himself back upwards and managed to hit his opponent's undefended helmet so hard that he ended up leaning even further backwards, until he unceremoniously fell out of his saddle to the ground with a loud thud.

John rode off around the arena with his sword in the air to celebrate his victory to the cheers of the crowd as the trumpet was blown, whilst Sir Mathew staggered to his feet shaking his head, clearly not happy with the manner of his defeat.
After brushing himself down as he walked over to fetch his horse, Sir Matthew then removed one of his gauntlets to gallantly shake hands with his victor.

After being rather surprised by the relative ease with which John had won his first duel, Sir Stephen wasted no time in mounting his horse to impress on his opponent that he was ready and very confident for their upcoming fight.

Within about five minutes the introductory formalities were over and the trumpet blown again to announce the start of the second challenge.
Both knights quickly engaged each other in a vicious sword fight with Sir Stephen appearing to hold the advantage as John repeatedly eased off from his opponent's continuous onslaught.

Sensing victory, Sir Stephen attacked even harder, until John suddenly pulled his horse away and rolled himself out of his saddle onto the ground, where he landed on his feet with his sword in his hand ready to continue the fight.

Although unsure if this was yet another trick, Sir Stephen still decided to dismount too and confront John without his horse.
He soon realised however, that this was a mistake, as John's armour was much lighter than his own and allowed him greater agility with his fighting moves.
Their strength versus speed unrelenting duel continued for another five minutes, with neither knight getting the upper hand, until the trumpet was blown and the lieutenants rode into the arena to halt the fight.

Both knights backed away from each other disappointed not to win, but shook hands as Sir Warwick announced that the result of their duel was a draw.
It was also agreed that John would leave the arena with his honour enhanced, which proclamation brought a huge cheer from the partisan crowd, whilst both teams of knights banged their swords against their shields in salute.

The lieutenant then signalled for the trumpet to be blown twice, after which two cannons were fired from the castle walls.

Sir Warwick thanked everyone again for attending, before declaring that the tournament was finally over.

An hour later inside the castle courtyard, Sir John and his cavalcade were almost ready to leave on their short journey back to KLOPTON, with the extra horseback soldiers put in place to guard the coach carrying all four ladies and also to escort the second carriage transporting the three dead soldiers bodies.

Lady Agnes was delighted that her son John would also be coming back home to stay with them for a while, as they had a lot to talk about since he left home at the age of sixteen.

In addition, Sir John and Sir Salisbury had agreed that Sir James could stay a few days at the KLOPTON Manor House before he returned back to Middleham Castle in Yorkshire, in order that he and Kathryn could spend some time with each other, whilst Kara would act as chaperone.

After a final goodbye to their hosts and other family guests, the ladies where helped into their coach and once the men had mounted their horses, they all set off through the castle Gatehouse on their journey back to Stratford-upon-Avon.

Meanwhile, Sir Warwick and fifty of his knights returned to join the garrison in Calais due to the ongoing conflict between the Yorkists and Lancastrians.

White Rose of York & Red Rose of Lancaster

HOUSE OF LANCASTER
- 15th Century -

Chapter 20 : **Wars of the Roses**

The return journey to KLOPT0N was uneventful and on their arrival Sir John led the cavalcade to a small fenced-off paddock in one corner of a large field on the edge of the estate, where as organised beforehand there was a group of people and a priest waiting to meet them.

The coach paused to let the funeral carriage with the soldiers on horseback pull in front, before they all stopped at the entrance to the field, where the coffins were lifted out and placed next to three holes dug in the ground, each of which bore a small wooden cross with a name and date on.

Meanwhile the four ladies in the KLOPT0N coach were escorted by one of either Sir John, Kane, John or Sir James over to where the coffins lay and they joined in the prayers read out by the priest.

After the simple service had finished Sir John said some very heartfelt personal words of immense gratitude on behalf of his family to all of the mourners attending.

Everyone then stood silent with their heads bowed as the coffins were lowered into the ground, whilst a trumpet was blown three times.

Once the trumpets had gone quiet, Lady Agnes went over to console the three grieving widows who were in tears and she also gave each of them a purse full of silver coin to help them financially.

Sir John then led the four ladies back to the coach and after the men had mounted their horses, their cavalcade completed the remainder of its journey to the Manor House where the servants were waiting in line to help everyone as needed.

With more guests staying than before, the sleeping arrangements in the House had to be changed slightly with John having his original room back, whilst Kane would share with Sir James during his short stay.

Over the next few days Kathryn & Sir James got to know a lot more about each other as their love grew even stronger, especially as Kara kept her chaperone duties very discreet and distant whenever she could. Unfortunately however, Kathryn knew she could not tell Sir James about her Klopton history, although it would be a very difficult secret for her to keep.

She did console herself though by promising that she would tell him everything in the future after they were married.

Too quickly it was time for Sir James to go home and although the date for their next reunion in October was arranged before he left, Kathryn was clearly upset as he rode off and began crying in Kara's arms as she tried to comfort her.

In the meantime, Kane and John also got to know each other well and exchanged many stories about each other's journeys and adventures in 14th Century Plantagenet England.

This included how they had both separately met Edmund and how John, whilst concealing his true Klopton family identity, had managed to learn about Edmund's murderous intentions when he was out drinking in the local taverns and then followed him through the cavern waters on the night of the full red Moon to help thwart his future plans.

Just as intriguing to Kane was how John had kept himself from being recognised due to his evident family likeness, which John explained he did by maintaining a ruggedly poor appearance including untidy long hair and beard whilst he worked on the KLOPTON farm as a labourer.

Indeed, when Kane thought back, he recollected seeing John around the estate on several occasions, although they never spoke nor even acknowledged each other since they moved in different circles due to their apparent status at that time.

Whilst Sir James was away, it was all agreed that John would join their small family social group when they were out riding or walking around the less guarded parts of the estate.

This was considered especially necessary whilst Edmund was still after the KLOPTON keys that Kara wore around her neck, as they needed to stop him from gaining control over all future passage through the main cavern waters.

Additionally, if anyone wanted to leave the estate to visit Stratford-upon-Avon or any other places nearby, they were to also be accompanied by the six horse soldiers assigned by Sir John to help protect them.

A couple of weeks later Sir John received news from Sir Warwick that tensions had peaked again between the Lancastrians and Yorkists, resulting in the significant probability of a battle taking place imminently between the two sides as they both raised more troops to increase the size of their armies.

A few days afterwards, Sir Salisbury together with three of his sons including Sir James, left Middleham Castle with a 5,000 strong army to march to Shropshire, where he was to meet up with both the Duke of York and Sir Warwick's troops near Ludlow in order to subsequently engage with the Lancastrian army.

Unfortunately, Sir Salisbury was intercepted on route by a force of 10,000 men sent by Queen Margaret and led by Lord Audley, which confronted his army at the **Battle of Blore Heath** on **23rd September 1459** in Staffordshire.

Despite being significantly outnumbered, Sir Salisbury's greater experience in warfare strategy eventually prevailed as his troops killed Lord Audley and then routed his forces as they were led by his second-in-charge Lord Dudley.

After a day to re-organise, Sir Salisbury took his remaining troops to join up with the Duke of York and Sir Warwick forces, after which they all planned to continue onwards together to London.

They soon discovered however, that their route ahead was blocked by a large Lancastrian army, forcing their Yorkist army to Worcester instead.

From there they retreated back towards Shropshire and then enhanced the defensive fortifications alongside the nearby river crossing, in readiness for the next day's **Battle of Ludlow** on **12th October 1459**.

Despite Sir Salisbury's previous victory he had lost many hundreds of men during the fighting, which resulted in the total number of Yorkist troops being significantly less than the combined size of King Henry VI and the Duke of Buckingham.

The Yorkist position was subsequently made even worse after a pardon was proclaimed by the King to any soldiers who changed sides to support him and this gambit resulted in many troops defecting to join the Lancastrian army.

That evening the Duke of York, Sir Salisbury and Sir Warwick realised that they could not win the upcoming battle and so, after telling the remainder of their troops that they were retiring to Ludlow Castle for the night, they all left instead and fled across the border into Wales.

The following day all of the abandoned Yorkist forces knelt down in front of King Henry and after swearing their oath of allegiance, were pardoned and joined his forces.

In the meantime Sir Richard, Duke of York with his son Sir Edmund, Earl of Rutland, secured passage over to Ireland where they still had strong support and could prevent themselves from being captured by the Earl of Wiltshire, who had been appointed as Lieutenant of Ireland in Sir Richard's place.

Sir Warwick, Sir Salisbury and the Duke of Yorks' eldest son Sir Edward, Earl of March sailed down the west coast instead, from where they borrowed a boat off Sir John Dynham in which they all crossed the sea to Calais.

All the troops and officials still supported Sir Warwick as Captain of the garrison in place of the Duke of Somerset, who was subsequently appointed by King Henry but been unable to take control of the city port.

Sir James had also fled, but decided to stay in England and initially took refuge in Middleham Castle before alternating his main place of refuge with Warwick Castle.
His choice of castle depended on which was the safest location across the regions for him to stay in whilst sending both his father and brother up-to-date reports on the Lancastrian troop movements.

Over the next couple of months Sir James also managed to see Kathryn quite often at KLOPTON, including on the 15th November 1459 which was her 17th birthday.
It was agreed they could have lunch out together in Stratford without Kara acting as chaperon on this occasion, although half-a-dozen horse soldiers still provided them with a guard on their coach journey from the Manor House and back as Edmund had still not been apprehended.

Upon their return to the estate, the day turned into a double celebration as Sir James, with the prior permission of both Sir Salisbury and Sir John, asked Kathryn to marry him.
Unsurprisingly, she was overjoyed in tears as she accepted both his proposal and also the beautiful diamond engagement ring he gave her.
That evening an extra special family dinner was held at the Manor House in celebration, with a group of minstrels in attendance to provide music and extra encouragement (if needed!) for everyone to join in with the dancing on such a joyous occasion.

A wedding date of 12th March 1460 was quickly confirmed by Sir James & Kathryn, which was also the same day as his upcoming 20th birthday.
Previously unknown to Kathryn, plans had already been agreed for this to take place at Warwick Castle, with a small family wedding ceremony inside the old private Chapel originally built in the 12th Century during the reign of King Henry II.
The reception and meal would be held in the Great Hall afterwards.

Sir Warwick & Lady Anne were delighted to provide the castle for the celebrations, particularly as it also ensured suitable security for all the Neville family members in attendance whilst the Yorkist war against the Lancastrians was ongoing.
Sir James & Kathryn spent as much time as they could together over the next few months whilst organising the rest of their wedding, although when Sir James was away on his travels, both Lady Agnes and Kara were only too pleased to help Kathryn instead, especially with choosing the wedding dress and their own new outfits!

Christmas soon came around once again, but with the weather being quite mild that year, both Sir Hugh and Sir Thomas managed to visit KLOPTON to share in all the family festivities and talk to their younger brother John about his travels over the four years he had been away.

The atmosphere in and around the Manor House over the next few days was one of great joy with everyone getting on very well with each other, especially those sharing rooms who were often heard talking excitedly through the night and into the early hours.

In the meantime, Sir Salisbury and Sir Warwick still remained in Calais, where they not only utilised their garrison troops to twice repel the Duke of Somerset's army from re-capturing the city port for the King, but also planned their future battle strategy against the Lancastrian forces via subversive communications with Sir Richard of York.

These plans included their future return to England and control over London, but to do this they first needed control of the English Channel.

At the **Battle of Sandwich** on **15th January 1460**, Sir Warwick ordered a flotilla of ships from his Calais fleet under the command of Sir Dynham, to attack the Lancastrian ships moored in the Kent port.

Arriving at dawn, the Lancastrian officers were still asleep and the battle that followed was short as Sir Dynham's soldiers quickly defeated the Lancastrian forces and captured several of their ships virtually intact.

Upon receiving the news of their conclusive victory, Sir Warwick steadily dispatched around 2,000 of his troops from Calais to first secure control of the Sandwich port and then the rest of the town.

Once this objective was achieved, other ancillary matters were put in place in readiness for the Yorkists subsequent planned attack a few months later, when the Channel waters were much calmer for the other troops arriving by ship.

Chapter 21 : **The Wedding Party**

The 12th March could not come quickly enough for Kathryn and when it did arrive she was up early that morning, although truth be known, she had been so overexcited the whole week before that she barely slept at all that night.

Kara was thrilled to be Kathryn's main bridesmaid and together with Lady Agnes they both did their best to calm her down now her Wedding Day had finally arrived, especially as she was becoming very anxious about everything that lay ahead of her.
Thankfully, with the wedding service at Warwick Castle not due to start until 12 noon, they did not need to leave KLOPTON until an hour before and therefore had plenty of time to get Kathryn ready - they hoped!

After Kathryn had finished a light meal brought to her bedroom, she moved over to sit in the chair by the side of her bed and gaze out of the window overlooking the Manor House gardens below, whilst she waited for Kara and Lady Agnes to get dressed in their own rooms before joining her.
Kathryn soon became lost in her thoughts however, as she had dreamt about this day ever since she was a young girl.
Sadly her parents were now far away in another time and although she could still remember their faces clearly, she knew they could not be with her on this special day.
She missed them both very deeply.

Suddenly, the bedroom door swung open and in entered both Kara and Lady Agnes, who were talking excitedly about the day ahead and how it was time for Kathryn to get ready.
Kara went over to where Kathryn was sitting and after helping her put on a pair of delicate ivory leather shoes, she took hold of her hands and lifted her up slowly out of the chair, before they both walked over to where Lady Agnes was waiting next to a full height mirror, ready to take her part in getting the bride dressed.

Kathryn stood still in front of the mirror for a few moments before removing her white linen sleeping robe, whereupon Kara brought over the exquisite ivory silk wedding gown that had been hanging on the bedroom dressing rail.
Together with Lady Agnes, the two of them carefully lifted the gown up over Kathryn's head and through her arms, before allowing it to drop slowly down from her shoulders over her unspoilt petite body, until it came to a rest just level with her dainty feet.

The dress height was simply perfect, as Kara fetched over the beautifully embroidered long lace train and after fastening this onto the back of the gown, spread it out behind Kathryn as far as she could over the bedroom floor, to reveal hundreds of small rose pink crystals embossed in the shape of seven symmetrically conjoined hexagons.

In the meantime Lady Agnes had gently brushed Kathryn's long brown hair back into the style she had chosen for her wedding and once this was done, she went over to the dressing table to open up an old oak box she had brought into the bedroom with her.
On top of this box's lid and embossed in silver, were the seven letters of the name KLOPT0N in a line, each enclosed by a separate hexagon shape carved into the wood.

Kathryn looked on intrigued as Lady Agnes lifted out of this box a perfectly smooth silver chain carrying a single exquisite large hexagonal rose pink crystal pendant encased in silver, which she placed around her neck.
As Kathryn held the pendant up to the light to examine it even closer, she saw that buried deep within the crystal was a red vein formed in the shape of the '0' phi symbol.

Lady Agnes next took out the box another piece of jewellery for Kathryn to wear, which was more stunning and intriguing than the necklace.
This was a multi-layered magnificent hexagonal shaped silver tiara, on the front of which was another even larger single hexagonal rose pink crystal, whilst on each of the other five sides was a similar but slightly smaller hexagonal crystal.
Lady Agnes held the tiara up to the light to reveal that the red vein deep inside the front crystal formed the shape of the letter 'K', whilst the red veins contained within the other five smaller crystals each formed the shape of one of the remaining five letters of KLOPT0N.

She told Kathryn how both these precious heirlooms had been passed down through time by the descendants of the original founding knights and were only for a true daughter of KLOPT0N who bore the hexagonal birthmark, to wear on her Wedding Day.
Lady Agnes then lifted the tiara gently onto Kathryn's head and whilst doing so, explained to her how it had been foretold in the ancestral KLOPT0N parchments, that by wearing both of these special silver and rose pink pieces together, would ensure the bride's fertility!

This historical prediction raised a warm smile from Kathryn which was shared between all three of them, but very soon she became overcome with emotion as she stood there in front of the mirror, mesmerised by the beautiful gown and exquisite jewellery she was wearing.

A tear of sheer joy started to roll slowly down her cheek as for the first time that day she fully appreciated the enormity of was actually happening and how soon she would be marrying the man she loved.

After what seemed like just a couple of hours the bedroom clock struck 11.00 followed by a knock on the door, both of which awoke Kathryn from her drifting thoughts, as Sir John spoke from outside in the corridor "Ladies, it is nearly time for us to leave and if you are all ready, please may I come in?"
Lady Agnes replied, "Yes, dear husband, you may".
As the door opened, the handmaid Jane entered first carrying two large wicker baskets full of rose pink & white roses, followed closely behind by Sir John, who for that special day was delighted to accept responsibility for walking Kathryn up the aisle in her father's absence.

Upon seeing his distant relation's niece in her wedding gown for the first time, Sir John bowed his head as he kissed the back of her hand and in a gentle voice said,
"Kathryn, you look absolutely beautiful and it is my greatest privilege to be able to look after you on your Wedding Day and escort you down the aisle to marry Sir James",
Her smile lit up the room as she responded with a curtsy, followed by a few words of her own,
"Sir John it is you who do me the greater honour and it is one for which I will be forever thankful".

Meanwhile, Lady Agnes and her handmaid sorted out all of the roses.
This included a corsage for herself; single rose button holes for Sir John and each of their three sons plus Kane; a medium sized bouquet for Kara; plus a single rose stem for each of the four younger bridesmaids who were waiting over at Warwick Castle with their mothers.

Finally, she made the biggest bouquet for Kathryn, which comprised seven large white roses intermingled with seven smaller rose pink roses, all of which had been tied together by a silver braid embroidered with a series of random hexagons each containing a letter 'K'.
Whilst this stunning bouquet was destined for Kathryn to carry with her on her journey to Warwick, she could not resist but to take hold of it now and stand in front of the bedroom mirror to look at herself with her whole wedding ensemble now complete.

It was abundantly clear from the happiness in her face how thrilled Kathryn was and as she turned around to look at Lady Agnes, she said,
"I cannot thank you enough for the overwhelming kindness you have shown me since the first day I arrived in your House.
I will forever be grateful for everything you have done for me".

Lady Agnes walked over to Kathryn and gave her a kiss on the cheek as she replied,

"It has always been my absolute delight to help and I wish you every happiness in your future life to come, but it is now time for us all to set off if you don't want to keep your fiancé waiting".

Kathryn responded with a cheeky smile, "We had better get going then!"

She passed the bouquet over to Kara, before carefully lifting up the bottom of her bridal gown from the floor and joining Sir John at the door. He proudly smiled at Kathryn as he gently took hold of her by the arm and they set off together down the stairs, where the others from their wedding group were waiting for them in the courtyard.

Once in the hallway Kara helped carry Kathryn's gown for her, as she and Sir John made their way over to the pristine wedding coach, which was harnessed to six magnificent white horses, all draped in the red & black colours and family crest of the House of KLOPT0N.

As soon as Kathryn was seated inside, Lady Agnes, Kara and Jane quickly joined her, whilst Sir John had a few last words with his three sons before they mounted their horses and he stepped into the coach.

Sir Thomas and Sir Hugh lead the private procession over to Warwick, whilst Kane and John rode immediately behind them.

All four men were impeccably dressed in their finest polished armour and seated on thoroughbred white stallions, which were also draped with the red & black family colours.

To the rear of the coach were sixty soldiers all patiently waiting on their perfectly groomed black horses, half of which men were from the KLOPT0N estate, whilst the other half from Warwick Castle who had joined them to help ensure a safe journey for the wedding party.

Seeing that everyone was ready, Sir Thomas gave the order for them to depart and as soon as they had exited from the main courtyard, all of the soldiers unfolded the coloured flags they were carrying to display their respective House crests.

As they proceeded down the streets of Stratford, crowds of town folk appeared from their houses and cheered them on their journey.

Both Kathryn and Kara could not resist but to wave back through the coach windows to acknowledge all their good wishes.

Meanwhile, Sir James was waiting at Warwick Castle, where he had been joined a couple of days earlier by his half-brother Sir George Neville, who was appointed Bishop of Exeter in 1458.

As the wedding officiant, Sir George looked splendid in his bishop's luxurious gold & red cassock with matching mitre on his head, and both of them were delighted he would be delivering their marriage ceremony.

Unfortunately however, two of his other half-brothers Sir Thomas Neville and Sir John Neville could not make the wedding as they had been captured by the Lancastrians at the Battle of Blore Heath in September 1459 and were still imprisoned inside Chester Castle dungeons.

Also, no one yet knew whether his eldest half-brother Sir Richard Neville of Warwick, who was meant to be his best man, would be able to attend the wedding along with their father Sir Richard Neville of Salisbury, since they were both still apparently taking refuge in Calais.

Sir Warwick & Lady Anne's two daughters Isabel (aged 9) and Anne (aged 4) were Kathryn's youngest bridesmaids, along with Sir Salisbury's daughters Eleanor (aged 13) and Margaret (aged 10) who together with Lady Alice had arrived at Warwick Castle two days earlier.

All four young girls looked simply gorgeous in their white & rose pink dresses and they were so excited at being bridesmaids that their mothers were struggling to keep them calm.

Suddenly, a fanfare of trumpets sounded out from the castle ramparts and upon hearing this, the girls all went very quiet as they stood totally still wondering what was going to happen next.

Thinking that Kathryn had arrived early, Sir James started making his way inside the castle, only to stop on the steps as a single knight on horseback entered the courtyard to make an announcement.

Both Sir Warwick and Sir Salisbury with their personal bodyguards of over a hundred knights and soldiers, had just arrived in Warwick and would be joining them within a few minutes.

Their journey across the town however, had come to a virtual standstill as the welcoming crowds grew so large they blocked the route, whilst their raucous voices could be heard cheering loudly by everyone waiting inside the castle courtyard.

Immediately assessing the problem, the main knight ordered the soldiers to push their horses steadily forward through the crowds and to create a line on both sides of the main street in order to hold all the people back.

The way ahead was gradually cleared and the cavalcade able to proceed onwards again until they reached the castle grounds, where they were greeted by another fanfare of trumpets and dozens of foot soldiers who had lined the driveway all the way to the drawbridge.

Sir Warwick and Sir Salisbury entered the castle courtyard in front of their men and rode straight over to see their wives and daughters, who were overjoyed to see them.

Realising that time was short however, the two men quickly dismounted and after several hugs especially for their children, they walked over to meet Sir James who warmly greeted them both.

Sir Salisbury was the first to speak to Sir James and asked him
"I hope you did not think I would miss my son's wedding?",
to which rhetorical question Sir Warwick added one of his own
"... and I hope you did not think I would miss being my brother's best man neither?".

Sir James replied to both of them with sheer joy in his voice, as he said, "I am absolutely delighted that you have both made the long journey to be with me here on my Wedding Day, although with just five minutes to go I must admit I was beginning to wonder if you would make it on time.

Kathryn's arrival however, is imminent and we all now need to make our way into the Chapel with Sir George so we can quickly go through all the service proceedings, whilst we still can".
This observation prompted Sir George to join in with the conversation by adding,
"Yes, we only have about five minutes left before the wedding is due to start and as the groom cannot by tradition see the bride as she arrives, please all follow me inside straight away".

They instantly turned around and started up the outside steps, when a single trumpet sounded out from the ramparts to announce the arrival of the wedding procession in Warwick, which brought a huge sigh of relief from Sir James as he wasn't sure Kathryn would be there by noon.

Outside in the town centre the soldiers were still lining the streets as the crowds thronged up close to the coach to try and catch a glimpse of the bride inside, with Kathryn overjoyed to see so many people clapping and cheering her on her way to her wedding.
As soon as the coach entered the castle grounds however and she saw the portcullis entrance up ahead, Kathryn became a lot more anxious and Kara gently took hold of her hands to help calm her down.

Less than a minute later the horses crossed over the drawbridge and upon arriving in the courtyard, the coachmen stopped the coach next to the steps leading up to the main inside hallway.
A squire from the castle opened the coach side door and Sir John was first to exit, quickly followed by Lady Agnes and Jane, whilst Kara stayed inside with Kathryn to allow the rest of the party time to adjust their attire.

In the meantime Sir Thomas, Sir Hugh, John and Kane dismounted their horses and passed the reins to the squires, before joining Lady Alice and Lady Anne who were busy with Lady Agnes and Jane sorting out all of the white roses they brought with them, including those for the four young bridesmaids.

The twelve of them all stood together in front of the main entrance, whilst Sir John walked back over to the coach to help Kathryn as she stepped out into the glorious sunlit courtyard.

Kara meanwhile followed on close behind carrying the bottom of both the silk gown and lace train, to stop them from getting soiled.

Once they had all made their way up the steps into the main entrance hallway, everyone stopped to allow time for Kara to release Kathryn's wedding dress onto the polished stone floor, after which Lady Agnes passed them their bouquets of roses to carry.

They all then set off along the imposing corridors and through the Great Hall, until they reached the Chapel entrance.

Sir John and Kathryn stopped next to two large pedestals of yet more rose pink & white roses placed either side of the door, whilst everyone else apart from the bridesmaids, went inside to take their places.

All around them everything went very quiet, prompting Kathryn to look over nervously at Sir John, who gave her a reassuring smile.

Suddenly the silence was broken, as the old clock inside the Great Hall chimed and virtually at the same time the bells from St Mary's Church in the town centre began to strike, to announce it was 12 noon.

Upon hearing them both, Kathryn became so excited that she wanted to set off up the aisle straight away, but it wasn't time yet and so Sir John gently took hold of her arm to stop her.

Subsequently, once both the clock and church bells had finished, Sir George asked everyone in the Chapel to stand up again.

Next, as the harpist began playing an appropriate wedding melody, he signalled for Kara to bring the other bridesmaids up the aisle with her.

Before setting off however, each of the four young girls were given a small wicker basket full of loose rose petals to carry with them.

They were all obviously delighted to be told they could throw these petals over the floor as they walked towards their mothers, who were waiting for them in the pews.

Kara walked behind the girls and once their baskets were empty, she went over to stand on one side of the altar to wait for Kathryn.

Meanwhile, Sir James stood next to Sir Warwick on the opposite side, where he looked down towards the door entrance, trying to get a first glimpse of his bride.

Sir George now signalled for Sir John to bring Kathryn into the Chapel and at that moment she was clearly ready to sprint up the aisle!

However, it was only a short distance in such a small building and Sir John held her firmly to ensure that she walked slowly enough to always remember this special moment when her Wedding Day was over.

Kathryn took a deep breath as she set off towards the altar and soon reached Sir James, where they looked deeply into each others eyes.

He then moved up even closer towards her for a few of seconds, as he whispered into her ear how beautiful she looked.

Some warm words of welcome were next said by Sir George to the couple, before he took hold of Kathryn's bouquet and passed it over to Kara to look after.

He then gently lifted Kathryn's hand out of Sir John's and symbolically placed it into Sir James' hand, after which Sir John stepped backwards from the altar to join his wife and sons in the pews.

The wedding service continued with a short prayer, a hymn and then a reading, followed by the vows and exchange of rings, after which Sir George announced the couple to be husband and wife, prompting them to give each other a kiss.

This moment brought a loud applause from everyone inside the Chapel as they both shared a huge smile with each other, although Kathryn could not contain herself and also shed a few tears of sheer joy.

Upon seeing these slowly trickle down her perfect face, Sir James removed an initialled silk handkerchief from inside his sleeve and passed it over to Kathryn to wipe her eyes with.

As she took this from him however, she immediately realised it was the same white handkerchief she had tied to his tournament lance on the day they first met and she squeezed his hands even tighter as she leant over to whisper how much she loved him.

It was now time for Sir James & Kathryn to sign the marriage register whilst the harpist played again, after which Kara and Sir Warwick also both signed as the couple's witnesses.

With the official formalities now over there followed another hymn, plus a short prayer and a final blessing, before everyone was invited to be upstanding for the bride & groom, as they prepared themselves to walk back down the aisle as husband and wife.

Everything went relatively quiet for a few moments whilst all of the congregation stood up and the couple turned around to face their family and friends who were there with them.

Kara then handed Kathryn her bouquet back and also spread out her gown's long lace train over the aisle floor behind her.

Upon seeing that everyone was now ready, Sir George signalled over to the two soldiers standing at the Chapel entrance to get their trumpets ready, as he announced in his grandest aristocratic voice,

"Please all join me in joyously welcoming your new bride & groom, Sir James & Lady Kathryn Neville".

As the soldiers started blowing their trumpets, the whole congregation began clapping loudly.

The couple instinctively took hold of each other's hand and slowly set off side-by-side down the short aisle, saying just a few words to as many people as they could whilst they walked along.

As the couple continued past each pew end, they were then joined behind by their family guests in turn, until everyone had left the Chapel.

They all then followed in a procession as they were led through the castle corridors by two knights, one carrying the colours of the House of KLOPTON and the other the House of Salisbury.

Upon reaching the Great Hall they were all escorted to their tables and once in their correct places, Sir George blessed all the food before he invited Sir James & Lady Kathryn to be seated first.

Everyone else then sat down too, whereupon drinks and a sumptuous meal were served as some minstrels played in the background.

A few hours later after they had all finished eating, there were a few short speeches, with the final one being by Sir Salisbury.

He concluded proceedings by saying,

"Both Lady Alice and I wish our son Sir James and his beautiful new wife Lady Kathryn, the greatest of happiness together".

Everyone applauded his words, but instead of sitting down Sir Salisbury remained standing until the clapping had stopped.

He then spoke again, although this time with melancholy in his voice.

"Unfortunately, it is with deep regret I have to announce that both Sir Warwick and I must say farewell to you all, as we now have to leave.

We have a long journey ahead of us and we need to be on our way before any Lancastrian spies discover that we have arrived in Warwick for Sir James' wedding.

I would ask you all to please remain here in the Great Hall after we go, apart from my sons and Sir John who will be accompanying us outside for a few minutes, after which they will come back inside to rejoin you".

At that moment he leant down to kiss his wife Lady Alice and their two girls goodbye, whilst Sir Warwick kissed his mother and sisters too, plus also his wife Lady Anne and their two girls.

Without any further adieu, all the men promptly walked out of the Great Hall and along the corridors until they reached the main courtyard, where their knights were keeping guard.

Upon seeing them appear, the castle lieutenant in charge immediately confirmed that the other knights and soldiers were still patrolling outside the castle walls and also along the town perimeter, but there had been no reported sightings of any Lancastrian forces.

Sir Warwick thanked his lieutenant, after which the men moved closer together so they could talk in private, with Sir Salisbury speaking first.

"We journeyed here last night from Ireland, having travelled there the day before from Calais to meet with Sir Richard of York and discuss our future plans against the Lancastrians.

From the outcome it seems very likely there will soon be further conflict and battles ahead, so everyone must remain vigilant and keep our castles secure until either Sir Warwick or myself sends you notice of our return to England, where we will join up with our other forces.

Unless any one of you have any other pressing matters, we must now depart on our long journey to the west coast, where we have a ship waiting to leave by dawn before we are discovered and from there take us back to Calais".

With nothing else to say, they all shook hands as the lieutenant instructed the squires waiting in the courtyard to bring over the two new thoroughbred horses he had specially selected for Sir Salisbury and Sir Warwick.

Before mounting their horses however, they both knelt down in front of Sir George who said a short prayer for their safe journey, after which they were ready to depart.

The lieutenant signalled for the trumpets to be blown from the ramparts, so that all the other knights and soldiers in the town would know they were leaving the castle and to rejoin them on the road out of Warwick.

Within an instant they had trotted across the drawbridge and were gone. Sir John then led Sir James and Sir George back inside the castle to rejoin their respective families in the Great Hall to continue with the remaining wedding celebrations.

The rest of the afternoon went by far too quickly and much sooner than anyone had expected, the old clock in the Great Hall struck 6.00.

Upon hearing the chimes finish, Sir John stood up and in a jovial voice made a short speech,

"I would once again like to thank Lady Anne and the rest of the Neville family who have been with us today, for their tremendous warmth and hospitality shown to all of my family who have also managed to join us on this wonderful occasion.

It is unfortunately now time for our departure and for us to make our way back home to KLOPTON before dusk.

In doing so however, we will be leaving behind in Warwick, one of our most treasured family possessions with Sir James for safe keeping.

Yes, I am talking about my beloved niece Lady Kathryn!".

Upon hearing this Kathryn again shed a tear of happiness, prompting Sir James to stand up and respond.

"I know that I also speak for my wife when I say how we cannot thank you and your family enough Sir John, for all the kindness and love you have shown Kathryn during her time with you in KLOPTON, and also for the way you have welcomed me so warmly into your family".

At that moment everyone stood up and after another round of applause, they all started walking around the room to shake hands with each other as they exchanged their farewells.

As soon as they had finished, Sir John & Lady Agnes' family group left the Great Hall along the corridor to the courtyard, where the coach, horses and soldiers were waiting for their return journey to KLOPTON.

Lady Alice, Lady Anne and their family group followed outside next where they too stopped and waited on the main entrance steps, until Sir James & Lady Kathryn appeared for one last farewell that day.

Once the KLOPTON cavalcade was ready, Sir Thomas led them all out of the courtyard.

Kara gave Kathryn & Sir James one last frenetic wave through the coach window, whilst Kane was riding on horseback from where he gave them both his best sword salute.

After they had crossed over the castle drawbridge, Lady Anne walked the newly married couple over to Guy's Tower which was to be exclusively theirs for the next couple of weeks whilst they stayed in Warwick.

She then gave Sir James the key to the tower's entrance door and said goodnight, before heading off back to the Great Hall again.

Once the couple were inside the tower alone, they locked the main door behind them and for the first time that day they were alone together.

This immediately prompted them to kiss each other, before Kathryn with a twinkle in her eye eventually spoke first,

"I hope you do not think that I have forgotten your birthday present dear husband, as there will be a special surprise waiting for you to unwrap in our bed chamber, although you will have to stay here in the sitting room for a few minutes longer until I call you upstairs".

They both gave each other a huge smile, as Kathryn made her way slowly up the staircase in her wedding gown, whilst James watched on for a few moments more until she was out of sight, whereupon he fetched a couple of drinks from the cabinet and nervously waited to hear her soft voice again ....

Chapter 22 : **Desolation of Battle**

The following week a messenger arrived at Warwick Castle with sealed letters from Sir Salisbury and Sir Warwick for their wives, which both confirmed that they had arrived safely in Calais and all was well, much to the grateful relief of Lady Alice, Lady Anne and their children.
Meanwhile, the newlyweds Sir James & Lady Kathryn were enjoying married life in and around the castle, as they explored the grounds along the walls and River Avon with a good level of privacy.

They would also occasionally wander through the bustling Warwick town centre to browse for items to buy from the shops or visit the magnificent St Mary's Church for prayer, although they would always have a couple of soldiers discreetly following them from a distant to make sure that they were safe.

When Sir James was away scouting for any Lancastrian troop movements however, either Lady Alice or Lady Anne would usually keep Lady Kathryn company, occasionally with their young daughters who now enjoyed playing with their new 'Aunt' ever since they were her bridesmaids.

Back over in KLOPT0N, Kara & Kane often helped out around the estate. In their spare time they would also be joined by John and all three of them would ride off into Stratford-upon-Avon town together for extra security, especially when the local market was taking place and thieves were about.

On other occasions they would visit one of the small villages and taverns further out in the countryside, although being mindful of the dangerous times they were living in, they would also wear their KLOPT0N armour when undertaking such journeys.
This included Kara too, who now had a suit of sturdy but light-weight armour with a helmet specially made for her, whilst she also carried a good sized sword so any potential attacker would not realise that she was a woman and be much less likely to confront her.

John was quite surprised how well Kara could yield such a sword and also wear armour whilst riding a large horse, that he was keen to join them both on one of their jaunts away from the estate and test their sword skills against each other in a secluded woodland duelling contest. Kane & Kara already knew each other's fighting abilities very well, so they were pleased to let John also take part in one of their private duels, especially when he quickly learnt to his discomfort not to underestimate Kara again!

It was the end of June before some significant news arrived by messenger from Calais that Sir Warwick, Sir Salisbury and Sir Edward York would very shortly be arriving back in England with their troops.

When they subsequently landed at the port of Sandwich, they marched on to London, where Sir Salisbury took charge of organising a siege of **The Tower of London** on **2nd July 1460** after the main Lancastrian supporters had taken refuge behind the heavily fortified stone walls.
Once the siege was secure, Sir Warwick and Sir Edward were joined by Lord Fauconberg and they marched up north with their troops to face the Lancastrian army waiting for them.

Meanwhile, back in Warwick Castle more soldiers were being organised to head off east and meet up with the troops, whilst Sir James was trying to console a very sad Lady Kathryn as she dutifully helped him put on his battle armour in readiness for him to set off with the soldiers.
As soon as he was ready, she held him tight for a moment and then said softly,
"Please come back to me safely James, as I cannot imagine living without you should you not return".
He replied to her in the gentlest of voices,
"I will never willingly leave you Kathryn, but if something was to ever happen to me in battle then you must promise that you will try and find happiness again with another, as you are far too young and beautiful to mourn for me forever".

His traumatic words prompted a tearful response,
"I could never love another man and you also have to come back to me for a second reason as I am now carrying our child".
Upon hearing this momentous news, Sir James was overcome with emotion and struggled to know what to say, but after a few moments he took her in his arms instead and they kissed passionately.
"When did you find out?" he eventually asked,
"Only yesterday" she replied, which prompted them both to give each other a beaming smile of joy.

Suddenly however, this beautiful moment was ended abruptly, as outside in the courtyard a trumpet sounded and they both knew that it was now time for Sir James to join the other soldiers.
They held each other by the hand as they walked slowly outside to where the troops were waiting and after one last quick kiss goodbye, Sir James mounted his horse.

Upon seeing that everyone was ready, the lieutenant in charge signalled for the trumpet to be blown again, after which he raised his arm and led them all out of the courtyard across the castle drawbridge.

Lady Kathryn could not stop the tears rolling down her cheeks as she just stood there watching the last soldiers leave, whereupon both Lady Anne and Lady Alice walked over to take her inside with them to the drawing room for company.

A week later they received news that the **Battle of Northampton** started on **10th July 1460** between the Yorkist forces and the Lancastrian army led by King Henry VI.
The heavy rain that day had fortuitously rendered the Lancastrian cannons ineffective and the Yorkist troops were able to breach their lines after their commander Lord Grey of Ruthin defected.

The Lancastrian army was comprehensively defeated and their leaders the Duke of Buckingham, the Earl of Shrewsbury, Lord Beaumont and Lord Egremont were all killed.
With the battle over, Sir Edward York and Sir Warwick captured King Henry VI and returned with him to London to take control of the Government and also end the siege of The Tower of London.

A few weeks later Sir Richard York arrived from Chester and entered Parliament to try and claim the throne, but without sufficient support he instead accepted an Act of Accord whereby he would govern as Lord Protector of England until King Henry's death, when he or one of his heirs would become King.

News of the Yorkist victory was received at Warwick Castle with great relief and when Sir James returned a few weeks later with some of the soldiers, Lady Kathryn was overjoyed to see him and even happier when he told her that he was not injured.
Later that evening whilst helping to bathe James however, she saw that he had a few deep cuts and large bruises over his body.

Although she tried to be brave as she tendered to these for him, he could see the anguish etched across her face and took her in his arms as he told her that she must not worry about his battle wounds since they would soon heal.
Being back together as their baby grew inside of her however, was much more important and a time of great happiness for them both, as they held each other in a loving embrace and kissed.

After a period of rest in the castle for Sir James to fully recover, Lady Kathryn wrote to KLOPT0N House to tell them the wonderful news that she was pregnant, upon receipt of which Lady Agnes immediately invited her and Sir James over to stay with them and join in the family celebrations.

Arrangements were quickly made for the following week and it was agreed that soldiers from Warwick Castle would escort them for the first half of their journey, after which soldiers from KLOPTON House would take over for the remaining distance.

The day soon came and they set off from Warwick in the coach accompanied by a lieutenant and two dozen soldiers, until as arranged, they met up along the road to Stratford-upon-Avon with the KLOPTON soldiers, who were led by three knights in full armour bearing the red & black family crest.

Lady Kathryn was disappointed that Kara was not also there with them to greet her and she remained in the coach with Sir James, as two of the knights rode forward to meet the lieutenant and take responsibility for escort duty on the rest of the journey.
Meanwhile, the third horse rider rode directly over to the coach instead and began speaking to them both as the visor on the helmet was lifted to reveal that it was Kara!

She was so happy to see Kara and replied how wonderful she looked in her armour, whilst Sir James was so taken aback that he was initially lost for words.
Kane and John soon joined them and after a few exchanges, they told the coachmen it was time for them to go and with that they set off along the road to KLOPTON, whilst the other soldiers returned to Warwick.

Lady Kathryn stayed with them in the Manor House for most of the next few months as the baby started to show.
Sir James was frequently away checking on the Lancastrian troop movements, with John often joining him as they became good friends.
When Sir James was not there, Kara and Lady Agnes both took great delight in making a huge fuss of Lady Kathryn and as Christmas began to get closer, they used this as a happy excuse to start buying numerous baby items such as a wooden cot and pure linen sheets, to put in the bedroom in readiness for the birth.

Sadly however, these joyous times did not last much longer, as the week before Christmas several hundred soldiers arrived from Warwick Castle with their lieutenant to advise Sir John that final preparations were now under way for a battle at the end of the month against a Lancastrian army gathering in West Yorkshire.

The urgency of their journey was preceded by the **Battle of Worksop** on **16th December 1460** when some Lancastrian soldiers attacked and defeated a small section of Sir Richard York's army, which had become separated from the main force on their way to York.

As Sir Warwick had stayed in London to maintain control over the city, this meant that Sir James was to leave KLOPTON straight away and join their father Sir Salisbury at Sandal Castle instead, where he had arrived with Sir Richard York and his son Sir Edmund of Rutland on 21st December.

Whilst the servants quickly arranged some drinks for the soldiers, Kara went with Sir James to find Lady Kathryn and tell her what was happening, which they both knew would be very distressing for her to hear.
Thankfully, she seemed to handle this news quite well and as they held each other tightly she told him that he had to come home safely, not only for her sake but also for that of their unborn baby.

As they kissed each other goodbye she could not stop a tear from rolling down her cheek, but wanting to appear brave she wiped this away before he saw it, as he gently pulled himself away and told her how much he loved her, to which she replied the same.
Sir James then mounted his horse and with one last look back at Lady Kathryn, he turned around and rode off out of the courtyard with the other soldiers.
Kara quickly walked over to comfort her as she stood there so forlorn, just watching as Sir James disappeared into the distance.

It was nearly a week before a message was delivered from Warwick Castle informing Sir John that the **Battle of Wakefield** had started on **30th December 1460**, but there were no more details at that time.
After telling the whole family what the brief message said, all they could do for now was continue looking after Lady Kathryn whilst they waited for more news.

A couple of days later a sole knight arrived early in the morning at KLOPTON, where he immediately asked to speak to Sir John in private.
It was the worst possible news and Sir John straight away fetched Lady Agnes from her room to join him, before going off together to find Kara and Lady Kathryn who were reading in the study.

Meanwhile, Kane and John had been outside in the stables helping groom their horses in readiness for a planned ride that afternoon, but upon hearing of the knight's arrival they quickly returned to the Manor House and soon everyone was together.

Sir John spoke with quite a somber voice as he introduced the visiting knight.
"This is Sir Stephen from Warwick Castle who has just informed me of the most distressing news.

203

Both Sir Richard York and his son Sir Edward have been killed at the Battle of Wakefield, where their troops were defeated by the combined forces of a large Lancastrian army led by Sir Henry Somerset and Sir Henry Northumberland.

Tragically, Sir Richard Salisbury was executed, but not before both his sons Sir Thomas and Sir James were also killed whilst valiantly trying to protect their father from being captured".

Upon hearing this Lady Kathryn stood up from her chair visibly shaking and with one of the most heart wrenching of saddest voices ever heard, she cried out uncontrollably,

"No, this cannot be true, you must be mistaken?

James promised me and our unborn baby that he would return home safely to be with us both!".

After a brief moment of quiet, Sir Stephen produced a white handkerchief from inside his pocket and as he passed it over, he replied "I am truly sorry Lady Kathryn for your tragic loss, but with Sir James' last breath to the soldier who found him mortally wounded on the battlefield, he handed over this handkerchief bearing your initials, together with his dying wish that it be retuned to you with all his eternal love".

Lady Kathryn recognised it straight away, but as she held the silk handkerchief up close to her face she saw that it was splattered with some dried blood.

Upon realising this must belong to Sir James, she became so overcome with grief that she collapsed in front of Kara, who thankfully caught her before she could hit the floor.

Kane immediately went over to help his sister and after lifting Lady Kathryn into his arms, he carried her upstairs to her bedroom followed by Kara and Lady Agnes, who both stayed to look after her.

Once Kane had returned back downstairs, Sir Stephen shared some more distressing information with the three of them, which he had not wanted to discuss in front of the ladies.

"Sadly, I have also been given the unenviable task of telling you that none of the Salisbury or York deceased families bodies will ever be available for formal burial.

Sir Richard Salisbury and Sir Thomas plus Sir Richard York and Sir Edmund were all either killed or captured and then barbarically beheaded, with their heads impaled on the gates of York whilst their remains thrown into the animal waste pits.

Sir James' body was however left on the battlefield where he died with the other soldiers and their bodies devoured by wild animals, whilst their remains left to rot.

In the circumstances, Sir Richard Warwick has given instructions for a private Neville family memorial service to be held inside the Chapel at Warwick Castle, until appropriate family tombs have been built and suitable resting places organised at a later date, when a full church service and mass can be held.

Unfortunately, he will not be able to attend this Chapel service himself as he must remain in London for the foreseeable future due to further upcoming battles against the Lancastrian forces and therefore Sir George Warwick who will be taking the service, will also arrange the date as soon as possible".

After a moment's silence, Sir John responded in a very solemn voice,
"This is the most horrendous news indeed and please pass on all of our deepest condolences to Sir Richard, Lady Anne and Lady Alice.
Please be sure to also let us know when the date for the memorial service has been decided so we can all attend",
after which he shook hands with Sir Stephen before asking Kane and John to escort him back outside to where his horse was waiting and bid him farewell.

The next couple of weeks were agonisingly difficult for Kathryn, who's only real solace was she was carrying James' baby inside her.
She also no longer wished to be called by her title anymore whilst around her family, but would wait until after the memorial service was over before deciding whether to use this again, since her husband had gone forever and she could never even be buried beside his body.

Over this period, everyone in the Manor House took it in turns to keep Kathryn company and try to comfort her.
It was during this time that John told her how he and Sir James had become very good friends, so much so he asked John to promise he would help look after her and his unborn baby if he ever failed to return back home from battle.

The day of the memorial service day on the 14th January soon arrived and after a light breakfast in each of their own rooms, all the family got suitably dressed in mourning wear and met downstairs in the hallway entrance.
All of the ladies wore full length formal black dresses and thick coats due to it being a cold winter's morning, whilst Kathryn also covered her head with a black veil made from fine embroidered lace as she did not want anyone to see her cry.

Meanwhile, all of the men were wearing full ceremonial suits of black armour including swords and everyone stood solemnly as Sir John took Kathryn by her arm and escorted her to the coach waiting outside.

The two of them were quickly followed by Kara, Lady Agnes and Sheila into the black coach, whilst Kane and John were last out of the House.
Once all the ladies were settled, Sir John signalled over to the lieutenant in charge of their soldier escort and they all mounted their black horses in readiness for departure.
A single trumpet was then blown and Sir John led the entourage off, whilst all the estate workers lined the courtyard driveway quietly with their heads bowed.

The cavalcade continued along the main road through Stratford-upon-Avon and then into Warwick, where they could see the castle's flags blowing in the wind at half mast.
A few hundred local residents also waited in silence to show their respect to the KLOPTON family as they arrived for the memorial service.

Once through the outer wall and onto the castle driveway, they were met by a couple of dozen soldiers all standing to attention.
As the coach slowly passed by in front of them, they each bowed their head as they drew their sword in turn and knelt down with its point touching the ground to signify the cross of Christ.

The procession entered the main courtyard and stopped in front of the castle steps, where Sir George Neville was waiting for them all in his ceremonial Bishop robe.
Upon seeing him Kathryn could no longer contain herself, as she took hold of Kara's hands for comfort and sobbed uncontrollably,
"It has been only ten months since James and I were at this very same Chapel getting married.
I miss him so much Kara and I can't see my life continuing without him".

Kara replied in her gentlest of voices,
"Kathryn, you must be strong for James's baby inside of you and once today is over, it will be less than two months before you bring a beautiful new life into this world, which we will all help you to look after".
Meanwhile, Lady Agnes called for one of the servants to bring some drinking water over and they all stayed in the coach together for a few minutes longer to give Kathryn time to regain her composure.

After a short while Sir George walked over to the coach to fetch everyone inside, but Kathryn would not let go of Kara and so the two ladies slowly walked to the Chapel together.
Once there, they sat down in the pew at the front next to Lady Agnes, whilst the three Klopton men sat in the pew just behind them.
On the opposite side of the aisle sat Lady Alice with her two daughters and son Sir John Neville Montagu, whilst Lady Anne and her two daughters sat in the pew behind them, all dressed in black.

The three ladies' handmaids Sheila, Jane and Julie all sat together, whilst a few local dignitaries and close friends of the Neville family sat in the remaining pews.

Unfortunately, not all of the family members could make it to the Chapel memorial, but instead sent messages of condolences and confirmed that they would be attending the Church service and full funeral mass at a later date.

Sir George gave a very moving memorial service, whilst Sir John Montagu said a few meaningful words and read out a personal message from their brother Sir Richard, who had already advised them that sadly he would not be able to make it that day.

These were followed by speeches from both Sir John KLOPTON and afterwards by his son John, who spoke about the close friendship he had built up with Sir James and how he would always talk about how much he loved Lady Kathryn and the happiness she brought him.

These heartfelt words unsurprisingly made Kathryn shed a few more tears, but this time she gently dabbed them with the white handkerchief she carried inside her sleeve.

This simple piece of embroidered silk material meant so much to both James and her during their short time together and remained very precious to her.

Warwick Castle private Chapel

Once the service was over Sir George led everyone out of the Chapel and down the corridor to the library room, where they all talked for a couple of hours until it was time for the KLOPTON family to return home.

After they had all exchanged their most solemn farewells outside in the courtyard, Sir John led the entourage out of the castle grounds and back to the Manor House.
Kara took Kathryn straight away up to her bedroom to get some rest, after what had been a very stressful and tiring day for her.

As the weeks passed by and the new baby inside Kathryn kept growing, everyone took it in turns to keep her company to ensure that she was focused on the impending birth and also eating enough for two.
One of her most frequent visitors was John, who was determined to keep his promise to his late friend and would sit with Kathryn for long periods, retelling the stories of their adventures together whilst out riding across Warwickshire and checking the Lancastrian positions.

Meanwhile, Sir Richard Warwick and Sir Edward York were both busy plotting revenge for the death of their fathers at the Battle of Wakefield, whilst also making plans to not only retain but enhance their present positions, by keeping the Lancastrian armies apart from each other.
Accordingly, whilst Sir Richard stayed to protect London for the Yorkists, Sir Edward took the sizeable force he had amassed at Wigmore Castle in Herefordshire, to engage the Lancastrian army led by Sir Owen Tudor at the **Battle of Mortimer's Cross** on **2nd February 1461.**

As dawn broke, both armies started watching the spectacular winter sunrise whilst they readied themselves for the start of the battle, but were amazed when they saw three identical Suns rise up side-by-side in unison on the horizon, instead of just the usual single Sun.
This parhelion of nature also made the morning sky and clouds glow even redder than usual for that time of the day.

Sir Edward York convinced all his forces that this unique apparition was in fact the Most Holy Trinity of God, who was there with them as a sign of their forthcoming victory over the enemy.
With this inspirational message he roused the courage of his men and led them to an overwhelming defeat of the Lancastrian forces, including the beheading of Sir Owen.

Upon being told about the Yorkists' success and the early dawn rising of the three Suns, both Kane & Kara remembered seeing a sketch drawing of such a unique astral occurrence within the KLOPTON 'L' scroll, which they had found inside the rock face passageway alcove and opened on their visit during the last full lunar eclipse.

208

At that time they were both unaware of its meaning, since neither of them could decipher the parchment's medieval text, nor had they encountered such an unusual phenomenon before during any of their previous journeys.

They agreed therefore, that this parhelion must have been a sign from across time, to reaffirm there would be three more battles before the Sun never rose again over the House of Lancaster.
Instead, the Sun would then rise over a future era of the House of York, whose family was destined to take the place of the Lancastrians.

Kara also recollected from having read one of William Shakespeare's plays whilst they were living in the 20th Century, that the Bard wrote about King Richard IV and in Part 3 how this included details of the parhelion sighting at the beginning of the battle of Mortimer's Cross.

Kane too had studied English history whilst at school and in particular the Wars of the Roses, so much so he knew there would soon be a second **Battle of St Albans** on **17th February 1461**, when a Yorkist army led by Sir Richard Warwick would seek to prevent Lancastrian forces led by Queen Margaret from entering London.

This battle was won by the Lancastrians and King Henry released from captivity, but despite their victory the soldiers reputation for pillaging made them unwelcome by the local people, who blocked the city gates shut to keep them out.
Having also lost a significant number of troops at the previous battle of Mortimer's Cross, Queen Margaret decided to turn her Lancastrian forces back north instead of trying to enter.

Subsequently, both Sir Richard Warwick and Sir Edward York returned to the city together and on 4th March 1461 seized the throne of England for King Edward IV, as the first Monarch of the House of York.

This claim however, was fiercely contested by the House of Lancaster until the decisive two day bloody **Battle of Ferrybridge & Towton** on **28th & 29th March 1461**, which was eventually won by the Yorkists after many thousands of soldiers were killed on both sides.

This overwhelming victory resulted in Sir Edward York being affirmed as the new lawful monarch of England through the Right of Conquest in place of the former King Henry, who fled to exile in Scotland.

Chapter 23 : **Dangerous Foes**

Neither Kane nor Kara had discussed the future with Sir John in order to prevent any possible impact on their history, but unless there was a full lunar eclipse before the end of March they would both be trapped in the House of York era, as there was no KLOPTON 'Y' key available for them to continue their journey through time with.

Furthermore, what were they going to do about looking after Kathryn and her new baby which was due in March, especially now her husband Sir James was dead?

The following morning Kane & Kara went to see Sir John about these matters and although they could not tell him everything, he already knew they had arrived two years earlier in January 1459 and that the next red Moon would be rising soon to allow them access through the cavern waters again.

The three of them sat down together in Sir John's private room so they would not be interrupted and he spoke before either of the twins had the chance to say anything.

"So what are your plans for both Kathryn and yourselves when the next red Moon appears in the sky over KLOPTON?"

They all smiled at each other and Kane replied,

"We were told by our parents when we first set off through the red cavern waters at the age of sixteen, that it was our destiny to complete a journey through KLOPTON time and although this is still our intention, our main concern for now is Kathryn's wellbeing and also that of her new baby".

Sir John responded,

"You both need have no concerns whatsoever if Kathryn wishes to stay with us and you have to leave, since we will be delighted to care for her as one of our own and let her live here with us for as long as she wants. However, it appears you have not yet discussed this with Kathryn, as from what I understand she has already made her mind up about what she wants and I think you may be quite surprised by her decision".

Upon hearing this, Kara could not contain herself and in her quite often impatient manner asked,

"Please tell us Sir John, what is it we do not know?".

After her candid interruption he continued,

"Kathryn has told both Lady Agnes and I, that with Sir James gone forever she no longer wishes to remain here without him and instead would prefer to travel onwards in time with you through the cavern waters to your next destination.

To undertake such a journey she must do so whilst the baby is still inside her, so she can protect it through the precarious red waters.

If her child is born before the red Moon appears however, then they will both have to stay here with us until the child turns sixteen.

In either circumstance, I have been told that my son John has fallen for Kathryn and she too has developed feelings for him, but as she is still in mourning they both accept that it is too soon after Sir James' death for them to take any new relationship forward too quickly at this time".

Neither of the twins knew how to react to this unexpected news and after a moment's silence, it was Kane who spoke next,

"May I please ask you Sir John, what are your and Lady Agnes thoughts about such an arrangement?".

After a glance over to his wife, Sir John replied,

"Kathryn is a lovely girl and the tragic circumstances of her husband's early death before the birth of their first baby was so cruelly unjust, that we both agree she deserves someone new to fill her life with love and happiness again, as soon as she is ready.

As for John, we have never seen him so intense about anyone else before and he has matured so much during his time away, that we know he will be a very loyal husband to Kathryn and also a wonderful father to her baby, which he will be honoured to bring up as his own".

Kara responded enthusiastically to what she had just heard,

"I genuinely believe that Kathryn & John will be perfect for each other and I am so pleased for them both, but especially for Kathryn.

Although she loved James very deeply, I know she has ample space in her heart for John too and will come to love him just as much, once she has finished her period of grieving".

Kane then added,

"Yes, I too agree that Kathryn & John will be ideally suited and I am also delighted to therefore give their future union my full blessing",

to which Sir John replied,

"Everything is agreed then and I will leave it to both of you to let them know the good news!".

A couple of weeks later, after Kane & Kara had spoken to Kathryn & John about their future plans, the second **Battle of St Albans** took place and this reminded them all yet again that time was running out if they were going to be able to leave that era together.

The following days passed by and they were beginning to give up hope, when suddenly one morning Kara ran into Kane's room wearing only her thick winter night robe, in which she jumped onto his bed to wake him up.

Blurry eyed and half asleep, Kane asked her what had happened, in response to which Kara did not speak but instead simply showed him that the rose pink crystals contained within both of her KLOPTON key pendants were glowing red.

"It's time!" uttered Kane excitedly, as he immediately checked the colour of the crystals in his 'K' signet ring, before grabbing his night shirt and stood up to hold Kara in his arms whilst he said,
"Let's both get dressed as quickly as we can and if you fetch Kathryn whilst I get John, we'll meet up in the dining room to find out which letter the dial on the wooden KLOPTON clock is pointing to".
Kara nodded her head in agreement and after giving each other a quick kiss, she was out of his bedroom door as quickly as she had come in.

The tall clock in the hallway struck 8.00 as all four of them entered the dining room together, where they were surprised to find Sir John & Lady Agnes already waiting for them, sitting in a pair of armchairs next to the fireplace mantlepiece.
Before any of them had the chance to speak, Sir John knew exactly what it was they wanted to know and without any hesitation he said out loud enough for them all to hear him say,
"The silver dial on the KLOPTON clock is pointing to the letter 'T' and do any of you know where this new passageway in time through the cavern will lead to?".

Kane & Kara looked at each other unsure how best to answer this question, whereupon sensing their hesitation Sir John spoke again directly to the twins.
"I know what you both told me when you first arrived at our House about Kathryn's past is true, but I have also since realised that neither of you are originally from the era you said you were.
You need not worry though, as I fully understand why you could not reveal to me your true birth timeline, since I gave my son John the same instructions as your parents gave you, before he too left home through the cavern waters all those years ago".

Sir John did though have one specific question he wanted an answer to, as he continued,
"I would like to know however, if you can please tell both Lady Agnes and myself, whether this new era in time to which you all intend to journey will be any better than where you are here with us now?".

Kane answered,
"We are both very sorry that we could not disclose our true origin to you when we first arrived here in KLOPTON and we greatly appreciate that you understand and accept our reasons why.

What we can tell you is that the letter 'T' refers to a very colourful and exciting period in English history spanning more than a hundred years.

Although this era does include some difficult times, overall there will be many advantages such as discoveries in medicine and science, which make this future destination a much safer and more productive place for all of us".

Sir John replied,

"Thank you Kane for sharing this revelation with us".

He then turned to speak to his son,

"John my son, with Kathryn's baby due very soon, your journey through the cavern passage together during the full red Moon will be even more dangerous than usual.

Although the red spring waters will help protect them both, we know you will do everything you can to keep them safe especially whilst swimming in the underwater current.

Your mother and I are so both immensely proud of you and we wish you every future happiness with Kathryn in your new era together and although we will miss you immensely once you have gone, we hope that one day we may meet up yet again".

John hesitated for few moments before replying,

"Dearest father & mother, you have both been the most wonderful parents and please be assured that it is my every desire and intention to devote myself to Kathryn and her new baby once we all reach our new destination in KLOPTON time.

Kane & Kara will also be with us of course and just as you welcomed them into your home, our future relatives living in the Manor House will no doubt look after us too, although they will never be able to replace the love we have shared during our time together".

At this juncture it was Lady Agnes' turn to shed a tear as she walked over to hold John tightly, whilst Sir John went over to give Kathryn a gentle hug and wish her well.

Not wishing to interrupt this tender family moment, Kane & Kara made their way out of the dining room to get something to eat.

They also knew there were still many things for them to sort out in readiness for their departure later on that day, after the red Moon had started to rise in the sky over the KLOPTON estate.

It was not too long before John & Kathryn went to join them, after which they agreed the girls would help each other sort out their possessions needed for the journey.

Meanwhile, the men would go and check that the passageway was intact, especially as no-one had seen Edmund for over a year since the ambush on the road to Warwick.

Kane and John finished first and after returning to their rooms to put their armour on, they met again outside with Sir John, who was waiting there with both his lieutenants and forty soldiers all dressed in armour.

Turning to his first lieutenant, Sir John instructed that he kept a guard around the Manor House using half the soldiers for at least the next twenty-four hours, ensuring Lady Agnes, Kara, Kathryn and Shiela were protected at all times.
In addition, the outbuildings were to be regularly searched by the squires, who were to be armed and given the task of patrolling the estate in groups of at least four for their own safety.
Sir John was being very cautious after his previous bloody encounter with Edmund and this time wanted to be ready for a fight if necessary.

He then turned to his second lieutenant and together with Kane, John and the other twenty soldiers, they all rode off towards the Oat Hill woodland covert next to the edge of the overgrown rock face.
Once there, they all stopped and dismounted to tether their horses to the trees close by the field stream, where four soldiers would remain to build a fire and light some wooden torches needed to explore the darkest areas along the inside passageway.
Everyone else slowly made their way over to the jagged rock face which was obscured by thick bramble bushes and wild shrubs, so much that Sir John ordered his lieutenant to take half of the soldiers to the other side of this thick overgrowth and approach from that direction instead.

Within a short time they all reached the hidden crevice together, where they discovered that not only had the ground in front of the rock face been flattened recently, but there was a large boulder blocking the gap to the entrance.
Sir John immediately ordered two soldiers to fetch some lit torches, whilst the lieutenant and six other soldiers were ordered to go back around to the front of the thick overgrowth and create a defensive perimeter to protect them from any potential attack.

The remaining soldiers pushed the boulder out of the away and into the thick bramble, after which John and Kane were first to enter once they had removed their armour, due to the crevice gap being too narrow for them to squeeze through whilst wearing it all.
Once inside, their armour was passed back to them piece by piece to put on again as quickly as they could, but upon realising that this was going to be difficult for him due to his larger size, Sir John decided to stay on guard outside for now and let the other slimmer soldiers enter instead.
By the time the two soldiers had returned with the burning torches, all the others apart from Sir John were inside with their armour back on and the torches were passed to them one at a time.

It was very quiet inside the passageway except for the sound of running water somewhere up ahead.

Although now partly lit by the torches and a few red crystals sparkling in the rock walls around them, this extra light helped prevent any element of surprise they may have encountered by a possible foe waiting inside.

With John and Kane both taking the lead, the soldiers drew their swords in case they were needed and slowly followed them in single file down the passageway.

They soon reached the glowing red stream running down alongside the rocks at its edge, which they were all told was very dangerous and to keep their distance away from.

They all carried on walking just a bit further inside until they reached a rock wall, where the red water stopped up ahead.

Meanwhile, the passageway veered off into the entrance of a small cave, which Kane and John had both seen when they first arrived nearly two years earlier.

Along the side of this wall Kane could make out amongst all the sparkling crystals lit up by their torches, a silver edged crystal lined hexagon with the empty shape of the letter 'L' at its centre.

Most of the soldiers reacted hesitantly to encountering such strange surroundings, but no sooner had they began talking amongst themselves about what they could see, when they heard some ominous growling sounds coming from somewhere amongst the dark shadows at the back of the cave.

"Quiet" ordered John, but after a short pause he added,

"Quickly everyone, create a tight defensive curved line formation and be ready to fight whatever enemy there is waiting for us inside this cave".

The growling noises started to get much more menacing and in the flickering light to the front of them, they could now see at least half a dozen sets of menacing blood-shot eyes and pointed white fangs moving slowly ever closer.

Their foe soon appeared from out of the shadows, whereupon John and Kane realised they were up against a pack of large wild dogs which had clearly been starved and were desperate for food, with the men evidently being their next intended meal!

Without any further hesitation the vicious hounds attacked, but they were too weak and no match for trained soldiers who hacked them down with comparative ease until they were all dead.

Cautiously, but with their swords still drawn and a few scrapes to show from the short fight, the soldiers all spread out in pairs around the inside perimeter of the cave with torches, to check if there were any more animals or even some people hiding within the crevice shadows.

Thankfully, all they found were some remains of what appeared to be a couple of partly devoured human carcasses.

Whilst Kane returned to the entrance to tell Sir John what had just happened inside, John ordered the soldiers to move all of the dead animal and human remains outside the passageway entrance to the woodland, so they could be disposed off on the fire.

Sir John instructed his lieutenant to join them once John had also arrived at the entrance and after a short discussion, all four of them agreed that the wild dogs must have been trapped inside the passageway by the boulder and stayed inside the cave after being lured there with some human bait.

The animals would then be left with stream water only to go hungry and attack whichever KLOPTON family member entered the cave next.

The despicable person who attempted this brutal plan must presumably have been Edmund and everyone on the estate was to remain at their most vigilant for the sign of any strangers over the next thirty-six hours, especially whilst the red Moon was overhead in the night sky.

Sir John left the lieutenant in charge of guarding both the passageway entrance and the woodland to ensure that the horses were kept secure and the fire burning at all times, with a supply of wooden torches also made ready to be lit.

Six of the soldiers accompanied the three of them back to the Manor House and then returned shortly afterwards with some fresh meat from the kitchen for the other soldiers' meals.

As soon as Sir John arrived back at the Manor House, he immediately went to review all of the security arrangements with his other lieutenant, whilst Kane and John went straight into the lounge to check on Kara and Kathryn, who were talking with Lady Agnes.

The two men told them all what had happened that morning, but assured the ladies that with all the extra soldiers protecting the estate they would be perfectly safe.

Furthermore, once the four of them had left through the underwater cavern that night and closed the passage behind them, everyone in the Manor House should no longer be in any danger from Edmund as the KLOPTON keys would have gone and he would have to flee Stratford-upon-Avon in order to avoid being captured.

The day sped by quickly and it was soon time for the four of them to make they way to the passageway before it started getting too dark and the full red Moon rose higher over the horizon.

Also, as Kathryn was now quite large with her baby due, they wanted to cross the fields slowly, with both John and Kara fastening their horses to hers to prevent any unexpected stumble or jolt during the short ride.

Fortunately, Kathryn had completed the journey through the stream and cavern once before so she knew what to expect.

Carrying a baby this time however, made the underwater section a lot more daunting and it was agreed that John and Kara would both swim with her through the strong current.

Meanwhile, Kara passed the two KLOPTON pendant keys she held over to Kane, so he could open and close the various locks whilst she helped look after Kathryn.

Once all four of them had finished hugging and saying fond farewells to Lady Agnes, they each mounted their horses, whereupon Sir John together with another dozen soldiers, escorted them from the courtyard. They soon reached the rock face without any mishaps on the way and dismounted in a small clearing near to the entrance.

Kane removed four large woven bags he had tied onto another horse, which contained all of their armour and other personal possessions they needed to carry with them through the stream and cavern.

Sir John had also removed his armour this time and slowly squeezed through the crevice gap first, before being followed by his lieutenant who brought lit torches with him.

After Kane had entered next, the four bags were passed to him one at a time through the narrow entrance, until he had hold of all of them.

The lieutenant passed him a lit torch and the men carried the bags down the passageway to the rock wall, where the stream was glowing red and the crystal hexagon 'L' key device was located.

In the centre of the cave was a pile of logs which had been built by the soldiers earlier that day and Kane decided to light this as it was still dark and damp inside.

The soldiers had also left some extra wooden torches, although these would be of no use once they were underwater, but thankfully by the time the four of them set off, the red Moon would have risen overhead and the whole main cavern brightly illuminated by thousands of red sparkling crystals and glowing stream water.

A short time later Sir John went further down the passageway with Kara, Kathryn and John to join Kane, whereupon they all encouraged Kathryn to sit down so she could have a short rest before the next stage of their journey.

As it would not be safe however, for the lieutenant to remain at the far end of the passageway once the red steam water levels increased, he went back to the crevice entrance to put his armour on again and help maintain guard with his soldiers, until Sir John returned.

217

It was not much longer before the crystals and stream water started glowing even brighter red and they all knew that the full lunar eclipse of the Moon had risen directly over KLOPT0N.

The time had now come for each of them to say their final farewell to Sir John, but with everything having already been said that morning between them, this was nothing more than a last quick kiss on the cheek with the girls and a handshake between the men.

Kara and John helped Kathryn climb down the rocks along the edge of the passageway into the stream and once there with her, they all watched on as Kane placed the 'L' key in the palm of his right hand directly in front of the crystal lined hexagon device, where it flew off into the empty 'L' letter key hole in the rock wall.

Kane waited a few moments before taking hold of the silver key stud on top of the 'L' pendant and turned it anti-clockwise, whereupon they all heard a loud thud from somewhere in the depths of the stream water beneath them.

They all knew that the gap in the rock wall had now opened and by doing so would provide them with the underwater passage they needed to enter the main cavern via the strong current this created.

Kara and John both took hold of Kathryn, as the three of them started swimming along with the stream, until they all dived together below the surface into the underwater current and let themselves be pulled through the large gap in the rock wall.

Thankfully, they all soon reached the main cavern, where they resurfaced as quickly as they could to help Kathryn wade out of the water and onto a raised area of drier ground, where she could rest.

John then waded back into the water close to where the current was flowing to wait for Kane and the four bags of their possessions he had hopefully managed to bring through with him.

Meanwhile, back in the passageway, Sir John tied the four bags together with a single rope and then lowered them down to the edge of the stream for Kane to pull along behind him, whilst also handing him a small knife in case the bags became trapped underwater in the rocks and he had to cut them loose.

Whilst Sir John held on to the end of the rope, Kane went back over to the rock face hexagon where he took a firm grip of the 'L' pendant stud, but this time did not turn the key around and instead pulled it out of the hole to put on the chain around his neck, with the 'K' key.

Kane then returned to the edge of the passageway and reminded Sir John that it would be several minutes before he was able to close the gap again from the other side, but once Sir John heard the thud from below the rock wall and seen the stream levels go down again, he would know that all four of them had made it safely to the main cavern.

Upon taking a firm grip of the rope and making one final grateful acknowledgement to Sir John, Kane climbed down the rocks into the stream and as the strong current started to pull him along, he quickly dived under the water followed by the bags and was gone.

Thankfully, the four bags did not cause Kane any real difficulty as he swam with them through the underwater gap and soon resurfaced inside the cavern, where John was waiting to help him as arranged.

Together, they grabbed all the bags and dragged them out of the water, where Kane looked around and was delighted to see both Kara and Kathryn waving at him so he knew they were safe.

Kane then walked over to where the seven hexagon device was embedded in the rock face and after removing the 'L' pendant from the silver chain around his neck, placed it in the palm of his hand from where it flew off into the empty 'L' key hole.

With the key now in place, Kane turned its silver stud clockwise until it locked into position and a loud thud was heard as the underwater gap in the rock wall shut to.

They all realised that once the stream water in the passageway had returned to its original level, Sir John would know the cavern entrance was secure and Edmund had not been able to follow the four of them to their next destination in time.

The soldiers would then cover the rock face crevice entrance again with brambles, whilst Sir John returned back to the Manor House to tell Lady Agnes they had all left safely.

Meanwhile back in the cavern, the 'T' hexagon and corresponding key in the seven letter hexagon device were both still glowing bright red.

Kathryn had rested long enough and was now ready to continue on the next part of their journey, which the twins told them was the era of the House of Tudor in the 16th Century.

A couple of minutes later, Kane and John dragged the bags across the cavern floor and into the shallow water at the edge of the stream.

Here they lassoed the end of the rope around a large protruding boulder for Kane to grab and pull the bags along with, once he was ready.

They both rejoined the girls and it was agreed that Kara, John & Kathryn would set off together to the shallow edge of the stream, where they would wait for Kane to open the new underwater passage.

As soon as Kane saw the three of them were in the correct place, he turned the 'T' key stud anti-clockwise and after a loud thud in the rock wall was heard, the water level quickly rose enough for them to swim with the strong current. Shortly afterwards they all reached the rocks along the stream and climbed out.

Once they were gone, Kane removed the 'T' key pendant from the seven hexagon device and placed it back around his neck.

He then walked over to loosen the rope wrapped around the boulder and after taking a firm grip of this, he swam off in the underwater current with all four bags trailing behind him.

Kane soon pulled them through the underwater passage and upon reaching the stream surface, John helped him climb up over the rocks before dragging the bags onto the passageway, where they were thankfully still all intact.

After a short respite, Kane then walked over to the single 'T' hexagon device on the rock wall which was still glowing bright red and he locked this with the 'T' key from off its silver chain.

They all heard the thud sound again and as the stream level started dropping, they knew this underwater gap was now closed.

Both Kane and John remained standing there for a few minutes with their swords drawn however, in case anyone else had somehow managed to follow them into this new passageway.

Whilst they waited, Kane took the 'T' key from out of its hole and together with the 'K' key and chain which he still had, handed them all over to Kara to wear around her neck again.

Thankfully, after waiting for some time, no-one appeared and with all of them now feeling much safer, both men knew they could leave Kara who always carried her sword, with Kathryn for a short time whilst they checked everywhere else.

They went inside the small cave first and and then down the passageway towards the outside entrance, as these areas were still lit by the red light reflecting from the full lunar Moon.

They soon returned and as it was quite mild inside the small cave compared to outside, they all decided to rest there until they set off to the Manor House at sunrise the following morning.

Despite having found nothing of concern, the men still decided to keep a look out overnight at the crevice entrance and after tossing a coin between them, Kane took first watch.

Church of the Holy and Undivided Trinity

Part 6

HOUSE OF TUDOR
- 16th Century -

Chapter 24 : **Date with Life ...**

A few hours later, the rose pink crystals along the passageway walls and the stream water further inside, all stopped glowing bright red.
Instead, they returned to their natural colours as the full lunar eclipse ended and the Moon disappeared over the horizon in the morning sky.

John had taken his turn to sit on the rocks next to the narrow crevice entrance, where he kept watch outside and saw the early morning Sun as it began to rise from the east.
The daylight started to shine through the gap in the rock face as he saw numerous bushes and brambles covered with new green leaves and he knew they had arrived during the spring.

At that moment he suddenly heard footsteps from behind him and instinctively turned around with his sword in his hand, only to see that it was Kane walking towards him, having been woken up when the light in the passageway changed.
John told Kane that it was all clear outside and so he went back to fetch the girls who were also both now awake, with Kathryn in particular feeling very hungry.

As they knew they had travelled forward in time to the House of Tudor era, both the men and Kara decided to wear their KLOPT0N armour, so they would be easily identified by the soldiers on guard when they reached the main courtyard.
This would also free up their hands to enable Kara and John to support a very pregnant Kathryn on their walk down across the uneven fields to the Manor House, whilst Kane would carry the rest of their possessions.

Finally, to avoid any confusion when they met up with the present KLOPT0N estate owners, they had already agreed and rehearsed their individual histories to tell them, which they hoped would endear them as much to this new family as they had been to their previous ancestors.

It turned out to be a mild spring morning as the four of them left the covered up rock face crevice entrance behind and set off slowly down the slightly damp hillside.

The Manor House soon came into full view and they saw that the property they had previously stayed in during the 1450's with Sir John & Lady Agnes Klopton, had been rebuilt to a more ornate design and also appeared larger in size.

As they walked around the lake and into the east facing courtyard, they were approached by five soldiers in formation, so they stopped to wait for them to arrive and hopefully speak first.

The officer at the front quickly spotted the KLOPTON crest displayed on their armour and instantly ordered his men to stop and stand to attention, before he said,

"Welcome all of you to KLOPTON and if you would please accompany me to the north entrance of the Manor House, I will fetch Sir William Klopton for you"

They all nodded in acknowledgement and without speaking, followed the officer and his men to the front door, above which the name KLOPTON and the family crest were etched into a large piece of oak.

After they had all come to a stop, the officer spoke again.

"Please wait with my soldiers whilst I go inside, although may I have your names first",

to which John replied,

"If you would please inform Sir William that Sir John Klopton has arrived with three other members of his family, that should be sufficient for now", whereupon the officer turned around and entered the Manor House before closing the door behind him.

A minute later the front door re-opened and the officer accompanied by a couple of servants appeared from inside, as he said,

"Please accept my apologies for leaving you all outside so long and if you would follow me into the sitting room where the lady with child may rest herself, the servants will serve you all with refreshments whilst you wait for Sir William & Lady Anne Klopton to join you very shortly".

John entered the grand hallway first as Kane helped Kara escort Kathryn inside, where they followed the officer through to the sitting room which was much grander than that of the previous Manor House.

On top of the original stone fireplace mantelpiece however, they were pleased to see the old wooden KLOPTON clock was still on display.

Kathryn was especially delighted to be able to sit down in a comfortable armchair after their long tiring journey and they were all equally grateful when the maid brought them a hot tasty drink each.

Kara was still wearing her armour, having decided to leave it on as long as Kane and John both wore theirs, or at least until they had been introduced to the estate's new Klopton family owners.

223

They also hoped that Sir William would let them all stay in the Manor House until the time of the next full red lunar eclipse.

As Kara sat there waiting, she took hold of the 'T' key pendant from the silver chain around her neck and looked at the wording on the longest stem, which for this key read,

'only the time ... will life inherit'

Again, there was also an unusual small symbol etched onto both sides of the stem end, which on this occasion looked like the combination of the number '2' and an elongated '+' joined together side by side.

Kara leant over closer to her brother with the 'T' pendant to discuss these etchings with him, when at that moment the double doors were opened and in walked a smartly dressed manservant.

Once inside the room he stood to attention and with the most reverent of voices, said to the four of them,

"May I please request that you all be upstanding whilst you welcome your most honourable hosts, Sir William Klopton & Lady Anne Klopton".

Kara quickly glanced over at the others and gestured as to how they were expected to greet their new hosts when they entered the room.

John and Kane decided they should all just bow their heads and so Kara agreed to do the same, especially since her armour made her appear to be a man.

Kathryn however, had sunk deep into the soft armchair and due to her uncomfortably large size, was unable to lift herself back up to curtsy.

She would therefore remain seating and simply nod her head instead.

Sir William looked quite formidable as he led his wife into the room.

He too was wearing a magnificent suit of highly polished silver armour with the red & black KLOPTON crest embossed on its chest plate, whilst he carried a daunting metal sword around his waist in a silver sheaf.

Lady Anne was equally dressed to impress in a beautifully embroidered full length dark red velvet dress with an exquisite black & red laced waisted bodice top, which from its large waist size demonstrated that she too was heavily pregnant.

Around her neck she wore a necklace displaying a series of seven polished rose pink crystals, each encased in a single silver hexagon.

Kara was so impressed with both their outfits, that she felt like they were in the presence of KLOPTON royalty!

Once they had both stopped still in front of the four of them, Sir William instructed his manservant to leave the room and to ensure they were not disturbed, to which he bowed in acknowledgement before closing the lounge doors behind him.

Sir William then turned back towards his visitors and after a reassuring warm smile, he said,
"My wife and I are sorry for keeping you waiting, but we are delighted to welcome you all to KLOPTON on this unexpected visit, although we assume it must be as a result of the full red Moon we saw overhead last night?", upon which he paused as they each nodded in turn to confirm.

He then continued to say,
"In the circumstances, I suspect you are anxious to know that today's date is the 10th April 1564.
It has been almost six years since her majesty Elizabeth Tudor became Queen of England, after her sister Queen Mary died in 1558.
May I now request that each of you in turn please introduce yourselves to both of us.
We would be especially interested to know the era you have travelled from and which of our most recent ancestors you are related to".

John, who was standing closest to Sir William & Lady Anne, took the lead and replied first,
"On behalf of all four of us, I would first of all like to thank you both for the very gracious way in which you have so warmly welcomed us into your home.
I am Sir John Klopton and was born during the reign of King Henry VI of the House of Lancaster, to my parents Sir John & Lady Agnes Klopton.

This young lady seated with child is my betrothed Lady Kathryn Klopton, who was born during the reign of King Edward III of the House of Plantagenet, to her parents Sir Frederick & Lady Khloe Klopton.
Tragically, Kathryn's husband Sir James Salisbury was killed during the Wars of the Roses at the Battle of Wakefield whilst fighting alongside his father and very sadly left Lady Kathryn widowed whilst pregnant.
It was therefore my greatest honour, after an appropriate length of time since Sir James' memorial service, to offer my hand in marriage and accept her baby as my own once born, to which she has graciously accepted".

At that point Lady Anne looked solemnly over at Kathryn, before speaking to her in the warmest of voices,
"Lady Kathryn, I am sorry to hear of your recent tragic loss, but delighted that you have found such an honourable knight as Sir John to become your future husband and the father to your unborn child.

I am also glad to see that you look so well after your long and difficult journey through the cavern, especially as in view of your size I assume your baby must be due very soon?".

Before responding to her kind comments and question however, Kathryn looked over at Sir John and reached out towards him, whereupon he walked over to hold her hand as she replied,

"Thank you so much for your kind words Lady Anne and I am indeed very fortunate to have met such a wonderful loving man as Sir John and I look forward very much to marrying him quite soon, as my baby is due within a couple of weeks.

May I also take this opportunity to ask you about your own new baby's pending birth, as from your size it appears you too must be due soon?", to which Lady Anne replied with the warmest of smiles,

"You are indeed correct Lady Kathryn, my baby is expected within the next couple of weeks and it therefore looks like we are both going to be very busy quite soon!".

Kane was next to continue with the introductions, as he said,

"I am Sir Kane Klopton and I was born earlier in the reign of King Edward III, with my parents being Sir Richard & Lady Katrina Klopton", to which Sir William responded

"It is our pleasure to meet you too, Sir Kane".

Finally, as he looked over towards Kara, Sir William asked,

"... and who may I ask is the third knight with you here today, yet again wearing another splendid suit of polished KLOPTON armour?".

Kara had been looking forward to this moment ever since she entered the Manor House and as she mischievously smiled to herself under her helmet, she knew it was time to show her true identity to their hosts.

After bowing slightly, Kara gradually lifted her helmet off her head with both hands, until she revealed her clear complexion underneath plus her dark brown hair, which was bound tightly behind her head to help disguise her true gender.

She then kept hold of her helmet in just one hand, whilst with the other she reached around to the back of her head and carefully unfastened her hair grips, after which in a moment of pure theatre, she started slowly shaking her head from side-to-side.

After a few moments, her long hair became loose and dropped down to unravel over her shoulders.

Kara stood still for a moment as everyone in the room remained quiet, until she looked back up towards Kane and spoke out in a bold dramatic voice, so there would be no confusion,

"I am Lady Kara Klopton and also the beloved wife of Sir Kane Klopton!".

226

Sir William & Lady Anne were taken aback by this totally unexpected disclosure they had just witnessed and for a few moments both of them remained still as they looked at each other, clearly uncertain at what to say next.

In the circumstances, Kara decided to continue speaking.
"I too was born during the reign of King Edward III, but my parents were Sir Andrew & Lady Kathleen Klopton, whilst Lady Kathryn is my niece.
Please forgive me for not revealing my true self to both of you earlier, but after the many dangers we encountered during the Wars of the Roses, we did not know what awaited us all when we arrived in this era. As I am proficient with a sword, we decided that it would therefore be safer if I also dressed as a knight in armour, in case we had to fight off any potential foes".

Upon hearing this their hosts managed to regain their composure, as Lady Anne responded first and said,
"I totally understand your reasons Lady Kara and there is certainly no need for you to apologise.
May I also say what beautiful young ladies both you and Lady Kathryn are and I will be delighted to help organise some more comfortable and appropriate garments for you to change into".

Kara responded instantly,
"That would be very kind of you, especially as Lady Kathryn and I have been wearing these same outfits for nearly two days now and we would both very much welcome some fresh clothes".

Sir William then spoke again,
"We assume that you have nowhere to stay in this era and we will therefore be delighted to offer accommodation in the Manor House to all of you, for as long as it is needed.
At this moment however, we only have two spare bedrooms and in the circumstances, may we suggest that the two men have one room, whilst the two ladies share the other until Lady Kathryn's baby is born and we can then review the available options again".

Sir John responded whilst looking at both of them,
"It is very kind of you to invite us to stay in your wonderfully improved Manor House and on behalf of all of us, I will be pleased to accept your most generous offer".
Lady Anne turned towards her husband and whispered something to him, whereupon he walked over to open the lounge door and was immediately met by his manservant waiting outside.
After Sir William gave him some instructions, he went back inside the lounge to explain to everyone the plan for midday,

"Lunch will be served at 12 noon in the dining room, where we will also be joined by the rest of our family.

In the meantime, our manservants and ladies-in-waiting will escort you all to your bedrooms, where they should be able to provide you with most things you need for now.

If however, you require anything else, we will arrange for such items to be collected from Stratford-upon-Avon for you by this afternoon".

Kara helped Kathryn out of the soft armchair she was sitting in and together they walked out of the lounge towards the grand staircase, where the ladies-in-waiting took them upstairs to their bedroom.

Inside the room the bath was already filled with some scented hot water, whilst hanging on the clothes rails was a delightful selection of various different sized ladies garments for them to try on after they had finished bathing.

Seeing all of this, Kara gave Kathryn a huge smile and said
"I think this is going to be a most enjoyable couple of hours",
to which Kathryn cheekily replied
"yes I agree, as you are definitely in need of a good soaking!",
prompting Kara to splash her with the bath water as they both giggled.

Meanwhile, Kane and John followed the manservants upstairs to their room, which only had lukewarm bath water waiting for them, but otherwise the selection of men's attire for them to choose from was similarly impressive.

The morning quickly passed by and shortly before noon there was a knock on both bedroom doors simultaneously, as the servants called out for them to make their way to the dining room where Sir William, Lady Anne and the rest of the family would be joining them in ten minutes.

Upon hearing this message, the men went over to fetch the ladies from their bedroom, where they would escort them both downstairs together into the dining room.

Kara was now wearing the wedding ring she was lent by her father Richard, back in the 14th Century.

Upon both men entering the ladies' room, she could not resist but to hold out her left hand to show Kane what she wore on her third finger.

With a huge smile on her face, Kara then playfully said,
"Kane, my devoted husband-to-be, it is wonderful to see you in my boudoir today, especially as you look so handsome in your elegant new formal suit and silk cravat",
to which jovial comments a beaming smile appeared across his face.

Once a few seconds had passed, Kane responded to her in an equally joyful manner,
"Kara, my loving and most obedient wife-to-be, I am everyday in awe of your stunning beauty and to see you here in front of me wearing such a gorgeous silk and lace gown, is a memory that will last with me forever".

Over the following moments, both of their fixed warm smiles changed into expressions of devoted love for each other and as they stood frozen in time wondering what to say next, they simply stared into each others matching eyes as they glazed over.

After what must have seemed like ages, John knew he needed to change the mood and coughed out loudly, before saying in a jolly voice,
"Time for lunch everybody and if the two of you set off first, I will take Kathryn down the staircase afterwards so we both have someone soft to land on if we slip on the steps!".
This lighthearted quip had the desired effect, as both the twins started laughing again and Kane turned towards John to answer,
"Yes, we must all now be going".

He then looked back over at Kara and as he held up the palm of his hand to her waist level, he said,
"If you would please take my hand Kara, it will be my honour to escort you downstairs for lunch".
Without saying another word, she gently lifted her hand into his as together they slowly left the room and down the staircase, followed closely behind by John & Kathryn.
Once outside the dining room they were all met by one of the manservants, who asked them to wait for a moment until he was ready to formally introduced them to everyone inside.

The servant then opened the doors and as they entered he called out their names to Sir William & Lady Anne, who both stood to welcome them whilst they sat down around the table with the rest of the family.
Sir William remained standing however, as he introduced his three young children, who each in turn upon hearing their name called, stood up to either bow or curtsy.
The youngest girl needed a slight helping hand from her nanny though, which caused a lovely warm "aaarrhh" response of approval, especially from all the ladies present.

With everyone now seated, Lady Anne spoke first,
"I expect Lady Kathryn and I will have much to talk to each other about after lunch, but the meal is now ready to be served and if you would all please let the servants know what you want to drink, they will also organise this for you straight away.
Bon appetite everyone!".

It was over an hour before they finished their lunch and the children were taken off by their nannies to their rooms to play.

At the same time, the adults all moved into the sitting room and spent the rest of the day talking amongst each other, whilst also taking the opportunity for a walking tour of both the rebuilt Manor House and the recently landscaped gardens.

Over the next week and days, everyone in the household waited anxiously for the arrival of the two new babies, with even a sweepstake being started by the servants and soldiers on the estate as to who was going to give birth first and the sex of the babies.

Upon discovering this, John, Kane and even Sir William were delighted to all join in with a small wager too!

Early in the morning on 23rd April, Lady Anne went into labour first and the local midwife was fetched by carriage from Stratford-upon-Avon, whilst the ladies-in-waiting and maids took care of her.

Being her fourth child however, Lady Anne was clearly managing to stay much calmer than most of those around her who were supposed to be helping.

During the next couple of hours there was a lot of frenetic activity in and around her bed chambers in the west wing of the Manor House, when suddenly a loud knock on the door was heard and a very excitable young maid rushed in forgetting the correct protocol, to announce that Lady Kathryn had also gone into labour.

Without any hesitation, Lady Anne instructed one of her ladies-in-waiting and a couple of other maids to go and help attend to Lady Kathryn immediately in the east wing and to stay with her as long as long as they were needed.

She also asked the midwife to check on Lady Kathryn's condition and only return back to her bed chambers when appropriate.

Meanwhile, over in the east wing of the Manor House, Kathryn had obviously not been in the mood to wait too much longer herself, especially after receiving the news of Lady Anne's change in circumstances, and within the next two hours she also went into labour!

Upon being told about Kathryn's latest situation, both John and Kane wanted to help too, but Kara quickly sent them out of the bedroom with clear instructions for them to stay downstairs in the sitting room with Sir William, until they were called for.

In the meantime Kara stayed with Kathryn doing her best to help, but she was very grateful when the midwife and Lady Anne's ladies arrived to provide their much greater experience.

It was several hours later that the joyous sounds of a healthy new baby could be heard crying loudly throughout the house from the west wing, as Lady Anne gave birth to a beautiful girl and Sir William immediately took their other children with him upstairs to the bed chamber to meet their new baby sister, who they named Margaretta.

Unfortunately, for Kathryn however, giving birth was not going as smoothly for her as it had for Lady Anne.
The various screams heard coming from her east wing bedroom were clearly not being those of a new baby entering the world, but instead the shrieks of pain from it's mother-to-be enduring the agonising various stages of her first childbirth.
As these unintentionally shared personal cries increased in frequency, Kathryn also started to include an array of unladylike expletives as she became ever more vocal, until later that afternoon everything suddenly went quiet.

In that instance, everyone else in the Manor House stopped whatever it was they were doing and waited in silence, including John and Kane who became increasingly anxious as they paced up and down in front of the fire in the sitting room, waiting to hear some news of Kathryn.
Then just as the tension was becoming unbearable, the glorious sound of a new baby crying out at the start of its life, bellowed all around them from upstairs in the east wing.
In that moment the whole house came alive again with excitable noisy chatter everywhere, quickly followed by some sporadic loud cheering, especially from John and Kane.

Without waiting any longer to be called for, the two men ran up the main staircase and along the corridor to Kathryn's bedroom, only to be greeted outside the closed door by a maid standing guard, who had strict orders that they were not to come in until asked to do so.
Looking at each other, they both knew better than to argue with Kara's instructions, but thankfully they did not have to wait too long as the baby's crying soon stopped and the door was then opened by Kara, who with a beaming smile on her face invited them both to enter.

Over on the bed they could see a very tired, but clearly overwhelmed Kathryn, staring in the most loving way possible at her new born baby, which was sleeping very content and quiet in its mother's gentle and very protective arms.

The lady-in-waiting and maids all stepped forward to welcome the two men, before telling them that they could only have ten minutes with Kathryn for now, as she was very tired and needed to get some well earned sleep.

231

They both nodded in acknowledgement and after the ladies went outside to freshen themselves up, Kathryn heard the door close shut behind as she looked up and saw her three best friends smiling at her.

With sheer joy beaming from all over her face, Kathryn slowly lifted her new baby up in her arms for them all to see and with the deepest feelings only a mother could possibly have, spoke quietly so not to wake her up again,
"Isn't she just absolutely perfect.
I have named her Khloe Sofia after my mother, who I wish was here today with Frederick, Ryan and James, so all of them would have also been able to greet her and say hello".
Suddenly a flood of tears started running down Kathryn's face, as Kara quickly walked over to try and comfort her with a gentle embrace.

Kathryn's raw mixed emotions poured uncontrollably out of her however and Kara could also not stop but to shed a few tears of her own.
Both men looked on clearly moved by the moment and not quite sure how best to handle it, until John calmly said,
"Kathryn my beloved, whilst none of your family are here with you today, they will always be remembered as a very important part of your life and also that of your daughter as she grows up.
This day is a time to rejoice at the birth of your beautiful daughter who you have brought into our lives and it would be my greatest honour to help you raise Khloe as her father, if you still wish to marry me?".

Upon hearing this, Kathryn reached out to John whilst cradling her baby in her arms and replied,
"With all my heart I wish to marry you John and I will also be so very proud for Khloe to have you as her father", whereupon he leaned over and kissed them both as her weeping turned to tears of joy.

At that moment there was a knock on the door and in walked Lady Anne's lady-in-waiting with two new maids, as she spoke authoritatively to everyone in the room,
"It is now time for both mother and daughter to get some proper sleep without being disturbed, so I must ask for the men and Kara to all leave. Two of the maids will stay overnight to watch over them both and everything from then on can be sorted out in the morning".

The three of them smiled over at Kathryn and wished both her and Khloe a good night's sleep, before thanking the lady-in-waiting and all together went downstairs to the dining room for an evening meal.

Chapter 25 : **Date with Celebration ...**

That week should have been chaotic with two new babies in the Manor House and their baptisms plus a wedding to organise, but Lady Anne was quickly back on her feet and calmly sorted everything out.

They all agreed that Sir John & Lady Kathryn would get married that Friday 25th April in the small chapel on the second floor.

This place of worship was added to the KLOPTON Manor House in the 15th Century by Sir Thomas Klopton, after his father got permission off Pope Sixtus IV in 1474 for its use in the celebration of divine service.

On the following day 26th April, both girls' baptisms would take place in the Church of the Holy Trinity, which side aisle chantry contained the KLOPTON family burial chapel where many tombs of their ancestors lay.

Friday morning soon came and everyone was busy helping out with the preparations for the Manor House's first wedding to be held inside its private chapel.

After helping Kathryn to get dressed into a beautiful ivory white silk wedding gown which Lady Anne had arranged for her, Kara was again to be her bridesmaid and this time wore a dress made out of white lace.

On this occasion however, Kara was also given the added responsibility of carrying baby Khloe down the short aisle in a white wicker Moses basket, in the hope that a recognisable face might help keep her subdued if she was to wake up during the service.

The clock in the bedroom sounded out a single chime to signify it was 11.45 and this was immediately followed by a knock on the door as Sir William entered the room, clearly delighted to have the responsibility of escorting Lady Kathryn up the chapel's small aisle to the altar.

After exchanging a few warm words with each other, Sir William presented Lady Kathryn with the ancestral rose-pink crystal silver KLOPTON necklace and tiara for her to wear, not realising that she had worn these at her wedding to Sir James a century before, but which in Kathryn's timeline was only a year earlier.

Upon seeing this family jewellery again, Kathryn's face glazed over for a moment as she was uncertain how to react.

Kara too recognised the significance of both these jewellery pieces and immediately went to comfort her, whilst also explaining the situation to Sir William who apologised profusely for his oversight.

Thankfully, Kathryn soon managed to compose herself as Kara helped her put the jewellery on for a second time and then passed over a large bouquet of rose-pink lilies to carry, which had been specially pre-ordered from the flower market in London a few days before.

Kara had a smaller bouquet made from the same colour lilies and also fastened a couple more onto the side of her hair.

Everyone was now ready to leave as Kara picked up Khloe, who was thankfully still fast asleep and all four of them set off out the bedroom door and along the corridors for their short walk up the main staircase to the second floor on the opposite wing of the Manor House.

Over in the small chapel Sir John was stood at the altar, immaculately dressed in his polished suit of KLOPTON armour, whilst his best man Kane was next to him wearing a black formal outfit with a rose-pink coloured cravat and matching single lily in his button hole.

Lady Anne was sitting in the second row of pews with Margaretta, as she waited for Sir William to join them, whilst the first pew was left empty for Kara and Khloe to use once they arrived.

On the opposite side of the aisle the first pew was left for Kane to use, whilst the ladies-in-waiting sat in the second row behind with Lady Anne's other three children to even up the numbers.

Upon reaching the chapel entrance, Sir William signalled their readiness to enter and as the violinist started playing a melody specially requested by Lady Kathryn for the occasion, everyone stood up.

The walk along the short aisle to where Sir John was waiting only took eight very small steps and after the local vicar from a nearby Church had welcomed them, the wedding service and shortened mass began.

Less than half-an-hour later, the newly married Sir John & Lady Kathryn Klopton walked back down the aisle together, this time carrying Khloe in her wicker basket.

Everyone followed them and made their way downstairs to the Great Hall for a celebratory meal, accompanied by some light entertainment.

The day soon passed by and Kara had previously moved all of her possessions into Kane's bedroom that afternoon, whilst Sir John had switched all of his in the opposite direction to Kathryn's.

It was time for everyone to retire to their respective rooms, although for this night only Kara & Kane agreed to let Khloe stay with them.

The following morning of the 26th arrived and thankfully Khloe had only woken up twice during the night, so Kara & Kane both managed to get some sleep and were ready for Kathryn when she came knocking on their door to collect her daughter.

After giving Khloe a big hug and kiss, Kathryn thanked them both again for looking after her and reminded them that she would be downstairs in the sitting room just before 10.30 for the Church baptism in Stratford-upon-Avon later that morning.

With a huge warm smile on her face, Kathryn walked back off to her bedroom whilst singing quietly to Khloe who she cradled in her arms.
The twins looked at each other and were both delighted to see how happy she was, before they went downstairs together for some food.

Sir William and the rest of his family had already started their morning meal in the dining room, whilst a lady-in-waiting kept a watchful eye over Margaretta who was asleep in her wicker basket.
Upon seeing Sir Kane & Lady Kara arrive, Sir William stood up to greet them both and requested that they also eat at their table, which offer the two of them graciously accepted.

Almost an hour later after everyone had finished eating and the children returned to their rooms, Sir William had some more news for them.
"As you know, both girls' baptisms are scheduled to take place in the Church of the Holy Trinity this morning at 11.00, but last night I received a message from the vicar informing me that another parishioner and good friend of mine John Shakespeare, had also welcomed a new baby into the world this week.

John Shakespeare is a town Alderman and he resides on Henley Street in Stratford-upon-Avon with his wife Mary.
Their new baby boy William, was born on the same date of 23rd April as both Margaretta and Khloe were.
This happy coincidence prompted the vicar's request to allow the boy's baptism to be held at the same time as our girls' and I happily agreed".

Kara & Kane looked towards each other in sheer disbelief at what they had just heard and struggled to contain their excitement.
Although they were in KLOPT0N time, the date was still the 26th April 1564 and in just over two hours they would be attending the baptism of William Shakespeare!
The staggering significance of this occasion was something no-one else in that time would even possibly begin to comprehend and yet they could not tell anyone they knew.

Upon Sir William seeing their reactions however, he asked a question,
"I see from both your faces that you appear somewhat displeased with my decision?".
Kane immediately replied, whilst Kara shook her head,
"No, not at all Sir William, it is marvellous news.
We both realise however, that we have to finish getting ready and also check on Kathryn & John to see if they need any more help with Khloe.
Once again, we greatly appreciate all your hospitality, but must both return upstairs until we meet up again later on in the entrance hall".
Whereupon, they both stood up and slowly left the room.

As the wall clock on the landing struck 10.00, Kane & Kara left their bedroom and walked over to join John & Kathryn in theirs, but upon arriving all they could hear was Khloe crying.

Knowing that time was running short however, they decided it best to knock on the door and also call out to see if they could help.

Upon realising they were both outside her room, a clearly flustered Kathryn replied to let themselves in and once inside, she immediately passed a distraught Khloe over to Kara and asked her to comfort her.

Kathryn then promptly disappeared into the adjoining room to get ready for her daughter's baptism.

Kara quickly took control of the situation in her stride and within a few minutes had calmed Khloe down until she stopped crying altogether, much to the obvious delight of both John and Kane who gratefully acknowledged how very impressed they were.

She then lifted Khloe into her wicker basket and after rocking this gently for a bit longer to make sure she was fast asleep, turned to look at both of them with a beaming smile and said,

"That is how you look after a crying baby and next time Khloe needs comforting, it will be the turn of you brave men to step up to the task!".

At that moment Kathryn re-entered the main room and upon seeing that Khloe was asleep, she looked over at Kara to say,

"Well done cousin, you are clearly going to make Khloe a wonderful god-mother!".

Kathryn then picked up the wicker basket in one arm, whilst with the other she took hold of John and said "Time for us to go!".

Kane instantly took hold of Kara, as all five of them made their way downstairs together into the entrance hall, where Sir William & Lady Anne were waiting with Margaretta and the rest of their children, plus a couple of ladies-in-waiting.

After one of the manservants had opened the front door, Sir William's family went outside and stepped into the largest of the two waiting coaches, followed by Sir John's group who boarded the second coach.

As soon as everyone was seated comfortably, Sir William signalled to both coachmen and they quickly set off together, with the two sets of horses riding along at a canter behind each other down the driveway.

It was not too long before they were both heading through the streets and into the town centre, from where they could see the tall church spire up ahead in the distance.

From there they continued along the side of the River Avon, until they reached the main doors of the Holy Trinity Church with ten minutes still remaining and saw the vicar John Bretchgirdle waiting outside for their arrival, along with a few dozen local well-wishers.

236

The coachmen quickly brought the horses to a halt and then opened the coach doors for everyone to alight.

Once outside, they accompanied the vicar through the church entrance to where John Shakespeare was already waiting inside.

Upon seeing each other, Sir William and John walked over with their respective families in order to exchange brief introductions before the service began.

Kane & Kara where so delighted at meeting William Shakespeare's parents however, that the vicar had to interrupt their questions so everyone could take their seats in time for the proceedings to start.

The Church had a long aisle and whilst John Shakespeare took his wife and children to sit in the right-hand side pews, Sir William made his way with all his family members up the left-hand side so they could stop in front of the private KLOPTON chantry Chapel.

Upon reaching this, the three men all knelt down on one knee and bowed their heads, whilst the ladies curtsied as the vicar joined them in a short prayer to their ancestors.

After a further brief period of quiet reflection, Sir William stood up first followed by everyone else, before they all made their way along the rest of the aisle to the front two rows of pews where they took their places.

The three baptisms went smoothly over the next half hour, although each baby in turn was clearly determined to try and cry the loudest as the vicar blessed them all with Holy water.

After they had finished, everyone stood up as the vicar concluded the service with one last prayer, whereupon the families left back down the main aisle together.

Once outside they all said their farewells to each other, before setting off in their coaches to their respective homes.

That evening after dinner, when Kane & Kara had retired to their room, neither of them could stop talking about the baptism they had just shared with the Shakespeare family for their son William, long before he grew up to become so famous!

Chapter 26 : **Date with Death ...**

Over the next couple of months, as life around the KLOPTON estate returned to normal, both babies and mothers settled into their new daily routines and the whole of the family in the Manor House were very content.

Unfortunately, this brief period of tranquility was all about to change however, as on the afternoon of the 11th July that year, a horse rider arrived in the main courtyard with a sealed letter for Sir William from the vicar of the Church of the Holy Trinity.

The apparently unremarkable initial contents of this letter, advised that during the morning an apprentice weaver named Oliver Gunn, who lived on the High Street in Stratford-upon-Avon, had tragically died.

Much more critically significant was the reason for this man's death and on the next line of text the vicar copied the following words, which he had written next to his entry in the church burial records:

'*hic incepit pestis*' (ie: '*here begins the plague*')

Upon reading this, Sir William realised the overwhelming importance of this unexpected letter and immediately called the whole family together in the sitting room, to tell them about its contents and also to issue new instructions,

"I have just received the devastating news that the plague has returned to Stratford-upon-Avon with the death of a local resident and I cannot emphasise to all of you enough, the need for everyone to confine themselves within the Manor House and inner secure boundaries of the estate until further notice.

No one is to meet with anyone else from outside of the family or the usual house staff, especially if they either arrive from the town or are not known to us.

This particularly includes all of the children, who must not be allowed to play outside with any of the other estate children.

If anyone from the household does show any signs of illness, they must be isolated immediately and locked in one of the empty rooms on the second floor".

By this time, all three of the ladies were hugging the children and understandably looking very distressed, whereupon he added,

"We must try not to worry ourselves too much, as if we look out for each other this should all be over soon and we will be able to get back to our normal lives again".

Sir William then beckoned John and Kane to join him outside and all three of them walked out of the room into the hallway, where he spoke to them very seriously.

"I will be relying on both of you over the next few months to help me keep the Manor House safe and to ensure that our families are protected until the plague has gone.

This will also involve keeping the whole estate secure and ensuring that all of the workers are well looked after, since we do not want them going into town and bringing the plague back with them".

They both nodded their acknowledgement, before following Sir William outside into the centre of the main courtyard.

Once in position, Sir William stood to attention with John and Kane either side of him and in his most authoritative voice, ordered that all of the house staff and estate workers had to stop whatever it was they were doing and to join him in the courtyard immediately.

It took a while for everyone to arrive, as Sir William's instructions had to be passed around to all of the outside workers, including those tending to the livestock in the nearby fields.

As they all gathered together, obviously very concerned by what was so important, John kept the house staff to one side of the courtyard, whilst Kane organised the estate staff on the other side.

When everybody was standing ready in their required places, Sir William calmly told them all about the local Stratford-upon-Avon man who had died that morning from catching the plague.

His unexpected and distressing news, immediately prompted some anxious discussions between them all and needed much reassurance from Sir William before he could continue with his future instructions.

"From now on, the whole of the KLOPT0N estate will be in lockdown until I tell you anything different.

All fences around the estate are to be made fully secure with every gate locked and all livestock moved into the closer fields and paddocks, whilst extra soldiers will patrol the perimeter every day.

No outsiders will be allowed to enter the estate and force will be used to repel anyone if necessary.

Everyone is to bathe regularly with the ladies using the main lake, whilst the men will use the streams and ponds.

Once everyday, a coach will go into town to organise all necessary supplies and any other essential items needed, some of which will be delivered no further than the outer guarded gate entrance.

It is therefore everyone's responsibility to notify the soldiers stationed outside the main front door every morning, of anything that is needed to be sourced from town that day.

From here on, Sir John will be in charge of all matters regarding the Manor House, whilst Sir Kane will be in charge of those issues relating to the estate, but if neither of them are available then do not hesitate to tell me immediately of anything urgent.

We will all pull through this very difficult situation together and eradicate the plague from our doorstep, if we look after each other.

I thank each and everyone of you for your loyal service to KLOPTON over the years and it is at times like this we will do our best to show our gratitude and repay your trust by helping keep you safe too".

Upon Sir William's rousing finish to his speech, everyone outside in the courtyard started clapping as he turned around and went back inside, whilst Sir John and Sir Kane remained to organise all of the respective responsibilities with the various workers.

The next few weeks turned into months and everyone became increasingly concerned, as news of the plague and deaths spreading across Stratford-upon-Avon and Warwickshire reached the estate.

Thankfully however, none of the family or workers had caught it yet, although some people had tried to enter the estate grounds to escape the town or steal food, but they were quickly driven away by the soldiers who threatened them with immediate execution if they did not leave.

Then one day during October tragedy struck the Klopton family, as a coach arrived at the exterior driveway gate of the estate, with Sir William's brother-in-law Sir Richard seated next to the coachman.

He was clearly very distressed and insisted that the soldier grant him immediate access to the Manor House.

Looking inside the coach, the soldier could see laying on the back seat what appeared to be a lifeless body, wrapped in a white shroud.

Realising that something was seriously wrong, he challenged Sir Richard, who said it was his daughter Charlotte, dead from the plague.

The soldier immediately drew his sword and refused him entry to the estate, whilst a second soldier rode off up to the Manor House to advise Sir William of the situation and get his instructions.

The arrival of the horse rider galloping into the courtyard instantly caught Sir John's attention, who with his sword drawn went over to grab the horse's reins as he shouted for the rider to go no further.

As soon as the horse had been brought to a halt, Sir John recognised the soldier and let him dismount, whereupon he told Sir John about Sir Richard's arrival at the main gate and his daughter's dead body laying inside the coach.

Sir John told the rider to return straight back to the entrance and to ensure the gate remained closed until Sir William ordered otherwise.

By now, Sir Kane had been notified of all the commotion in the courtyard and upon seeing Sir John hastily making his way back towards the Manor House, he went over to join him.

After a brief discussion, he ordered a guard to fetch Sir William immediately, who quickly appeared at the front door and as soon as he had been appraised of the situation, gave instructions to Sir Kane.

"As you are already wearing your KLOPTON armour, please fetch your horse and together with four of my soldiers, ride off to the Church of the Holy Trinity without any further delay.

Once there, you are to explain to the Reverend John Bretchgirdle, who you met at the christening, what has happened here today and that I will be arriving very shortly with Charlotte Klopton's body, which needs to be entombed immediately.

Unfortunately, her mother Lady Eleanor won't be able to join us, but her father Sir Richard will and he will also be the one responsible for carrying their daughter's body into the church from the coach.

In the meantime, the vicar is to empty the church and lock all of the outside doors, which will be guarded by my soldiers.

He is then to fetch the keys he holds for the outer vaulted gates of the ancestral KLOPTON chantry chapel and the inside steps down to the underground family vault and tombs".

As soon as Sir William had finished speaking, Sir Kane nodded his understanding and hurried over to fetch his horse from the stables.

He also quickly organised an officer plus three soldiers to join him and they all set off with a gallop out the courtyard and quickly into Stratford.

Sir William next turned to Sir John and gave him his instructions too,

"I need you to stay here and be extra vigilant, with additional soldiers posted around the Manor House and estate whilst I am gone, in case there is any trouble once the local people hear of the family death and mistakenly think the plague has arrived here in KLOPTON.

I am now going to put my armour on and you should do so too, but first of all make sure that everyone in the family is informed of what is happening and tell them they must all stay indoors until I return.

Please also have my horse ready for me by the time I have got changed and that my lieutenant plus three additional soldiers, are all waiting to accompany me down to the main gates and into town".

Meanwhile, Sir Kane soon arrived at the church and after finding the Reverend John to explain the tragic family situation to him, quickly had everyone else leave and the soldiers guard all the doors, pending the arrival of Sir William and the coach carrying the young girl's body.

With all the commotion caused, several dozen townspeople started to gather outside wondering why a knight of KLOPTON was standing at the main doors with the vicar and who it was they were waiting for that prompted the church to be emptied of people and guarded?

The answer soon became apparent however, as Sir William Klopton and his soldiers galloped into view followed by the coach and upon reaching the church, the soldiers quickly dismounted.
Together with the lieutenant, they immediately moved all of the crowd further away by creating a defensive line, with strict instructions that they must keep their distance.

As soon as the area outside the church was secure, the coach pulled forward and stopped in front of the main doors, which Sir Kane and the vicar unlocked in readiness.
Sir Richard climbed down from next to the coachman and opened the coach door to step halfway inside.
A short time later he stepped back out and in his arms he was now carrying twelve year old Charlotte's body, which was fully draped in a white shroud bearing the red & black crest of the House of KLOPTON.
The Reverend John said a quick prayer over her body and then slowly led the way through the church doors accompanied by Sir William, who was followed by Sir Richard with Charlotte, and Sir Kane last to enter.

Once they were all inside, the lieutenant pulled the doors shut behind them and turned around to tell the small crowd outside the church to be quiet and show respect for the duration of the entombment service for a young daughter of KLOPTON.
He then ordered the soldiers to form a line with him outside the church doors, where they drew their swords as they knelt down and placed the pointed end on the ground to signify the cross of Christ.
They all solemnly bowed their heads and were to remain there until the short service was over and the doors re-opened.

Meanwhile, inside the KLOPTON chantry chapel, the large slab covering the entrance had been lifted and Sir Richard slowly descended the stone steps with Charlotte in his arms, until he reached the underground passageway to the family vault.
Amongst the numerous tombs he found an empty alcove in one of the thick walls, where he stopped to lay his daughter's precious body.
Sadly, he only had sufficient time to prepare a small wooden cross engraved with her name on, but for now Sir Richard placed this on top of the crested shroud she was draped in.
He whispered to her a final tearful "Goodbye, my beautiful daughter", after which he turned around and stepped back up into the chapel, where the slab was laid back in place and firmly closed shut to again.

They all stood together next to the chapel railings as the vicar re-locked the gates and after one final prayer, they made their way back down the aisle to the main church doors.

Once outside, they said their farewells as Sir Richard climbed inside his coach and the coachman rode off with him back to his family home on the edge of Warwick.
Meanwhile, the lieutenant and soldiers stood up again and proceeded to mount their horses at the same time as Sir William and Sir Kane.
They all rode off together at a steady pace back to KLOPTON, where they were met with expressions of sadness from everyone, although thankfully there had been no trouble on the estate whilst they had been at Charlotte's entombment.

By the end of the week just as everything had calmed down, tragedy hit the Klopton family again.
This time, Sir Richard & Lady Eleanor's ten year old son Edward was struck down by the plague, just like his older sister had.
A similar entombment service was quickly organised within the chapel at the Church of the Holy Trinity as it had been for Charlotte, but this proved to be much more traumatic than anyone could have possibly imagined.

As Sir Richard entered the underground family vault carrying Edward's body, that was also draped in a white shroud with the KLOPTON coloured crest, he was confronted by a harrowing sight no father should ever have to witness.
There, down below him in the candlelight, he saw Charlotte's corpse laying upwards over the bottom few steps, with sheer anguish embedded across her once perfect young face.
Upon encountering such a heart wrenching scene, Sir Richard became totally distraught and lost his footing, whereupon he fell down the remaining few steps into the passageway below.
In doing so, he landed on top of Charlotte's body, whilst at the same time unwittingly letting Edward drop from his arms onto the vault floor.

It took Sir Richard some time to regain his composure from the utter despair of this nightmare situation.
Gradually, he managed to pull himself back upwards and although one of his knees was badly injured from the fall, he could still bend down to collect Edward in his arms.
He slowly hobbled over to find an empty alcove in the wall and placed his son's body next to where Charlotte's had been a few days earlier.
He then went back over to the bottom of the steps where his daughter's corpse now lay and saw that her exposed limbs were covered in cuts and dried blood.

Evidently, Charlotte was not actually dead when they entombed her in the family vault and afterwards she fell out of her alcove in the pitch black, before crawling along the stone floor to climb back up the steps. After scratching with her finger nails on the underneath of the slab in a desperate attempt to claw her way out, the poor girl ended up tragically dying alone in the most distressing and cruelest of circumstances.

Sir Richard shed some tears for his daughter as he picked up her body for a second time and carried it back along the passageway to the same empty alcove, where he wrapped it up again in the KLOPTON shroud which he found laying on the vault floor and replaced the wooden cross. He also took out of his pocket a similar wooden cross he had made for Edward that morning and laid this on top of his son's body in the next alcove, before saying a short prayer for both of his beloved children and then returning back up the steps to the family chantry Chapel above.

Klopton family Chapel in the Holy Trinity Church

Over the next few months, everyone on the KLOPTON estate remained unsettled by further reports of more people dying across various parts of Warwickshire, but they all still continued with their duties diligently. Thankfully, the food supplies and livestock were very well managed and there were no significant food shortages.
The soldiers maintained their regular patrols around the estate to keep any would-be thieves and trespassers out, whilst the few specific goods needed from the traders around town were delivered to the guards at the main driveway gates, who took them up to the Manor House.

As December came, Sir William was so pleased with everyone's efforts to keep them all safe from the plague, that he instructed there to be a large banquet outside in the courtyard on Christmas Day for the whole estate to partake in, as a thank you from all of the Klopton family.

Upon hearing this, all of the soldiers, household staff and other workers cheered up noticeably and were eager to help as much as they could with all the preparations and work involved, which Kane & Kara were both only too delighted to be given overall responsibility for organising.

During the next couple of weeks, Kara helped the cooks with arranging all the food needed and got Sir William's permission for the number of cattle and poultry required to be slaughtered, whilst sufficient winter vegetables and mixed fruit, plus extra bread dough were all either sourced or ordered for delivery on time.

Kara also sorted out all the entertainment for the day, although she had never realised before how many talented musicians and different types of entertainers there were amongst the workers on the estate.

They were all very keen to take their turn performing and Kara did her best to arrange a schedule so most of them would get the chance.

Finally, she especially wanted some small Christmas presents for all of the youngsters on the estate and got all the parents to provide their children's names and ages in order that gifts could be organised.

Lady Anne and Kathryn were also delighted to help with sourcing and wrapping all of these.

Meanwhile, Kane was busy ordering sufficient wine, mead and all other drinks needed, plus ample jugs, glasses and goblets to enable everyone to celebrate the festivities throughout the day.

Next, he arranged for two large fires to be built at either end of the courtyard in order to help keep them all warm outside in the winter weather, especially once the evening got colder.

Numerous barrels of water from the lake were also to be stored nearby in case either of the fires got out of control so close to the house!

Additionally, a large cooking spit was needed throughout the day for the outside hog roast Kara had organised, with plenty of wood chopped up and kept close by to ensure that the flames would be kept burning.

This was kept well away from the Manor House on the opposite side of the courtyard for safety reasons, but all the tables and benches were set out in a large circle close by so everyone could easily fetch the cooked meat as required, whilst also enjoying the entertainment.

Christmas Day quickly came and everyone on the estate was clearly in high spirits, especially as apart from a light morning mist over the lake and surrounding fields, the weather was dry and very mild for that time of the year.

245

The courtyard had all been made ready the day before and whilst the cooks were busy preparing all of the festive food, the plates and cutlery were being set out on the tables together with the various drinking vessels and jugs.

At noon, Sir William & Lady Anne walked out of the front doors with the rest of the family and signalled to the lieutenant waiting outside to blow his trumpet, so everyone knew it was time to stop whatever it was they were doing and to join them in the courtyard for the festivities to start.

The whole day was a great success and ended at 9.00 with a final message from Sir William who said "Good night and Merry Christmas to each and everyone of you".

Before he and his family had the chance to turn around and re-enter the Manor House however, the lieutenant in charge of the household staff and soldiers stepped forward to shout out loud,

"Three cheers to Sir William, Lady Anne and the rest of the Klopton family", to which everyone enthusiastically joined in and followed this up with a huge round of continuous applause.

The whole family stood there quite overcome by this spontaneous warm gesture of gratitude and affection which lasted several minutes.

After everyone had finished, the family looked towards each other and without needing to say a word, responded by putting their hands together and applauding back in acknowledgement of the appreciation.

Once they had finished, they all then took it in turn to say "Thank you and Merry Christmas", before slowly walking back inside through the main door which was closed behind them.

New Year soon came, but very few celebrations were held as a number of deaths from the plague were still being reported across Stratford-upon-Avon and the surrounding villages.

It was not until the first week of February that a horse rider arrived at the main gate to deliver a sealed letter for Sir William, which he quickly opened and immediately called the whole family together in the lounge to tell them of its contents.

"I am delighted to tell you all that I have just received a letter today confirming there have been no more deaths from the plague around Warwickshire for more than two weeks.

Accordingly, the epidemic is officially considered to be over and everyone can therefore now go about their normal lives again.

Whilst this should be a time for us all to be joyful however, it should also be a time for reflection as we mourn together with all of those families including our own, who have lost loved ones.

Over 200 people have been recorded as dying during the six months since the plague first arrived amongst us all.

This Sunday, Reverend John Bretchgirdle will be holding a special memorial service at the Church of the Holy Trinity for all of the Stratford-upon-Avon townsfolk who have died, to which all of the local gentry plus town officials are invited.

We will be attending, but without the children who will remain at home.

For now however, please ensure that all of the workers and soldiers on the estate are told of the news that the plague has gone.

If any of them need to visit their families sometime over the next few days or weeks, they should arrange this with the stewards, as we cannot unfortunately allow everyone to leave at the same time".

On the day of the memorial service, the church was completely full and the main doors were therefore left open so that the many hundreds standing outside could also listen.

It was a very solemn occasion with everyone wearing something black and Sir William invited by the vicar to be one of the few dignitaries to read out a passage from the Bible to the whole congregation.

It was a long and very meaningful service, which the vicar ended with a message of hope followed by a suitable rousing hymn to try and help lift their spirits. All of the townspeople outside joined in with the singing and for that moment in time the whole community came together, in what was a truly genuine heartfelt act of remembrance.

Once the service had finished and they were all back outside through the church doors, Sir William and the rest of the Klopton family were overwhelmed by the number of people simply standing there subdued, as they looked so sad and helpless.

Overcome with sympathy by such a distressing sight in his home town, Sir William immediately instructed his lieutenant to fetch a couple of bags of silver from his coach.

The contents were to be divided also with Sir John and Sir Kane, so all three of them could hand out the silver coins to those most in need.

Realising what was happening, Lady Kara stepped forward as she too wanted to help.

Whilst Sir William was only trying to be protective in case someone in the crowd got too over eager, he quickly remembered that Lady Kara could look after herself and promptly split the silver into four bags.

Whilst Lady Anne and Lady Kathryn waited inside their coach as they watched Sir William's generosity with admiration, the others walked off in a close group through the large crowd until the coin was all gone.

As Kara climbed back into their coach, the men mounted their horses and together with the soldiers returned back to KLOPTON before the thick grey clouds overhead brought down some heavy rain.

Chapter 27 : **Date with History ...**

A couple of months later April came around again and with Kathryn getting so over excited that it would soon be Khloe's first birthday, John decided to give Kara the almost impossible job of trying to keep her calm!
As Lady Anne's daughter Margaretta was born on the same day, it was agreed there would be a joint birthday celebration in the Manor House, although in all reality both babies would be far too young to know what was going on.

The 23rd arrived and a small mountain of birthday presents for the two girls was waiting in the lounge as 2.00 struck and both Kathryn and Lady Anne ceremoniously arrived with their daughters awake in their cots, although thankfully neither was crying.
It soon became obvious however, that the parents and older children would have to open all of the presents as neither baby understood what was expected of them, although Lady Anne already knew this from her other children but did not have the heart to tell Kathryn beforehand.

Fortunately, everything went smoothly and it was a couple of hours later that the girls started getting tired and after everyone had sang "Happy Birthday", they were both put back into their cots ready to be taken to their respective bedrooms for some well earned sleep.
Kathryn was so happy as she thanked everybody for such a wonderful party and left with John and Khloe back upstairs.

The summer months turned out to be glorious that year and the family spent a lot of time outside together in the gardens playing with Khloe and Lady Anne's children.
Kane & Kara would also ride off to explore the surrounding countryside and find secluded places where they could continue honing their sword fighting skills against each other, without being disturbed.
It was after one such journey that they retuned back to the Manor House to find John & Kathryn sitting by the lake with Khloe fast asleep in her cot, when they called them both over to come and join them.

After Kathryn had asked them how their day had gone, she quickly changed the subject as she really wanted to talk about their ongoing journey and if they would be leaving them at the next full lunar eclipse.
Kane & Kara looked at each other, already knowing the answer, although it was Kara who answered first,
"Yes, unfortunately we will, as we still have to complete the journey through KLOPT0N time which our mother set us on after our return to England when we turned sixteen.

We do anticipate however, that there are only three more periods in time left for us to discover and hopefully after exploring each of them, we will find the answer to our true destiny".

John then joined in with the conversation, as having travelled through KLOPTON time himself, he too was fascinated by the whole experience. He also knew that now he and Kathryn had Khloe, they could not take her with them through the red cavern waters until she was sixteen and would therefore instead be making a new life for themselves where they were for the foreseeable future.
"What can you tell us about your journey so far?" he asked.
Kara was delighted to have other family members with which to discuss their travels, although she knew they could not disclose anything about the future.

"You both know about the seven letters of KLOPTON from the dials on the old wooden clock above the fireplace and it appears from the four eras we have visited so far, each of these letters correspond with a different period of time in history.
If we are correct, then we still have three more eras left to visit and although we assume that the letter 'N' refers to the House of Normandy period, we are not aware from our limited knowledge of English history what era the letter 'O' may relate to.

We also remain uncertain about the purpose of the '0' as this is not a standard letter and may instead represent either the ancient Greek letter 'phi', or alternatively signify the mathematical number often referred to as the 'golden ratio'.
If not, then it could refer to the unseen energy force known as 'magnetic flux', which we physically encounter every time we place one of the keys next to a hexagonal key hole embedded within the rock face, during the full red Moon".

John looked towards Kathryn inquisitively, but she shook her head back at him, prompting his response,
"Unfortunately, neither of us know anything about what you speak and cannot help you with this part of your conundrum".

Kara said for them both "Not to worry" and then proceeded to discuss the various text etchings visible on each of the KLOPTON keys,
"There is another puzzle you might know the answer to instead.
Engraved in an unusual italic styled font on either side of the longest stem of the four KLOPTON keys we have obtained so far during our travels, is a short two-part inscription".
Kara removed the two pendant keys she was wearing around her neck and passed one over to Kathryn, whilst the other she gave to John.

After allowing them a short time to examine their respective keys, Kara swapped each other's pendants over so they could look at both of them, before she continued,

"Individually, all of the inscriptions we have seen to date, appear to reflect different aspects of our journeys across time.

Furthermore, the first letter of the last word on the initial side, matches the letter of the key it is engraved upon and we suspect therefore that this will be the same for the remaining three.

Apart from this however, neither of us can find a hidden message within any of the text and presumably we will have to wait until we have seen all seven inscriptions, before we can determine if there is something else to discover".

With Kara having finished, John & Kathryn looked across at each other and both of them disappointingly shook their heads, to signify that once again they could not provide any additional input.

It was now Kane's turn to join the discussion, as he told them both with a smile,

"It's not time for you to give up yet!".

He then proceeded to explain about a further discovery he and Kara had found on the keys, but which again they were unable to completely understand.

"If you have another look at the very end of the longest key stem, you will find an unusual symbol etched onto each of them.

On the 'K' key stem this is a crescent shaped object, whilst on the 'T' key the symbol looks like the number '2' fused with a long '+' sign".

"Yes" replied John excitedly,

"I can see the crescent symbol on the tip of the 'K' stem, which I suspect represents the visual shape of the partial eclipsed Moon, before it rises high in the night sky to be seen in its entirety.

I do not recognise the other symbol however, etched as you describe on the 'T' key stem".

Kane replied, "You are indeed correct about the 'K' key symbol, whilst I have seen the 'T' symbol when I was at school, where it was drawn on an ancient astronomical manuscript to signify the planet Jupiter.

Kara and I have also seen two more key symbols so far, with the one on the letter 'L' signifying Saturn and on the 'P' symbol the planet Venus.

Accordingly, we assume that the remaining three key symbols will similarly refer to the other three planets, which collectively represent what historically were known as the 'Seven Classical Planets'.

All seven of these were thought to travel around the Earth together, since at that time our planet was considered to be the centre of the Universe".

250

"Yet again, neither of us have any specific information to help you with further" said John, "although I do know something that my father told me when I was a young boy, which may be relevant.

Whilst growing up on the KLOPT0N estate, I was always fascinated by the night sky and not just when the glorious red full Moon was overhead, but also because of the thousands of glistening stars visible on a clear night when there were no clouds.
My father would sometimes take me onto the hills during such a night and we would just sit there in the grass near the rock face, looking up at the numerous constellations these stars formed, whilst he would tell me the wonderful fables behind many of their unusual names.

Once I got a bit older, he pointed out five particular bright lights in the sky that I had always thought were stars, but which he said were in fact planets and he told me what they were each called.
Over the years I watched these five planets regularly, until I realised how they slowly moved across the night sky to different locations.
It was not until I turned sixteen however, that my father told me a story, which he said had been passed down over time by many generations of our KLOPT0N ancestors".

Kane & Kara's expressions changed upon hearing this and they were intrigued to hear what else John had to say, as he continued,

"It was apparently told in KLOPT0N legend, that during every millennium, seven of the celestial bodies comprising the red full Moon, the five planets and the Sun, would come together in the night sky at the same time, to create a perfect vertical alignment with the Earth, pointing directly at KLOPT0N.
During those few Earth hours, KLOPT0N time would stand still whilst the rose pink cavern crystals and spring waters glowed bright red, as the underwater passages all opened up together.
Our ancestors would then appear inside the cavern at the same time to crown a new First Knight born of the true KLOPT0N bloodline, who would watch over and protect all of the family past, present and future, for the next 900 years".

Kane immediately asked first, before Kara got the chance,
"Is this legend true John, as neither Kara nor myself have ever heard anyone in our family speak of it before?",
to which he replied,
"I have always thought it to be something my father just made up to keep me interested, but having since travelled through the red cavern waters and listened to what you have both told me, I must admit to wondering whether there could indeed be some truth in what I was told.

251

If so, then the journey through time you are now on, could be the quest you were set to complete and possibly discover your future destiny?".

It was just at that moment that Khloe began to stir and as Kathryn picked her up she said,
"We will have to talk about this some more another time, as I must now take Khloe inside to be changed and fed", whereupon John stood up too and after everyone said a quick "farewell", the three of them went back over to the Manor House.

Meanwhile, Kara & Kane sat looking over the lake for a bit longer, as they both reminisced about when their mother Katrina told them of their upcoming journey all those years ago.
At that time, she had made a specific point of saying she could not tell them anything more, and was because she did know about the legend?

Over the following months they continued to talk about this between themselves, until eventually Kane & Kara decided to ask Sir William if he knew anything, but he was not very forthcoming and would only say that he had heard of the story, before changing the topic.

September soon came and early one morning before breakfast, Kane & Kara went into the sitting room as usual, but on this day they saw the dial on the wooden clock pointing to the letter 'O' whilst its rose pink crystals had turned bright red.
Both of them instantly knew the red Moon had now risen again and later that afternoon it would be above the KLOPT0N Oat Hill woodland rock face, where their next journey in time would continue.

They immediately sent a servant to deliver Sir William the news and request that he post some extra soldiers outside the rock face as soon as possible, so no-one else could enter the crevice passageway during the period of this full lunar eclipse.
In addition, they asked for both Sir William & Lady Anne to join them in the dining room, before sending a separate message informing John & Kathryn of what was happening and for them to meet in the same room.

The six of them were soon sitting down together around the breakfast table, but with so much to talk about, it took a long time before everyone had finished their food and drink.
Afterwards, it was agreed they would all meet up again that afternoon for dinner, whereupon Kane & Kara went back upstairs to sort out which of their few belongings they would be taking with them on their journey.

The two of them instantly agreed to wear their armour again, as they did not know what to expect from wherever the 'O' key took them in time.

252

Later at 1.00 they heard the clock chime in the hallway, prompting Kane & Kara to make their way back downstairs into the dining room, where everyone was waiting for them as previously agreed that morning.

Whilst the servants started serving lunch, it was soon evident from the sombre atmosphere within the room that no-one was particularly in the mood for eating and very soon Kathryn could no longer contain herself, as tears started running down her cheeks.

She slowly stood up and after gathering Khloe in her arms, walked over to where Kara was sitting so both of them could give her a poignant embrace, before saying,

"I know you have to leave us to continue with your journey, but Khloe and I are especially going to miss you so very much".

Despite wearing her armour, Kara held them both as close to her as she could, whilst tears also began to appear in her eyes and with deep emotion in her voice she replied to Kathryn,

"We will try to come back and see you all as soon as possible, but you have a wonderful loving husband to look after you both, so be very happy together and have as many more children as you can!".

This final comment brought a moment of light relief, as they slowly released each other from their embrace and followed this up with a warm smile, despite their obvious mutual sadness.

In the meantime, John had gone over to shake Kane by the hand, but instead Kane reached out to take hold of him in an awkward man hug.

Afterwards, he asked John why he was also wearing his KLOPT0N armour, to which he replied,

"As I can safely enter the red glowing passageway and stream during the period of the red full Moon, I want to help protect you both from any possible intruder.

I will therefore remain to guard the open underwater passage access after you have swam through it, until I hear the gap shut again and see the red waters recede, so I know you have arrived back safely in the main cavern",

to which Kane said,

"Thank you John, that will be very much appreciated".

Kane next joined Kathryn and Khloe for a gentle hug each, which ended after a final few warm words and a kiss on both cheeks.

He and Kara then walked over to Sir William & Lady Anne and thanked them once again for all their generosity and kindness during their stay, before adding the words "God be with you".

They also asked them both to say farewell on their behalf to all of their wonderful children, who they had come to know so well and would miss seeing grow up.

Meanwhile, they saw Sir William wearing his armour to and upon asking him why, he explained that he was also going to join them inside the passageway and would stay there with John until they had safely left, in case his help was needed as well.

It was now time for the four of them to leave and once through the main door of the Manor House, they were joined outside by several soldiers waiting in the courtyard.
After a quick word from Sir William, they all set off together at a steady pace across the fields to the Oat Hill woodland and nearby rock face, whilst a sad Lady Kathryn watched on from her bedroom window until they were out of sight.

Upon reaching the crevice entrance which Sir William's other soldiers had been guarding since that morning, the three men removed their main body armour in order to squeeze through the jagged gap in the rock face, whilst the soldiers lit some wooden torches to pass them as they entered the passageway.
The three of them then replaced their armour, whilst Kara made her way through the crevice without having to remove hers, as she had now gained a slimmer figure.

They all walked slowly along the passageway until they were next to the red glowing stream on one side and the poorly lit small cave on the other, which Kane & Kara had stayed in with John & Kathryn when they first arrived.
It was this cave however, that gave them the most concern and with their lit torches held in one hand and swords in the other, they checked this to ensure no one was hiding inside, but thankfully it was empty.

Satisfied they were safe, it was time for Kane & Kara to depart on their journey and whilst John helped Kane climb down the rocks alongside the stream, Kara made her way over with Sir William to where the red glowing single hexagon was in the rock.

Once there, Kara took the 'T' key pendant from around her neck and placed it into the empty 'T' hole hexagon, where she turned it anti-clockwise.
After a very short wait, a loud thud was heard in the rock wall as the underwater passage opened and the water level started to rise, whereupon Kara pulled the 'T' key back out of its hole and replaced it onto her silver chain again.

They both then walked over to the edge of the stream, where John helped Kara climb down the rocks to join Kane, who reached out to hold her hand and then steadied themselves in readiness to leave.

Just before they did however, John asked
"Have you both forgotten to remove your body armour before you swim off in the stream?",
to which Kane replied
"We will be fine thank you, as we have been practising wearing our armour underwater for many months now and with the strong current to also help pull us along, we will be quite safe.
Take good care of yourselves and your families, and hopefully one day we will all meet again, but until then it is now time for us to leave".

Just as Sir William and Sir John were about to say one final farewell, Sir Kane & Lady Kara dived off into the stream together and quickly disappeared under the water
- they were gone!

Less than a couple of minutes later, the twins re-surfaced from the underwater current into the flowing waters of the illuminated cavern, from where they waded out onto a part of the surrounding rock plateau.
Initially, they both just stood there for a short time whilst they took a few deep breaths and reminded themselves of the sheer magnificent spectacle the red glistening crystal cavern provided.

They then walked over to where the seven hexagon device was on the rock face and Kara replaced the 'T' key into its hole, before turning it clockwise to close the underwater passage.
The usual loud thud sound quickly followed and as the water level started to recede, they knew Sir William and John would both realise that they had arrived safely.

Kara now changed her attention to the bright red crystals in the letter 'O' hexagon, where she took hold of the 'O' silver stud top and turned it anti-clockwise.
This action caused a loud thud to be heard coming from within the rock wall again, but this time from a slightly different location, which would be the new direction they would be leaving from.

As soon as the water levels had risen sufficiently again, Kara pulled the 'O' pendant key out of its hole and placed it on the chain around her neck, whereupon both her and Kane waded back into the current and dived under the water to their next destination in time.

Sir Alfred with the scroll of Lady Osburh

Part 7

HOUSE OF OSBURH
- 9th Century -

Chapter 28 : **Fidelity to Bloodline**

A couple of minutes later, Kara & Kane re-surfaced in the red glowing stream and climbed out over the rocks to the passageway above, where all of the walls were again lit up by red sparkling crystals.

On the opposite side was an illuminated small cave, similar to others they had seen before and being aware of its potential hidden dangers, both drew their swords and cautiously walked over to check that it was empty, which thankfully it was.

 They next found the single hexagon shaped device on the rock wall, which displayed the bright red glowing empty letter 'O' hole.
This prompted Kara to remove the matching 'O' pendant key from the chain she was wearing on her neck, as she readied herself to close the underwater passage again.

Before Kara got the chance to do this however, they both heard some muffled sounds echoing around the empty passageway walls.
These appeared to be men's voices originating from somewhere beyond the crevice entrance and so both of them stood perfectly still to listen more intensely.

After waiting for a short time, Kane whispered to his sister,
"It sounds to me like there are a number of people talking near by and although it could be dangerous for us to discover who they are and the era we are in, we need to know these answers before we can continue on our journey".
"I agree" replied Kara in a low voice, "but I also suggest we do not lock the underwater passage with the 'O' key for now, so we can escape quickly back through the red stream into the main cavern if necessary".
"Yes, that's a good idea" said Kane.

They both drew their swords and set off stealthily towards the glowing light coming from the full red Moon outside.

Upon reaching the rock crevice entrance, they realised the men's voices were not as close by as initially seemed, whereupon Kane proceeded to remove the body section of his armour so he could fit through the narrow gap, whilst Kara went ahead first.

Once outside in her shining armour, Kara quickly crouched down behind some overgrown bramble bushes for cover, through which she glanced out over an eerie red coloured landscape, edged along one side by a line of tall woodland trees.

Further down on the other side of the sloping fields next to a fast flowing stream, there were dozens of burning log fires surrounded by hundreds of soldiers encamped under the glowing red night sky.

Meanwhile, Kane had made his way through the crevice entrance too, where Kara rejoined him and explained what she had just seen.

After a few moments of thought, Kane replied,

"As I mentioned previously, there seems to be no other option for us but to welcomely engage with these soldiers, if we wish to continue with our journey.

I do think however, that we can use the red Moon light pointing directly at us in front of the rock face, to our advantage.

I suggest that we step out from behind the bushes in our highly polished silver KLOPTON armour, with our helmets on and visors down.

We then walk at a slow pace away from the rock face, until after finding some prominent but level ground, we stop to point the tips of our swords downwards, whilst keeping their silver handles facing towards the soldiers.

Next, we wait for them to see us, if they have not already done so and hope that they are intimidated by our glorious apparition, as our armour shines bright red from the reflection of the full Moon".

"This sounds a rather interesting idea" replied Kara, "but if instead of cowering in awe at our sheer brilliance, what do we do if they they treat our presence with contempt and simply decide to attack us instead?".

"Then we will have to fight!" said Kane with the clearest determination in his voice, to which Kara responded,

"To the death, dearest brother?".

To which Kane replied "I sincerely hope not dearest sister, as I have no wish to ever lose you",

"Nor I to lose you" replied Kara, as they both held each other tightly for a few moments before setting off.

It soon became obvious that it had not taken too long for some of the soldiers to see Kane & Kara walking down the red Moon lit field, as they started shouting amongst themselves and more soldiers stood up to see what all the commotion was about.

Looking back to see how far they had already walked, the twins both agreed that the distance was still close enough to the rock face to give themselves a reasonable chance of escape, should they have to retreat back through the crevice gap into the passageway.

They quickly found some relatively flat ground to stand on and turned to face the Moon with their swords held vertically, after which they stood next to each other whilst they watched several dozen soldiers gather in formation below to presumably await their instructions.

A couple of minutes later, three horsemen rode over to join the other soldiers, before stopping in front of them to shout out some orders.

Shortly afterwards, the horsemen started to ride off at a slow trot towards Kane & Kara, whilst the foot soldiers followed on behind at a brisk pace.

It did not take very long for everyone to come into clear sight, which revealed that the horsemen were wearing cloth tunics with a leather cuirass and long cloaks plus conical caps, whilst their shields were circular in shape and appeared to be made from wood.

The foot soldiers where dressed quite similar too, but without any added cloaks.

Neither of the twins had ever encountered such unusual military uniforms before and in the absence of any metal armour, agreed they must have travelled back hundreds of years in time to a medieval era.

As the soldiers got closer, both Kane & Kara were pleased to see that none of them had drawn their swords and were also not approaching in any obvious threatening manner.

It was at this distance the leading horseman lifted his right arm slowly into the air and spoke with a rather unusual dialect.

He seemed to instruct everyone else to stop, as all the other horsemen and soldiers came to an abrupt halt behind him.

The three horsemen dismounted together, whereupon the man at the front walked forward on his own, until after a few steps he paused and slowly withdrew his sword from its sheaf.

Instead of pointing this at them however, he stood it vertically onto the ground in front of him to match the way Kane & Kara had already placed their swords and after also laying his shield by its side, he waited there looking at them both for a few moments before bowing his head.

These actions took the twins by surprise, but before they had chance to decide how to react, it prompted an even more unexpected reaction from the other horsemen and soldiers.

They all drew their swords to place them on the ground with their shields, before bowing their heads and also bending down on one knee.

After taking a few moments to appreciate the surreal red lit Moon scene that had unveiled itself in front of them, Kane & Kara both lifted up their helmet visors to show him their faces.

Kane then spoke out clearly and slowly to this horseman who was presumably the leader, in the hope he might understand what he said,

"We are knights of KLOPT0N and we are pleased to meet you here on the night of the full red Moon".

Once Kane had finished speaking, the man lifted his head back up to look at them both, before replying equally slow in an unusual strong dialect which thankfully the twins could interpret,

"I am Sir Alfred and it is my pleasure to greet you both here in your splendid armour on this significant day, although I am disappointed that you have arrived too late to witness my being crowned as the next First Knight of the House of KLOPT0N for 900 years.

If you look up into the night sky, you will still see the seven classical planets shining brightly above the Earth.

A few hours ago these were all in a vertical line with the Moon, Sun and each other, pointing directly at this place in time.

These celestial bodies are no longer perfectly aligned however and this is the reason why our KLOPT0N ancestors have already returned back to their own eras.

Once they had left, all of the cavern passages were closed, until you just re-opened the letter 'O' stream gap for your journey here".

Upon hearing this, Kane bowed his head and after removing his helmet, looked back up to introduce himself,

"It is our honour to be here with you on the day you were crowned the First Knight of the House of KLOPT0N and we apologise most sincerely for not being on time for such an auspicious occasion.

Please let me introduce myself first, as I am Sir Kane Klopton and we have both come here from your future".

It was then Kara's turn to remove her helmet, causing her hair to come undone and drop down over her shoulders.

When she looked up in readiness to also introduce herself, Sir Alfred fell to his knees and she was shocked as he called out,

"Lady Osburh, I never thought I would ever see you again!".

Kara took a few moments as she stood there quite bewildered, before politely answering back,

"I am sorry Sir Alfred, but I do not recollect we have ever met before?",

which prompted him to reply further,

"It is I, Alfred your son and although I am now sixteen years old and a knight, do you not still recognise me?".

Kara was totally taken back by this comment, but gradually replied,
"Unfortunately, you are mistaken, as I am Lady Kara Klopton.
I was born on the same day as Sir Kane in 1899 to our mother Lady Katrina Klopton and I have never had any children.
Sadly therefore, I cannot be your missing mother Lady Osburh to whom you refer".

Sir Alfred slowly stood back up whilst he continued to stare at Kara, evidently still convinced she was his mother, as he began to provide her with some more details about his family history.

"The year you have arrived in is 865 and if what you say is true, then you have both travelled more than one thousand years into the past through the red crystal cavern of our ancestors and also passed the time of the next great alignment in order to be here with me today.

Lady Osburh married my father Sir Aethelwulf before he became King of Wessex in 839.
After having given birth to six children including myself, I was told our mother tragically died in 856 when I was only seven years old.
However, there is a small cloth drawing of my mother and I together before she was deceased and from this you must be able to see the close likeness between you both?".

After Sir Alfred passed the picture over to Kara to look at, she stared in disbelief for several moments before also showing it to Kane, who was equally astonished by his sister's similarity to Sir Alfred's mother Lady Osburh.

Kara slowly nodded her head in acknowledgement as she handed the drawing back to Sir Alfred and said,
"Upon seeing this picture of your mother I understand why you could believe I am she, but sadly we were both born to different parents in different eras and this remarkable resemblance between us must be something passed down through our ancestral bloodline".

Sir Alfred tried his best to hide his disappointment, but continued with the story.
"Following-on from Lady Osburh's death, none of us were ever shown her body and after our father married his second wife Judith later that same year, the six of us decided to create a permanent memorial to Lady Osburh in recognition of being both our Queen and our mother.

We knew she carried the same hexagonal shaped birthmark on her right arm as we were all born with and that we inherited this directly through the bloodline of our KLOPT0N ancestors.

It was therefore agreed that Queen Osburh and all of her future descendants, would forever be blessed with being part of the House of Osburh whenever they used the KLOPT0N letter 'O' key during the red full Moon, which you both did when you travelled here tonight".

As soon as Sir Alfred stopped talking, Kara took hold of the 'O' key pendant to show him the symbol etched onto the end of its longest stem, which looked like the letter 'o' fixed to an arrow pointing mid-northeast.

Sir Alfred knew straight away what this etching represented and quickly explained,
"This symbol is identified with the celestial body known as Mars, being one of the seven classical planets seen in the sky tonight".

Realising that such an opportunity may not occur again very soon, Kara continued with another question,
"As you obviously recognise the celestial symbols Sir Alfred, do you also know the reason for the seven individual cryptic messages engraved on the longest stem of each corresponding letter key.

For example, on the KLOPT0N letter 'O' key I have, the text reads,

'only the origin ... will blood eclipse'

Separately, every message we have read so far on five of the pendant keys has had a different meaning, but we both suspect that upon having seen the other two as well, something else significant will also reveal itself?".

Sir Alfred hesitated for a few moments before replying,
"Yes, you are correct, but you will only discover this when you have seen all seven of them and found the hidden text contained therein.
It will then be for you to decide whether you wish to continue on any further journeys or not and meet more of your KLOPT0N ancestors.
Unfortunately, it is not my place to tell you anything else about your future, since it will be up to each of you individually when the time comes to choose your own destiny".

After an inquisitive look from Kane & Kara towards each other, Sir Alfred continued with his own story,
"When I became 16 and was told more of the secrets about the House of KLOPT0N, I began to wonder if Lady Osburh did actually die in 856, or if instead she managed to escape elsewhere through the cavern once she learnt of Aethelwulf's decision to marry Judith that year.

Following-on from the wedding, my father subsequently died only two years later in 858, after which my eldest surviving brother Aethelbald replaced him as King of Wessex and then also married Judith, but he too only lived for a short time afterwards and died in 860.

Aethelberht was my next brother in line for the crown and he ruled for the following five years, until he died in battle during the spring of 865.
My last remaining brother Aethelred then became King and it was his decision that I, as the only other remaining son, should become the First Knight of KLOPTON in his place on this wondrous night.

It is this great honour that has prompted me to try and find out if my mother is still alive somewhere in KLOPTON time.
Then, on the very night of my being crowned, I see the beautiful Lady Kara standing here in front of me, looking identical to how Lady Osburh did when I last saw her, with the same long brown hair, blue eyes and graceful stature.
In the circumstances, you must surely understand why I find it so difficult to accept that you are not my mother, despite your insistence to the contrary?".

Upon listening to all of this, Kara stood there looking at Sir Alfred for a short while as she was uncertain what else she could say to convince him otherwise.
She definitely decided however, not to tell him how much her mother Katrina and her also looked very much like each other!

Kara then regained her line of thought and continued by saying,
"Yes, I do fully appreciate your rationale Sir Alfred, but unfortunately this cannot be true as I have already tried to explain.
There could be another reason for our likeness though, if I am instead directly related to your family bloodline as seems more possible.
Whilst you say there should be over 1,000 years between us, if Queen Osburh did manage to escape through KLOPTON time as you have suggested, she could have changed her name to protect her true identity and by shortening the future timeline, blessed her descendants with her distinctive good looks?".

Sir Alfred was pleased to hear Kara's suggestion, as he replied,
"This seems a very plausible explanation thank you, which gives me renewed hope that I will eventually meet my mother again one day".

He then spoke to both of them on a different matter.
"Looking up into the night sky, it is now time for me to leave this place with my soldiers before the red full Moon sets again and I recommend that you should also continue on your journey as soon as you are ready.

Be aware however, that over the coming months it will probably be a lot safer for you both if you return back through the cavern from where you have just come and also whilst the red Moon remains overhead, so the underwater passages you need can still be opened.

I tell you this because you may not know about the Great Heathen Army of Scandinavian warriors that landed on the shores of East Anglia only a few months ago, with the clear intent of conquering our lands.
A large splinter force from this large army have now started pillaging and foraging across Mercia in this direction.
I have therefore been sent out together with my soldiers to monitor their positions and help prepare our defences against them.

Whilst I would greatly welcome your help in this upcoming war, this brutal fight is not of your time.
Furthermore, with the sheer size of the invading army facing us, there is little doubt that over the next few years many thousands of our soldiers will die, before we eventually secure victory".

Upon hearing this news, Kane & Kara turned towards each other and after a short conversation, Kane spoke to Sir Alfred again,
"Thank you for informing us about the Great Heathen Army's intentions, but as we need to complete our journey through KLOPT0N time, we will take your advice and be on our way back through the red glowing stream waters, instead of staying here on this occasion.
One day in the future however, we look forward to meeting up with you again, especially so we can hear about all your great victories over the Scandinavian hordes".

With the decision to return having been made, it was now time to leave and after the two men removed their gauntlets, they both stepped forward to reach out and firmly take hold of each other.
After they finished shaking hands, it was Kara's turn next.

Sir Alfred however, had already pre-empted this moment by bending down on one knee in front of Kara and taking hold of her outstretched hand instead, which he gently kissed the back of.
Kara responded to this lovely gesture with a warm smile and not to be outdone, waited until after he had stood back up again, to give him a big kiss on his cheek which made the young man blush!

Both the twins then said,
"Goodby Sir Alfred, until the next time we meet!".

To which he courteously replied,
"It has been my privilege to welcome you both here today".

Sir Alfred then turned around and walked over to remount his horse with the other two riders, after which he signalled for his soldiers to stand up as they went off together to rejoin the rest of the troops camped below on the KLOPTON fields.

Kane & Kara watched for a couple of minutes as the soldiers left, before they then made their way back up the short distance to the crevice entrance in the rock face.
Kane went ahead first after temporarily removing his chest armour to squeeze through the outside gap, whilst Kara kept watch until she heard him call out that it was safe for her to follow.

Once both inside, they walked along the passageway until they reached the red stream, where they took a deep breath before diving in and swam off through the underwater passage, which they had left open about an hour earlier.

They soon resurfaced inside the main glowing cavern and straight away waded over to where the seven hexagon device was located amongst the rocks, so Kara could replace and lock the 'O' key hole to now close the gap in the underwater rock wall behind them.
After the usual loud thud was heard, they rested whilst the red water level began to decrease again and soon realised which period in time they would be visiting next.

Back in the seven hexagon device, the only other letter key crystals still glowing bright red belonged to the 'T' key and the twins were both delighted they would be re-joining John, Kathryn & baby Khloe again so soon after they had just left them.
Kara immediately unlocked the 'T' key stud and removed it from its hole, whereupon the loud thud was heard as the previous underwater passage in the rock wall opened up to let the cavern water rise again.

They soon waded back into the deep red glowing water and were both quickly swimming along with the strong stream current through the gap, before climbing out over the rocks onto the passageway again.
Kara locked the single hexagon 'T' hole in the rock wall with its key and the underwater passage shut behind them with another loud thud.

As they rested for a couple of minutes whilst the stream level decreased yet again, Kane took the opportunity to discuss with Kara some of the history he had learnt about Sir Alfred whilst they were younger.

"I am not sure if the English medieval lessons you had at your school covered the same eras as mine did, but do you realise who we have just actually met?".

Kara looked at her brother rather quizzically, before replying,
"Apart from everything I now know about Sir Alfred and his family after what he just told us, I do not recollect being taught anything specific about his period in history at my school",
which response prompted Kane to briefly tell her what he knew.

"The thirteen year war against the Great Heathen Army was eventually won in 878 by Sir Alfred, who had become King in 871 after his brother died.
Subsequently, after numerous other victories in battle during his rule, he was later bestowed with the title of 'Alfred the Great' due to his success in defeating the vikings, but also transforming many aspects of Christian life and society across parts of Britain for the better.

It therefore makes me wonder if Alfred used his position as First Knight of KLOPT0N to visit the future to learn other things, including what his enemies plans were and thus helped him defeat them all?".

"Now you mention this" replied Kara, "I do remember hearing of his titled name and from what you say about his many great feats, it could indeed be true that he travelled through KLOPT0N time to gain the information needed and if so, it is evident that he used such knowledge very wisely!".

The bright red Moon light coming through the gap at the end of the passageway started to go dull and realising that they had only just made it back in time to that era, Kane & Kara started to make their way along to the rock crevice exit.

After only a few short steps however, they both suddenly noticed someone else standing up ahead of them in the shadows, but not recognising who this was and therefore fearing the worst, they both immediately drew their swords in readiness to defend themselves as necessary.

Part 8

HOUSE OF TUDOR
- 17th Century -

Chapter 29 : **Tales of Tragedy**

With their swords gripped tightly in their hands and helmet visors closed, Kane & Kara set off again slowly towards the person stood between them and the outside gap.

As they got closer, a man's voice which they seemed to recognise called out to them,

"Is that you Sir Kane & Lady Kara who I see both wearing such splendid glistening KLOPT0N armour here in the remaining red light of this ever darkening passageway?".

The twins looked at each other quite puzzled as they tried to identify who the voice belonged to, but they were both unsure as Kane shouted back to the man who was also wearing a suit of shining armour,

"Yes, it is us, but due to the dark shadows you are standing in and your voice being muffled by the surrounding rock walls, neither of us are able to tell who you are from this distance Sir knight?",

to which the man spoke again, but this time a lot louder,

"I am Sir John Klopton, husband of Lady Kathryn and I have been coming to this passageway during the period of every full red Moon for the past thirty-five years since you departed KLOPT0N, just waiting for the day you would come back to rejoin us".

They were both totally surprised and also unconvinced by the man's statement, with Kara being the quickest to reply,

"We do not understand what you are saying Sir Knight, as we have only been gone from this passageway and time for just over an hour!",

to which the man responded further,

"Whilst you may have departed from here in 1565, the year you have arrived back in is now 1600!

If however, you do not believe what I am saying, then both please step forward a few more yards and remove your helmets, whilst at the same time I will also come out of the shadows towards you.

We can then all see each others faces and also talk more easily without having to shout".

Kane & Kara nodded to each other and after replacing their swords in their sheafs, they took their helmets off and walked further down the passageway.

Ahead of them they saw the man move from out of the rock face where he had been standing and into a much better lit area.

After several moments of just staring at each other in the dim light, the man edged forward a few more steps before speaking again,

"I am delighted to see that it is indeed the two of you as I hoped it would be, although neither of you appear to have aged a single day since you left here all those years ago!".

This seemed a very strange comment for the man to make, until both the twins realised that although he looked old due to his grey hair, he did have many of John's facial features.

After further hesitation, Kane made an unexpected comment,

"If this really is you John, then you definitely seem to have aged quite considerably since we last saw you".

"Yes, it is definitely me, although I am clearly much older than either of you will remember" the man replied, before continuing to briefly explain,

"I am 59 years of age this year, whilst Kathryn is 54 and we have had four children including Khloe, who is also now married and has three children of her own, plus two young grandchildren!".

Kane & Kara just stood there for a while in sheer disbelief at what they were hearing, before they walked up even closer to where he was standing and after one further look into his eyes, they were finally convinced that he was indeed the same John Klopton they said goodbye to earlier that night.

They both then gave him huge welcoming smiles as Kane reached out to greet him first with the firmest of handshakes, after which Kara followed this with the warmest long embrace.

"How can this have happened?" asked Kara after she eventually released John from her grip, to which he replied

"We do indeed have a great deal to talk about as a lot has happened since you left, but I think it would be best if we leave the passageway before it becomes too light outside on this brisk winter's morning.

Kathryn and I now live in one of the KLOPTON estate cottages on the other side of the Manor House and ideally we should make our way over there quickly whilst there are still very few people about, so you are not seen for the time being".

"Please lead the way" said Kane and the three of them soon squeezed through the narrow gap in the crevice on the rock face.

Once outside, they looked down across the fields covered by an early morning frost and could see smoke rising from the chimneys of the Manor House in the near distance.

From there, John led them through the Oat Hill covert and briskly across the open field down to Stony Hill, where they followed the edge of the trees until up ahead they could see a couple of small cottages, one of which was their destination.

No one appeared to have seen them as they reached the front door and John went inside first, whereupon he heard Kathryn call to him from upstairs.
After responding so she knew that it was him, he quickly invited Kane & Kara to come in and wait in the lounge whilst he went to fetch her from their bedroom to join them.

As they waited, Kara turned to Kane and asked,
"As Kathryn is now aged 54, she too will also look much older than when we last met and what are we supposed to say to her when she sees us both still looking so young?",
"I am not sure" replied Kane, "but we do have to be positive about their elderly appearance and try to let them do most of the talking, since we have only been away for less than a day in our time, whilst they have decades of history to tell us about in theirs!".
At that point they heard John & Kathryn coming downstairs and both of them stood there waiting for the sitting room door to open.

John walked in first whilst holding his wife's hand as she tried to conceal herself behind him, but once they were both inside the room John gently pulled her forward next to him, before speaking,
"Kathryn, please welcome Kane & Kara back into our house after their thirty-five years absence from us".

Slowly, she lifted her head upwards and upon seeing them both in front of her, stared in sheer disbelief not knowing what to say, which after a few moments prompted Kara to speak first,
"It is so wonderful to be here with you again Kathryn after all these years and to see that you are keeping so well".

A few moments later Kathryn released her hand from John's and made her way across the room towards Kara, where she stopped just in front of her and reached out with both arms.
Tears started rolling down Kathryn's face, as in a very emotional voice she replied,
"Kara, it really is you!

269

I could hardly believe what John was telling me until I saw you for myself, but I am so very happy that both you and Kane have come back to share your lives with us again",

The two ladies hugged each other as Kara started crying too and it was some time before they released each other, upon which Kathryn walked over to greet Kane and also give him an affectionate long embrace.

After releasing him too, she turned to both of them and said,
"It is obvious that you are still wet and cold from your journey through the cavern waters this winter's morning.

You must please follow us upstairs to our spare bedroom, where we will sort you both out some dry clean clothes and pour a bath of hot water before you get changed.

It was nearly noon before the twins returned back downstairs, looking quite different out of their armour and even slightly older themselves in the old fashioned clothes their distant cousins had organised for them to wear.

Upon hearing them back in the hallway, John called for them both to come and join him in the dining room where a log fire was burning brightly and also somewhere they could talk whilst Kathryn was busy in the kitchen cooking lunch for everyone.

John was impatient to learn about their latest journey through the cavern, but before Kane & Kara had chance to tell him that much, it was time to fetch their dining plates from the kitchen.

They agreed to talk more about their great ancestor Queen Osburh later that afternoon.

After Kathryn had returned with them to the dining room, John organised some wine and everyone sat down to eat the wonderful meal prepared for them all.

Once they had finished, Kara was first to thank Kathryn and with a broad smile on her face she said,
"I did not realise you were such an excellent cook and I look forward to eating here with you again as often as possible!"

This comment prompted Kane to add,
"Yes Kathryn, that meal was superb and you must find the time one day to teach Kara how to cook even half as well as you can!",
which banter prompted a hand cloth to be thrown playfully across the table at Kane by Kara and in doing so helped everyone laugh for the first time that day since they had all been together.

After this relaxed change in mood, Kane decided it was the right time to ask John & Kathryn more about their lives over the past 35 years since they left,

270

"Whilst we were with John in the passageway early this morning, he told us both a little about your enlarged family since we last saw you and we would be delighted to hear much more about all our new relatives",
to which Kathryn happily replied,

"As you already know, Khloe is our eldest daughter, but she now has three daughters of her own plus two grandchildren and they all live in a house in Stratford-upon-Avon with her husband Steven, who owns a gentlemen's outfitter shop.
Two of our other daughters Kathryn and Sarah are also married with two daughters each, but they have both moved away with their husbands Richard and Mark to live in London and Cambridge.

We also had a fourth daughter named Alice, but we lost her in terrible circumstances when she was still a teenager",
at which point a deep sorrow surfaced in Kathryn's voice as she stopped speaking and John continued with the rest of their sad story.

"Our second eldest daughter Alice, was just fifteen when we let her go into Stratford-upon-Avon with a few friends on her birthday, but after she had stayed behind in my shop for a couple of minutes longer before returning home, she was kidnapped by two men after she walked out on her own and no one apparently ever recognised either of the culprits responsible.
It soon became evident that these men knew who she was, as later that evening a note arrived at the Manor House demanding we pay a ransom or else Alice would be killed.

Sir William generously offered to pay the money for us in full and an exchange was arranged, but unknown to us he also decided to set a trap with his soldiers to try and capture the men after Alice was safe.
Tragically however, his plan went badly wrong, as the men must have had an accomplice who saw the soldiers and warned the kidnappers, who rode off with Alice before they could be captured.

Both the soldiers and myself gave chase, but upon seeing us in pursuit, the men threw Alice off Clopton Bridge into the river below in a brutal act of defiance, before riding off as fast as they could along the road out of the town.

Whilst the soldiers continued after the men, I immediately dismounted and jumped into the River Avon to try and rescue Alice.
Tragically, she had got herself tangled up in some underwater reeds and by the time I got her free and back up to the surface, she was no longer breathing.
I desperately tried to revive her, but there was nothing I could do as she died in my arms".

271

Once John had finished, both he and Kathryn shed a few tears as they held each other tightly, whilst the twins could only sit there and watch on with the deepest sympathy, as the sheer trauma of this raw memory was etched across their cousins faces.

After a few moments Kane whispered something over to Kara, before both of them stood up as he said,

"Kara and I are going to take a break in the sitting room for a while and when you are both ready to rejoin us, please do so",

to which John quietly said "thank you", as they left the dining room.

It was almost an hour later before John & Kathryn walked in to join them again and apologise for their enforced absence, to which Kara replied,

"You both have nothing to be sorry for, as we appreciate how deeply saddened you must be after such a tragic loss".

John gently smiled back at them in reflective response, before saying,

"We now wish to tell you both about what else has been happening in KLOPTON during your long absence, since you will be with us here in this era until the next full red lunar eclipse occurs and there is much you need to know".

Kara & Kane looked at each other as they sat there waiting in quiet anticipation for what else they were going to be told, as John began to recall some of the previous years events,

"Back in 1564, you will remember that all four of us attended Khloe's christening in the Holy Trinity Church, which was also held at the same time as that of both Margaretta Klopton and William Shakespeare.

Since then, Khloe got married in 1581 and William a year later in 1582, with both of them holding their small wedding services in the private Chapel at KLOPTON House, where Kathryn & I previously got married thirty-six years ago.

Margaretta never got married however, as the man she fell in love with would not do so and eventually in 1592, she discovered that he already had a wife and two children who he lived with in the village of Alveston.

She was so distraught by her lover's betrayal, that from that day onward she decided to call herself Margaret instead and later that evening she packed a few of her possessions in readiness for her to leave Stratford-upon-Avon and start a new life somewhere else.

The following morning, as she sat in the lounge considering where to go, she saw the KLOPTON clock on the mantelpiece reveal a full red Moon was rising that day.

With having the hexagonal birthmark displayed underneath her arm, Margaret decided that she would travel through the crystal cavern to a different timeline instead, where no-one would know her.

That afternoon after lunch and once everyone else had left the Manor House, Margaret placed a personal letter on the mantelpiece addressed to her parents Sir William & Lady Anne, telling them where she was going and that they were not to worry about her anymore.

As the Sun started going down, Margaret entered the passageway through the crevice gap in the rock face and walked over to where the glistening red stream water was flowing.
Along the side of the rock wall, she found the crystals in the single letter hexagon device glowing bright red and Margaret took hold of the key stud to turn it, but it would not move no matter how hard she tried.
After a while, she got so upset that she started frantically hitting the key with a rock, but this too had no effect.

Margaret had never actually tried to enter the cavern during a full red Moon before, so she convinced herself she was wrong about having to turn the letter key and instead there must be another way in.
After some thought, she decided that swimming through the glowing red waters to the underwater passage in the rock wall, would allow her to reach the crystal cavern and her next destination.
Without any further delay, she climbed down the rocks along the edge of the stream and feeling no fear, dived straight in.

Within a few moments, the red waters began to swirl around her body and as the current got stronger, Margaret began to spin out of control in a downward spiral.
She frantically started to flap her arms as she realised she was being dragged deeper under the water, but it was too late to save herself as she was flung around against the underwater rocks and knocked unconscious, where she drowned all alone.

In the meantime, Sir William arrived back at the Manor House and upon walking into the lounge found his daughter's letter and immediately fetched me to accompany him to the rock face to find her.

After we had entered the crystal lit passageway through the gap in the rock crevice, we made our way up to the edge of the stream where we saw a lady's body floating face-down on top of the red glowing water.
Sir William instantly fell to his knees as he cried out,
"Margaretta my beautiful daughter, is that you?".

By this time, I had already climbed down the rocks into the stream and swam over as quickly as I could to recover the lifeless body, which I recognised as being that of Margaretta.
After lifting her out of the water and up over the rocks, I walked over to lay her carefully on the passageway floor in front of Sir William.

He was still kneeling down as I placed the dead body on the ground and upon realising that it was definitely his daughter, Sir William became completely distraught.

As he started gently stroking her cold wet face with his hand, he started talking to her as if she could still hear him speak,

"Margaretta, you were born of my KLOPTON blood and you cannot therefore have died in these red stream waters during the full red Moon, so you must have been killed elsewhere and your abused body thrown into the stream afterwards.

I promise you my beloved daughter, I will find the pathetic wretch who did this despicable deed and avenge your tragic death".

Sir William then picked Margaretta up in his arms and once back outside the passageway in the red Moon lit night, placed her body on his horse, before accompanying her all the way down the field to the Manor House.

Upon his arrival, he personally carried her upstairs to the private Chapel on the top floor, where he laid her down on the altar and said a prayer.

Afterwards, he ordered his lieutenant to gather up all the men available with horses to track down the murderer and bring him back alive, so he could be fed to the dogs!

Unsurprisingly, no one was ever caught for this traumatic murder and although Sir William bitterly accused Margaretta's lover of being the man responsible, he was in a Stratford-upon-Avon Inn at the time with several witnesses and therefore had to be acquitted.

He was still blamed for at least having a part in her death however and soon forced to leave town to avoid the threats of retribution.

After the funeral, Sir William did not want anyone else from the Klopton family to die in the flowing spring waters ever again and whilst still very distraught, he ordered that the whole outside stream section down the hillside from the rock passageway, be channelled underground instead.

This concealed tunnel was subsequently dug all the way to a new concave shaped brick well, which Sir William had especially built on the eastern edge of the Manor House rear gardens.

From here, the remaining stream would resurface through an iron grill fixed across the new well front and so prevent anyone from gaining access into the running water at that end.

The resultant new shallow stream then flowed through two small ponds, before finally entering the main garden lake.

Additionally, the jagged rock face previously visible within the Oat Hill covert was covered over with soil and sown with wild grasses.

Extra bramble bushes were also planted across the front of the narrow crevice entrance so it would be even more difficult to find and access.

From then onwards, both the passageway's location and the cavern's existence were only disclosed to the next first generation House of KLOPT0N family descendants who lived in the Manor House.

Finally, in everlasting memory of their daughter and to honour the wish in her farewell letter to them both, Sir William & Lady Anne christened the new well 'Lady Margaret's Well', being the name she had chosen for herself to be forever remembered by.

Although the actual reason behind Margaret's death was different to this, all the facts were never revealed to Sir William during his lifetime due to the distress it would have caused him and the rest of the family.

This is however, something we believe you should both now know".

John paused for a moment, before then continuing to explain what happened after Margaretta's lifeless body had been brought back to the Manor House and laid upstairs in the Chapel, on that fateful night.

"I subsequently took Kathryn with me to pay our respects and after remembering what Sir William had said in the cavern when he saw her dead body, we lifted up Margaretta's right arm to examine the hexagon birthmark underneath.

It was then we found out that this was still coloured dark brown and had not turned bright red as it should have done for all children of KLOPT0N once they reach the age of puberty and enter the red Moon water.

Furthermore, upon closer examination, we saw that this was not like either of our birthmarks, but instead more like a scar from an incision, for which there could be only one reason, it was not real.

This meant that Margaretta was not born of KLOPT0N blood nor was she Sir William's daughter and hence why she tragically drowned upon entering the red glowing stream on that night of the full Moon.

We never said anything at the time, but later that year after Sir William had also died, we spoke to Lady Anne about our discovery and she confessed that she had an affair during one of her husband's many absences, but that Margaret's true father was still living in Stratford and if she told us we must not tell anyone else.

Sadly, Lady Anne died in 1594 and we are relieved that we finally now have the chance to share this with someone else in the family, since we have never told either of the other two remaining daughters Joyce and Anne, despite the man still being alive and known to all of us".

At that moment, Kara, who had been listening intensely to John's fascinating story, suddenly spoke out to say

"Yes, you must tell us who the real father is!".

John looked over at Kathryn for re-assurance and after she nodded in agreement, he replied .....

"Margaret's true father was John Shakespeare, which also means that she was the half-sister of William Shakespeare, who were both born on the same date to two different mothers and we were all there together at both their christenings!"

Kane & Kara did not know what to say, as they could hardly believe that one of their ancestors was directly related to William Shakespeare, who they knew was going to become in the future one of the most famous men in British history and across the World!

Whilst the significance of this news was still registering with the twins for future reasons unknown to John, he could sense that they were clearly distracted by what he had told them and so decided to leave them alone for a few minutes, whilst he and Kathryn went into the kitchen to fetch everyone another drink.

Upon returning back to the lounge however, John said that he still had further brief, but important news to tell them, prompting an attentive posture as they both waited to hear more about what else happened, during what they originally thought was only an hour's absence!

John continued,

"When Sir William died eight years ago, he had no direct male heir and whatever he owned was left to his surviving daughters Joyce and Anne. However, as you know, only men are allowed to own property and so their husbands acquired everything between them.

Joyce was born in 1565 shortly after you left here and she married George Carew in 1580, who was knighted in 1586 and subsequently appointed 'Lieutenant General of Ordnance' for England in 1592, following-on from his distinguished service to Queen Elizabeth.

He acquired the majority of the KLOPTON estate grounds upon them being bequeathed to Joyce, but they only stayed in the Manor House occasionally due to their oversea travels, especially in Ireland.

Meanwhile, Anne, who was born in 1577 and therefore the youngest daughter, married her distant cousin William Klopton from Durham in 1586 when aged only nine and she inherited the Manor House on behalf of her husband, although they also do not live here and only rarely visit.

It was agreed that Kathryn & I could stay in this estate cottage for as long as we live and in return we manage all of the estate affairs on both husbands' behalf.

This responsibility enables me to also ensure that the crevice entrance in the now hidden rock face to the passageway, is unblocked every time the full red Moon appears, in the hope that one day you would return to us, which of course you now have.

The only other remaining news I can think of to tell you about at the moment is that William Shakespeare's only son Hamnet died in 1596 at the age of eleven, leaving behind his twin sister Judith and elder sister Susanna.

Kathryn & I were the only Klopton family members available to attend the funeral service and although we both again briefly met William and his father John Shakespeare at the church that day, it was neither the time nor place to try and discuss other family matters, so we have still never spoken to either of them about Margaretta or Lady Anne since their deaths".

This final bit of news from John resulted in Kane replying,
"I think we should all talk more about this matter again at another time, as my immediate personal view is that William should be told about his half-sister if his father has never done so, although deciding on an appropriate opportunity could be quite difficult".

Both John & Kathryn nodded their heads in agreement with Kane, as did Kara.

The rest of the afternoon was spent with Kane & Kara talking about their journey back to the year 856 and their meeting with Sir Alfred of the House of Osburh, which ancestors neither John & Kathryn had ever previously heard about and they found this part of their KLOPTON history really fascinating.

During their subsequent discussions, it was agreed by them all that the 35 year difference between Kane & Kara leaving and then returning to their current KLOPTON time, was probably caused by the Moon and Earth's change of alignment from when they first entered the cavern compared to when they both subsequently left, although they did not really know for sure.

At this juncture Kara stood up out of her chair and said,
"I think this is now enough talking about KLOPTON history for one day, so instead I would like to help Kathryn with preparing our evening meal, during which we can then change the topic, as I for one would love to hear all about your now extended family and to discuss plans for when we can meet them all during our stay with you".
"That is an excellent idea" said Kathryn, as they left the room together and headed for the kitchen.

Meanwhile, the two men took the opportunity to organise themselves another drink, prompting Kara to mutter under her breath with a wry smile on her face,
"Yes, typical of the men!",
although she didn't really mind that much.

William Shakespeare the 'Bard of Avon'

Chapter 30 : **To Be Shakespeare**

Over the next few weeks, all four of them spent most of their time together, as Kane & Kara looked forward excitedly to Christmas Day and meeting up with John & Kathryn's much larger family, who were all coming over for an extended midday dinner and to also share in the usual yuletide festivities.

The cottage was unfortunately a lot smaller than the Manor House and it was therefore going to be a much cosier affair than they had been used to at their other previous parties in KLOPT0N, plus there would also be no servants to help them!
Kane & Kara however, really wanted to contribute as much as possible with all the preparations and also on the day, so the four of them agreed on how to best split all of the different jobs to be done between them and needless to say, everything was well organised and ready on time.

As soon as Christmas Day morning arrived, so did all of the family members and it was a real pleasure for Kara & Kane to meet all of their three children, seven grandchildren and two great-grandchildren!
The day was very hectic at times, but they all took everything in their stride and it was a hugely enjoyable experience for everyone.
Kara was especially happy when she handed over some extra little secret presents she had bought for the young children and saw the sheer joy in their faces as they hurriedly unwrapped them to play with.

Later that evening, after all the family guests had said their farewells and set-off back home, the four of them tidied up before slumping down into the armchairs in front of the roaring log fire to have a rest.
Together with a good supply of mainly alcoholic drinks, they reminisced about what had been a really wonderful Christmas Day for all of them.

The discussions soon moved onto another related topic however, as Kathryn took over the conversation and targeted their two distant cousins by saying,
"It was wonderful watching how Kara was so good with all the younger children here today, being just the same as I still remember her from thirty-five years ago when she helped me so eagerly with Khloe after she was born.

I also see how very close you both are when together and the way you look with such passion into each others eyes, so much so you must please forgive me for asking the following question.
As you clearly both love each other so deeply, why have you still not got married and had children of your own yet?".

Kathryn paused as Kara immediately blushed a bright red and Kane clearly flinched as he tried to find the right words to say in response, until after a few uncertain moments he managed to speak

"Yes, there is no denying that Kara and I have very strong feelings for each other, but you should remember that not only are we brother & sister, but we are also twins and on many occasions we can sense each others most inner thoughts and emotions.

These factors bond us together in a special loving relationship that only other similar twin siblings would ever understand.
You must also be aware that it could be unsafe for siblings to have children together.
We do not therefore believe this is something we should pursue at the moment, especially as we still have our journey through time to fulfil and children would not be able to survive if they too journeyed through the red glowing stream".

Kathryn was not totally convinced by Kane's answer however, but not wishing to be anymore intrusive into their private lives, she replied,
"I understand your desire to complete the journey you are both on and appreciate your hesitation, but from the immense satisfaction John and I have gained in having our family, I can only hope that you do not leave such a decision until it is too late, as there is no doubt in my mind that you would both regret never having the joy of bringing your own children into your lives".

This time, it was Kara who spoke,
"Thank you for your considerate thoughts Kathryn and let me assure you that what you say is very much on our minds, but as Kane has said, we must finish our travels through KLOPTON time first and once this task is completed, we will then be able to make such a momentous decision on our future lives together".

They all then agreed it had been a tiring day and therefore time to say goodnight, whereupon Kane & Kara went upstairs to their room first and after a short conversation, held each other in their arms until they both eventually fell to sleep.

The next day after they finished breakfast, John had some very exciting news to tell everyone,
"This morning I received a letter from the Manor House steward informing me that Sir George & Lady Joyce Carew, plus the next generation Sir William & Lady Anne Klopton, will be coming over to stay at KLOPTON for a few days over the New Year period and we have been invited to join them all for their New Year's Eve festivities".

Kara replied,

"I think this would be a wonderful idea if everyone else agrees, although one question I have is regarding both Joyce and Anne, since they must have been told about us by their parents who got to know us very well when we were here with them thirty-five years ago.

Whilst both sisters were born after we left and have therefore never met us, I still wonder what might be said when we meet up and they see Kane & I not only looking so much younger than you both do, but also not even close to the age they would expect us to be?".

Kathryn respond,

"I too would love to go and am not as concerned about your true ages, since these can be made less obvious by changing your appearances.

For example, John & I will give you both some of our more dated evening clothes for you to wear, whilst you can also add some grey colouring to much less flamboyant hair styles and apply heavy face make-up.

In addition, I notice that Kane has not shaved for a couple of days and I suggest that he should continue to let his stubble grow and then to colour this grey too, which will also hopefully make him look more distinguished and older".

"This sounds like an excellent ruse to me and one which should make the New Year festivities even more entertaining"
said Kane, as he eagerly joined in with the plans for the evening,
"There is also one further matter I think we should discuss too, which is our names, as it is quite probable we have been talked about since we left and some of the staff who were here during that time, may also still remember us.

Fortuitously, since we arrived I do not remember formally introducing ourselves to anyone at the Manor House and there should therefore be no-one who knows our true names.

In the past, Kara & I have on occasion adopted the names of our parents Richard & Katrina when the necessity arises and I suggest that apart from when we are together on our own, we should do the same from now on as required until we leave?".

"Yes" said John, "I agree with this and in fact, it is something we should have thought about before now.

Thankfully however, as Kane rightly says, no-one on the KLOPTON estate has yet been told who you actually are and I will therefore send our acceptance letter on behalf of all four of us, with your names stated as you have suggested".

Kara also nodded her head in agreement.

Over the next few days, Kathryn and Kara had lots of fun experimenting with as many different mature hair styles as they could for Kara's long dark brown hair, as well as trying on numerous of Kathryn's more fashionable older evening gowns available for Kara to wear that night.

Meanwhile, John quickly sorted out one of his dated dining suits for Kane to wear which fitted him quite well, whilst he was also responsible for organising the Manor House stewards and ensuring that the estate was in good order for the owners' imminent arrival.

It was during the afternoon of the 30th December that a coach carrying Sir George & Lady Joyce arrived at KLOPTON, followed a couple of hours later by Sir William & Lady Anne in their own coach.
Upon being advised of their presence, John went over to greet all of them and after confirming a few last minute changes for the following day's festivities, he left them shortly afterwards in the capable hands of their stewards and staff.

Once back inside his cottage, John had some very interesting news about the other guests who would also be joining them for the festivities, as these now included William & Anne Shakespeare who were coming instead of John & Mary Shakespeare, as he was poorly and needed to stay at home.
Kara & Kane looked at each other with great excitement at the thought of being able to spend some time talking to 'the Bard' about his plays and maybe even joining in a dance with them both during the evening.

The 31st turned out to be a very mild winter's day and after an early lunch, Kathryn and Kara both went upstairs to get dressed together, whilst John and Kane also started preparing themselves, although in the end they took a lot less time to get ready than the ladies did!

A few hours later as the men waited in the sitting room, both fitted out in their very smart black dinner suits, they heard the ladies talking as they came down the stairs and stopped outside the door in the corridor.
Kathryn called out that they were both ready as she walked into the room first, followed several moments afterwards by Kara, who for more dramatic effect also added a couple of twirls to her step to show off the red embroidered black silk full length evening dress she was wearing.

Upon seeing both of them so beautifully dressed, the men started clapping their warm approval and accompanied this with numerous compliments, which brought big smiles to both ladies faces.
John then went over to take Kathryn in his arms for a warm embrace, whilst Kane reached out to take hold of Kara's hands with his, as he swirled her around again a couple of more times, before whispering a few tender words,

282

"Kara, you look so amazingly different and if I ever had any doubt about not loving you quite as much as I do now when we are both old and grey, I know this will never be the case as your beauty transcends age and I will always love you as intensely as I do now".

Upon hearing this, a few tears appeared in Kara's eyes as she replied,
"Kane, you too look just as handsome as you always have and I never realised I could still love you so much with grey hair and matching beard, that I might even let you keep them this way after we have left this era in time",
whereupon she released her hands from his and instead threw her arms around him as she gave him a passionate kiss, forgetting for a moment that Kathryn & John were both still in the room with them!

Suddenly, upon remembering that they were not alone, they both stopped kissing and stepped away from each other, before looking over to see Kathryn & John initially pretending not to have noticed, until Kathryn light-heartedly said,
"You do realise that I will now have to replace some of the face make-up I put on the two of you earlier!".
They both smiled, as Kara replied,
"well, if that's the price we have to pay for a kiss, that's fine by me!",
prompting all four of them to laugh out loud.

Half-an-hour later, there was a knock on the front door as the coachman arrived to take them all the short distance to the Manor House in Sir William's coach, which he let them borrow.
After putting some thick winter coats on, they climbed up the steps into the coach and set-off at a slow pace over to the main courtyard, where they stopped outside the front door and were shown inside by one of the stewards.
Once in the hallway they removed their coats, before being escorted into the main dining room and formally introduced to all of their hosts and the other evening guests.

Kara was absolutely thrilled to be seated next to William Shakespeare and whilst Kane also tried to listen-in on their conversation, another lady sitting next to him on his opposite side to Kara was very talkative.
Since Kane could not be rude and ignore this other guest, he found it very frustrating at not being able to hear them talking instead of her.

What happened next however, cheered Kane up immensely.
After the main meal had finished and the servants were clearing all the tables in readiness for the next course, William suddenly stood up and asked Kara to join him for a dance as the minstrels started playing one of his favourite melodies.

Although initially taken aback by this totally unexpected request, Kara was delighted to take hold of William's hand and promptly rose out of her chair, as they slowly walked over to the centre of the room to wait for the dancing to begin.

Emboldened by what he had just seen, Kane also stood up and after excusing himself from the lady on his right, walked past the two now empty chairs between him and where William's wife Anne was seated.
After introducing himself, Kane asked if she would like to join him in the dancing with their respective partners, which request she was pleased to accept and soon all four of them were standing with each other in the centre of the room, just talking.

In the meantime, many other guests had risen from their chairs to take part too and as soon as the floor area was full, Sir George instructed the minstrels to start playing the same piece of music again from the beginning and the dancing began.

It was well over an hour later, after the final food courses had been served and all the drinking goblets refilled, the music was temporarily stopped by Sir William as he stood up and announced,
"I know we have all had a wonderful evening so far and I would therefore like you to join me in thanking the jugglers, jesters and musicians for keeping you thoroughly entertained whilst you enjoyed the delights of this sumptuous meal prepared for you by our excellent kitchen staff".

This request prompted everyone to stand and after a couple of minutes applause to show their appreciation, they all sat down again except for Sir George who had an announcement of his own to make,
"Although the dancing will be starting again very soon and continue until just after midnight when the festivities will sadly have to end, I am delighted to tell you all that we have a wonderful extra surprise for you.

Our guest of honour this evening, for those of you who may not have yet recognised him mixing amongst us, is none other than one of England's most renown dramatists.
Only last year, he finished building his magnificent new Globe Theatre in London, from where he now has a much more fitting arena to perform all of his many wonderful plays.

We are therefore very fortunate to have him here with us tonight and he has also very graciously offered to share with us for our pleasure, several of the latest sonnets he has written.
Please all remain seated as you welcome to our improvised circular stage floor area, the one and only William Shakespeare!".

284

Everyone immediately turned to where William was now standing and after a very flamboyant bow, he slowly walked over to the centre of the room whilst waving his arms about theatrically as he went.
Upon stopping, he then raised his arms up further into the air to acknowledge the ecstatic cheering and traditional table banging coming from all of the men, plus the more refined but equally enthusiastic clapping from the ladies.

Unsurprisingly, for someone with William's talent, he began reading out all of his short sonnets with such a dramatic gusto, that after each one he received a resounding applause.
This elation became even louder after he had finished all six of them and everyone also stood up whilst he bowed majestically.

William eventually returned to his seat and Kara could hardly contain herself with excitement at what she had just witnessed and the thought of how all the 20th Century school friends she made in Stratford-upon-Avon would never believe her, if she was to meet them again of course!

The dancing then continued on through midnight, as the New Year was welcomed in with some rather over-exuberant celebrations.
After the music eventually quietened down, William approached Kara & Kane and unexpectedly asked if they would join him in another room before they left, as he wished to discuss something in private with them.
Intrigued by what this could possibly be, they both eagerly accepted his invitation and followed him into the sitting room, where they found some empty chairs in the corner away from anyone else, whilst Anne stayed behind in the dining room talking to Lady Joyce.

As soon as the three of them were seated, William started to speak,
"Through my father, I came to know the previous Sir William Klopton very well before he died eight years ago, so much so that he graciously gave permission for Anne and myself to marry in the small private chapel on the top floor of the Manor House ten years earlier.

I still remember though, how he used to tell me some fascinating stories of his family history both past and present, but one in particular about a young couple named Kane & Kara Klopton.
They both stayed with him on the estate for a number of years, during which time they also attended my baptism in the Church of the Holy Trinity on the same date as their baby cousin Margaretta, who later in life tragically drowned.

Subsequently, in 1565 whilst the full Moon shone bright red overhead in the night sky, they suddenly left to continue elsewhere on an ancestral quest and he was not sure if he would ever see either of them again.

Coincidently, last month I saw a recurrence of this full red Moon phenomenon over the estate hills and then this evening I meet you two unknown KLOPT0N family members, who I have never seen or heard of before.

Additionally, for reasons I do not profess to understand, you are both wearing face make-up and grey hair colouring, which I see actors wear on stage to make themselves look much older than they are.
You also have very clear eyes similar to people half your proclaimed age, whilst you are unable to disguise your youthful voices and have young unblemished hands.
Please forgive me for being so forward, but I find all of this so intriguing that I have to ask who you both really are and I solemnly promise to never disclose anything you tell me?".

The twins turned to look at each other for a moment, before Kane responded,
"William Shakespeare, you are indeed as perceptive and intelligent a man as we knew you were and it has been an absolute pleasure for both of us to meet and talk with you here today.
The reason for our disguises however, is simply because we would prefer that neither Sir George Carew nor Sir William Klopton recognise who we truly are.
In addition, we will not be staying in Stratford-upon-Avon for much longer, as we continue on our journey along the same family path our distant cousins Kane & Kara took all those many years ago".

Then thankfully, before William could ask them anything else, the minstrels stopped playing and the steward announced that the festivities were now finished, with the coaches waiting in the courtyard to take everyone back to their homes.

This interruption however, gave Kara the chance to say,
"William, thank you very much for your wonderful company tonight and we both look forward to meeting up with you and Anne again sometime in the future".
William stood up and leaned over to kiss Kara on the cheek, before then shaking hands with Kane and replying,
"I would thank you both likewise for helping make this evening so enjoyable and I hope that we will indeed get the chance to meet up again before too long and continue our conversation".

The three of them then walked out of the sitting room together where William found Anne and departed, whilst Kane & Kara found John & Kathryn before all four of them said goodbye to their hosts too and made the short journey back to the cottage.

Once through the front door, they said goodnight and went upstairs to their respective rooms, where Kara was still over-excited after the party, probably in part due to the amount of wine she had inadvertently drank.

After quickly realising that she was incapable of unfastening her full-length evening gown, Kara decided to ask Kane for his help, who having also drank too much alcohol, enthusiastically agreed.

They soon started giggling as both of them struggled with the tight buttons down its back, never mind the smaller ones on the front of the bodice section.

Eventually, they managed to undo them all as Kara wiggled herself out of the dress and it dropped onto the floor, after which she reached behind her head to remove a dozen clips and shake her long hair loose over her shoulders.

It was then she noticed in the mirror that she was standing in front of Kane with just her undergarments on, whilst he was still fully dressed in his smart evening outfit.

Without any hesitation, she eagerly asked him if he also wanted any help in removing his suit, to which he readily agreed.

After some more giggling whilst they found all of the numerous buttons and Kane managed to remove his clothes, they started kissing each other in a loving embrace and soon the candles were blown out as they jumped onto the bed.

It was later than usual the following morning before anyone in the cottage stirred, but as the winter cloud cover cleared and the Sun managed to shine through their window, Kane & Kara awoke.

They just lay there on the bed looking at each other for a short while, until Kane asked rather sheepishly,

"As we obviously both drank a bit too much last night, I am wondering if we maybe also did something else neither of us had originally planned on doing?",

to which Kara replied with a huge smile on her face,

"Yes, I seem to remember we did, but do not worry as it was a safe time for me".

Her comment prompted a cheekily joyous response from Kane,

"well in that case, you will have to let me know when the next safe time comes around again!",

which playful remark prompted Kara to laugh out loud, as she also picked up her pillow to lightly hit Kane with.

After that moment, neither of them were in any rush to get anything to eat that morning.

Chapter 31 : **Play on Names**

After just a couple of extra days staying at the Manor House, both Sir George Carew and Sir William Klopton left with their wives to return to their other homes, which allowed Kane & Kara to go outside the cottage without having to worry anymore about being seen around the estate by any of them.

For the remainder of the year they spent most of their time exploring the Warwickshire towns and countryside villages on horseback, sometimes with Sir John joining them when he had the time.
Thankfully, the plague which ended in 1565 when they originally left Stratford-upon-Avon, had not reoccurred and they found that the places they visited were now much less violent and threatening under the established rule of Queen Elizabeth.

Kane & Kara still wore their KLOPT0N armour when away from the estate however, as it gave them a lot of prestige with other noblemen and the local folk, whilst they also carried their swords just in case these were needed, but otherwise they both enjoyed their new found freedoms and being able to spend much more time alone together.

On the 7th September that year as autumn approached, a messenger arrived at the cottage with an urgent letter for Sir John Klopton from William Shakespeare, which contained the tragic news that his father John Shakespeare had died that morning.
The funeral service would be held in the Church of the Holy Trinity at 1.00 the following afternoon, to which all members of the immediate Klopton family were invited to attend.

Sir John instantly went over to the Manor House, where he despatched horse riders to both Sir George Carew who he knew was currently in London, and also to Sir William who only lived less than a couple of hours away.
He then gave instructions for the estate stewards to ensure that the stablehands had the ceremonial KLOPT0N black coach ready in pristine condition, together with eight black horses fittingly groomed and draped in the red & black crest colours, by the morning of the next day.

Both Kane & Kara became very inquisitive as to what was happening, but Lady Kathryn knew there was nothing they could do except wait in the sitting room until Sir John's return from the Manor House.
It was a couple of hours later before he arrived back at the cottage and upon hearing him enter through the front door, Lady Kathryn called for Sir John to join them all in the lounge.

Her husband was clearly out of breath after racing over to the Manor House and back, but soon recovered sufficiently to tell them all the sad news, whereupon they agreed that once the funeral was over and before William Shakespeare returned to London, they must find the time to discuss with him the truth about Margaretta (*aka Margaret*).

In the circumstances, Kane & Kara would once again have to both wear facial make-up and colour their hair grey for the day, whilst also calling themselves by their parents' names when necessary.
Furthermore, although Sir John and Kane (*aka Sir Richard*) would be wearing their KLOPTON armour for the duration of the funeral service, Kara (*aka Lady Katrina*) would need a formal black mourning dress instead of her armour.
Once they had finished discussing this matter, Lady Kathryn took Kara upstairs to sort out appropriate outfits for each of them to wear on such a somber occasion.

The next day was soon upon them all and just after dawn a messenger arrived with a brief note for Sir John, which confirmed that Sir George Carew would be riding from London for the funeral with his lieutenant and they should be at the Manor House before noon.
Unfortunately though, his wife Lady Joyce would not be able to join them on this sad occasion, as it was too short notice for her to travel such a long distance on horseback and a coach would not have made it to Stratford-upon-Avon on time.

A couple of hours later however, Sir William Klopton and his wife arrived at the Manor House in their own private coach.
Whilst Lady Anne went straight upstairs to her bed chambers to freshen up after their journey, Sir William joined Sir John outside to review all necessary travel arrangements for the funeral.

After they had checked the ceremonial KLOPTON coach and black horses were ready, it was agreed the three ladies would travel in this together with Sir George, who would be tired after his long trip.

Meanwhile, the two of them plus Sir Richard (*aka Kane*), would all ride their horses at the front of the coach driven by two coachmen, to ensure that it had a clear path to the church door, whilst Sir George's lieutenant would keep guard at the rear.

As Sir William went inside to join his wife and freshen up, Sir John borrowed his private coach to fetch the other three from his cottage.
Upon returning back, the ladies went inside the Manor House as Sir John and Sir Richard (*aka Kane*) waited outside with the KLOPTON coach for Sir George to arrive.

Just after the main hallway clock had struck 12.00, two horsemen could be seen riding up the long driveway, who they soon recognised to be Sir George and his lieutenant.

Upon reaching the courtyard, the two men quickly dismounted and whilst a couple of squires took hold of their horses, Sir William appeared through the front door to join Sir John and Sir Richard (*aka Kane*) in greeting them, before going inside for some refreshments and a short rest after their long journey.

Twenty minutes later everyone came back outside to take their respective places, either inside the coach or on the horses as previously arranged and they all set off on the short ride into town.

As they approached the Church of the Holy Trinity their coach came to a virtual standstill due to the hundreds of towns people lining the streets surrounding John Shakespeare's coffin, whilst it lay outside the main church doors in an open hearse waiting to be taken inside for the service.

Not wishing to injure anyone, Sir William instructed that all the horses be brought to a halt where they were, after which the men dismounted and once Sir George had stepped out of the coach, they helped all the ladies to alight too.
Whilst the lieutenant and coachmen stayed with the coach and horses, Sir George led the three couples slowly on foot through the centre of the crowds up to the church doors.

Once there, the doors were opened and William Shakespeare appeared as he stepped outside to meet them all.
After a solemn greeting with each of them separately, he turned to Sir Richard (*aka Kane*) last and asked a special request from him,
"Unfortunately Sir Richard, I am one coffin bearer short and I would be grateful if you are able to please join me in taking my father's body up to the altar for the funeral service?".
"It would be a great honour for me to do so", he replied without any hesitation.

Sir Richard (*aka Kane*) then turned to ask Sir George for a favour,
"May I ask if you would please accompany my wife Lady Katrina (*aka Kara*) to her pew for me, as William has just requested my help in carrying his father's coffin into the church?".
Sir George readily agreed and promptly took hold of her arm, after which the six of them stepped through the open doors and made their way up the aisle at a dignified pace, to where several spaces were reserved for all of them.

As the time reached 1.00, the vicar stood up at the altar and asked for everyone to be upstanding.

A solitary trumpet was blown outside and the townsfolk who were watching all bowed their heads as John's coffin draped in the Shakespeare colours, was carefully lifted out of the hearse in readiness to be brought inside.

By this time, the vicar had walked down the aisle to meet the coffin at the church doors where he said a short prayer, before turning back around to lead William Shakespeare and the other five men slowly up to the altar, where they lay the coffin down on top of a large ornate block of stone in the centre of the aisle.

The men then all stepped to one side whilst William took his father's sword from out of its sheath on his belt and placed it on top of the coffin lid, after which they all took their places in the pews.

It was a long and moving service, during which William also read out a couple of poignant and meaningful sonnets he had specially written in honour of his deceased father.

After the service was finished, everyone stood up as William with the help of the other five men lifted the coffin up again.

This time they made their way at a steady pace through the side door of the Church to the graveyard outside, where a burial plot had already been excavated in a secluded corner and John Shakespeare was finally laid to rest after another short prayer from the vicar.

With the funeral now over, most of the mourners soon started to leave the church yard.

Once the number of remaining guests had decreased, William & Anne Shakespeare walked over to introduce both their daughters Susanna and Judith, his mother Mary, sister Joan and brothers Edmund, Gilbert and Richard plus their children, to the Klopton family attending.

After much conversation between them all, it soon became time for Sir George and Sir William & Lady Anne to be on their way back to their respective homes, as it would be dusk in a couple of hours and they had a long way to travel.

As soon as they had left, it was Sir John and Sir Richard (*aka Kane*) plus their wives turn to depart next.

Whilst they prepared for their short trip back to the KLOPTON estate cottage, William Shakespeare briefly interrupted them with a specific request,

"I have decided not to leave Stratford until tomorrow morning and I would instead welcome the opportunity to discuss something very important with you all, before I return back to my lodgings in London.

I am hoping therefore, that I may come over to the Manor House this evening after dinner and we can speak on a very private matter?".

Sir John was quickest to reply,

"Yes, tonight will be fine for us, although to ensure that we have the privacy you require, I would like to invite you over instead to the estate cottage where I have been living most of the time since the previous Sir William Klopton died.

How would a time of 8.00 suit you?",

to which William responded,

"Yes, that will be ideal thank you and I look forward to meeting you all again", whereupon they said their farewells and set off back to their respective homes.

Once back in the cottage, the rest of the afternoon soon passed and after an early dinner they all waited patiently in the lounge for William Shakespeare to arrive, whilst they discussed what they assumed would be the main topic of conversation that evening.

Just before 8.00 they heard a horse galloping up the cottage pathway before it came to a halt outside and as Sir John opened the front door he saw that it was William, whereupon he immediately helped him to tether his steed in the small paddock before they both went inside quickly to get out of the cold.

Upon entering the lounge, the others all stood up to greet him again, whilst Lady Kathryn got him a drink and they all then sat down together, with William given the chair closest to the fire so he could get warm again before his journey home later.

William however, took them all by surprise, as he began telling them something they had not expected,

"I have been to the Manor House many times with my father since I was young and I always enjoyed exploring the unique building and lovely gardens, so much so I was delighted that the previous Sir William Klopton agreed to let me marry Anne in the private family chapel on the top floor when I was eighteen.

We were also graciously invited to stay the night in one of the bedroom suites on the first floor.

In the morning, after I opened the windows to take in some air and look out over the glorious inner symmetrical courtyard below, I realised how good the acoustics were and how clear I could hear the members of family talking on the ground below me.

It was this occasion that influenced me into designing aspects of the Globe Theatre for the sound benefit of both the actors and audience, which I recently finished building in London for the future performance of all my plays.

One such play I have still yet to finish writing is called 'Hamlet', which name I specifically chose in memory of my only beloved son Hamnet who tragically died when he was only eleven years old.

This new play includes a female character I have created named 'Ophelia', who dies by drowning after her lover deserts her.

I was inspired for this part of the play's tragic storyline by the sad drowning of Lady Margaret Klopton, who is remembered by a concave brick well built at the end of a small stream on the edge of the garden.

You will no doubt know that she was born to the previous Sir William & Lady Anne Klopton and christened Margaretta in the Church of the Holy Trinity, which events both happened on the same dates as I was born and then christened by the same vicar.

Lady Margaret (*aka Margaretta*) was of course, the sister of Lady Joyce Klopton who is now married to Sir George Carew, and also sister of Lady Anne Klopton who is married to her cousin Sir William Klopton.

In view of all these related circumstances, it has always been my desire to hopefully perform a few scenes from this new play within the inner courtyard of the Manor House, where a well is also located.

Before I had the chance to make such a request of you however, another matter which I did not want to believe could be true was revealed to me by my father whilst he lay on his death bed.

What I am about to tell all of you must never be told to anyone else, especially whilst my mother Mary is still alive, as if she was to ever find out then she would become even more distraught than she is today and may not therefore survive such a revelation".

Sir John responded,
"I can assure you that none of us will ever disclose what you wish to tell us here today, so please continue",
which statement prompted William to look over at the other three of them as they all nodded their heads in agreement, whereupon he took a deep breath before saying,
"I sincerely regret having to tell all of you this, but Lady Margaretta (*aka Margaret*) was not the daughter of the previous Sir William Klopton, despite everyone I know always believing she was.
In fact, her true birth father was none other than my own father John Shakespeare, which incidentally makes Margaret my half-sister!".

As he paused hoping for a response, the four of them all sat there motionless without saying a word, thus ensuring that William was next to speak again,
"Please forgive me for asking, but from your reactions, was this family secret kept hidden from all four of you too?", which question led Sir John to reply,

293

"It was I who found Lady Margaretta's body all those years ago and upon my discovering the false KLOPTON birthmark etched on her arm, I realised Sir William could not be her birth father, but I did not tell him this at that time, nor did I know who her true father could possibly be.

Subsequently, when Sir William died two years later, Lady Anne confided in me about her relationship with your father and I promised to never disclose this fact until after both of their deaths, hence why I could not tell you anything about this matter before today".
"I fully understand and respect you Sir John for honouring your word to Lady Margaretta's mother",
replied William, before he then asked them another equally significant question,

"In view of this unwelcome situation we are now all aware of, I would very much like to know if any of you think it would be at all beneficial to talk about this indiscretion with anyone else?
Such a revelation would also have to include Lady Margaretta's two sisters, my four siblings and also most importantly, my mother Mary?
I personally believe that whilst the truth is important, there is nothing to be gained that I can see, by any of us revealing this very private matter any further than amongst ourselves.
Furthermore, such a lack of disclosure would also avoid the public and family embarrassment otherwise inevitably caused".

The four of them looked over at each other and in turn all nodded their heads in agreement, whereupon Sir John replied on their behalf,
"We concur with you William, there is definitely no need to cause any sort of scandal and we therefore all solemnly promise to take this family secret with each of us to our graves".

Their answer prompted a short sigh of relief by William, who responded,
"I thank you all for your understanding.
Unfortunately however, I no longer think it would be appropriate for me to perform the scenes from my new play in the Manor House inner courtyard, as I previously mentioned.
Instead, all of you must visit me in London one day and when you do, I will be delighted to organise some tickets for you to come and see the whole of 'Hamlet' being performed at my new Globe Theatre".

William then stood up and said,
"It is now time for me to leave, but I thank you all for your hospitality and I look forward to us meeting again sometime in the future".
Whereupon, the four of them also stood up to say farewell to William, after which Sir John took him outside to untether his horse, from where he was soon heard riding off back to his house in Stratford-upon-Avon.

Upon returning inside the cottage, John joined the others in getting himself another drink and then sat down again in front of the log fire hoping to relax, but this only lasted a couple of minutes as Kane started talking loud enough to ensure everyone heard what he was saying,
"It has certainly been a very intriguing night for all of us so far, but the revelation by William Shakespeare has prompted Kara & I to agree it is now time for us to disclose something important we have previously withheld from you, for reasons which will soon become apparent.

After all the years we have known you both, we consider you to be our closest and most trusted friends.
We have therefore decided we must try to help you keep safe once we have set off again on our journey through the cavern, but before I begin I must know if you are aware of the doctrine told to everyone born of the KLOPT0N bloodline, which is to never change events in time?".

John & Kathryn both looked over and nodded to each other, before confirming to Kane,
"We were told this by our respective parents when we came of age",
whereupon he continued,
"You will understand therefore, why you must both consider your future actions in this matter very carefully, once I have finished telling you what Kara & I already know".

Kane suddenly hesitated for a few moments as he became uncertain how best it was for him to start, until he just blurted it out instead,
"Neither Kara nor myself were from the time period in your past which we originally told you we were, but instead we were actually both born several hundred years later in your future and hence why we know that Queen Elizabeth will die in the year 1603.

By then, Sir William & Lady Anne will have sold their share of the KLOPT0N estate to Sir George & Lady Joyce who will own it all, but they rarely come to visit the Manor House and once James of the House of Stuart has become King of England, Sir George subsequently rents out the estate to Ambrose Rookwood.

Afterwards in November 1605, Ambrose together with several other co-conspirators, will try to blow up King James and the House of Lords with gunpowder, but they will not succeed and are either captured or killed, with Ambrose being executed the following January.
This failed plot will lead to numerous other significant repercussions and although neither Sir George nor William Shakespeare, who both knew some of the conspirators will be implicated, we nevertheless recommend that you are very vigilant during this period and avoid any possible suspicion falling on you due to living on the estate at the time".

After a long pause to reflect on what they had just heard, John eventually spoke,
"Thank you for warning us both of this potential risk to our future lives and at least we now have plenty of time to decide on what course of action we should take, without threatening the timeline which you have revealed to us.

Indeed, this conundrum proves why such a doctrine exists and therefore, particularly in view of our ages and large family, we may simply do nothing and instead just wait to let time happen, thus avoiding any possible negative implications on our future".

Kara also had something to add,
"This option you suggest John, may indeed prove to be the wisest solution for everyone, but whatever you ultimately decide, we know we can trust you both to take the right path and not change the future.
You should also realise that we too find all of this very frustrating, as for example, we would love to talk more with William Shakespeare about his future as we know what it is, but we cannot.

Yet when he met us, William knew that neither Kane nor I were of the age we pretended to be in his presence and when we have gone, it is very likely he will ask you some more questions about us, to which you will have to get your answers well prepared".
All four of them sat there quietly for a while and after finishing their drinks, agreed they would retire and try to get some sleep, although after what had been discussed that night, they knew it would probably be quite a difficult task.

Christmas and New Year soon came around again, but this time there was no party in the Manor House, but John & Kathryn's extended family did come to the cottage on Christmas Day and another joyous time was had by everyone.

Once spring arrived, the four of them realised it would not be too long before the next red Moon appeared overhead again and Kane & Kara would have to continue on their journey together.
Kathryn especially did not want Kara to go, even though she knew they both must, since that might be the last time they would ever see each other again.

The full red Moon 'Classical Planet'

Part 9

HOUSE OF KLOPT0N
- 18th Century -

Chapter 32 : **Ancestral Alignment**

It was a late September morning when a weary-eyed Kara was woken up by a bright red light glowing from the rose pink crystals contained within the KLOPT0N key pendants.
She usually wore these on the silver chain around her neck, but to avoid discomfort whilst sleeping she would place these on top of her small bedside table overnight.

Upon reaching over to find out which one of the keys had started to turn red, Kara was totally surprised to see that they both were and she immediately shook Kane vigorously to wake him up, so he too could look at them glowing red together.

Wondering why Kara was being so overexcitable at such an early hour however, Kane rather sleepily tried to simply ignore her, but instead she reacted to his overwhelming lack of response by firmly placing the two pendants into his hands, as she said to him,
"Kane, it is important that you have a look at the bright red light coming from both my 'K' and 'T' key pendants, which is something they have never done before at the same time!".

To this instruction Kane opened his eyes and upon seeing the bright red crystals, he immediately realised what this double occurrence probably meant, as he replied to Kara,
"I can only think of one reason for this, but I will need to go to the dining room first and see all the dials and crystals on the old wooden KLOPT0N clock, which John has fortuitously brought over to the cottage from the Manor House, before I know if I am right or not".

He quickly jumped out of bed and grabbed a thick night shirt as he headed towards the bedroom door, which sudden activity prompted Kara to say,
"You are not going downstairs without me Kane, as I need to look at the crystals too",
whereupon, she too put a night gown on top of her undergarments and together they hurriedly made their way to the dining room.

298

Upon entering through the already opened door, they both looked over to where the clock stood on the mantelpiece and were taken aback as all seven of the KLOPT0N letter hexagons glowed bright red.

From what the two of them had learnt over the past number of years, such a full display of red coloured crystals could mean only one thing, they were now finally approaching the end of their lengthy journey through the many centuries of KLOPT0N history.

The time they believed they were destined to visit was upon them.

At that moment, both John & Kathryn also arrived in the dining room, having heard Kane & Kara run noisily down the stairs a few moments earlier and upon seeing all the glowing red crystals on the clock face, John asked rather cryptically,

"Is it actually going to happen, after all this time?".

Kane immediately understood what John was referring to, as he replied, "Yes, it appears so and as we have discussed before, this evening when the full Moon of the lunar eclipse glows bright red directly above the crystal cavern, all the seven different passageway doors in KLOPT0N time will open together.

Meanwhile, the 'seven classical planets' will vertically align with each other and the Earth for the first time in 900 years.

During this perfect convergence in the night sky, the coronation of the next First Knight of the House of KLOPT0N will take place".

John quickly had a few words with Kathryn, after which he said, "Both of us have decided we would like to go with you to the cavern this evening, so we too can witness this once in a lifetime event.

We also hope we might meet up with some of our family who we have not seen since we left our original homes to join you in KLOPT0N time, especially as we will probably never get another chance again".

Kane responded first, "It would be wonderful for both of you to come with us tonight, but as we all have a lot to do, may I suggest we return to our rooms for now and after getting more suitably dressed, we meet up again at noon for something to eat and another talk".

Everyone excitedly agreed and returned upstairs.

After the clock in the hallway struck 12.00, they all met up in the dining room for a good hearty lunch and to discuss everything they could think about for the evening ahead, with Kara starting first, "We should all set off together late in the afternoon before dusk and probably go via the Stony Hill covert in order to reach the Oat Hill woodland, thus hopefully avoiding anyone from the Manor House or outbuildings seeing us.

This would be particularly important as it will still be quite light at that time with no clouds about, whilst the setting Sun and rising full Moon will both help illuminate the clear night sky.

We will also be fairly conspicuous in our polished KLOPT0N armour, which no-one would be expecting to see us wear around the estate during a normal day in the 18th Century, unless there was an armed conflict or a ceremonial occasion they were aware of".

To which John replied,
"Yes, this sounds fine to us, with only Kathryn wearing a more appropriate evening garment to help keep her warm, on what will probably be a long cool evening before we subsequently return back to our cottage a few hours later".

After lunch was finished, they all helped tidy up the meal dishes and then rested again for a short time in their bedrooms, before meeting up in the hallway at 5.00, being the time they had agreed to set off at.

Outside, the late afternoon sky had started to glow with a red hue from the full Moon as it started slowly rising over the distant hills.
They could also see some of the 'classical planets' starting to glisten like small stars up above, as they all set-off at a pace over the fields to where the grass covered rock face stood within the Oat Hill covert.

Thankfully, there was no-one about and once they arrived, they quickly found the rock crevice hidden behind the thick overgrowth and bushes.
Kara went through the gap first whilst still in her armour, before being followed by Kathryn wearing her evening clothes, as they were both slim enough to get through the narrow entrance whilst still fully dressed.
After both of the ladies were inside, the men had already removed their body armour and one at a time carefully squeezed their way through the gap also.

Soon, all four of them were together again inside the passageway, where they discovered that the rose pink crystals along the rock walls had already started glowing a red colour.
By the time the men had put their armour back on, everyone's eyes had adjusted to the dimness of the passageway and they all started walking slowly up to the rock wall.

Once there, they found that the red glowing stream level was higher than usual and the strong underwater current clearly visible.
Realising the underwater passage must therefore be already open, Kara knew she did not need to use the 'T' pendant key to unlock this and instead left it securely on the silver chain around her neck with her other 'K' key.

They all then carefully climbed down the rocks at the side of the stream together, but as it had been a very long time since either John or Kathryn had swam with the strong underwater current, it was agreed that Kane would lead whilst the two of them swam next and Kara last.

Thankfully, they all reached the cavern without any problem and as they waded out of the water, they noticed a few of their KLOPT0N ancestors had arrived before them and were already standing on some of the flatter rocks which stood out above the water level across the floor.
They all decided to find themselves a similar platform to use, but first of all set-off in the direction of the seven letter hexagon panel device concealed within the rock face.

Once there, they immediately noticed that although all the seven hexagons crystals were glowing bright red, three of the keys were missing, two of which Kara was wearing around her neck and the other being the 'phi' key.
They decided to reinsert the 'T' key and after removing it from around her neck, Kara put it onto the palm of her hand close to the hexagon and watched as it was pulled away straight into its hole.

When in position, the key faced in the same direction as the other four keys, which Kara knew was not their usual locked position, but would probably help to explain how all of the seven passageways were being kept open at the same time that night.

Kara also then realised that they could have a look at the 'N' key, which they had not been able to during any of their journeys so far and after agreeing to do this with Kane, she took hold of the 'N' key and it easily came out of its hexagon hole without having to be unlocked.

With this in her hand, Kara & Kane were able to see the inscription on either side of its longest stem, which text read,

'only the night ... will moon arise'

 In addition, they also saw the symbol etched onto the end of the same stem, which had a circle 'O' in the middle, with a sideways letter 'c' on top and a downward pointing cross '+' underneath.

Both Kane and John recognised this symbol as representing the 'classical planet' Mercury, being one of the celestial bodies which would be aligning in the sky that night with the Earth.

Kara then replaced the 'N' key back into its hole, but decided to keep hold of the 'K' key for the time being.

Without it, they would never be able to return through the KLOPT0N passageway link in time to Clopton, where they believed their parents Katrina & Tarak were still both living in the 20th Century, ever since Kane & Kara had left on their quest together.

Upon the four of them turning around to walk back over to the centre of the cavern, they saw that even more of their family ancestors had now arrived and so quickly found themselves a suitable rock platform to stand on whilst there were still a few such perches left.

As they waited for the evening proceedings to begin, the red glow from thousands of sparkling wall crystals reflected onto the glistening stream waters covering most of the rock floor.

This glow was accentuated further by rays of red light shining through the cracks in the ceiling from outside, which all combined together to illuminate the whole of the cavern in a magnificent bright red colour.

The overall result was more glorious than anything they had ever seen before during their previous journey through the passages of time.

Kane & Kara stood there silently as they looked on in awe at this most wondrous spectacle all around them, which unexpectedly reminded them both of a mystical kingdom they had once read about in a fantasy drawing book their mother gave them when they were young children.

After discussing this further between themselves, they also remembered some of the other storylines told in their child's book and for the first time realised how these contained even more similarities.

All of a sudden, the quiet was broken by a loud thud coming from amongst the rocks in the centre of the cavern.

This familiar sound was quickly followed by red glowing spring water shooting upwards out of the ground, whilst covering the silhouette of a knight wearing shining armour embossed with the KLOPT0N crest, who appeared at the same time.

The knight was standing on top of a large boulder, which lifted him up above the waterline of the cavern floor and after the spring waters had subsided, he began speaking with an authoritative booming, but very distinguished voice which everyone could clearly hear,

"I welcome every one of you to this ceremonial gathering of our KLOPT0N ancestral dynasty, on the night of the full red Moon in 1765 during the reign of King George III of England & the House of Hanover.

You have all been invited here this day to assist me in approving your next First Knight of the House of KLOPT0N, who will take my place.

For those of you who have never met me before, I am Sir Alfred of the House of Osburh.

900 years ago on this same day in 865, during the last alignment of the seven classical planets, I was crowned First Knight by my predecessor.

Subsequently, in the year 871, I was also crowned King of England, although those of you born after the Reformation period of the 16th Century, may know of me as 'Alfred the Great'.

Very soon this evening, the seven classical planets in the night sky will once again align directly with this most wondrous of places on Earth, which according to legend was first discovered several millennium ago by our original KLOPT0N ancestors.

This was also a long time before many of our descendants decided to settle permanently on these hills to become our Clopton relations, but in doing so this also caused most of them over the subsequent centuries to lose their previously inherited hexagonal bloodline birthmarks.

Once the perfect alignment of the planets occurs, a single beam of bright red light will form and shine down into the cavern through a crystal covered hexagonal shaped hole hidden in its roof.

Upon doing this, the hole will create the outline of a red hexagon on the rock floor surrounding the spring water for most of the next hour.

It is within this hexagon that the next First Knight will be chosen by either mutual acclamation of those in attendance, or else by a duel between opposing claimants.

Once decided, I will place the crown of KLOPT0N which I currently wear, onto the victor's head.

Thereafter, my time as your First Knight will end and a new 900 year era for the House of KLOPT0N will begin".

Chapter 33 : **Deadly Duels in Time**

Shortly after Sir Alfred had finished speaking, a beam of bright red light appeared through the previously unseen crystal hexagonal hole in the cavern ceiling and the selection process began, as he announced,
"Whichever knight here amongst you believes they are worthy enough to be crowned the next First Knight of the House of KLOPT0N, should now step forward into the hexagonal red lit arena and state their claim".

Everyone stood perfectly quiet for what seemed like a long time, until suddenly a loud voice broke the expectant wait as someone shouted out "I do!".
A knight, who was also wearing a highly polished suit of silver armour displaying the red & black KLOPTON crest, began walking across the cavern floor towards Sir Alfred.

Once he had entered the red illuminated floor arena, the knight stopped still and removed his helmet, after which he introduced himself with a very commanding voice,
"I am Sir John Klopton and I was born in the 18th Century during the reign of King William III of the House of Stuart, with my father having been Sir Edward Klopton.
My only son who was also named Edward, has recently died and my daughter Lady Frances bore no male children, thus making me the last direct hereditary male of our ancestral family line.
Through my legitimate birthright, I am therefore clearly the rightful claimant to become the next First Knight of the House of KLOPT0N".

After he had finished speaking, Sir Alfred responded,
"You have all heard Sir John Klopton's claim to the crown and if there is any amongst you who wish to contest this, then you must declare your intentions now".
His statement prompted an unexpected immediate response from someone concealed within the shadows of the rock face crevices, as a very bombastic voice shouted out,
"I will challenge this unfit pretender for the KLOPT0N crown!".

As a gasp arose from around the cavern in reaction to this statement, a large stocky knight wearing an old shabby suit of armour stepped forward into the red light and in a deliberately confrontational manner, slowly walked past very close to where Sir William was standing.
The knight eventually stopped several feet away within the perimeter of the red hexagon, where he removed his large sword from its sheaf and started waving it around threateningly in the direction of Sir William, before he lifted up his visor and announced,

"I am Sir Edmund Klopton and I was born in the 14th Century during the reign of King Edward III of the House of Plantagenet and I am the only surviving son of Sir Stephen Klopton.

I served with my father in the King's army and I bear the KLOPTON birthmark to prove my claim".

Kane and his three companions were very disappointed and dismayed to see that Edmund had managed to make his way into the cavern that night for the ceremony and that he was prepared to challenge Sir John to become the new First Knight.

Before Kane could say or do anything however, Sir Alfred spoke again,

"There are now two new claimants for the House of KLOPTON crown and first of all I must ask if either of them are prepared to step aside, or whether they choose to fight each other instead".

In response to this question, Sir John was first to reply,

"I will fight, as I will not yield to this clearly unworthy challenger".

This comment prompted an equally robust and intimidating response from Sir Edmund,

"and I will fight too, as I will not concede the crown to such a feeble old man!".

After making their alternate statements, Sir Alfred spoke out loudly so everyone in the cavern could clearly hear his next announcement,

"Both of these knights have chosen their right to fight for the KLOPTON crown, but if during their duel either of them step outside the perimeter of the red hexagonal arena, they will be deemed to have lost.

Alternatively, if I call for the fighting to stop and enter the red hexagon with my sword raised, both knights must put their swords down immediately or else forfeit their challenge.

It is now time for me to take my place on top of the boulder adjacent to the arena edge, where I will lower my sword onto the rock floor as a sign for the duel to start".

Sir Alfred walked over a few paces to his new position, whilst everyone watched on as both knights held their swords ready and once all three of them were standing in their correct places, he proclaimed

"Let the duel begin and may the most honourable knight win!".

It all went very quiet around the cavern in anticipation, as Sir Alfred lowered his sword onto the face of the rock floor as his signal.

There was an immediate loud clash of swords as both men quickly stepped forward and tried to land the first blow against the other, but with Sir John being much quicker than Sir Edmund had anticipated, he managed to land several blows against Sir Edmund without receiving any back in return.

However, after a short while, it soon became apparent that Sir John's over-exertions were not having any noticeable effect against Sir Edmund's bulk and his forays became less frequent and unaggressive as he weakened.

Upon sensing his opportunity, Sir Edmund suddenly lunged forward and struck Sir John with a heavy blow from his sword, which instantly made him recoil backwards.

Seizing the advantage, Sir Edmund thrust forward again and this time knocked Sir John to the ground, from where he valiantly tried to get up off his knees.

Sir Edmund however, was not going to show him any mercy and with both hands swung his sword through the air with all his strength to decapitate Sir John, with his head rolling off into the red waters covering that side of the cavern floor.

Sir Edmund immediately held his sword up in the air to celebrate his victory, but with everyone present having witnessed such a brutal and unnecessary beheading, a loud chorus of disapproval erupted throughout the cavern, prompting Sir Alfred to step forward and formally announce,

"Sir John Klopton has lost this duel and I have no choice but to therefore declare Sir Edmund Klopton the victor.

However, it is now up to a new challenger from amongst you all to step forward, or else it will also be my duty to award Sir Edmund Klopton the crown of KLOPTON".

After listening to Sir Alfred's declaration, Kane immediately turned to look at his sister and said to her,

"You know how much I will always love you Kara, but I cannot let Edmund become the new First Knight.

We both set out on our long journey together through KLOPTON time for a purpose and I now believe that it was for me to take the crown with you by my side.

I must therefore fight Edmund in a duel and I know with your love and support I will defeat him".

Upon hearing Kane's words, Kara slowly lifted up his visor before she opened her's too and then leant forward to give him a kiss, after which she defiantly declared as bravely as she could,

"Kane, I have no doubt that you will beat Edmund, but I also want you to kill him so he will never trouble us or our family ever again.

I will love you forever Kane and after you are crowned the new First Knight, I will remain by your side until the day we die together in each other's arms".

Kane smiled as he looked deeply into Kara's eyes for a few moments, before he then stepped to one side and lifted his sword above his head as he shouted out for everyone to hear,
"I will challenge Sir Edmund for the crown of KLOPTON!".

He then walked over to where Sir Alfred was standing and after acknowledging him with a quick bow of the head, Kane stepped forward into the red hexagonal arena where he spoke out again,
"I was born Sir Kane Klopton in the 19th Century during the reign of King George V of the House of Windsor, and through the bloodline of my mother Lady Katrina who is a daughter of KLOPTON.

I first met Sir Edmund in 14th Century KLOPTON, where unknown to me, he followed both Lady Kara and myself through time, until over a hundred years later he paid some outlaws to attack us in order to try and steal the two KLOPTON keys my sister wore around her neck.
Accordingly, I denounce him as a brigand and a treacherous coward, who is totally unworthy of becoming the First Knight of KLOPTON".

Once Sir Kane had finished speaking, Sir Edmund stepped forward very aggressively towards him with his sword raised and retorted,
"You are a liar and I will prove this by decapitating you too if you dare think you can fight me for the crown!".

As Sir Kane stood there looking quite composed despite Sir Edmund's obvious attempt to try and intimidate him, Sir Alfred spoke out aloud,
"Sir Edmund Klopton you must put your sword down now and move away from Sir Kane Klopton into your allocated position, until the duel begins.
Be assured that I will not tolerate any unchivalrous behaviour and if this does happen again or the rules of engagement I have stated are broken, then I will disqualify the offending knight instantly".

After both knights were back in their correct places and their face visors closed, Sir Alfred formally announced,
"Let the duel begin and may the most honourable knight win!".
He then lowered the point of his sword onto the rock floor for the fight to start.

During the previous duel, Sir Kane had noticed that although Sir Edmund moved slowly around the arena due to his bulk and heavy armour, these factors did provide him with a physical advantage when it came to defending himself against Sir John's rather predictable attacks.
It was also evident that Sir Edmund could yield his large sword with quite significant force and he was therefore a dangerous opponent who must not be underestimated.

This assessment prompted Sir Kane to concentrate his tactics on using his agility and sword skills to provoke Sir Edmund into lashing out in frustration and hopefully make some mistakes.

Once they began their duel, Sir Kane soon took control of the tempo of the fight, with Sir Edmund quickly becoming annoyed by Sir Kane's speed as he easily avoided any of his attempted heavy blows.
Upon sensing Sir Edmund's growing irritation, Sir Kane started moving around with even more effect and began landing his sword with some force and frequency, especially against Sir Edmund's helmet and weaker joints in his armour, making him have to defend himself for longer periods of the fight.

Sir Edmund clearly did not like doing this and in an attempt to stop Sir Kane's more regular attacks, he changed tact and focused all of his pent-up aggression into abruptly swinging his sword around wildly towards Sir Kane, causing him to step backwards in order to avoid being struck by its blade.

Taking this as a sign of weakness in Sir Kane's fighting ability, Sir Edmund felt encouraged enough to use his weight and push his way forward in defiance of Sir Kane's blows to his armour and started to become even more frantic, until Sir Edmund eventually managed to back Sir Kane into one of the hexagon's inner corners.

Remembering that he would forfeit the duel if he stepped outside the perimeter edge, Sir Kane tried to use some of his quick footwork to escape this annoyingly simple trap he had let himself be caught in, but by doing so he forgot how wet that section of stone floor was and slipped over as he lost his footing.

Delighted by his opponent's stumble, Sir Edmund seized the opportunity and with both hands lifted his sword upwards in readiness to bring it down with all his strength onto Sir Kane's helmet below.

Seeing this imminent attack coming, Sir Kane swiftly lifted his own sword upwards over his head to defend the incoming strike, but he was still unfortunately off-balance.
Realising this, Sir Edmund decided instead to take his body weight onto his right leg, whilst he used his left one to kick Sir Kane hard in his chest as it was unguarded.

Before Sir Kane could react, Sir Edmund's powerful kick sent him reeling backwards out of the arena, where he hit his helmet with a thud against a large rock and fell down onto the ground close to the boulder where Sir Alfred was standing.

Sir Edmund knew he had won the fight, but in his over eagerness to make sure of his victory by decapitating Sir Kane, he similarly lost his balance as he too slipped on the wet stone.

With nothing to grab hold of, he also ended up landing outside the perimeter edge of the red hexagon.

Whilst Sir Kane had still not moved since striking the rock, Sir Edmund struggled to pick himself up off the floor again due to his bulk and after reviewing the position, Sir Alfred spoke out loudly,

"With both knights having breached the perimeter boundary of the red hexagonal arena, I declare this duel to be forfeit and for there to be no winner yet.

Furthermore, as Sir Kane Klopton is clearly injured, I will allow a five minute break for both knights to recover from their falls.

If Sir Kane Klopton cannot continue by that time however, then another challenger must step forward or else Sir Edmund Klopton will be crowned the new First Knight of KLOPTON due to his initial victory.

If either knight has a seconder who wishes to come forward and help them recover, now is your opportunity to do so".

Kara immediately asked John to help her with Kane and together they walked straight over to where he was still laying motionless on the ground.

Upon getting up really close, they saw that some blood was trickling through the visor covering Kane's face and upon removing his helmet, realised that he was unconscious with a large bleeding gash on his forehead from where he had struck the rock.

They both lifted Kane up together and carried him over to where the glistening red spring waters were so they could bathe his wound, knowing that its healing powers would help him recover.

As Kara knelt down and rested Kane's head on her lap, John scooped up some of the red water in his hands, with which Kara gently washed away the blood and then cleaned out what was a bad cut.

After a couple more minutes Kane slowly opened his eyes and upon seeing that Kara was there with him, he quietly spoke,
"It is wonderful to see you again, but what has happened?".

Kara hugged him with sheer relief at hearing him talk, before replying,
"The result of your duel has been forfeit as both you and Edmund stepped over the hexagonal arena perimeter.
Sir Alfred has however, given you five extra minutes in which to recover and continue with your duel, or else Edmund will be crowned First Knight unless another challenger comes forward instead".

After hearing this Kane tried to lift himself up, but he was still far too weak as his arms gave way and he slumped back onto Kara's lap.

Upon realising that he was not able to continue with the duel, John spoke to them both,

"Unfortunately, Kane has not been able to regain enough strength within the short time available for him to fight again and as we cannot let Edmund claim the KLOPT0N crown, I will challenge him instead".

Kara instantly looked at Kane for his response to John's proposal, which prompted him to shake his head slowly as he spoke just loud enough so they could both hear what he was going to say,

"I am truly sorry John, but it cannot be you who fights this duel, even though you are more than worthy a knight to take the crown.

Sadly, old age has now caught up with you and being no longer fit enough to defeat Edmund, he would undoubtedly kill you too and in doing so leave Kathryn on her own and totally distraught at having lost both of her husbands in battle.

It is now apparent to me that it was never my destiny to take the crown and instead the honour clearly falls on Kara to defeat Edmund.

Furthermore, in doing so whilst carrying our unborn child, Kara will also restore the true KLOPT0N ancestral line for at least another 900 years".

Kara was taken aback by what her brother had just said, but before she had the chance to say anything in reply, Kane took hold of both her hands in his and spoke again,

"Through our shared twin senses Kara, I know you have just recently become pregnant and whilst at all other times I would be there to protect you both, it has evidently been your destiny to become the First Knight of the next KLOPT0N dynasty and why Edmund has to lose here today by your hand alone.

We only have a very short time left to talk until Sir Alfred will want the duel to continue and before the planetary alignment comes to an end, so we must quickly discuss a few important tactics.

You will have seen during both of Edmund's fights that he tries to intimidate his opponent with his bulk and strength, but you are much more agile on your feet and quicker with your sword than even I am, so keep him at a distance and do not let him force you up to the perimeter's edge.

His main weakness will be his arrogance, especially as he is fighting a woman, so if you feign the occasional mistake such as slipping like I actually did, he is likely to get even more over confident and give you the opportunity to attack him where and when he least expects.

Also, his armour may be strong, but not all of its leg joints are anymore, particularly those just below his hips and you can use this to physically weaken him if you can breach the right spot with your sword.

I know you will defeat him Kara otherwise I would not let you fight and as long as you believe this too, then you will win!".

Kara was just about to reply to Kane, when Sir Alfred suddenly spoke again,

"It is now time to continue the previous duel, unless either knight is no longer able too".

This announcement prompted Sir Edmund to immediately lift his sword above his head and declare,

"I, Sir Edmund Klopton, am ready to finish fighting Sir Kane Klopton for the crown!"

Sir Alfred then looked over to where Sir Kane was still laying on the ground, but before he could say anything, Sir John lifted him up off the ground and started carrying him over to where Lady Kathryn had remained, so she could help to continue bathing his head wound in the red waters.

Upon seeing this, Sir Edmund shouted out excitedly,

"I have defeated Sir Kane Klopton and I therefore claim the KLOPTON crown as mine!".

This statement prompted Sir Alfred to instantly respond,

"Before any such proclamation can be made, I must first of all ask if there is any other here amongst you tonight who will challenge Sir Edmund Klopton to a duel, otherwise I will now have to proceed and name him as your new First Knight of KLOPTON?".

Lady Kara was stood up already and having composed herself, she knew what she had to do.

As she lifted her sword up in the air, she took a big breath and then with as threatening a deep voice as she could muster, she shouted out defiantly,

"I will challenge this brutal thug and in doing so preserve the integrity of the crown of KLOPTON!".

This unexpected announcement caused much loud chatter around the cavern, as it seemed everyone was asking about the identity of this brave new challenger who again wore the highly polished armour of the House of KLOPTON.

Lady Kara then replaced her sword into its sheaf and closed her visor again, before she slowly made her way over to the red hexagonal arena where Sir Alfred was and once there bowed her head out of respect, prompting him to say,

"I seem to recollect having met you somewhere else before Sir Knight, but I am uncertain where this was and will you please therefore introduce yourself to me and everyone else here in the cavern".

After taking a few moments to ready herself, Kara tilted her head forward before taking hold of her helmet in both hands and after slowly lifting it off, dramatically shook her head to loosen her long brown hair and let it drop over her shoulders, as she had done in the past.

She then stood up straight again and shouted out loudly, but this time in her usual voice,
"I am Lady Kara Klopton and the sister of Sir Kane Klopton, who I have travelled through time with from the 20th Century to be with you all today and fulfil my destiny to become the First Lady Knight of KLOPTON by defeating this false claimant to the crown!".

Upon seeing Lady Kara standing there, Sir Alfred could not contain himself from asking her,
"Lady Osburh, is that you?",
which prompted Lady Kara to shake her head whilst smiling back at him as she replied in a low voice, so only he could hear their conversation,
"No Sir Alfred, it is I Lady Kara Klopton again, who you met back in 865 when I was with Sir Kane on the ancestral hills during the night of you gaining the KLOPTON crown".
After a few moments, Sir Alfred said,
"Yes, I remember you well with your helmet removed, as you have hardly changed since then and still look like my mother Queen Osburh".

Suddenly, the two of them were interrupted by Sir Edmund as he started laughing loudly whilst pointing towards Lady Kara, before also mocking her as he shouted out so everyone could hear him say,
"You cannot seriously expect me to fight this weak and pathetic woman for the crown of KLOPTON!",
to which Sir Alfred raised his voice as he angrily replied,
"Sir Edmund Klopton, your disparaging remarks against Lady Kara Klopton are not worthy of a true knight and I will disqualify you from any further involvement in these duels if you continue to show such disrespect again.
Do I make myself clear!".

Sir Edmund begrudgingly nodded his head in acknowledgment, after which Sir Alfred then made an announcement,
"I am not aware of a Lady Knight having ever fought for the KLOPTON crown before and in the circumstances I would ask for everyone here present to show their agreement to Lady Kara's participation in this duel, by way of acclamation".

As soon as Sir Alfred had finished speaking, the applause started instantly and quickly reached a crescendo which vibrated throughout the whole cavern, upon which Sir Alfred raised his arm to signal for quiet and after the noise had subsided, he declared,

"Lady Kara Klopton your desire to challenge for the crown of KLOPTON is hereby acknowledged and accordingly Sir Edmund Klopton, do you now wish to step aside, or alternatively do you wish to accept this challenge?"

Sir Edmund unsurprisingly responded,
"I will fight Lady Kara Klopton, but in doing so she must be aware that I will show her no mercy!",
to which statement Kara strongly retorted,
"I would never expect any favour from you Sir Edmund and equally I will not show you any when I dispatch you with my sword".

Upon hearing such a combative reply, Sir Alfred glanced over at Lady Kara with sheer admiration in his eyes at her courage, before he looked back around and announced,

"A challenge for the crown of KLOPTON has now been made and accepted.
Both knights must now step apart before turning around in their places to face each other again, after which I will lower my sword to the ground for the duel to begin and may the most honourable knight win!".

The contest started with Sir Edmund slowly walking towards Lady Kara with his sword in one hand, whilst he tapped its blade repeatedly against the palm of the other and uncompromisingly said,
"Surrender now, or you will die by my sword".
Lady Kara simply ignored his obvious attempt to intimidate her and calmly stood there waiting for him to come closer.

Very soon he was only a few feet away but she would still not react, whereupon Sir Edmund lifted his sword upwards to show her that he was going to attack, as he said,
"Are you just going to stand there, or do you want me to come over and kill you?",
to which Lady Kara boldly replied, "I would like to see you try!".

This goading prompted Sir Edmund to snarl at her as he took another step forward and thrust his sword directly towards Lady Kara's head, but at the last moment she dropped down low onto one knee, causing him to completely miss striking her and for the force of his lunge to throw him off balance.

313

Seeing this, Lady Kara instantly jumped back onto her feet and twisted behind Sir Edmund, from where she took hold of her sword in both hands and swung it with all her strength against the rear side of his helmet.

This strike made Sir Edmund stumble forward and slip over where he fell flat on his face, allowing Lady Kara the time to take several steps backwards and create a safer distance between them both.

She then looked on as he slowly dragged his heavy armour and bulky frame back up off the floor until he was standing upright again, from where he saw Lady Kara just watching him and realised that she was taunting him, whereupon he could no longer contain himself and aggressively called out to her,
"Come and fight me like a man, instead of like the feeble girl you are!".

Lady Kara however, would not be baited that easily and instead decided to provoke him further by beckoning him with her hand to step forward,
"You can come over here and fight me whenever you want Sir Edmund, if of course you still think you can beat me!".

This response clearly had the desired effect, as Sir Edmund instantly lifted up his sword again and began swinging it around in Lady Kara's direction whilst heading straight towards her, obviously with the single intent of striking her down.

Lady Kara had been waiting for Sir Edmund to adopt this tactic since she saw him use it against Sir Kane and as he got closer, she began to move sideways around him to stop her from getting penned in too near to the hexagon perimeter.

As Sir Edmund kept changing direction to follow her around the arena, Lady Kara simply moved even quicker, causing him to lash out wildly as his sword continually failed to hit its intended target.

Sensing that he was now getting tired, Lady Kara took him by surprise as she waited for another of his frantic wayward swings to miss and then suddenly stopped moving on his primary undefended side.

Before Sir Edmund had time to react, Lady Kara immediately jumped forward a couple of steps and with a precision strike, plunged her sword deep into a weak point she had noticed at the joint between his body and leg armour, after which she quickly retreated to avoid any possible counter thrust.

The resultant leg wound soon started bleeding quite visibly, causing Sir Edmund to slow down in his ongoing pursuit of Lady Kara as he had to take most of his weight on the other leg, whilst hobbling around on the injured one.

Realising this was her opportunity, Lady Kara stepped forward directly in front of Sir Edmund again, but still just out of his reach in order to deliberately goad him once more.

He promptly lifted up his sword and tried to re-continue with his attack, but she was far too quick for him as he struggled with his injury to move around the floor and instead, he could only continue to lash out even more erratically.

After a while, the blood began to flow faster down Sir Edmund's leg and Lady Kara could see from his eyes through his loose visor slot, that he was becoming light headed.

She knew it was time for her to move in for the kill and end the fight.

As Lady Kara waited for the right moment when his defence was distracted elsewhere, she suddenly changed direction and swiftly took a few steps backwards.

Then, to the sheer amazement of everyone watching, she rolled forward over the arena floor and used her momentum to leap through the air.

With a single summersault she landed on top of Sir Edmund's shoulders and wrapped her legs around the front of his helmet, dragging his body down under her weight to the ground below.

A few moments later, after he landed on his back and also hit his head against the rock floor, Sir Edmund realised his visor was being lifted up and saw Lady Kara sitting on top of him with her sword in both hands, pointing straight down at his face.

He frantically tried to reach up and grab hold of her, but before he could free his arms from under her due to him being too shaken and weak from his blood loss, she said to him with sheer venom in her voice,

"Farewell Edmund, you deserve to die!".

Without any further delay, she plunged the blade of her sword with all her strength directly into his head through the visor gap, upon which his body initially shuddered before going totally limp.

Lady Kara sat there for a while, not quite believing that Sir Edmund was actually dead, but then slowly stood up over him and removed her sword from his helmet to wash off the blood in the red glowing water.

Once her sword was clean, Lady Kara lifted it up in the air and with a huge release of emotion, shouted out loudly for everyone to hear,

"I Lady Kara Klopton have vanquished the treacherous Sir Edmund Klopton here today and in doing so, I claim the crown of KLOPTON!"

This triumphant announcement prompted a chorus of ecstatic cheering and loud applause from throughout the cavern, with some of the men also banging their swords against the rocks in acknowledgment.

Chapter 34 : **Crowning Victory**

As the full extent of her victory against Sir Edmund started to fuel the feelings building up inside of Kara, she looked over to where Kane had been resting after his duel and upon seeing him standing there as he joined in with the loud cheering, she could no longer control herself and burst into tears.

It was at this moment that Kara realised she still had her visor closed and after first replacing her sword in its sheaf, she lifted her helmet off so Kane could see the relief etched across her tearful, but joyous face.

Upon seeing Kara so emotional, Kane immediately set off across the cavern floor to be with her and as he got closer, she started walking over to greet him with her arms stretched out.

Very soon they were holding each other tightly, whereupon Kane spoke first,

"I am so very proud of you Kara and always knew deep in my heart that it was your destiny to be victorious here today, but we must now let Sir Alfred complete your crowning before we can celebrate any further".

Kara replied,

"It is wonderful to see that you have recovered from your injury Kane and once the ceremony is over, we obviously need to have a long conversation regarding our future together and that of our forthcoming child, which you already seem to know about!",

to which Kane lovingly said,

"Yes, we certainly do and also the rest of our lives as a family".

As the celebratory noise from all around the cavern started to diminish, Sir Alfred interrupted Sir Kane & Lady Kara's heart warming moment together, as he announced,

"Every knight and daughter of KLOPTON present here with us today, has just witnessed Lady Kara Klopton win with great skill and honour her duel against Sir Edmund Klopton.

Before I can proclaim that she now becomes the next First Knight of KLOPTON however, I must ask that each one of you either confirm your acceptance of her rightful claim to the crown or else challenge her to another duel".

As soon as Sir Alfred had stopped speaking, each knight in turn, including Sir Kane, lifted their sword up in the air and shouted out

"I accept Lady Kara Klopton as First Knight",

before subsequently bending down on one knee and bowing their heads towards her.

Once all the knights had finished doing the same, each lady then took their turn to call out the same few words, before they curtsied and bowed their head.

After a subsequent few moments of reflective silence, Sir Alfred formally announced,
"Every ancestor of the House of KLOPTON here with us today during the alignment of the classical planets and full red Moon, has confirmed their acceptance of Lady Kara Klopton as the new First Knight.
You may now all raise your heads again to watch whilst I undertake her crowning, but please remain as you are until I ask you to stand".

Next he beckoned Lady Kara over to join him and as soon as she was by his side, he led her into the centre of the hexagonal arena, which was still being displayed on the cavern floor by the red beam of light shining through its ceiling.
Sir Kane had already positioned himself in one corner so his sister could see him throughout the ceremony.
Sir Alfred knew that time was now running out and quickly directed Lady Kara to kneel down in the place where she stood, whilst he lifted up the crown he was wearing and held it out in his hands above her head for everyone to see.

He then spoke very clearly with the regal presence of a past King of England, to ask her,
- "Do you Lady Kara Klopton, as an ancestral daughter of the House of KLOPTON bloodline, hereby accept the position of First Knight of KLOPTON until the time of the next alignment of the seven classical planets?",
to which she calmly replied "I do".
- "Do you also confirm to abide by the Knight's code of chivalry and to always protect the House of KLOPTON with your life if necessary?",
she again replied "I do".
- "Do you also accept the crown of the House of KLOPTON and to wear this with all due reverence and honour?",
Lady Kara now quite excitedly stated "I do!".

Sir Alfred slowly lowered the crown onto her head and then stood silent for a few moments with his head bowed in acknowledgement of her succession.
He next removed the sword of KLOPTON from its sheaf which he was still wearing and carefully placed its blade on each of her shoulders in turn to complete the ceremonial formalities.

Sir Alfred then indicated for Sir Kane to join them and asked him to take Lady Kara's hand with his as he helped her rise to her feet again.

317

Once Lady Kara stood up, Sir Alfred passed her over the sword and spoke quietly to them both for a few moments, after which Sir Kane released her hand and knelt down on one knee in front of her.
Sir Alfred then spoke out loud enough so everyone else in the cavern could also hear his next words,

"For my penultimate act as First Knight of KLOPTON, it has been agreed that Lady Kara Klopton will take a a guardian knight to help protect her and she is delighted that Sir Kane Klopton has accepted such an auspicious role.
It is therefore my duty to ask of him for the following affirmations,
- "Do you Sir Kane Klopton, as a knight of the House of KLOPTON, hereby accept the position of guardian to Lady Kara Klopton, the new First Knight of KLOPTON, until the time of the next alignment of the seven classical planets?",
to which he replied "I do".
- "Do you also confirm to abide by the Knight's code of chivalry and to always protect Lady Kara Klopton with your life if necessary?",
to which he assertively said "Absolutely!",
which positive response brought a beaming smile of gratitude and love across Kara's face.

Sir Alfred then signalled to Lady Kara, who instantly placed the sword of KLOPTON on each of Sir Kane's shoulders in turn and pronounced,
"It is with my eternal gratitude that I, Lady Kara Klopton the First Knight of the House of KLOPTON, hereby accept you Sir Kane Klopton as my guardian knight until the day we both die",
whereupon she reached her hand out towards Sir Kane who kissed the back of it, before he then stood up beside her again.

The three of them then turned around to form a horizontal line facing the cavern in front of them, whilst at the same time Sir Alfred instructed everyone else to also now be upstanding.
Once they were all in their right places, Sir Alfred glanced over to Lady Kara and with the warmest of smiles quietly said to her,
"Are you sure that you are really ready for this moment?",
to which she looked back with great joy etched all over her face and replied "Most definitely!".

Sir Alfred then took a single step forward and with his most booming majestic voice proclaimed to everyone,
"Whilst it is my formal duty, it is also my greatest honour and privilege as your previous First Knight, to present to you all the Lady Kara Klopton as your new First Lady Knight of the House of KLOPTON!".
He started clapping loudly and everyone immediately joined in, as the acclamation echoed throughout the cavern, even more than it had done after her victory over Sir Edmund.

Sir Alfred and Sir Kane stepped backwards to let Lady Kara take all of the applause which she had truly earned, as she stood proudly showing off her new crown and also held the sword up in the air.

Although still overwhelmed by the sheer magnitude of this incredible occasion, Lady Kara suddenly thought of her mother and became upset at her not being there to share this once in a lifetime coronation with her. Nevertheless, she was determined to keep smiling and not to let any such other feelings show through.

After a few minutes, the bright red light beam coming through the ceiling crystals down onto where Lady Kara was standing, started to diminish and soon the red hexagonal shape being silhouetted onto the cavern stone floor had completely disappeared.

As Sir Alfred looked upwards he knew that the seven classical planets had now moved out of alignment with each other and the single red beam of light which only this phenomenon could create, was no longer visible in the night sky above.

The cavern however, still remained well lit due to the continuing bright red glow of the full Moon reflecting onto the rock crystals and sparkling water, but this red light would also be gone before too long and everyone had to start returning home through their respective passages to their own era.

Sir Alfred walked over to join Lady Kara again, from where he made another announcement to everyone,

"The full Moon will no longer be glowing red anymore in the next couple of hours, so Lady Kara and I will soon be re-opening each of the underwater passages in turn so you can all find your way back to your own specific timeline.

Please listen carefully when we call out the century you are from and quickly come over to confirm which year you wish to return to, or else you could end up arriving back in the wrong time".

They then both set off to where the seven lettered hexagon key device was concealed on a rock face.

On their way there, Sir Alfred took off the key pendant he wore around his neck and handed it over to Kara, before telling her,

"I now present you with the final KLOPTON key pendant for you to keep safe, as being the most powerful of the seven keys, it is always the specific responsibility of the First Knight to protect.

The 'O' and 'I' letters which you see combined on the top of the key are often referred to as the symbol 'phi' which is an infinite mathematical number.

319

When this key was handed to me in 865 it was known as the 'Forever' key and this is therefore the name I have always called it by, although this is now your choice.

On either side of the longest stem of this key is its text inscription, which reads,
'only the one ... will life conquer'

 Also etched onto the very end of this same stem is a symbol which once again comprises a letter 'O', but this time with a single dot in its centre and when these are combined together, they represent the Sun.

Whilst the Sun was always considered to be one of the 'seven classical planets' by our ancestors, we both now know it is not actually a planet but in fact a star and also the centre of our planetary system instead of the Earth, which everyone previously believed".
"Yes, I am aware of all this" replied Lady Kara, before she added,

"There is however, another question which neither Sir Kane nor myself have yet been able to unravel and that is the hidden message contained within the seven cryptic inscriptions on the various key stems. Although you have only just given me the final key with the remaining text inscription which I was missing, I am no closer to deciphering the answer yet, but suspect that you are not going to tell me?".

"Unfortunately Lady Kara, you are right about this" replied Sir Alfred, "as if I did let you know what you are seeking, then you will no doubt ask me even more questions which are no longer my place to answer.
Once again, it will be for you & Sir Kane to discover the path you are able to follow and then decide whether or not you wish to continue along this on your next journey together through time".

As the two of them approached the rock face containing the keypad, Kara saw that Kane was already standing there with a lady who had her arms wrapped around him, but not recognising who this was made Kara suddenly feel quite jealous.
After getting much closer, Kara was just about to call out to Kane, when her twin senses made her think of her mother again and suddenly she realised that it must be her he was with.

She immediately called out Katrina's name, prompting her and Kane to both turn around and look towards her, whereupon Kara saw for definite who it was.
Upon seeing her daughter smiling back at her, Katrina released Kane from her grip and instead reached her arms out to greet Kara.

It was only a few moments before the two of them were hugging each other tightly, as tears of sheer happiness started running down both their faces and Kara said,

"Mother, it really is you and I am overjoyed beyond words to see you again after all the years that have passed by since we last said our farewells to each other".

Katrina responded, "Yes Kara, it is definitely me and it is so wonderful to see how you have grown into an even more confident young lady than you were when you first set off on your quest with Kane.
I am very proud of how you defeated the brutal thug Edmund and for me to be watching you as you were crowned the First Lady Knight of KLOPTON, is just amazing".

Kara replied, "I can hardly believe it myself and to have you with us both here on what has been such a momentous day, is something even more special than my receiving the crown of KLOPTON".

It was just after this emotional exchange, that Sir Alfred approached them to say,
"Please forgive me ladies for interrupting your obviously joyous reunion, but Lady Kara and I must proceed with getting everyone back to their own ancestral timelines before the full lunar eclipse finishes".

As the two of them separated from each other so Lady Kara could join him, they both turned to face Sir Alfred, but before they could speak he immediately went down on one knee and spoke first,
"Lady Kara, you must please tell me if this lady you are with is your mother, as she not only looks just as beautiful as you, but is also identical in appearance to my mother Lady Osburh when slightly older!".

With all that had just happened, Lady Kara had forgotten about their family resemblance and remembering the story he had told her about his own mother, she replied,
"Sir Alfred please meet my mother Lady Katrina Klopton",
to which introduction he bowed his head and said,
"It is a great honour to meet the mother of Lady Kara and I am delighted that you have been able to join us today to see your daughter win her duel and be crowned the First Lady Knight of the House of KLOPTON".

Lady Katrina replied,
"Thank you for your kind words Sir Alfred.
I will leave my daughter with you for a short time to fulfil her duties, whilst I go and rejoin my son Sir Kane",
upon which she walked over to find him, as Lady Kara went off with Sir Alfred to the seven hexagon key device amongst the rocks.

Along the way however, Sir Alfred could not contain himself from repeating how identical the three ladies looked to each other and how their two families must without doubt be descended from the same House of KLOPT0N ancestral bloodline.

Lady Kara knew he had to be right and that this also probably helped explain why it was her destiny to take the crown from him.

Upon reaching the hexagon device, Sir Alfred explained to Lady Kara how she would use the 'Forever' key together with another letter key, to open an underwater passage to a specific year of her choice.

Each of the seven lettered KLOPT0N hexagons displayed a group of different sized circles around the key hole in their centre, along the rims of which were a series of notches that were etched with Roman numerals, similar to those seen on many old clock faces of that period.

Each of these notches would identify the day required in time by the individual settings selected from its century and decade year numbers, through to its actual date.

They both decided to begin with their House of Lancaster ancestors and after removing the 'L' key from its hole, Sir Alfred asked for everyone from the 15th Century to come forward and tell them the date they wished to return home too.

Two separate couples approached, the first of which asked for a date in 1402 and the second for a date in 1438.

Sir Alfred showed Kara how to set the first date using the two appropriate keys and then as she finally locked the 'Forever' key in place, a loud thud could be heard coming from the underwater rock wall, prompting the first group to swim off back to their home through the passage which had just been re-opened up for them.

Five minutes later, Kara adjusted both of the keys to the date requested by the second group and after another loud thud was heard, they too swam off back to their specific time.

The next sets of ancestors to return home originated from a couple of dates during the House of Normandy period and after they had all left, it became the turn of those family members from the House of Tudor to rejoin their individual timelines.

This meant that Kane & Kara would unfortunately now have to say farewell to John & Kathryn yet again.

Although it was sad to leave them, they knew the next time they visited would be on a chosen date and therefore promised to make the trip on Christmas Day so they could share this with all their family once more.

After Kara had amended the required key positions, the four of them had a few last hugs before John & Kathryn swam off through the passage and back to their cottage on the estate.

The House of Plantagenet ancestors were next to leave, with several couples and groups coming forward before also setting off in turn to rejoin their respective families in time.

It took nearly another twenty minutes before the only few remaining ancestral family members still waiting to return home were from a different timeline.

Kane & Kara were especially intrigued to meet Sir Robert de Clopton from the 13th Century who had originally re-discovered the KLOPTON crystal cavern during the period of the War of the Barons and was granted the estate lands and old Manor House by King John, due to his bravery and loyalty to the Crown.

With time now running out, they only had the chance for a few more words before these ancestors also had to leave, after which Sir Alfred would finally have to say his last ever farewell.

Before that significant moment came however, he went over to Katrina to discuss Kara's pregnancy and about Kane being the child's father.

Upon telling him how the twins had been born after she crossed the void of time, Sir Alfred responded by explaining why neither of them need ever worry about their new baby's wellbeing.

He also told Katrina to tell them both how much they were perfectly suited for each other due to their enhanced bloodline birth.

Furthermore, it was evident to him that destiny had chosen them to have as many children together as they desired and in doing so, create the foundation for the next generations of the House of KLOPTON.

After saying goodbye to Lady Katrina, Sir Alfred went over to bid farewell to Kara & Kane, before he returned back to the House of Osburh in 899. This was the date he died in true time and where his soul would finally come to rest with the passing of the last full red lunar eclipse he would ever see.

It was now time for the twins to leave the cavern and they both decided to initially continue on their travels through KLOPTON time with Katrina.

Sadly, their adopted father Tarak had died during WWI in India, whilst their grandparents had died soon afterwards, thus leaving their mother to remain on her own if they left her to return to her existing time.

Additionally, with Kara being pregnant, Katrina wanted to help them both raise their first child together and so they decided to go to the House of Plantagenet era instead, in the hope that their birth father Richard might still be alive after Kara & Kane left him there in 1349.

As Kara could now set a specific date in time by using the 'Forever' and 'P' keys together, they all agreed to return during the first week of February 1351, since they knew the Great Plaque would have subsided across England by then and it was therefore safe for them to do so.

Kara & Kane decided to keep the 'K' key for KLOPTON with them for now and then set the destination date they agreed using the other two keys, resulting in the usual loud thud sound being heard coming from within the rock wall.

After subsequently removing these keys from their individual hexagon holes again, Kara placed them both on the silver chain around her neck with the 'K' key and together with Katrina, they all walked over to enter the red glowing stream waters.

A few steps later, Kara noticed Kane was carrying a scroll of parchment in his hand which she had never seen before and upon asking him what this was, he explained,

"Sir Alfred showed me the location of a large rectangular alcove concealed in the rock face near to the seven hexagon device, which can only be opened with the 'Forever' key.

So when you were busy I used this key to open it with and then removed this scroll from inside, whilst at the same time I replaced both the crown and sword of KLOPTON that Sir Alfred had taken out for him to use during your coronation".

Upon hearing this, Kara instinctively put her hand on her head to find that her crown was indeed no longer there, whilst she also felt around her belt to discover that she did not have her sword neither.

Seeing Kara looking a bit concerned by this, Kane said,

"Do not worry Kara, as Sir Alfred told me they would both be safe inside the locked alcove and that after we have studied the scroll, we should return that next time we are in the cavern during the night of the full red moon".

"Thank you Kane for dealing with this for me", replied Kara, "although I never knew you had such a good slight-of-hand that you could remove both of these items from me whilst I was still wearing them!".

Kane raised a smile, as he replied,

"I have to keep some of my many talents hidden from you Kara, or how else could I keep on surprising you every now and then!".

Kara responded by leaning over to give him a kiss on the cheek, before saying,

"Yes, that is fine by me Kane and also the very same reason why I keep some of my best secrets from you too!".

This jovial exchange between her two children led Katrina to join in the banter and say,

"Although you both keep telling me how much older you have grown since I last saw you, I had not realised that this meant you were going to give me even more trouble now than when you were younger!",

which motherly comment prompted all three of them to start laughing.

Just before they were then about to dive off into the stream current together, Kara took one last look back over to where she had been crowned a couple of hours earlier and suddenly realised that she could no longer see Edmund's body laying there.

Quickly calling over for Kane to join her, Kara stepped back onto the cavern floor where the red hexagonal arena had previously been illuminated during the classical alignment and said to Kane,
"Edmund's body has gone!".

Kane began frantically searching around the cavern floor area and amongst the rocks, but he too could not find his body anywhere, before saying,
"Sir John Klopton's headless torso is no longer to be seen neither and presumably they were both swept away when the red water levels rose whilst each of the different passages in time were re-opened".

"Yes, let's hope so!" replied Kara, trying to sound convincing as they both walked back over to join Katrina at the waters edge, from where the three of them swam off on their journey together ....

Rose-Pink KLOPT0N Crystals

HOUSE OF KLOPT0N
- A Name Lost in Time -

Epilogue

The journey back to 14th Century England for Kane, Kara and Katrina was going to cause mixed emotions for each of them and although they all wanted to meet up with Richard again for their own various personal reasons, Katrina's desire to see him after such a long time was clearly very significant to her.

Meanwhile, the most important issue for Kane & Kara was the future well-being of their first child together, but they also had many questions that needed answering about their own true conception as 'twins', their baby's birth and how they would move forward as a family in time.

Additionally, Kara now had her new duties and obligations to fulfil as the First Lady Knight of KLOPT0N, including the next ancestral destinations to visit with Kane and also their pathway together to the new world which was still to be revealed by the cryptic inscriptions on the seven keys.

The next nine hundred years until the alignment of the 'Seven Classical Planets' occurred again was going to be a very long time for Kane & Kara to travel and they were therefore determined to discover what their ultimate destiny would be a lot sooner than this.

* * *

The next book of this intriguing series about the **HOUSE OF KLOPT0N** continues to once again draw inspiration from history, as Kane & Kara continue on their journey through time together, where they explore new places and discover more about their ancestors.

- Legend - Fact - Fiction -

Ancestral Lineage

13th Century:

Mathew Parker & Janet

Sir Robert *de* Clopton & Marsha   Richard Parker

Sir John *de* Clopton & Arabella   Sofia   Kate

14th Century:

Sir James *de* Clopton & Susan

Sir Frederick *(Johnson)* Clopton   Sir Stephen *de* Clopton
& Khloe Clopton   & Christine

Kathryn   Ryan   Edmund

15th Century:

Sir John & Agnes Clopton

Thomas Clopton   Hugh Clopton   John Clopton

16th Century:

Sir William & Anne Clopton

Joyce   Anne   Margaretta

16th Century:

Sir George *(Carew)* Clopton   William Clopton of Durham
     & Joyce Clopton   & Anne Clopton

17th Century:

Sir John & Kathryn Clopton

Steven & Khloe   Richard & Kathryn   Mark & Sarah
  nee Clopton   *nee* Clopton   *nee* Clopton

18th - 20th Century:

Sir John *(Ingham)* Clopton & Karen Clopton
|
Sir Thomas *(Lloyd)* Clopton & Katherine Clopton
|
Sir Andrew *(Warde)* Clopton & Kathleen Clopton
|
Dr Tarak Singh & Lady Katrina Clopton

Sir Kane Clopton   Lady Kara Sofia Clopton

Sir Arthur & Eliza Hodgson
|
Reverend Francis & Elizabeth Hodgson
|
Avis Hodgson

*NB: It was often the practice over the centuries for the same
forenames to be given by parents to their children and
explains why this Ancestral Lineage may be confusing.*

Cecil P Saunders

Author

During World War II, many thousands of young men joined the British Army to fight for King George VI and Country, but tragically too many of them died by the time the War had ended.
Thankfully, I was amongst all those soldiers who survived and soon managed to return back home to a civilian life in England.

Shortly afterwards, I met my wife-to-be and we celebrated by taking a coach journey with some of our closest friends on a couple of days visit to Stratford-upon-Avon.
Whilst there, we looked around the Shakespeare houses and also saw where the 'Bard of Avon' was laid to rest inside the Church of the Holy Trinity on the River Avon, with his body entombed along the main aisle close to the Chantry Chapel of the aristocratic Clopton family.

Several months later I joined the Legal profession, before then marrying my wife Mavis and over the next few years we were blessed with three wonderful children.
Throughout my career, I would read as much literature as I could find about these two famous Stratford-upon-Avon families, but it was only after I retired that I had the time to delve a lot deeper and discover even more about them both, including how their lives overlapped.

With the benefit of some less well known historical manuscripts and other documents however, I also uncovered the now evidently forgotten, but remarkable legend of the ancestral HOUSE OF KLOPT0N.
I subsequently decided to compile all of the information and stories I had gathered to create this book for posterity and to include the events told across time by those original family descendants born into the long lost bloodline.

www.CecilPSaunders.co.uk